WATCH OVER ME

Books by

Christa Parrish

Home Another Way

Watch Over Me

WATCH OVER ME

CHRISTA PARRISH

BETHANY HOUSE PUBLISHERS

Minneapolis, Minnesota

Published by Bethany House Publishers
11400 Hampshire Avenue South
Bloomington, Minnesota 55438

Bethany House Publishers is a division of
Baker Publishing Group, Grand Rapids, Michigan.

Printed in the United States of America

Library of Congress Cataloging-in-Publication Data

Parrish, Christa.
    Watch over me / Christa Parrish.
        p.   cm.
    ISBN 978-0-7642-0554-5 (pbk.)
    1. Marriage—Fiction. 2. Parenting—Fiction. I. Title.
    PS3616.A76835W38   2009
    813'.6—dc22

                                                                    2009025126

For Jacob,
My baby in the rushes;
The Lord has His hand on you, too.

Chapter ONE

The kids slumped against the hood of his squad vehicle, not clinging to each other but wanting to. Their shoulders and hand-stuffed pockets pressed together, brown dust pasted to the toes of their sneakers. Benjamin Patil knew why. Blood hid under the dust.

"You kicked the towel?" he asked them.

"I fell over it," the boy said. "I didn't know what it was."

"Are we in trouble?" the girl asked.

Kids. They were fifteen, sixteen maybe, and he thought of them as kids. He was only ten years their senior. Only.

When did he get so old?

"You're trespassing," Benjamin said, taking his camera from the car. He snapped some photos of the bloody towel, of the red flecks across the grass. He listened to the chirps of his camera, the rustling beneath his feet, the Say's phoebe and dickcissel fluttering and chattering around him. "Want to tell me what you're doing out here?"

The teenagers both shifted from one hip to the other.

"I didn't think so." He pulled on a rubber glove, shook open a transparent evidence bag, and grabbed the balled-up towel. It unrolled, and a pulpy, grayish blob plopped to the ground.

"Oh, man. Is that a brain?" the boy asked.

"No," Benjamin said. "Get in the car, both of you."

"What—"

"Now."

He shoveled the towel and placenta into the evidence bag, dropped it through the open window of his nine-year-old Dodge Durango. Head down, he tracked the speckles of blood until they turned to drops, then splotches, leading him along a thin, heat-eaten stream. Something yellow was tucked in the slough grass on the near bank of a muddy pond. He strode forward, needle-and-thread awns snagging his pants, trying to stop him from finding what he knew he'd find. And then he was there, at the pond's edge, staring at a white grocery sack, yellow smiling face printed on it, two tiny feet twisted in the handles.

"Dear God . . ."

He dropped to his knees, clawed at the bag, the plastic stretching like skin, tight over his fingertips. It split, and he saw human flesh before a swarm of mosquitoes poured into the air. Benjamin swiped them away; one dove into the sweat on his forehead and bit him. He crushed it against his brow and, in the same sweeping motion, gathered an infant from the bag and into his hands.

Startled by the light and the rush of air against its body, the newborn scrunched up its face and wailed, fists flailing like a prizefighter's, knuckles bluish-gray and filmy. The umbilical cord hung from its— her—belly, a dirty shoelace knotted near the frayed end. Benjamin laid her across his knees, tugged at the buttons of his uniform, opening the top two and then yanking the shirt over his head. He wrapped the baby in it and sprinted to the car.

"Tallah, get up here," he said.

"It's a . . . a . . ."

"Just get in the front seat. And belt up." The girl did, and Benjamin gave her the baby. "Hold on to her, you hear?"

The girl nodded, her arms tightening around the bundle, and Benjamin flipped on his siren.

She was three, maybe four hours old, the doctor told him. A bit longer in the June heat and she would have been dead. Benjamin stared at her in the isolette, her new baby skin swollen with dozens of furious, nickel-sized welts. Mosquito bites. Black fly. Maybe some ant mixed in. She was wired and tubed and taped. And alone. The other babies born within the past forty-eight hours—seven, he'd been told—slept with their mothers in private rooms.

Her chest rose and fell with the beeps of the heart monitor. He put his hand through the hole in the side of the Plexiglas and stroked her arm with two fingers, once, twice, feeling her frailness beneath the downy lanugo. She shrunk away; his hands were cold. Always, lately.

Things like this didn't happen in Beck County. Women tossed away infants in other places—faraway places people around these parts heard about on the news but never visited. A New York City dumpster. A Chinese rice paddy. Not in the weeds at the west end of Hopston's beef farm. After Afghanistan, when Benjamin came home to South Dakota, he thought he'd gotten away from things like this, things that caused nightmares. But here they were, following him. God's judgment.

A nurse came in. Her purple rubber clogs squeaked as she walked. She checked the fluid bag and the intravenous line in the baby's scalp.

"How's she doing?" Benjamin asked.

"Holding her own, considering."

"The doctor said they might move her."

The nurse nodded. "To Sioux Falls. They got a NICU there."

Benjamin touched the infant's palm. She closed her fingers around his, and he stared at her shiny, pink fingernails, so small and perfect. He thought of Abbi, of all the times he'd looked at her hand in his own, her pale Scottish-Irish-English-and-whatever-else skin ghostly against his India brown. And he wanted to hear her voice, which surprised him almost as much as finding the baby.

"I'll be back tomorrow," he said, meaning his words for *her*, but the nurse nodded.

In the hospital lobby, he dialed home. One ring, two. Three. Abbi's recorded voice said, "Hey, we're not here. Leave a message." He pressed the receiver against his ear for several seconds, tapped it against his forehead before hanging up. He needed to get back to Temple, for the press conference.

He carried the evidence bags through the jumble of news vans, cameramen, reporters, and gawkers, and into the courthouse building. The temperature in the sheriff's office felt hotter than outside; Benjamin said so.

"Probably is. Cooling unit broke this morning," Deputy Al Holbach said. "You don't plan to talk to the press looking like that."

Benjamin still had on only his undershirt, the armpits yellowed with sweat, his stomach smeared with his dirty handprints and blood. The sleeveless, ribbed-cotton kind, the kind Abbi hated. She called them wife-beaters, told him she saw them and thought of the men who wear those undershirts as outerwear, and stand on their front lawns scratching and screaming at their women and children. Just one more thing she never did like about him.

"Can't we just send a press release?"

"Don't think those piranhas waiting outside would be happy with that," Holbach said. "I got an extra shirt if you need it. Might be a tad big."

"No. I have one." Benjamin wrenched open the bottom drawer of his desk. He grabbed a clean uniform shirt, another undershirt, and his black leather toiletry bag. In the restroom, he stripped off his dirty shirt and balled it under the faucet, drenching it with cold water. He rubbed his bare torso, his neck and head, and slathered deodorant under his arms. The clean shirts felt stiff, unyielding. The dirty undershirt, he tossed in the waste can.

"Where's the boss and Wes?" he asked, back at his desk, pinning his name tag on his pocket.

"They should be back any time now. Went out to the scene."

"They found the bag, then."

"Right where you told 'em."

Benjamin briskly rubbed the top of his head, wishing he had hair long enough to grab and yank. "Just—" He dropped his bag into the drawer and slammed it closed with his foot. Sighed. "Just . . . everything."

"You said it," Holbach said.

The press conference lasted twenty minutes—three minutes of prepared statement, and the rest questions from the mob, most drawing answers of "We can't say right now," or "We just don't know at this time." The reporters skulked away, unsatisfied. Benjamin knew the feeling.

Back inside the office, he bit down on the marker cap and pulled, drawing a diagram over the whiteboard, a squashed spider with an uneven black circle for a body and eight legs spread in eight different directions. Sheriff Eli Roubideau rolled some tape on the back of a Polaroid photo and slapped it in the center of the circle. The torn plastic bag.

"Gotta get one of the kid instead," Roubideau said, removing his hat and patting his hairline with a rag. "Somebody needs to get over to the school tomorrow."

"I will," Holbach said. "First thing."

Benjamin wrote *School* and *A.H.* on one of the empty lines. The office phone kept ringing; they didn't pick it up after hours, after the secretary went home. The answering machine kicked on, recording reporters or dial tones.

"That bag. The Food Mart uses them," Raymond Wesley said.

"And probably a dozen other stores," Holbach said.

"We can't do anything about the others, but I'll head over to the Food Mart, ask around. Maybe one of the clerks remembers someone coming through there pregnant."

"And I'll just start knocking on doors," Benjamin said, adding Wesley's and his initials to the diagram. "Covering the whole county is going to take a lot of time. Not much else to do, though, at least for now."

"Not much else, sure as shooting," Roubideau said. "Now go home. All of you."

Benjamin didn't. He drove around for twenty minutes, then let himself back into the station, into the holding cell. He took off his shoes and socks, his shirt, his belt, and crawled onto the bottom bunk, setting his watch alarm for four thirty. The sheriff didn't come in until close to six.

Chapter TWO

She hadn't trimmed her hair in six months. That was what Abbi was thinking when she saw the dull spasms of light beneath the haze. Heat lightning. She stopped, drank the air instead of breathing it. It tasted like rain, sort of mossy and gray. On either side of her, the hard red winter wheat stood unmoving, the humidity sponging up the wind. Harvest would begin in a month or so.

How her mind had wandered from prayer to hair, she couldn't remember. But it happened that way when she ran, her feet penitent against the loose stone at the start, her petitions spilling into the open space with each breath. And then, twenty or so minutes later, she slowed for a quick drink and realized she'd been making mental lists of glazes she needed to reorder, or replaying her conversation with Genelise from late the night before.

She unzipped her hip pack and swallowed her last mouthfuls of water from a stainless-steel bottle. It was too hot to run, she knew. But Benjamin had asked her not to go. Or told her not to; she couldn't tell the difference with him. He'd finished reading the front page article in the weekly *Beck County Register*—the one she read minutes before, about the rare humidity spell, the heat index over one hundred degrees, the three hundred dead cattle across the county—and said a couple jumbled sentences about the temperature and his concern, and how she could just skip a few days and jog when the swelter broke. She said, "Yeah, thanks," and hid in her studio until well after he'd left for work.

Back out on the paved road, she untied the bandana from around her hair and shook it open, smoothed it over the top of her head like a veil. It helped cut the sun a little. She walked now, her toes burning in her jute sneakers. The asphalt stretched ahead of her, shimmering in places as if wet, an illusion of the heat. A tractor putted by, loose hay jouncing in a trailer hooked to the back. Abbi hopped in the bed—she doubted the farmer noticed—and rode until the turnoff to her house. She jogged the remaining distance, gravel shifting under her feet.

They didn't live on a farm, but rather a misplaced street of ranch houses built in the '50s, seven in a row with less than a quarter-acre each, more than most had in town. Theirs was second to last, peach-colored with faux stucco siding. The Vilhausers, a quiet elderly couple who kept chickens and a goat, lived on one side. The wife, Marie, sold eggs to Benjamin; she wouldn't speak to Abbi, hadn't so much as looked at her since that day when Abbi's photo appeared in the newspaper, while Benjamin was gone, the one of her at the protest. The old woman had poked her skeletal finger into the ripple of bones beneath Abbi's neck and called her a fascist.

On the other side, Silas and Janet McGee. Janet had moseyed over the first week Abbi and Benjamin moved in three years ago—Pepsi cake with broiled peanut butter frosting balanced on one hand, an "Are You Going to Heaven?" tract taped to the domed aluminum foil. She had a collection of tracts, Abbi soon found out, all colors and lengths and for every occasion. Janet often left the glossy booklets in the Patils' screen door, mostly messages of praise or comfort, some-times reminders of the power of prayer, and once a "Be a Missionary at Home" tract that encouraged the use of more tracts. Abbi had a good chuckle over that one, but she did admire Janet's utter sincerity. She and her husband attended the same church as Ben and Abbi, and Abbi used to be able to call her a friend—sort of. Now, more often than not, she kept away from the windows when Janet came by, and didn't return her phone calls.

Once inside, she dumped her exercise clothes in the washing machine and took a cool shower. After drying, she began her getting-dressed ritual. Underpants. Bra. The stack of jeans came out of her nightstand. She pulled on the size-fourteens first, stood in front of the mirror attached to the top of her dresser. She gathered the extra material, first at the front, holding it in her fist at her navel, then at the back, and then let go and rolled her stomach like a belly dancer; the pants slid down her legs.

Twelves next. She buttoned them and tugged the waistband up as high as it could go, then released it and watched the denim settle low on her hips. She did this four, five, six times before stripping off the jeans and shaking out the folded size-tens. This pair fit perfectly—a little give in the seat, some room in the thighs, not too tight across the belly.

Abbi folded the jeans, put them away, and dressed in an elastic-waist skirt she'd made from a vintage tablecloth—all her homemade bottoms had elastic; she was a crafter with a short attention span, not a seamstress—and an ocean blue T-shirt. She draped a raku-fired pendant around her neck, a copper and turquoise leaf print on a black cord, and then changed her nose ring from the hoop she preferred to the little diamond speck most folks didn't notice. Before leaving, she gathered her hair into a loose ponytail knotted with an orange silk scarf. She didn't know why she bothered trying to look nice; she'd be wearing a yellow polyester smock the rest of the day.

⌐

The small grocery store buzzed with people, more people than Abbi usually saw during a Wednesday shift. They weren't shopping so much as congregating, standing with cans of Green Giant peas in their hands, talking in quick, gossipy bursts. She punched her timecard and tied on her Food Mart apron.

"So, your hubby's a hero," the other cashier, Jaylyn Grant, said.

Abbi shook her head. "I don't know what you're talking about."

"What's wrong with you? Don't you watch the news?"

"No."

Jaylyn rolled her eyes. "He found a baby. Some wacko dumped a newborn baby girl on Pete Hopston's land, and Deputy Patil found her. Probably left by an Indian. Maybe a drunk one."

Abbi pressed a button on her register. The drawer clanked open, and she dropped her money tray in. "Isn't your sister part Native American?"

"Sienna, yeah. Her daddy's half of one. That's the half that made him split, so my mother said."

Abbi bit the inside of her cheek, said nothing. She keyed in merchandise codes and slid the food to the end of the ramp, watching Jaylyn's back, her seventeen-year-old legs long and smooth in her cutoff shorts. The girl dropped bananas and two-liter bottles of soda on loaves of bread, flirting as customers passed by. The old men played along, the young men snuck glances at her body, and Abbi stood there like the Pharisee in the temple. *God, I thank you that I am not like these sad people.* And she despised herself for it.

Women wandered through Abbi's checkout line, heaping compliments on Benjamin. She said, "Thank you" and "I'll tell him" and "I know I'm lucky." But she just wanted to go home, and when her shift ended at six, she hurried to sweep and punch out, wadding her smock into a ball and tossing it on the shelf.

The house was still empty. On the answering machine, a red digital number one pulsed on, off, on. She pressed the Play button and heard static, then a dial tone.

She wasn't hungry, not really. But there was too much space

around her, inside her. She filled it with a sprouted-grain bagel and homemade hummus, two handfuls of raw almonds, a soy yogurt, and a chewy, double carob chip cookie. Before changing into her pajamas, she drank three glasses of prune juice, quickly, one after another, plugging her soft palate with her tongue to dim the taste. Then she snapped on the living-room lamp and made a sandwich for Benjamin—roast beef and Swiss; her stomach lurched as she picked the meat up between her thumb and forefinger, dropped it on the bread—in case he wanted something to eat when he came home.

In case he came home.

Chapter THREE

Other people woke to alarm clocks or crying babies or shouts from the apartments next door. But Matthew Savoie woke in silence, and in the minutes before he opened his eyes, he hid alone within his head, without distraction.

He thought in words, watched them scroll across the backs of his eyelids, ordering him to get up, get going. But the heat ground against him, wet and heavy, a mildewed blanket over his face, provoking his sleepiness.

The sheet stuck to his chest as he managed to turn over; he felt it peel away from his skin like a Band-Aid. Last night, he had taken the three cushions off the couch and lined them up on the floor. A narrow bed, yes, but his body was well accustomed to the width. He'd slept on the sofa here in his aunt's living room for the past five years. And the floor—where his feet flopped off the end of the cushions, and he could spread his arms for air—was cooler than if he folded his body to fit between the padded gold arms, his skin pressed into the hot velour fabric.

A little cooler, he tried to convince himself.

He felt the floor shake. Someone slammed the bathroom door. He opened his eyes and saw two of his cousins, Jaylyn and Skye. Irish twins, his grandmother called them, born eleven months apart in the same year. Two different fathers.

"Ma said you better get your lazy self up or you're gonna be late," Jaylyn said.

Matthew turned onto his stomach again, swept his arm over the carpet and caught his T-shirt on his pinky. He put it on, not wanting the girls to see his bare chest, pale as the moon and puckered with ribs. Too thin for a sixteen-year-old. Too thin for a boy, really. He stood, shrugged.

"What's that supposed to mean?" she asked.

He found his notepads in the denim shorts he'd worn yesterday, a sad pair of jeans Heather brought home from the Salvation Army, cut and hemmed by hand one night when she'd been feeling maternal. He flipped open the red one, spiral-bound on top like a reporter's, and wrote, What do you care?

"Retard. Come on, Skye," Jaylyn said, and twirled away, her smooth blond hair fanning around her shoulders.

Skye stood there looking dark and tired. She reached her hand across her chubby stomach and grabbed a knot of skin near her hip and, through her cutoff sweatpants, kneaded it. She seemed more distracted lately, quieter than usual. Matthew doubted anyone else had noticed, a symptom of living packed close together, eyes turned toward the ceiling or floor—at first to give each other a bit more privacy, then to have more privacy of one's own, until finally all anyone did was look up and inward and away.

Are you okay? he wrote.

"Yeah," she said, head dripping into her shoulder, her mouth still moving.

Unable to read her lips now, he scribbled, What? and held the pad in front of her face.

She looked at him. "Nothing. Sorry," she said, and followed Jaylyn outside.

He hated that. The *nothings* and *never minds*. As if it took too much effort to repeat the words, and he wasn't worth a minute more of conversation, another lungful of air. But he was used to it, too.

He couldn't go without breakfast, so he took the three steps to the kitchen and filled a bowl with cornflakes. Opening the refrigerator, he stood inside it while he poured milk on his cereal, indulging in the rush of cold around him, a few guilty seconds of luxury. He slid the near-empty jug back onto the top shelf and elbowed the door closed.

The cereal, a store brand that came in a huge plastic bag, lost its crunch before Matthew sucked the first bite off the spoon. Still, he finished it, the soggy flakes filling the pits in his molars. He dug the mush out with his tongue, a silvery pain shooting through his jaw as he brushed the cavity he needed to have filled. Then he drank the warm, gritty milk left in the bottom of the bowl and opened the cabinet again to get his pillbox, hidden on the second shelf behind a stack of dishes so Lacie wouldn't be tempted to play with it. Once he forgot and left it on the counter, and later found his youngest cousin twirling around the kitchen, shaking the blue plastic case like a maraca and singing.

With his thumbnail, he popped open the square labeled *Thursday Morning* and dumped the pills into his palm. Orange footballs, white capsules, and pastel wafers that look like Easter candies. Blood thinners and stool softeners, vitamin supplements and phosphate binders—he could take all eight in one gulp, and did, feeling as if he swallowed a handful of gravel and drinking a full glass of water to wash them all the way to his stomach. If not, he would belch up bitterness until lunch.

His noontime pills and between-meals pills he rolled in a paper napkin, to take with him for later.

He looked at the clock—already close to eight. In the bathroom he saw a speck of silver glittering at the bottom of the toilet and flushed. When the bowl refilled, the speck was still there, so he reached in and washed it and his hands with soap. Skye's earring, a skull-and-crossbones stud. Her favorite. He left it on her pillow.

Rushing now, he pulled on yesterday's shorts and stuffed his notebooks and medication into the pockets, then lifted the top off the Rubbermaid tote in the corner of the living room. All his clothes fit in there, and he shuffled through to find his collared shirt, a yellow polo style with a bundle of green, black, and white stripes banded around his chest. He put it on, stared for a moment at his good chinos folded at the top of the pile, then snapped the lid closed. His mother wasn't worth pants in near 100-degree heat. She wasn't worth a collared shirt, either, not worth a single drop of the sweat that would sprout at the nape of his neck and slide down his back beneath the heavy piqué fabric. But Matthew remembered the fifth commandment. *"Honor your father and your mother, as the Lord your God has commanded you, that your days may be prolonged, and that it may go well with you in the land which the Lord your God gives you."*

He flipped the lid off the tote again and took out a clean pair of shorts to wear.

He needed all the days he could get.

⟶

There wasn't a single taxicab company in Beck County. Not one in Castle, either. Matthew pedaled to the main roadway, stashed his bicycle in the tall grasses near the on-ramp, and waited. A car rattled by, then another, ignoring his outstretched thumb. Already his head and mouth felt fuzzy. He couldn't stay in the sun much longer.

Finally a pickup steered onto the shoulder. The driver rolled down his window.

"Where you going, son?"

Matthew opened his pad. He'd already written Hollings.

"You got a tongue in that mouth of yours?"

He flipped his pad over, showing the driver the words

already printed on the back cover. I'M DEAF. I READ LIPS.

"Deaf, eh?"

Matthew nodded.

"Foolish thing, hitchhiking. 'Specially when you can't hear nothing." The man took off his Twins cap, wiped his hairline with his cuff. "Get in."

In the truck, Matthew dropped his backpack on the floor and unzipped it, took out a bottle of water. He drank all of it, and half of another. Too much. He was allowed only four cups of liquid a day.

Goosebumps sprouted on his arms, his sweaty skin reacting to the air-conditioning like a vinegar and baking soda experiment. He flipped the vent toward the driver, who glanced at him and said something; Matthew couldn't read his sideways mouth but nodded anyway. The man slid the air control to low.

Matthew looked out the passenger window. He counted hay bales, four hundred and ninety-seven during the twenty-minute ride, his eyes flickering over the fields, grouping, estimating, the numbers adding themselves. In Hollings, he walked a couple of miles to the bus station and bought a ticket to Pierre.

Aunt Heather might have driven him to visit his mother on Saturday, if he'd asked, or she might have made her boyfriend do it. But he didn't want anyone to know. He'd been planning to go alone for nearly a year, and wasn't quite sure why he chose today to do so. He only knew that he had fallen asleep last night ready, finally, to take his trip. His aunt thought he was sitting in the high school computer lab, completing on-line classwork.

The bus crossed the bridge into Pierre, a gray city on a gray day, the street lined with gas stations and hotels and fast-food restaurants. Matthew got off at the station, walked to his mother's apartment building—three floors high, with the bottom floor half underground, the bluish siding a patchwork of dark and light stripes, newly replaced boards between the old. He prayed as he approached the main door. An elderly man with a cane stood just behind the glass, trying to push outside while dragging his wheeled shopping basket. Matthew rushed over, held the door open for him.

"Thank you much, young man," he said.

Matthew smiled and slipped through, trudged up the hot stairway and banged on his mother's apartment. The peephole darkened; Melissa Savoie opened the door, smirk on her face.

"This isn't *my* kid. He doesn't ever come see me," she said. "He's too good for me, that boy."

Matthew's hands shook as he fumbled to find a blank sheet in his notepad. Can I come in?

"By all means. This don't happen every day, you know. Is Heather with you?"

I came alone.

"You drive now?"

Bus.

He wiped his feet on the plastic runner, took off his sneakers and his backpack. The apartment had new carpeting since his last visit. Dark blue, almost purple, and plush. He sunk into it as he crossed the room to the small kitchen table.

"You want a drink?"

He shook his head.

"I have root beer. Well, diet. It used to be your favorite. You used to sneak it, and pour it over your cereal when you were little. That kind you liked."

Cocoa Krispies.

"Yeah, that. So, you want some?"

He had used root beer on his cereal because it was often the only beverage his mother had in the house. And she'd been too strung out to get up and make him breakfast.

He shook his head again.

"Suit yourself," she said, sitting across from him.

I'm Sick, he wrote, turning the words to his mother.

"Tell me something I don't know."

It's worse than before.

Her mouth pulled in, the lines around her lips giving her a toothy appearance, as if she wore her jawbone on the outside. "Heather told me."

I need a kidney.

"You think I'm gonna give you mine?"

He wouldn't ask if she would, fearing the answer. He knew she had loved him once; he remembered that, remembered her lifting him onto the handlebars of her rusty three-speed bicycle and pedaling seven miles to the T-ball field so he could play. They had no car then. They barely had food. But she tried, fighting for sobriety during those few summer months. She pedaled him to the school field after her double shifts at the catheter factory, sat smoking under the basketball net, watching the ball roll through his legs. Then Griese showed up, and any trying his mother used to do disappeared up her nose in a cloud of white powder.

I can't use yours.

She dropped her eyes to her lap, tugged at the collar of her gray T-shirt. "So, what are you doing here?" She whispered this; Matthew could tell by the way her face remained still while her mouth moved.

Where's my father?

"That dirtbag's not gonna help you."

I just want to ask.

"I haven't talked to him in years."

Does he have family? Someone who might be in touch?

"Forget about him."

You won't tell me?

"I don't know."

Fine, he wrote, standing and stuffing his notebook in his back pocket.

Melissa grabbed his arm and said, "Buffalo. New York. He was there, last I heard."

Matthew pressed his lips together and nodded.

Melissa let go of him. "You should have called. I don't got time for this today. I'm working now. Got to get there in forty-five minutes."

He nodded again, strapped on his knapsack and left, walking back to the bus station, to the ticket window. The bus to Hollings wouldn't leave for another three hours. He waited in the air-conditioning, buying two packages of Chips Ahoy from the vending machine and shaking the crumbly, stale cookies into his mouth straight from the bags. He read, worked a Sudoku puzzle in the newspaper someone left behind. After an hour, he wandered out to one of the cabbies lining the station curb and asked how much it would cost for a ride back to Temple. When the driver said two hundred dollars, he went back to the hard plastic seat to wait some more. He'd take the bus, even though it meant he'd be stuck on the side of the road when he got off in Hollings, praying for someone to stop and bring him home.

Chapter FOUR

Sitting at the kitchen table, his third cup of coffee empty, Benjamin stared at the Bible. He didn't remember the last time he opened it, had to blow the dust off it when he found it under his bed, having stuffed it under there when he couldn't stand it looking at him from the nightstand, accusing him of neglect. But he had dug it out today, opened to a random page somewhere in the middle, hoping for—he couldn't say what. He hadn't read more than a sentence, the blurry words drifting off the page, disappearing each time he rubbed his eyes to clear his vision.

He heard Abbi come out of the bedroom, the swollen door opening with a sticky pop. Everything swelled in the heat. Problems. Fears. Sins. All puffed with humidity and ready to rain out with the slightest change in air pressure.

As she passed, his arm moved on its own, reached out and cupped her loosely around her waist. She let him, and he tried to think back to the last time their touches weren't accidental bumps against one another while scurrying around the small bathroom in the morning, or brushed hips when passing too close in the kitchen. For months, they had each slept on their own side of the bed, backs to each other, their bodies two parentheses curving away from one another, refusing to close. When he came to bed. He hadn't last night. Or the night before.

"I didn't know you were home," she said.

"Came in late."

"You're sweating. Turn the air on."

"It's too loud. I can't hear myself think."

She spun away from him, opened the dishwasher. "You emptied it."

"Yeah."

"Where's the juicer?"

He pointed up, at the middle cabinet. "Where it always is."

She stood on tiptoe and stretched to reach it on the top shelf. Her arm uncurled above her head like a butterfly's proboscis.

She's beautiful, he thought, had thought hundreds of times. But not in a long time.

"What are you doing today?" he asked.

"Working. You?"

"Working. Probably late again."

She took two oranges and a lemon from the refrigerator, balanced them on the flat of her bare arm. "Want some?"

Benjamin shook his head, watched her slice through the fruit right on the counter, without a cutting board. Citrus filled the air as she pressed each half against the glass juicer, twisting and grinding the guts out. She rinsed her hands, wiped them on the back of her—his—boxer shorts, and drank right out of the collection cup.

He couldn't find words for her anymore. They used to talk—bicker—about anything, everything. Politics, religion, the price of corn on the cob at the roadside farm stand. But now it was fights with jagged words, or polite trivialities, or nothing. Mostly nothing, a wounded silence snapping at their heels.

Abbi rinsed the juicer, without soap or sponge, rubbing the pulp away with her fingers. She only used detergent on oils and baked-on crud. "It's the water that does the cleaning. The soap only helps it along, and a little elbow grease will do the same," she'd tell him if he complained. It drove him crazy. To him, plates weren't clean unless the sink mounded with bubbles. He got that from his mother. Commercial cleaners, difficult to get in India, at least where she had lived, were almost an addiction for her, and after coming to the States, his mother had filled her kitchen pantry with pastes and gels and sprays. Chemical fumes meant loving care; they comforted Benjamin almost as much as the simmering black-eyed peas and *garam masala* in his mother's *chavli amti*.

"The McGees invited us to dinner after church this Sunday," Abbi said, her back to him, wiping down the counter. "Again."

"What did you tell them?"

"That I'd ask you."

"I don't know. We'll see."

"It's Friday, Ben. I need to give them an answer."

"You're not going to Pierre?"

"I don't have to."

"What do you want to do?"

She sighed, scratched at a spot on the Formica with her thumbnail. "We should probably go sometime. Janet has been asking for the past three months."

"How about next week."

"Can I tell them that?"

Benjamin closed his Bible. The room had grown hot with questions, and he reached over and flicked on the air-conditioner. "I don't know."

"What else is new," she mumbled, throwing the rag in the sink. Then she left the room. He heard the bathroom door slam and the shower started.

"Stupid," he said, standing and shoving the chair into the table. He wanted their old life back. He crammed a bag of deli ham, the rest of the loaf of bread, and a squeeze bottle of mustard into his insulated lunch bag, tossed a freezer pack on it, and zipped. Repositioning the wad of lamb's wool—thick and yellow and slightly greasy, the kind

29

dancers use in their pointe shoes—in the front of his right boot, he tied his boots on. The wool kept his foot from sliding forward and crushing his remaining toes.

He shoved his keys in his pocket, but the shower went off, a dull thud echoing through the house as Abbi pushed in the single faucet. He leaned against the living room doorway, eyes closed, stretching his lower jaw in and out so his bottom teeth slid over his top ones, then popped back behind them with a painful scrape. Finally, he set his lunch on the end table and walked quietly down the hall, knocked on the bathroom door. Abbi opened the door, wrapped in a towel with a corner tucked between her breasts. And they stood there, both staring over the other's shoulder, until Benjamin said, "We can go, if you want."

She shrugged. "It's fine."

"Well, whatever. Just let me know."

"Yeah."

A drop of shower water made its way down Abbi's face from her hairline, catching a moment in her eyebrow before lazily rolling toward the tip of her nose. *Toward its demise.* He wiped it away with his thumb. That was twice he'd touched her today. "I'll see you tonight," he said, without thinking if that, indeed, would be the case.

She looked at him then. "Really?"

He was trapped. "Yes."

Abbi lifted the cuff of his shirt a little, turning his arm so she could read his watch. "You have time," she said, and she plucked at the tucked corner of the towel. It mounded at her feet. He glanced at her, shiny and fleshy and soft. Her body was the same as on their wedding day. He thought it was. He hadn't seen it in too long. His fault, not hers.

He turned his eyes away.

"Puritan," she said.

He blew one quick burst of air through his nose, a chuckle of sorts. "Liberal." And they smiled—tired, uncertain smiles that didn't reach their eyes—because they had begun this way, with insults and name-calling, and the flutters that came with a new love.

She sighed and sank back against the vanity, arms clamped across her chest, shoulders pulled in toward each other and legs crossed as if trying to disappear into herself. Benjamin wanted to touch her again, wondered if she'd disappear—*poof!*—if he did. Or crumble. Or leave.

Benjamin knew she was waiting for him to come to her. But he didn't, and she sighed again, gathering the towel from the floor and tying it around her waist. He watched her cross into the bedroom, his eyes tracing the lines of black ink growing from between the dimples on her tailbone, rising and curling over her spine, out toward her shoulder blades, her tattooed interpretation of Gustav Klimt's *Tree of Life*.

She closed the door behind her.

He found himself once again in Hopston's field, wandering circles in the thirsty grass. The sheriff had tied a small knot of crime-scene tape in a clump of weeds by the creek—yellow tape, like the bag, marking where it had been found. Benjamin still saw some blood, brown and dusty, but it would rinse away with the approaching storm. It drizzled now, one plump drop on the back of his hand, one on his ear, his boot. The air already felt cooler.

Interstate 90 sliced the cattle farm in two. It cut through the entire state, from one side to the other. Whoever left the baby might have simply been passing by. Benjamin shook his head, let out a low groan only the birds heard. He would never know who did this, not unless someone came forward.

Before Afghanistan, before Stephen, he would have prayed. Now his prayers were like his words, atrophied at the back of his throat.

And if they did come, if he forgot that he didn't want them to come, they'd drop to the ground in brittle, incoherent half phrases and clanging cymbals. For the best, probably. He was afraid of what he might say.

Yesterday he canvassed seventy-three houses; today he hit thirty before noon. No one had seen anything suspicious, nor could they think of any women who might have been hiding a pregnancy. He thanked people and offered them his card should they remember something. Not many took them, saying his number was already stuck to their refrigerators, printed on car-shaped magnets given out by the sheriff's department each June.

⌢

At the office, Wesley leaned back in his chair, boots on the desk, eating a bowl of chili, napkin squeezed between his collar and bullish neck.

"How can you eat that stuff? It's ninety degrees outside," Benjamin said.

"It's eighty outside, only seventy in here. And I like it." Wesley held the bowl above his mouth and scraped the last bit of tomato into it. "Any luck door knocking?"

Benjamin shook his head. "One hundred and three homes down, nearly fourteen hundred to go. I heard yesterday there was no luck at the school."

"Nope. Two pregnant girls there this year. One had her baby in May. The other, not due for another month."

"You sure?"

"Went to the house, saw her tummy myself."

"Anything else?" Benjamin asked, scratching the side of his nose, pushing down until it hurt.

"Got five other girls to check out. Names the guidance counselor heard through the grapevine. She said it's probably nothing, but she always keeps record of the pregnancy rumors, just in case."

"Well, let me know what you come up with," Benjamin said. "I'm going to Pierre."

"Again?"

"So what?"

"You could just call to see how the baby is doing. Save the gas."

"Then I wouldn't get the mileage reimbursement," Benjamin said, waving a form in the air before folding it in half and tucking it under his arm.

"Patil," Wesley said, popping open a can of Sprite. "You'll need to let this one go."

"Not yet."

He drove to the hospital in a rain so heavy it felt as if he were moving beneath the sea. Water sluiced around his tires, shimmying the car. He turned on his hazard lights, but didn't pull off onto the shoulder like the other, smarter, drivers. Through the downpour, he saw figures he thought were children dancing in their yards; it could have been the vibrating rain playing tricks on him, or shrubs moving in the wind. Maybe it was all in his head.

The baby was still the only child in the nursery, but out of the isolette and in a bassinet, cocooned in a white blanket. She wore a pink-and-blue-striped hat and mewed, kitten-like, her face flushed with hunger. "She's a fighter," the nurse said, holding a bottle. "Even the doctor's surprised she's come 'round so fast."

"She looks better," Benjamin said.

"Want to feed her?" Before he could answer, the nurse eased the baby from the bed and into his arms. "You can sit in that rocker. There, behind you."

The nurse poked the nipple between the infant's lips, let the plastic bottle slide into Benjamin's hand. He watched the baby smack and sigh, and couldn't help but start the chair rocking gently.

"You're a natural," the nurse said. "I'll be back in a few."

After the baby finished the formula, he lifted her to his shoulder and patted her on the back. She seemed to be in discomfort, fussing and arching. He laid her in the bassinet and changed her into a clean diaper no bigger than his hand, making sure to fold the top down under the umbilical stub, a mottled golden raisin in her belly button. The insect bites had faded to strawberry-colored smudges.

She cried earnestly now, mouth wide, legs bent into her stomach. Her hat slipped off; he left it, picked her up again, bouncing and walking the room, talking, telling her the story of how he found her, like Moses in the reeds. "The Lord's hand was on you," he said, and then stopped, thinking even saying the name of God might be too close to a prayer. His nose rested against the top of her head, his lips in her eyelashes. He felt a warm wetness run down his neck, into his shirt, and pulled her away. Curds of regurgitated formula hung on her chin. He wiped up the mess on her, on him, but could still smell the milky rancidness.

The nurse came back in and laughed. "She got you good."

"I think she feels better now."

The woman took the baby; today her clogs were blue, yesterday, coral. "I bet she does. Try club soda on that stain when you get home."

"Thanks, I'll do that."

"So, will we see you tomorrow, Deputy?"

"Maybe," he said. The baby's slate blue eyes were on him, drawing him in. Connecting him. He hadn't felt attached to something, someone, in a long time. "Yeah."

Chapter FIVE

They went to church on Sunday, and it didn't feel like a holy day. Abbi's hair was still wet from the shower and soaking the shoulders of her linen blouse as she leaned back in the passenger's seat beside Benjamin. He had buttoned his shirt crooked, left collar peak jutting into his chin and two buttons vying for one lonely hole. She tried to tell him, opened her mouth with the words *Ben, your shirt is buttoned wrong*, but somehow it came out as, "Slow down. My teeth are rattling."

"We're late," he said.

Ben, your shirt is buttoned wrong. "I was ready at ten to."

He steered onto the side of the road, between the bright orange cones, and jammed the shifter to park. She scrambled out of the car before him, wanting her slam to come first, and it did, echoing in the golden farmland around them. He untangled himself from the seat belt slowly, deliberately; he wouldn't look at her.

Ben, your shirt is buttoned wrong. How difficult was it to say? But she let him walk across the street without trying again, knowing everyone inside would notice but be too polite to mention it. That was what her marriage had become—unspoken fashion advice taped together by barbs, and vows she wasn't sure she should have ever said.

Their church was a sturdy Presbyterian congregation of about sixty meeting inside a metal building, the outside walls rippled and yellowish. The potato-chip church, she called it when they first moved to Temple three years ago. She'd liked the Catholic church better, a musty-smelling white chapel with a festive nun-organist, who wore Nikes and nylons beneath her habit, and Father Brendan, an Irish priest planted in the wheat fields. Every sermon, she said to Benjamin, was delightful in brogue. He wanted to go to Second Baptist because the worship team reminded him of the one in Vermillion, and when she asked him what was wrong with First Baptist, and why a town of five hundred needed two of the same church, he told her not to be so darn difficult.

This church had been their compromise.

They weren't late. The preparatory music hadn't started yet, and people mingled in the narthex and sanctuary; the casual scent of coffee and cookies swirled through the cloud of noxious glue fumes still loitering from the new carpet that had been installed during the week. Abbi's sinuses constricted, pressure building between her eyes, in her cheeks. She didn't know what was wrong with the old carpet; yes it had been Raggedy Ann red and twenty years old, but so what? Now she was Judas, complaining about using the perfume instead of selling it for the poor. Judas, of course, was a thief. She was just as self-righteous. She knew it.

She took a bulletin and sat in the last row, next to Benjamin, and saw the Communion table draped in a bulging white cloth. The second Sunday. She had forgotten, and ate breakfast. Usually, Abbi fasted on Communion days, or tried to, a conscious effort to remember those in poverty who went without. Some Sundays she made it through, pushing aside the thoughts of the two or three pounds she'd lose, like a woman spreading the clothes hanging in the closet to get the rarely worn coat in the back—the prayers for the hungry that should come with every growl and pang. Other Sundays she hated herself for considering the fast's effect on her weight and stuffed food in her mouth until she hated herself more.

By the time Communion began, she was concentrating more on keeping Benjamin out of her thoughts than keeping the words of institution in them. He hadn't partaken in six months. She leaned across him to pluck a cracker from the tray, her fingers hovering over the broken pieces before selecting the smallest she could find without seeming too obvious she was actually searching. Benjamin pinned his hands between his knees. Seven months.

The kids ran around after the benediction, collecting the little plastic cups from each seat, stacking them until their disposable towers swayed as they paraded to the trash can.

"I'm going to the bathroom," Benjamin said. He'd stay there until the building cleared.

Abbi didn't move. Women passed her, some smiled and nodded and said, "Hi, how are you?" but didn't wait for an answer. Others acted busy with their bulletins or hurried by without eye contact. Then Janet McGee stopped, knelt one floral-skirted knee on the chair next to her. "We missed you at Bible study Thursday night."

"I had to work," Abbi said, though they both knew the Food Mart closed at six, and Bible study didn't begin until seven, though it was more like seven fifteen once all the ladies got there and stopped talking.

"Think you can make it next week? It's not the same without your— What did Gail call it?"

"My unique perspective." And they both chuckled a little at the memory; seventy-nine-year-old Gail Galpin's shock when Abbi wondered aloud if perhaps the Sabbath should still be celebrated on Saturday, and then went on about anti-Semitism during the early Roman church. Abbi's brand of shaded belief baffled those with a more black-and-white Christianity; she knew that from college, but at least then she also knew many others who thought more like her. Here, not so much. That included Janet. But rather than retreating into her fixed faith, she and Abbi had often batted around ideas, doctrine, differences. Not that either of their minds changed.

"You certainly liven up the discussions," Janet said.

"I don't find out my hours until tomorrow."

"Well, I hope you can come," Janet said.

Ask me. Ask me why I stopped.

But she didn't.

They had done this each time they spoke lately, the dance of niceties, sidestepping with polite questions and non-answers, and then waltzing back center to go again. But Janet wasn't alone. If not her, then Claudia Martin; if not Claudia, then Rachelle Yates. Or others. The concern was there, but no one asked her straight out why she didn't attend the study and prayer meeting anymore, stayed away from the monthly ladies' tea, and avoided even impromptu fellowship. She couldn't say whether she'd tell them if they did. Abbi wasn't deliberately keeping secrets, but she didn't know how to outrun them anymore, and they gobbled her up into their silent belly.

She didn't feel right living as her husband rotted away, and more so because of the difficulty she had stepping back into things she'd withdrawn from. She didn't belong with these women anymore, having spent months underground, no longer engaged in their lives, not learning until weeks after the fact that Minnie's daughter had filed for divorce or Tabitha's father had succumbed to his Alzheimer's fog. The connection had been broken, and Abbi was too exhausted, too alone, to try to find her way inside again.

Janet switched knees and rearranged the pens in the front pocket of her Bible cover. She punched her knuckles against her hipbone, cracking them. "You seem . . . quiet today."

"I'm fine."

"How's Ben doing?"

"He's fine." *Left, right, together. Left, right, together.* "Just busy with this baby thing."

"Oh, tell me about it. It's horrible. Silas can't believe it, either."

"Yeah."

"We haven't really had a chance to chat lately. Anything going on with you?"

"No, I'm good."

Left, right, together. Left, right, together.

Two seats to her right, Benjamin's thin fingers slid onto the back of the green padded chair. Abbi didn't turn around, but Janet said, "Ben, I was just telling Abbi how Silas and I are still reeling over that baby. We can't believe it. No one can. It's really a miracle you were there to find her."

"You should be thanking the Wayne kid," Ben said. "And God, who apparently even works through a teenaged boy trying to get into his girlfriend's pants."

"And who thwarted both unhappy endings." Janet laughed. "Who says God doesn't have a sense of humor?"

"Simon Wayne, for one. He's grounded for the next two months."

Janet laughed more, too much, shifting knees again, popping knuckles again. "I feel like we haven't seen the two of you in ages. Are you sure you won't come for lunch today? We have plenty."

"We can't—" Abbi and Benjamin said together, then stopped. His fingers tightened on the chair.

"I'm heading up to see a friend," Abbi said.

"Oh. Soon then. Maybe next week."

"We'll let you know," Benjamin said.

"Well, I'll stop going on now and let you get out of here. Have a nice visit with your friend, Abbi."

Abbi nodded and left the building with Benjamin, his buttons properly aligned now. They got into the Durango. She didn't understand. Anyone with one working eye could see her husband withering away to a skeleton, the man who came back from Afghanistan wearing Benjamin's clothes and face and voice wasn't the one who went over.

She needed someone to say it first, to give her permission to cry out, "Yes, yes, you see it, too. I'm not crazy."

She knew these people cared about Benjamin, and her. Why wouldn't they help?

"You going now?" Benjamin asked, turning onto their street.

"Yeah. What are you doing?"

"I don't know. Something. Nap, maybe."

He pulled his squad vehicle onto the grass in front of their house so he wouldn't block her in and wordlessly walked inside. She started her own bumper-stickered Volvo and sped north, the road pink, as if sunburned. Insects pelted her window, exploding in sticky bursts of yellow and orange. She flicked on her wipers, trying to wash the blood away before it baked on in the heat.

⌒

"Abbi!" Genelise said, squeezing her as she arrived at the park on the edge of the Missouri River. Her friend wore her hair half blue today, brushed to one side and moussed in long spikes.

"Don't suffocate me. I just saw you last week. And we talked for an hour last night."

She pulled back. "You look tired."

"So do you."

For several months Abbi had driven up to Pierre on Sundays to help Genelise's church give out food and clothing and toiletries, or little things that had been asked for the previous week; one woman pleaded for a tube of lipstick, to feel pretty again—"At least my mouth will," she said—and a man wanted black socks because they looked less dirty after days of wash-less wear. And Lulu begged for a toaster. She had three already in her cramped, subsidized one-room studio in the senior housing building, but someone brought her another, which she petted and carried around under her arm like a prized Chihuahua, black electrical-cord tail dragging.

Lulu ambled over, shiny silver toaster hugged against her side. Her breasts swung long and heavy beneath a man's white T-shirt. "Yoo-hoo. You girl. Didja bring those plums again?"

Last week Abbi had brought bags of extra-ripe plums too old for the Food Mart to sell. She'd rescued them from the dumpster behind the store when she found out they'd been tossed; she would have asked for them—and Jerry would have given them to her—if she'd known before the overzealous stock boy decided to take his job seriously for once. No harm. The plums washed fine, and Lulu had eaten nearly half of them. Abbi had watched her, juice dripping from her chin, and couldn't help but think, *"Forgive me, they were delicious, so sweet and so cold."* Benjamin's fault. He'd read her William Carlos Williams's poems when they were in college, over and over, until she told him she was sick of wheelbarrows and chickens, and men dancing in front of mirrors and yellow shades.

"Sorry, Lu. No fruit today. I have some heads of cabbage, though."

"What do I want that for? I don't buy cabbage 'cause I don't like it, so why would I take it now it's free?" And she walked away in her sparkly blue jelly shoes, backs cut out to accommodate her swollen heels, lined with deep cracks, dried riverbeds splitting the thick, yellow skin.

"I'm sorry," Abbi called again. Lulu raised her arm and swatted at the air above her head without turning, but another church member came to her with an orange, and she bit away a hunk of rind, spat it on the ground, and continued to peel the fruit.

Abbi loved the action of these people around her, their living, breathing faith. Not like the amputated Christians she'd known, those who waddled about as if their limbs had been hacked off, unable to reach out into the world and be the arms of Jesus. She wished her own church could be more like this. Genelise kept trying to convince her to attend services here, but this group was a bit too left-leaning even

41

for her. Plus, Benjamin would never agree, and that seventy minutes on Sunday mornings was the only time they came face-to-face with a common purpose. Abbi needed at least that.

"Nice Monroe," she said, looking at the little gold ball protruding above Genelise's upper lip, on the right side, a metallic beauty mark.

"You like it? I wanted a Medusa." She flicked the groove beneath her nose. "But Clay talked me out of it."

"Men," another woman said.

"Tell me about it." Genelise sighed. "I might still go back and have it done."

The wind brushed over Abbi; she gathered her skirt tight around her legs and breathed in the muted river smell of algae and wet stone. And after she helped Genelise and the others pack up, her friend invited her back to her apartment.

The purple shag area rug and matching chair were Genelise's contributions to her boyfriend's otherwise modern décor—a khaki-colored, armless couch with sharp, rectangular cushions, beauty salon–style chairs, and a bleached wood coffee table with a top shaped, in Abbi's opinion, like Australia.

She had met Genelise in college, in her 2-D design class as a first-semester freshman. The next year her roommate convinced her to try a Campus Crusade meeting, and for a while she felt yanked in two directions—one night hands held high with Lauren, the next at a bar with Genelise, arms above her head again, but moving and shaking to La Bouche, not "Blessed Be the Name of the Lord."

Things jumbled up even more when she met Benjamin. Genelise ebbed away until Abbi needed her—on weekends Benjamin went to training exercises and Lauren went home. Genelise didn't mind. At least she acted like she didn't mind; she was used to being a backup plan. Like now. Benjamin wanted nothing to do with Abbi. Genelise did. She cared for Abbi—really, truly.

"Where's Clay?"

"He's in Vegas. With Neva."

"Wait. Neva? His ex, Neva?"

"That would be the one."

"Why didn't you tell me?"

Genelise waved her words away. "I didn't want to think about it. Still don't. Thirsty?"

"I can do some water."

"Me, too." She climbed up on the stove and opened the small cabinet above it, jumped down to the floor with a bottle of vodka in her hand. And then, after filling a tall glass of water from the tap, she filled another glass with the alcohol and held them both to the light, swirling them. "The neutral spirit. Just like water. No taste, smell, or color. No difference."

"Except one is forty percent alcohol."

Genelise shuffled the glasses, a magician playing sleight-of-hand tricks, sliding the cups around one another. "If it looks like a duck—" she said, picking up one glass and taking a swig. Sucked air through her teeth. "Oh, that burns."

"Did you and Clay break up?"

"Officially, no." She took a container of orange juice from the refrigerator and poured it into the vodka glass until it quivered at the rim. She leaned close and slurped the liquid down to a safe level. "But what part of us ever was official? I think he just gave me this ring so I would stop pestering him to marry me."

"Gen, you deserve better."

"Do I? I don't know anymore," she said, and then she guzzled the entire glass of vodka and juice.

"Are you nuts?" Abbi grabbed the bottle and spilled the remaining alcohol down the drain. "There were like four shots in there."

"Or six, or seven." Genelise held tight to the counter, stretched the collar of her shirt. "I'm hot."

"You're an idiot."

"I'm you're friend."

"Then you should have told me you and Clay were having problems."

"You have enough on your mind."

"That's such bunk. Anyway, I'd rather think about your garbage than mine."

"I didn't know we were having problems." She leaned over the sink. "My stomach is sloshing."

Genelise vomited a stream of thin orange liquid; it splattered on Abbi's bare forearms in tiny pings. She wiped her mouth on the hem of her shirt and staggered into the living room, drunk and loose with grief, and flattened herself on the floor, eyes closed.

Abbi crouched beside her and put one hand on her back. "Genelise?" Shook. "Genelise." When her friend didn't answer, Abbi pulled back one of her lids—her blue iris rolled up toward her forehead.

"Who put the carpet on the walls?" she said.

"Idiot," Abbi said again, let her eye fall closed.

"I don't know how to be alone."

"You learn."

Genelise flopped onto her back. "But not tonight. Stay here, okay?"

"Yeah, okay," she said, and Genelise threw her arms across her face, groaning a sleep sigh. "If I puke again," she told Abbi through her arms, "roll me over so I don't choke to death."

Abbi wedged herself into the hairy purple monster of a chair, her legs folded under her, her hip jammed against the padded arm. She read her Bible for a while and prayed for Genelise, for herself—for the deep, miserable alone they were both tangled in. Then she called Benjamin. She'd considered, for more than a moment and with spiteful pleasure, not bothering, thinking it might do him good to find a dark, empty house and know the feeling of wondering where she might be.

She used to wonder when he didn't come home, would let her mind conjure all kinds of horrible scenarios. She'd drive around at night, looking for his car, sure she'd find his body in it, gun stuffed in his mouth and the back of his skull missing. Finally, she worried herself out of worry, every last drop dried up, and began pretending he was still in Afghanistan, at war, with an excuse for deserting her.

In a way, it was the truth. He was stuck over there.

Benjamin didn't pick up the phone, of course. He might not even miss her if she didn't show up. But she left her message after the tone anyway, her voice hollow in her own ears.

Chapter SIX

He sat on the stoop, waiting for the medi-bus, the chipped cement scratching the back of his calves. His cousins fought over the one unbroken swing on the metal jungle gym—Sienna hung in the plastic seat on her stomach, fingers raking the dirt, while Lacie punched her in the back, shouting something Matthew couldn't make out. Finally, the five-year-old threw a fistful of grit in her sister's hair and ran to him, crying.

"Sienna won't let me swing."

Matthew didn't take out his pad; she couldn't read yet. But he hugged her to his side, pulled her up by the arm, and led her into the apartment, where he found a grape Fla-Vor-Ice in the freezer. He snipped off one end and gave it to her.

"Don't let Sienna have any," she said, and ran back outside to eat it in front of her sister. As soon as Sienna saw Lacie's treat, she stomped over to where he stood in the open doorway. Lacie hopped onto the vacated swing.

"I want some," Sienna said.

He shrugged and pointed inside. She grabbed two and flopped down on the couch, fished the remote control out from between the cushions and turned on the television. He watched Lacie squeeze the last of the purple sugar-juice into her mouth and, seeing her sister had deserted her, dropped the plastic tube on the dirt and charged toward the apartment. Matthew braced his arm across the door.

"What?"

Grabbing the top of her head, he gently spun her, pointed to the wrapper. Her shoulders heaved up and down. A sigh. Then she shook him off and dashed to pick up the trash.

A couple of other children came out on the playground, and Lacie, seemingly forgetting she had been heading inside, threw the wrapper on the ground again and climbed up the geodesic monkey bars with the Miller boys.

It wasn't much of a playground. The bars, one swing, and a sandbox—four two-by-twelves bolted together in the corners with a blue tarp stapled inside. Really, the whole courtyard was a sandbox; a few clumps of crabgrass sprouted along the walkways, otherwise just dirt. Two long three-family ranch houses sat on either side of the play equipment.

The bus drove into the cul-de-sac. Matthew pounded on the door, and Sienna said, "Yeah, bye."

He pounded again, and she lifted her eyes to him as he motioned out the front window. "I'll watch her."

He waved to Lacie before getting on the bus. She didn't see him. Darn that Jaylyn. She knew he caught the bus at one thirty, promised Aunt Heather she'd be home to watch the girls. He hated leaving them alone, a nine-year-old to look after a kindergartner. The driver honked. Matthew hefted his knapsack onto his shoulder and found his usual seat in the back left corner.

Straightaway on I-90, the trip to the dialysis center took twenty-nine minutes. But the medi-bus picked up four other people, adding almost an hour to the trip. He didn't mind so much in the summer; he went to the school to complete his on-line courses in the computer lab, got home in plenty of time. The rest of the year he needed to leave school early three days a week. The guidance counselor scheduled his electives in the afternoon—typing, health, art or gym on opposite days—so he didn't miss anything too important.

The other patients on the bus were older, a forty-six-year-old bank teller and three elderly ladies. Matthew kept his head turned toward the window so no one would try to start up a conversation. He had spoken a few times with all of them when he first started treatment a year ago. The women offered him butterscotch candies in gold wrappers and looked at him with the pity of lives long lived, patting his knee and assuring him that the good Lord had a plan for him, even if it didn't seem fair that he'd been stricken at such a young age. The bank teller talked only of the three B's—beer, broads, and basketball. Matthew had tired of wasting paper in reply.

After he was examined and weighed, Matthew settled in the dialysis chair, a beige vinyl recliner draped in a sheet, and offered his left forearm to his nurse, Denise. She wiped on a cleaning solution and, after three minutes, used a cotton ball to apply a topical anesthetic. It did nothing.

Denise slid two fifteen-gauge needles into his fistula, one to suck the dirty blood out of his body, one to spit it back in, clean and rosy. He tensed, clamped his teeth together as the metal poked through his skin with a pop, then slid into the vessel.

"All done now," she said, and he exhaled.

She strapped a blood pressure cuff around his right arm. "Want the TV on?"

Matthew shook his head, pointed to his school bag. Denise pulled out his books for him, hung the pack on the arm of his chair. "Good grief, Matt. Calculus? It's summer. Have some fun."

Math is fun, he wrote in his notebook. Anyway, I'm not doing calculus. I'm just reading about it. It's like a story. A history book.

"You have issues," she said.

He nodded and grinned at her, and he thought she laughed. It looked that way, her eyes crinkling at the corners, her shoulders heaving back and forward. And in his head he heard Woody Woodpecker. He closed his eyes and saw the crimson bird, speeding along in a car with Shaquille O'Neal. Then the basketball player disappeared and Denise was there, laughing Woody's laugh. *Ha-ha-ha-HA-ha. Ha-ha-ha-HA-ha.* A Pepsi commercial he saw when he was—what?—four, five years old.

Some sounds he had locked inside him, from television mostly. Not many. But sometimes he would see the flashing lights of an emergency vehicle and remember a siren he'd heard on *CHiPs* reruns, or he'd watch a dog bark and the *woof-woof* of a black-and-white Lassie would come back to him. Didn't matter if the dog was a German shepherd or a poodle, he heard the same bark. *Woof-woof. Timmy's in the well.*

He opened his book, read about Isaac Newton and Gottfried Wilhelm Leibniz, the two brilliant men who independently discovered calculus, and the battle of pride and plagiarism that ensued as a result. Calculus, the study of change. He lived that. Revolving homes, men coming and going—first in his mother's life, then his aunt's—new medications, new aches and pains. He clung to the God who was unchanging, the God of mathematics. The God of pi.

He remembered in middle school learning about pi, and it fascinated him. He read books, spent hours working the Brent-Salamin Algorithm, watching pi grow longer and longer, marching into infinity. He memorized pi to a thousand places—give or take—and found himself praying the numbers when he had no words. *Three point one four one five nine two six five three five eight nine seven nine three two three eight four six two six four three three eight three two seven five zero . . .*

In pi, he saw the reflection of God. Pi was constant, always the same—today, tomorrow, and forever. It was irrational, like the cross, foolishness to those who didn't believe. It was transcendental; no finite sequence of operations on integers could ever create it.

It never ended.

When his eyes tired, he leaned back on the padded seat and dozed, but not deeply enough that he didn't feel Denise check his blood pressure every thirty minutes. Finally, after three hours, the needles came out. The nurse covered his punctures with a gauze pad, and he pressed his hand over it. Two vampirish spots of red seeped through.

He was weighed again—lost five pounds, all excess fluid removed from his body. His temperature taken again, still normal. His blood pressure, standing and sitting. His pulse.

He climbed back on the bus, waited for the others to shuffle on. He felt a little weak, stiff from being tied to a chair for so long. And tired. Just so tired. He hoped the apartment was calm when he got home—no blaring television, no arguing over stupid things, like Jaylyn using his aunt's perfume, or Sienna twisting the heads off Lacie's Bratz dolls. Doubtful, he knew. There always seemed to be some sort of crisis at home, and if there wasn't, one of the girls found a way to make one. Nobody was happy if they weren't hurting each other. He wished they would just quit. He hurt enough for all of them.

Chapter SEVEN

Benjamin stared at a pile of letters—some opened, some not—stacked high and wobbly on his desk, the way he imagined the mattresses in that children's fairy tale *The Princess and the Pea*. He had more peas than he could count—Abbi, the baby, the case, his memories—those hard, insistent predicaments that poked at his soft places when he slept, and continued to follow him around while awake.

The letters came from everywhere—donations, offers of adoption, little prayer cards and notes of encouragement. Nothing captivated like the suffering of children. People were more likely to open their checkbooks for little, bald chemo heads and distended African bellies than—

What's wrong with me?

He'd never been a cynic, and he hated feeling the undertow at his feet all the time, battling to pull him down. So far, he had been able to keep his head from sinking beneath the crashing surf—barely sometimes—but each day he found himself struggling more. If he wasn't such a coward, he'd give up.

He scooped the letter into a manila envelope and took the stairs by twos and threes to the second floor, the family services office. Cheyenne Donaldson typed at her desk, twinkling in the fluorescent lights, cheap rhinestone rings layered on each finger. Thumbs, too. She wore her lavender blouse '80s-style, collar starched up, gold-tone fairy necklaces jangling against strands of pastel pearls.

"More mail," Benjamin said, spilling the letters onto a table next to her.

She sifted through them, picked one up, and tapped one end on brown laminate. When the letter settled, she tore off the other side, squeezed both edges of the envelope, and shook. A folded sheet of paper slipped out, and a check. Cheyenne skimmed the letter, stuffed it back in the envelope, and opened another. "Want to help? Mail in one pile, money in another. We opened an account for all the donations coming in."

Benjamin dug under the loose end of an envelope flap and yanked, and then stuck his index finger into the hole, sawing the paper open. He found four five-dollar bills in a glittery pink *Welcome, Baby* card and added the cash to the pile.

"No luck finding the parents yet," Cheyenne said, more statement than question, more defeat than hope.

"I doubt we will."

"She's leaving the hospital in a few days, Monday or Tuesday. Into foster care. You know." She paused, her plastic bangles clattering as she plowed through the envelopes again. "We have three licensed families in the county. You're one of them."

He sliced through another envelope, more quickly this time. "Abbi can't have children."

"Do you want to take her?"

Now he stopped. "Cheyenne, I don't think . . . There must be someone better."

"This isn't coming out of nowhere. You've been at the hospital, what? Every day? More than anyone else, she knows you."

"She's only ten days old."

"She knows you."

He couldn't. What did he know about babies, especially ones who'd been abandoned by their mothers? He and Abbi thought they'd be adopting an older child, if at all. The way things were between them now . . . If Cheyenne knew, she'd not be making this offer.

He could hardly keep himself from coming apart.

But new fathers knew nothing of babies, either. They learned and stumbled through. They made mistakes, and their sons and daughters turned out fine. And he'd found her. He went to the hospital every day because he still felt responsible for her. He was her protector. She was his redemption.

Some part of him wanted this.

"I'll need to talk to Abbi," he said.

"Think about it a couple days, and let me know."

⌒

He walked the unpaved quartzite of Lippman, the town east of Temple and smaller still. Benjamin had loved the sound of gravel roads as a child, closing his eyes and imagining great dragons gnashing the bones of their prey as the stones scraped and popped under car tires, or his feet. Of course he was the dragon slayer. The brave hero. Some boys grew out of this phase; that was what he heard his parents whisper to each other as he attacked giants in the tree trunks with twiggy swords and slept with his golden junior officer badge—his name engraved on it, a Christmas gift from Stephen's family one year—pinned to his pajamas. Things would have been a lot easier if he'd gone on to middle school and left the cops-and-robbers games in his fifth grade cubby with his Teenage Mutant Ninja Turtles lunch box his parents made him buy with his own money. A lot different.

A lot better.

He bounced as he walked, partly from his naturally loose gait, partly because his hip twisted as he pushed off with the ball of his right foot instead of his toes. Each step jostled his desire to bring the infant home, settling it deeper. It had been there since the beginning, though he had refused to admit it until now. He still needed to ask Abbi, and he had no right to ask anything of her.

Lippman's thirty or so houses clustered on less than six acres in the southeast corner of town, trying not to waste too much valuable field space. Benjamin started with the first house on the first street; many knocks went unanswered. He looked at his watch, the hour hand barely scraping two. Folks at work, kids at daycare. He left a preprinted note asking people to call if they knew anything. Those he did find home said they couldn't help him. No one seemed to be lying.

Some children laughed and bounced on a corroded trampoline in one front yard. They saw Benjamin and ran to him, pleading for him to show them his gun. He unholstered it and let them run their dirty fingers over the metal. They poked at it and jumped away, as if worrying it might come alive and bite them.

He walked away from the last house and decided not to bother with the farms today. No more procrastinating. The gravel shifted as his Durango rolled over it. *Chomp, chomp, chomp.* The only dragons left to slay were his own.

⟶

"I wasn't expecting you home," Abbi said when he entered the kitchen. "I didn't cook anything for you."

Benjamin said nothing, and she didn't turn around but kept chopping the cucumber into smaller and smaller pieces. He made her nervous, her knees locking forward, elbows drawn in against her sides. She brushed the cucumber into a bowl and from a green carton dumped tiny oblong tomatoes onto the cutting board. They collapsed as she tried to slice them, spitting watery juice and seeds over the counter. She mumbled under her breath, flinging the smooth-bladed knife into the sink before pulling a serrated one from the block.

"Abbi."

She exhaled, tilting her neck backward until it crackled. "What."

"I need to ask you something."

"So, ask."

"It's important. Turn around."

Knife still in her fist, she shifted, only half facing him. But that was Abbi—tell her to do something and she'd find a way not to.

"Cheyenne Donaldson wants to know if we would take the baby," he said. "The one I . . . you know."

"For how long?"

"I don't know. Forever, maybe."

"Maybe."

"It's all up in the air, Abbi. She'll need permanent placement. If we don't find relatives, someone has to raise her."

"Someone, you."

"No. Someone, us."

She rinsed the knife under the faucet and dropped it, blade down, into the dish rack. Swiped her hands on the back of her shorts. "There isn't an *us*."

It was the first time either of them had said it aloud, and the words stirred no emotion in Benjamin, no surprise. They were two halves now, no longer one flesh, put asunder not by man or circumstance, but by each other.

Abbi's hands trembled as she swept her vegetables into the bowl of couscous on the counter. She took a bite, shook on some salt, pepper, and took another bite. Her back still toward him, he read its twitches. Should he press her or not? He rubbed his thumbs over his sweaty fingertips. "Abbi."

"What, Ben? What? If you have something else to say, just say it. If not—" She shoved her bowl away. "I'm just . . . going to the studio."

"Wait," he said, jumping in front of her, and she flinched, a residual instinct from *that* day. Both their eyes found the uneven mango-sized spot in the living room wall. He had patched the hole with spackle and repainted it, but it still wasn't as smooth as the surrounding Sheetrock, the white paint brighter. "I found her."

"Oh, I get it. It's, like, finders keepers?" Abbi snorted. "You've lost your mind. She's not a quarter you picked up from the sidewalk. This is a life."

"I saved her life," he shouted. He didn't mean to, but it bubbled out. This time Abbi didn't back away; her gazed dropped to his waist. Hesitantly, she reached out and traced the silver buckle on the creased brown-leather belt he'd worn since before they met. It had become a joke between them. Every Christmas and birthday Abbi bought him a vegan belt to replace it, wrapped in the same-sized box so he knew what it was. After the first two times he'd figured out her routine, and he would shake the gift and make outlandish guesses—"Is it a bowling ball? Keys to a new Corvette?"—before untying the ribbon and acting surprised. He'd strap the belt around his forehead, or around his neck like a tie, and dance about the room, and they'd laugh together and end up in bed.

All those belts hung on the inside of the closet door—faux suede, jacquard nylon, canvas and hemp and vegetan—jingling each time someone opened it. He never wore any of them, each day sliding the battered leather through the loops on his pants. And now he watched her finger hop from one hole to the next; he was buckled to the seventh. The third hole was fat, a gaping wound from years of use. The next three were only slightly stretched. She lingered on the eighth and final hole. "And who's going to take care of her while you're at work?" she asked.

"I figured you could quit the grocery. And not go back to subbing in the fall."

"You're trying to bribe me."

He smiled a little, shrugged. "Yeah."

She dropped her hand, her face falling with it. "I guess we go see Cheyenne tomorrow."

"Thank you."

"Don't," she said, and went to her studio.

Chapter EIGHT

The smell of birth assaulted Abbi as she stepped through the doors of the maternity ward—a thick, sweet coat of lotions and latex gloves, and that pink toilet cleaner in the gallon bottles. She lagged behind Benjamin, passed by a glowing couple walking hand in hand, the proud papa lugging a blue-socked baby in a car seat, the wife still waddling with postpartum weight.

That's how babies should go home.

Benjamin didn't wait for her. He waved to the nurse through the window and slipped into the nursery. The woman came out, holding the door for Abbi. "Go on in," she said. Abbi waited, the door against her hip, and as the nurse swished down the hallway, Cheyenne clattered around the corner. "I'm here, I'm here," she said. She crowded Abbi into the room. Benjamin hoisted the baby on his shoulder, one of his brown hands cupped under her diapered bottom, the other eclipsing her back. Her thin, purple legs wriggled like night crawlers against his shirt, and Abbi winced at her shrill bleating. He draped her over his forearm, her head in the crook of his elbow. She calmed as he rhythmically pounded her back.

Abbi read the card taped to the bassinet. *Baby Doe.* But the *Baby* had been crossed out and above it *Angel* had been written in red marker. "Is that her name?"

"That's what the nurses have been calling her," Cheyenne said. "I think it's cute."

Benjamin strapped the infant into the car seat he had purchased before coming to the hospital, at Wal-Mart, along with a crib and clothes. Abbi had waited in the car. He looked at her. "If you can think of something better . . ."

"You want me to name her?"

Benjamin rubbed his palm over the top of his head, over the whirl where men went bald, though Abbi didn't know if he was losing his hair or not. He'd always kept it short, nearly shaven. It couldn't be described as fuzz. More like five o'clock shadow on his skull. "I'm sure you'll come up with something . . . nice. Don't take too long to decide, okay?"

The nurse returned carrying a mint green diaper bag dotted with Peter Rabbits. She filled it with the disposable diapers from the drawer beneath the bassinet.

"We won't need those," Abbi said.

"You'll go through lots of them," the nurse said. "Any extra will help."

"We're using cloth."

"Mmm." The nurse stuffed the remaining diapers into the bag and zipped it. Benjamin signed the necessary release forms, and the nurse embraced him quickly. "I'm glad it's you, Deputy."

He nodded.

"I'll be over tomorrow," Cheyenne said. "Around eleven. Just to make sure everything's in order."

"We'll be there," Benjamin said, and carried the baby to the car. Abbi followed; she drove home while he sat in the back seat with the infant. He spoke to her in hushed tones, coos, and sang in Marathi. She couldn't understand him, but, still, there was an openness in his voice that she hadn't heard in a long time.

He'd always wanted to be a father.

She'd ruined that for him.

They had been on the bed in their apartment in Vermillion—she studying for her art history final, he pretending to read, but more accurately trying to annoy her into stopping. He kept standing up and stretching, only to flop back down on the mattress, sending pencil and index cards bouncing onto the floor. He ran his foot up her calf, tickling her with his toenails, and reached across her to grab highlighters or sticky notes off her nightstand, brushing against her breast or blowing in her ear on the way back to his side.

She repeatedly slapped him and finally, biting the inside of her cheek so she wouldn't giggle, said, "Stop it."

"Sorry," he said, and would stare at her over the pages of his *Law Officer* magazine until she couldn't take his eyes boring into her. She looked at him, and he hid behind the glossy photos of motorcycle cops before peeking out like a child, sticking his tongue out at her and darting back behind the magazine.

"Fine, I give up," she had said, closing her notebook in the fat history text and dropping it on the floor. "But if I fail and have to spend another semester here because you're acting like a three-year-old who wants his mommy's attention, don't come crying to me."

"Oh, you're done studying?" he said, batting his eyelashes. "Let me just finish reading this."

"You jerk." She laughed, grabbed the magazine from him and tossed it over her shoulder. Then she straddled his legs, facing him. "I hope you have something better planned for tonight."

He stretched the neck of her T-shirt to kiss her collarbone. "Maybe I do. Maybe I don't. Though—" he kissed her neck—"we could—" he kissed her chin—"start working on that family we want."

"What?" She pulled back.

"I got offered a deputy's job today, in Beck County. It's about three hours from here, but only twenty minutes from Lauren's parents' farm. You'll be close to her when she and Stephen move out there, and we'll be in the little town we both want. It's perfect."

"You haven't even asked me," she said, and his eyes, bright seconds before, clouded over. She climbed off him, stood, but he grabbed her hand and tugged her back down. Laced his fingers through hers.

"What's wrong?" he asked.

"Nothing."

"Don't give me that."

"What do you think is wrong? I'm your wife, but, oh no, you're going along, making plans without me."

"They're our plans, Abbi. We've been talking about them forever."

"Well, maybe things have changed. Maybe I don't want to pull up my skirt and start squeezing out kids for you."

"Fine," Benjamin said, shaking his hand free of hers. He went into the bathroom, slamming the door behind him. She lay on her back on her side of the bed, her vision swimming in the pools atop her eyeballs. She scrunched her lids closed, and the tears rolled outward, into her ears. She heard the door open, and then felt Benjamin's hip against hers as he sat. He touched the corners of her eyes with his thumbs and traced the wet path to her hair. "Tell me," he said.

She hadn't meant to deceive him. They talked about having a family while they dated, and after, and she meant what she said. She thought they would try for a few years to get pregnant, and when nothing happened, they'd go to a specialist and get the bad news together, and she would act as surprised as he. That was *her* plan. But now she couldn't lie. She looked at Benjamin. "I can't have children."

If he was trying not to react, he did a good job. Only the lower half of his face betrayed him, lips and jaw trembling for a moment, until he unclenched them, then got up from the bed. Abbi thought he would leave, but he shut off the light and slid next to her, folding her against him as she wept into his neck.

They talked about it, of course, days and weeks later, in the light, when big things seemed somewhat smaller, more known and manageable. He mentioned adoption and she agreed; not because she wanted to—she believed her condition to be a sort of penance for her youthful indiscretions and thought she should bear her barrenness as a cross—but because she felt obligated. So they completed their paper work to foster-adopt and had waited.

And now this nameless infant slept in the back seat of the car. Abbi didn't want her, either. But Benjamin did, and he deserved to get something he wanted after all he'd been through. If it meant he would come out of . . . whatever it was he was in. She'd do anything to keep him from wasting away to that eighth and final hole on his belt. Or past it.

She owed him.

⌒

They lay in bed, sheets kicked at their feet, the baby between them. She sucked her lower lip, eyes shut. Benjamin had set up the crib in their bedroom, but the infant wanted none of it, screeching until he cuddled and swayed her to sleep. He promised to buy a bassinet tomorrow, in the hopes the smaller space would help settle her. Now he slept too, fatigue whistling in his nose.

Abbi couldn't find her way into dreamland, the springs of their shoddy mattress grinding against her hip. They bought it used at a bedding outlet when they first married, one of those hauled-away-for-free-when-you-buy-a-new-one mattresses, strips of duct tape stuck over each stain. She propped her head on her elbow, ear squished against her skull, and gently touched the top of the baby's head, tracing the soft, triangular divot beneath her downy black hair. *Who are you?* Abbi thought. And she remembered a vague snatch of Shakespeare. *"Who is Silvia? What is she . . . ?"* She had no idea of the rest. That was Benjamin's realm.

She flattened her palm against Benjamin's ribs, shook him. "Silvia," she said.

"Mmm. What?" he asked, opening one eye. He rubbed the other with the back of his hand. Yawned.

"Her name. Silvia. It's what I want to call her."

"You're kidding, right? Is she going to stick her head in the oven?"

"Not that Sylvia," Abbi said. "The one from Shakespeare. You know."

"Silvia. With two I's," he said, rolling to his elbow to look down on the baby. " 'Who is Silvia? What is she, that all our swains commend her? Holy, fair, and wise is she; the heaven such grace did lend her, that she might admired be.' "

"Yeah, that one."

He flopped back down on the pillow. "Okay."

"That's it? No argument?"

"I don't win arguments with you."

⁓

They didn't sleep more than a few unsettled minutes between the crying.

Both of them had practice with worry-induced insomnia. Forced sleeplessness was a different beast, the body and the mind craving rest and being refused. Benjamin walked the hallway beyond the closed bedroom door, but Abbi heard each peep and moan beneath her pillow. She began to doze when the noise stopped, and then it started again, jerking her from her half sleep. She looked at the clock. Seven minutes.

"Why won't you make her stop?" she said, stomping toward him.

"Right. I'm enjoying this at three in the morning." He moved between the kitchen table and the front door, baby across both arms, jostling her up and down. He wore his pants, belt open and jingling.

And socks. He didn't wear them to bed, or in the shower, but the socks went on before anything else, and off last.

"This was your brilliant idea."

"If you're not going to help, go back to bed."

"Like that's a possibility."

He took a bottle from his back pocket and pushed it into the baby's wailing mouth. She continued to cry around the nipple. "She doesn't want it."

"You just fed her half an hour ago." She went back into the bedroom to escape the penetrating noise, tried to ignore it for another few minutes, but couldn't. It wasn't maternal instinct but sheer exhaustion that moved her to take an old T-shirt from her drawer, cut it beneath the armpits, and stretch the fabric tube over her body like a sash. "Give her to me," she said, plucking the baby from Benjamin's arms. Abbi wrapped the shirt around her, hanging the infant in the hammock of sorts across her torso, and walked. The baby bounced naturally with each step Abbi took; she whimpered and hiccupped, but the screaming stopped.

"Finally," Abbi said.

Benjamin came close to her, close enough that the space between them was occupied only by the baby. He smoothed Silvia's tiny eyebrows. "Thank you," he said.

Abbi nodded. "I might as well keep her until she starts up again." She lowered herself into the couch, imagining this was how a pregnant woman moved, off-balance with the weight in her abdomen, flexing her knees and holding the couch's arm, and falling back on the cushions without folding at the waist. She lifted her feet up, bending her knees so Benjamin could sit on the other end. He closed his eyes, and Abbi hesitated only a minute before stretching her legs, resting her heels on his thighs. Benjamin lightly stroked her shin before dozing off, his hand suddenly heavy against her skin.

Benjamin went to work wearing fatherhood under his eyes and on his shoulder. After he left, Abbi dozed when Silvia dozed, and kept moving while the infant was awake—doing laundry, vacuuming, scrubbing the tub with the lemon rinds she saved during the week—because if she sat, she'd fall asleep. She carried Silvia with her to the mailbox, the sun giving her a bit of an energy boost, and pulled out an envelope of coupons and a phone bill. Closed the box with her elbow.

Marie Vilhauser dug in the flower bed along the split-rail fence separating their yards. She didn't look up as Abbi passed, but said, "First coupla weeks are hardest. But it stops, eventually, the crying does."

Abbi nodded. "Thanks."

Chapter NINE

The computer listed seven Savoies in the Buffalo area. Two lived on the same street. No James. No Jimmy. Two J's. Matthew copied them into his notebook, twice checking each letter, each number to be certain he'd not made a mistake. Then he figured the cost. Forty-one hours on a bus for eighty dollars—each way. By train, nearly a day and one hundred forty dollars, after he managed to get to the station in Minnesota. He jabbed his ballpoint into his pad, cutting the paper with deep, black lines. Threw the pen onto the table; it skidded off the end. He shouldn't be frustrated. He'd known it would be expensive.

But money meant time.

He tore the scored pages from his pad, rolled them between his palms, like a child forming a Play-Doh snake. The librarian scowled, tapped her watch. He relinquished the computer and found a desk in the back corner of the three-room public library.

He'd have to go by train. The bus took too long. He shouldn't miss a treatment, but could, had twice before. Once because of a snowstorm, and once when Lacie tripped and split her forehead open on the coffee table, and she wouldn't go to the hospital without him.

With taxi fares, he'd probably need at least four hundred dollars for the trip, if he spent the night in the train station and not a motel. He could do odd jobs—painting, maybe, shoveling in the winter—and collect bottles and cans for the refund. Another year of long, tedious evenings and bus rides and needle sticks.

He was being stupid. Bullheaded. His aunt could pick up the phone and, in ten minutes, find out if Matthew was kin to any of the names on his list. But it seemed rude to have Heather calling paper names, asking if they had a son they'd forgotten. And he wouldn't have some random relay operator do it—him sitting in the apartment typing out his life story while a stranger read it off a screen to another stranger in Buffalo, who may or may not care to know him.

Besides, he didn't just want a kidney; he wanted a father. That was something that needed to be done face-to-face, man-to-man.

The library closed at five in the summer, and it was close to that. Matthew thought of things he could do instead of going home. There weren't many. Too bad it wasn't a dialysis day.

He envied Jaylyn sometimes—she always had a place to go, had people who wanted her—until he considered the price she paid for those perks. She gave herself away to anyone who showed a bit of interest. Not worth it.

Dirk was cheating on his aunt, again; that was what the crisis had been this morning. Matthew had cooked eggs and toast for his two younger cousins and ate with them until Heather came storming from the back of the apartment, hurling her boyfriend's clothes out the front door. Dirk followed, grabbing her wild arms. She whacked him across the face with his sneaker; blood spurted from his nose, and Matthew had pulled the girls to a neighbor's apartment before biking to school to use the computer lab.

The lights blinked on and off, the ten-minute warning. He slipped on his backpack, passed Skye hunched in a desk cubby, her thick hair veiling her face. He watched as she picked the metal security strip from a magazine, stuck it under the desk. He tugged her sleeve and she jumped.

"Matty, don't do that. You scared the stink out of me."

Sorry, he wrote. You hiding out?

"Yeah. You?"

70

He nodded. What are you reading?

"Nothing. The newspaper." She shuffled the gray pages over the latest issue of *Seventeen*.

Want to get some ice cream? My treat.

"I'm kinda . . . not really eating ice cream right now."

You rather go home?

"Okay, well, maybe a pop. Let me just put this back."

She kept the magazine hidden beneath the newspaper and disappeared into the stacks for a minute. When she emerged, he saw the outline of a rectangle beneath her thin yellow T-shirt, the silhouette of a woman, the word *Maybelline*. He stood too close to her as they left, his stomach nearly against her back, so the librarian wouldn't see it, too.

They walked to Phil's Steak n' Bake, Skye scuffing her heels through the gravel.

New shoes? Matthew asked. She wasn't wearing her usual canvas tennis shoes, the black ones covered in pink hearts and top-hatted skulls. These were light blue with pointed toes and fat white soles.

"I found them in the back of Ma's closet. I'm going for the granny look. You like?"

Crazy.

"That's me."

The small restaurant, decked out in Old West style, was fairly busy for a Tuesday. Some locals, some travelers who pulled off the highway for food or toilet, and some families from the KOA down the road. They sat, and Skye pulled the magazine from her back. He flipped the page in his pad, but she snatched his pen. "Don't start."

He ordered a sundae, she a Sprite with two scoops of chocolate ice cream floating in it. She drank from three straws and paged through *Seventeen*. They didn't talk, weren't there for talking. Skye tore several uneven circles from the magazine and sucked up the foam at the bottom of her mug. He paid at the register, and someone bumped him.

"Hey, Matt. Long time no see," Jared Whalen said.

Matthew took a pen from beside the credit card machine and scribbled on the napkin, *Busy, busy.*

"I hear you," Jared said, stuck his finger through a hole at the hem of his dingy T-shirt. "Well, I don't hear you. But I, you know, get you. It. What you said. I mean, wrote."

Relax. It's all good.

"I know, Matt. Sorry. I think I must be fried from the sun." He'd rolled the bottom of his shirt into a fat sausage of fabric while he spoke, eyes flickering toward Skye, and then back to his nervous fingers. "Mr. Hoogendoorn hired me on for harvest."

You leave for college soon, right?

"End of August." The women behind the counter gave Jared two styrofoam containers. "Wouldn't have made it without you. You know that."

Nah. I'm not the only nerd around.

Matthew had tutored Jared in occupational math and chemistry last year, a favor for Skye. When she'd asked him, he protested a bit, wondering if her boyfriend might do better with a tutor who could actually explain concepts to him verbally. Skye batted away his worries. "He asked if you would do it," she said. "He likes you."

I like pie. That doesn't mean it should help me with my math homework.

"Like you'd ever need help. Seriously. You know how shy he is. Come on. Just do it for me."

That had been early October. By December, Skye had broken up with Jared. Matthew knew none of the details, except that Jared was clearly heartbroken, and Skye hadn't seemed too happy about it, either. He asked Jared if he'd feel more comfortable with another tutor. "Only if you would," he said.

So Matthew had spent every Tuesday and Saturday afternoon writing out equations and diagrams, and word problems asking for the width of a river if the length of line segment AC and angle ACB are known. Jared muddled through with C-pluses and made it into college—first in his family—for his mother.

"She's convinced the land killed my pops," Jared had said. "I think I'll find my way back to a farm, though. I'm not the desk-sitting type." Matthew had agreed; winter wheat filled Jared's veins, and that wouldn't disappear after a couple of years of lecture halls and frat houses.

Jared now picked up his food and tried one last time to make eye contact with Skye. She buried her head deeper into the magazine. "Well," he said, "I'll see you around. Tell your cousin I said hey."

Matthew returned to the table. Skye was leafing through his notebook. He held out his hand.

"Nope. Not until you tell me about this." She tapped the heart he'd doodled on the inside front cover, the one with the *E* inside it. "Who is she?"

Matthew flared his nostrils, snapped, pointed to the pad. She tore out a page, gave it to him.

I could just buy a new one.

"Yeah, but you want to tell me."

He grinned at her, wrote, Ellie Holt.

"Are you serious? She's a brain."

I know.

"She's not that pretty."

Yes she is.

"She's not. She has a mustache."

He rolled his eyes, blew a long puff of air through his lips, felt them vibrate with sound.

"She does. All the kids call her Stache."

You're worse than Jaylyn.

"How can you even say that?" She slung the pad at him. "You *are* a retard."

He shouldn't have, did it only to be hurtful because she made fun of Ellie. He knew she hated being compared to her sister and, really, they couldn't have been less alike.

Jaylyn was tall and beautiful and thin with youth, though Matthew could imagine her looking like her mother in another decade, with an extra twenty pounds of life clinging to her hips. But now, today, that didn't matter. Jaylyn strutted through the dusty streets of Beck County, expecting all eyes on her, and they were.

In another place, a place where not everyone lived paycheck to paycheck or harvest to harvest, Jaylyn might not have been considered much more than pretty white trash. But there was no preppy, rich in-crowd in Beck County, not like in those teen movies Sienna begged Jaylyn to bring home from the grocery; everyone smelled like sweat and farm, wore clothes from JCPenney or Wal-Mart, or hand-me-downs. So popularity depended less on money and more on beauty. And Jaylyn had that in abundance.

Skye could never keep up. She was her father's daughter, heavy all over, from hands to hair to gait. She could have been pretty, but she worked to be the anti-Jaylyn, letting her hair obscure her face and her dark, oversized clothes hide the rest of her.

Sorry, he wrote.

"Whatever."

Really.

"Well, I shouldn't have insulted your girlfriend."

She's not my girlfriend. He dragged the cap of his

pen through a blob of hot fudge he had spilled on the table, swirling the dark goo. You see Jared come in?

"Hard to miss."

He liked you. Still does.

"Old news. I'm so over it."

You won't tell me what happened with you guys?

"Nothing happened. I was just done. Learned from the best, right?"

He looked at the clock on the wall, the second hand jerking up a second, then twitching back a half, up and back, up and back. It's nearly seven. We should go. Walk or hitch?

"Hitch, definitely." She touched his arm. "I won't tell anyone about Ellie."

I know.

"No you don't. But I promise anyway."

⌒

The apartment glowed with one hidden light—the hallway light, oozing into the living room—and the television. The blinds were closed. Lacie and Sienna hugged their knees on the couch, skin blue in the cartoon glow, dark eyes dancing with yellow Sponge Bob irises. Heather sat in the dining area on a plastic lawn chair, feet propped on another, cigarette twined in her fingers.

"Nice of you to grace us with your presence," she said, took a long draw; the ash burned orange, then died. "Not like we needed anything from you tonight."

"We were at the library," Skye said.

Heather snuffed out the butt on her dinner plate, lit another. "I don't need this garbage from you, too, Skye."

"It's the truth."

Heather turned to look at Matthew. He nodded.

"Dirk's gone." Smoke leaked from Heather's nose, between her teeth.

"For how long this time?" Skye asked.

Heather ignored her. "I'm going to bed. Get over here and kiss me good-night."

Lacie skipped into the dining area, knocking the ashtray off the plastic chair while throwing her arms around her mother's waist. Heather pulled the girl off by the strap of her tank top, said something; Lacie's head flopped forward.

"I mean it. I better not find this mess in the morning," Heather said. She looked at Sienna. "You can't get your lazy self off the couch to say good-night?"

" 'Night," Sienna said.

"See how I jump for you when you want something." Heather turned down the narrow hallway, and Skye followed. Matthew felt two doors slam through his feet.

He found the spray cleaner from beneath the sink and gave a handful of paper towels to Lacie. He squirted the floor and she wiped, then he took her into the bathroom for a shower, her limbs dingy with the day's play. She dug around the laundry basket, finding a mismatched pajama top and bottom, put them on. He combed her waist-length hair, and she danced and stomped as he wiggled the plastic teeth through the snarls. She finally turned and said, "Matty, you're hurting me."

He tried to reply, "Sorry," but didn't know how it came out. Lacie seemed satisfied with whatever sound he'd made, and let him finish untangling her wet knots.

"Can I sleep out with you tonight?" she asked.

Matthew caught himself before he sighed, and nodded instead. She didn't ask often, but when she did, it meant the floor for him. Tonight wasn't exactly a night he wanted to give up the couch. He went into the living room and pressed the Off button for the television.

"Hey," Sienna said.

He pointed down the hall.

"Ma didn't say I had to go to bed yet."

He bent his arm and whipped his index finger toward the hall-way again. "Fine," she said, and shoved Lacie into the wall on the way by.

Matthew covered the couch with a sheet and tucked Lacie into it, covered her with another. Then he found a sleeping bag in the closet and unrolled it onto the floor, lay down. Lacie's foot hung over his head. He grabbed it, tickled the bottom. She jerked it back up on the cushion, and he wished he could hear her giggle.

Chapter TEN

Benjamin called his mother.

Usually she phoned him, once a week on Sundays; he made sterile conversation with her and his father—What's going on at the university? At church? How is this neighbor or that colleague?—fulfilling his obligation as a son. It wasn't that he didn't want to speak to them, but it took effort to act as if he was holding it together. Today something inside him remembered his Band-Aided knees and the *gharge*—fried, sweet pumpkin bread—she had made for him while he lay in bed with the chicken pox, and he realized he desperately wanted to feel that security again.

She answered on the third ring.

"*Aai*, hi."

"Benjamin. I am surprised to hear you. Happy, yes. But something is wrong?"

"No, no. Everything's fine. I just wanted to see how you were doing."

"I have much blessings."

"And how's *Ba*?"

"Good. Busy. You can come see us soon? I know he will like that much."

"I'll have to check with Abbi."

"If it is too much with that baby, we will come to you."

"I said I'd check with Abbi, see if she's up for taking a trip," he said, his words craggy.

Silence.

"Okay, I'm going now," he said. "I'll let you know about the visit in a couple days."

"Benjamin . . . give our love to Abbi."

"I will."

He had to admit, both his parents had accepted Abbi into their family more easily than he had expected. Sangita gave her a *mangala sutra*, the traditional Indian wedding necklace. Harish invited her to live with them during Benjamin's deployment. Both did whatever they could—whatever they were capable of, given their personalities—to make her feel welcome.

They had met Abbi several times when he had first begun dating her. He brought her to church and Sunday lunch, and afterward they would joke together about seeing his parents' heads explode if they ever married. But as the relationship became more serious, Benjamin stopped bringing her around; he didn't want his parents to see that Abbi had gotten inside him.

He proposed to her the night before his graduation, and after the ceremony his parents took both of them to dinner. And then he told them about the impending marriage, how he and Abbi planned a quick double ceremony at the courthouse with Stephen and Lauren. Neither reacted, except to offer congratulations. But the next day his father asked to speak with him and, without emotion or pretense, asked simply if Benjamin had considered "all facets of the equation."

"Facets of the equation? Come on, *Baba*. This is love, not chemistry."

"A marriage is more than fleeting feelings, which can come and go. If you do not know this, you will have difficulties."

"You just want me to have you find me a proper Indian girl? A nice mail-order bride, like Aai?"

"Benjamin, you misjudge us. If Abbi is whom you will marry, we will support you. But do not be so naïve to think your mother and I cannot understand what you feel because we not so American as you."

"I didn't say that."

"You did not have to," Harish said.

His father had come to the United States for college on a student visa, completed his Ph.D. in biochemistry at the University of South Dakota, and stayed on as a member of the faculty. There were no Indian women in Vermillion, though, except for a couple professors' wives and a handful of students—or, if there were, he had little time to search for them after his lectures and research. Harish didn't scour advertisements or pay some finder's fee to an arranged marriage company; he simply sent word to his relatives back in Maharashtra that he wanted a wife. And he found one—or, one found him. Sangita Mehta wrote a letter to him in early 1980, saying she would come cook and clean, and bear him a child, if possible. Well past marrying age at nearly forty, her first two husbands in the grave, she was ready to escape her rural home and the religious tensions in a country where Christians comprised less than one percent of the population.

Benjamin had been born two years later.

It was true; he had discounted his father's words. He thought his parents knew nothing of the foolishness of love. They respected and honored and served one another—but if they felt more than that, Benjamin hadn't seen it. He'd never even seen them kiss.

Harish hadn't been the only person with concerns about the match, though. Stephen came to him two nights before the wedding and said, "Are you sure?"

In retrospect, Benjamin understood where his friend was coming from. The young loved more easily, without looking ahead or behind, without considering those pesky nuisances that sprout up when two people shared space—she squeezed the toothpaste tube in the middle and let the excess gel crust up until the top wouldn't screw on; he didn't turn off the lights when he left the room, and ran the shower while he read on the toilet, forgetting how long he'd been sitting there. They became less pesky and more nuisance as time passed.

But there were bigger things between him and Abbi than toothpaste and wasted water, things defining them as people, wound so tightly around bone and blood vessel, which no surgeon would ever dare remove. These were the things Stephen meant him to consider, although Benjamin wondered if Stephen had the slightest notion of real differences. He and Lauren seemed perfectly matched in every way, like when God made them male and female, he took them apart from each other knowing full well one day they'd come back together.

Benjamin's blindness had been love-induced, yes. He loved Abbi for who she was. And he loved her because she was everything his family wasn't, which God knows was never good for a relationship. But there was a bit more truth hidden behind his shame.

They had dated a year before going to bed together, an accident, a moment of weakness, they told each other. But it happened every month or so—always unintentional—and one or the other would sneak away in the night and they'd ignore it, ashamed, not knowing quite how to deal with the aftermath of it, not quite wanting to give it up. And when he asked Abbi to marry him, he did it because he loved her, and because he'd slept with her. He couldn't imagine telling another woman he'd been with someone else.

Stephen knew him well enough to figure it out, Benjamin was fairly certain. Now he wished his friend had come out and said something directly, confronted him, peeled Benjamin's hands from his eyes and told him that guilt made bad glue. It wouldn't hold him and Abbi together. It wouldn't have stopped Benjamin from marrying her, but at least he wouldn't have been as surprised—as desperate—when the problems began.

Two tinfoiled pans sat on the kitchen table. He lifted the corner of one to find a tray of egg noodles congealed in condensed soup, gray mushroom pieces stuck to them. People had been dropping meals by all week, casseroles loaded with cheese and eggs and cream sauces; Abbi wouldn't eat them. He'd taken them to work to feed Roubideau and the deputies.

He found her at the computer in the spare room, Silvia limp across her knees. Abbi touched her finger to her lips.

"How long has she been out?" he whispered.

She clicked the Internet window closed. "Not long enough."

The infant stirred, rubbed her face against Abbi's denim-clad thigh. "I talked to my mother today," Benjamin said. "She wants to visit."

"You didn't tell her yes, did you?"

"No."

"Good. That's the last thing I need, her showing up here with her suitcase, ready to move in for six months." When they had first married, Sangita had grabbed—not patted—a handful of Abbi's stomach and shook it, saying, "Hurry with the baby, and I come stay to help." Abbi stood there, not knowing how to react. Benjamin explained to her that, traditionally, Indian mothers went to their married daughters' homes when a baby was born, and lived there for up to a year while the new parents adjusted. If the mother wasn't available—and Abbi's mother was not the live-in Mary Poppins type—the mother-in-law often took her place. He hadn't known about the infertility then. His mother still didn't know.

Abbi had a more difficult time adjusting to the role of daughter-in-law. Some of it was cultural. But a larger reason—though Abbi always denied it when he confronted her with the idea—was because she didn't know how to be a daughter. She and her mother had never had that kind of relationship.

"They don't have to come here," he said.

"So, what are you saying? You want to go see them, at their house?"

"I'm leaving it up to you."

"Are seeing them here and seeing them there my only two options, or can I pick door number three?"

"Look, see them, don't see them. Whatever you want."

"Whatever I want," she mumbled, squeezed her tangled ponytail through her hand and sighed. "Fine, have them come."

He rubbed the top of his head. They'd been at this for several days, since not long after Silvia came, sleeplessness not only dragging up their worst selves but making them more difficult to hide. "No, never mind. It's a long trip for them, and we're both exhausted. I'll tell Mom another time."

"I said to invite them."

"I can't win," he said.

"If you'd just listen to me, there wouldn't be an issue. You said pick. I picked."

"Yeah, but you don't want them here. I'm trying to be considerate."

"Considerate?" Abbi pushed the chair back from the keyboard. "Tell me, how is ignoring what I'm saying considerate?"

"You want them to come? Fine. I'll call them tomorrow and invite them for next weekend."

She yawned into the shoulder of her wrinkled shirt. "Wait. No. Have them come next month. I think we both need time to . . . settle in. But just, you know, make sure your mother knows this is only for the weekend."

"I will." He looked at her, suddenly ashamed of his outburst. "Abbi—"

"Here, take her," she said. "I'm going for a run. There's plenty of food out there, if you're hungry."

Silvia woke as Abbi lifted her into Benjamin's arms. She reached up toward his face, and he traced her chin, her miniature ears. Her eyebrows, one thin and straight as a fine-pointed marker line, the other feathering over the bridge of her nose. "Hello, beautiful," he said. "Are you ready for dinner? We'll go eat in just a minute. I promise." She stared at him with her murky blue eyes. He couldn't see himself in them.

He maneuvered the computer mouse, opened a Google window and scrolled through the browser history, clicking on Abbi's last site. A collection of soldiers' stories, told in their own words—about Iraq and Afghanistan, about coming home.

She was trying to understand him.

He could barely understand himself.

Chapter ELEVEN

She couldn't work with the baby around.

When Benjamin told her she could quit the grocery, Abbi had thought she'd have time for her pottery again. She found she had no spare minutes, after feedings and diaper changes and simply comforting the fussy baby. And Silvia fussed for hours at a time, as if she thought, eventually, her cries would bring the voice she expected to find after her birth, the voice she'd heard for nine months, the one that became warm and familiar as she sloshed around in the dark. Or maybe she just knew she wasn't wanted—not by her mother, not by her foster mother.

With all their time together, Abbi had begun to decipher Silvia's cries—terse and low-pitched when hungry, spastic whimpering when bored, and a continuous, droning whine when uncomfortable or overtired. She felt almost competent when she was able to tell Benjamin, "She just wants to be held," and Silvia quieted after he nestled her in his arms. And Benjamin almost noticed Abbi then, too, as if he thought she might be good for something other than reflecting all he didn't want to see.

She slid open the door into the backyard. Silvia napped in the sling Abbi wore over her shoulder and across her chest. Abbi paced off a three-foot square in the center of the grass, took a shovel from the shed, and stabbed the dry grass. She stood on the blade, stomping on it like a pogo stick, Silvia bouncing against her belly. When she tried to scoop the dirt from the hole, she knocked the baby in the head with the handle.

Dropping the shovel, Abbi went into the house, found an umbrella in the hall closet, and tucked a bedsheet under her arm. Back outside, she spread the sheet on the ground, wriggled the still-sleeping baby from the sling and shifted her to the sheet. Abbi opened the umbrella to shade Silvia and then continued to hack at the ground until the wailing began again.

"Oh, Silvie," she said, grabbing the shovel with both hands and plunging it into the dirt. She gathered the baby and folded her back into the sling. Inside, she filled a bowl with hot water from the tap, dropped a bottle of soy formula into it for several minutes, then fed Silvia, cradling her in the corner of the sofa. The baby sucked and grunted—like a piglet, Abbi thought. She picked a flaky scab from Silvia's black hair, another. Cradle cap.

A heavy pounding came at the door. *Great, more food.* Must be a husband; the women knocked much more politely. The banging started again, and Abbi called, "One minute," as she struggled off the couch with the baby. She held the bottle upright with her chin and reached for the doorknob, opening to see a scarecrow of a boy standing on the patio, his wind-whipped hair the color of straw and long over his ears. He offered a sheet of creased paper to her. She tucked the bottle into the waistband of her shorts and read, I'm deaf, but I read lips. Then, beneath that, Looking for bottles or cans to return, or any odd jobs.

"We don't drink soda," she said, giving the flyer back to him. "I've seen you, in Food Mart. You're Jaylyn's brother?"

Smiling, he took a pad and pen from his back pocket and wrote, Cousin.

"Oh, right. Sorry."

Me too.

A hot wetness gushed over Abbi's arm. She looked, saw regurgitated formula seeping beneath Silvia's pimpled chin, felt it dripping down her pants, between the toes of her left foot. She groaned, moved the baby to the other arm, and Silvia spit up again. "Lovely."

The boy snapped his fingers, pointed to the baby and held out his arms. Abbi hesitated, then unlocked the screen door. "Thanks. If you don't mind. It will just take a minute for me to clean up."

She gave Silvia to him, watched as he cupped the back of her head with one hand. Abbi stretched to the sofa without uprooting her feet, grabbed a burp cloth and dropped it on her toes, stepped on it. She got another from the kitchen and smoothed it around the boy's shoulder, under Silvia's face. "Just in case," she said.

In the bathroom, Abbi wiped her arm and stomach with a washcloth and changed, keeping the door half ajar so she could hear the baby, or the front door, should it open. Nothing. She came back to the living room with a clean T-shirt and diaper for Silvia. The boy hadn't moved. She took the baby and asked, "What's your name again?"

He pulled his pad out. Matthew.

"I'll give you fifty dollars to dig me a hole."

Matthew nodded eagerly.

"It might take a couple days."

He shrugged and nodded again.

"Okay, let me show you."

She led him to the backyard. "I need a hole three feet square. Or round. Whatever's easier. It just can't be any less than three feet deep. Shovel's there. And there's a pitchfork thingy in the shed."

Matthew picked up the shovel and dug. Abbi watched him from the kitchen as she massaged olive oil into Silvia's scalp, combed her hair with a soft brush. Then she bathed the infant in the sink, and Silvia cried, her mouth pulled in small, her lower lip in a pout. After drying, Abbi twisted an unbleached cloth prefold diaper and pinned it around the baby, tugged a recycled wool soaker—one she'd made from an old sweater after felting it in the washer—and gently bent her into a T-shirt. Then she settled Silvia in the sling again and carried a glass of water to Matthew. He took a sip.

"You okay out here? It's not too hot today."

He nodded.

"Is that a yes to you're okay, or a yes, it's hot?"

He laughed and nodded again.

"Well, let me know if you need anything."

Matthew flashed a thumbs-up, poured the remaining water over his head, and went back to work.

Abbi didn't intend to nap, but the nighttime feedings hadn't lessened, and even though Benjamin was the one who got up, she couldn't sleep while he paced and sang and shook the mattress as he pounded each air bubble out of Silvia. After swaddling the baby into the Moses basket, she dropped onto the sofa and dozed until she heard the sliding glass door slam. She jumped up, slapped her cheeks, and told Matthew, "You can wash in the bathroom."

He shook his head and showed her his pad. *I have to go. I can finish Thursday.*

"That's fine. Hey, wait. What are you saving for?"

A trip to NY.

"Like a class trip?"

Yeah, he wrote.

"Cool," Abbi said. "You're hitting the city?"

He hesitated, wrinkled his forehead. Nodded.

⁓

Benjamin came home from work and hid behind the baby. He swooped through the door and took her from Abbi, and didn't let her go for the rest of the night. He'd become adept at managing one-handed—his left arm around Silvia, his right used for eating and reading and taking the garbage to the curb. He chattered at the baby, but he didn't speak to Abbi, not really. He tossed random statements into the air—"She needs a diaper change" or "Her skin is clearing up a little"—and they landed willy-nilly around the living room floor while he continued to entertain the baby.

She hadn't wanted to disturb the fragile peace between them. He was at least, she told herself, coming home at night now, even if she wasn't certain she wanted him there. She'd found it easier to breathe before, when she had her night alone, and didn't have to pretend to be busy, or make the effort to give "Mmms" and "Uh-huhs" after Benjamin's comments. She found those wordless vocalizations more effort than words themselves.

"I'm going to take a run," she said. She changed to her running clothes and sneakers, tied back her hair, and left. The screen door hissed closed behind her.

She liked to jog at twilight, when the details began blurring into the horizon. Tonight the sky was wan with harvest, a haze left in the air by combines cutting wheat and trucks hauling the grain to bin sites or local elevators throughout the county. She'd come to love the exercise. She didn't run to lose weight now—she'd never be some little waif of a girl, never smaller than a size ten—but had in the beginning, eight years ago, the summer before college.

Then she ran every day, pushing herself for three, four hours sometimes. She liked how she looked when the pounds spilled off, liked it too much, her mood dependent on the scale's tattling. By the time classes began, she was always tired and irritable and half-starved, and no longer had the time or willpower to spend long hours in the gym.

Now she spent maybe an hour on the roads, her quiet time, though if she went much longer than three days without it, she began to feel a bit antsy. A bit fat. And then the laxatives tempted her.

She shook her head, prayed, her words timed to her stride, bouncing in her mind. *Step. Step. Step. Step. Lord. Please. Hear. Me.* Tonight they were for Benjamin.

Abbi thought he was fine when he first came home, when the days were busy with reporters and photographers, with relatives and well-wishers, with various ceremonies and speaking engagements. A little more pensive, a little less young. But still fine, after what he'd been through. Things hadn't been all that wonderful between them when he left—her fault, she could admit it now. But he had brought up none of that, and they worked at reconnecting. Going on dates and hanging out at old haunts in Vermillion, hiking the Badlands, making love. And then the phone stopped ringing, and friends stopped dropping by, and life returned to quiet normalcy. And Benjamin slipped between the cracks of the mundane.

It didn't happen all at once. More a gradual fading—like wallpaper too long in direct sunlight, and no one noticed until a picture was moved and hung somewhere else, leaving a big, vibrant square of color peering out from the center of the washed-out pattern, and people thought, *So that's what it used to look like.*

One night Benjamin didn't finish the plate of his favorite *biryani*, didn't laugh at his favorite movie, didn't lie on the couch with his legs thrown over hers, and turned his back to her when she reached for him in bed. Abbi had curled in a ball on the other side of the mattress, listening to him listen to her, replaying the past months, and realized she'd been losing him for a long time.

Then she had come home from the grocery to find him on the bathroom floor, toilet swimming with vomit, an empty bottle of Paxil—prescribed by the V.A. doctor—on the sink. He shouted at her to leave and stayed there all night, emerging in the morning showered and shaved, and went to work without discussion.

Abbi hadn't known he was taking antidepressants.

She was good at doing nothing. Too good. But now something needed to be done for the baby's sake. Abbi had grown up with two parents who spoke only of the price of gas and what color to paint the shutters, and retreated to private corners when the trivialities ended. She didn't want that for Silvia.

At home she showered and, in her pajamas, crept into the bedroom. Benjamin read, propped up on both pillows, his back to her. Silvia slept next to him, covered with a flannel receiving blanket, feet poking from the bottom. Abbi wiped her palms on her flannel shorts, licked her lips. "Why are you doing this to her?" she asked.

He stiffened, turned the page of his book. "What?"

"Us."

"There isn't an us. Remember?"

"You know what I mean."

"I don't." He snapped off the lamp, pushed one pillow to her side of the bed. His own he folded in half, burrowed both arms under it and hugged it to his head.

"I'll tell them about the pills."

He said nothing, but his left hand squeezed the pillow. His right snaked out, touched Silvia's shoulder.

"I'll tell them all the things you left out. And they'll take her away and give her to a happy family."

"Why are you doing this?" he said to the crib.

Because I love you. "Because it's time something was done."

"What would you suggest? Since you're so full of suggestions tonight."

Abbi sat on the bed, at Benjamin's feet, could see the outline of his toes through the thin cotton. *One, two, three, four, five, six,* she counted, *and a half.* "I don't know. Talk to someone, maybe."

"Talk," he said.

"The V.A. could recommend someone. Or maybe Pastor Bob. You said you liked him."

He said nothing, so Abbi asked, "So?"

"We'll see."

We'll see. Her mother used to say that to her all the time, when she meant, "No," but had no interest in dealing with the repercussions of her answer. She took a breath, turned her head. The closet was open, all Benjamin's belts hanging on it, vegan dreadlocks down the back of the door. What did he think about when he saw them each morning, if anything at all? "You'll have to do better than that," she said.

"Fine," he said, lifting Silvia over his body to the outside of the mattress and shimming her between his arm and rib cage, her head tucked in his armpit, not quite in her own sleeping space.

"She can't stay in the bed," Abbi said, though they'd slept with her between them several nights, despite it being a foster care no-no.

He ignored her again, and she got up to brush her teeth, lingered in the bathroom squeezing blackheads on her chin. Then she called Genelise. No one answered. Benjamin was still awake when she went back into the bedroom; his eyes were completely closed. When he slept, his lids opened halfway and his eyes rolled back into his head so only the whites could be seen. The first night they stayed together—in college, when she and Benjamin played chicken with temptation by *just sleeping* in the same bed—she woke up and thought he'd died.

She crept over to the very edge of her side, used to balancing there, but tonight the fall seemed so far. So she rolled back toward Benjamin and, keeping her body on her half of the mattress, lay on his pillow. Her nose close to the nape of his neck, she smelled sweat and scalp and the bitterness of dried saliva—inhaled deeply, trying to pull the thoughts from his head with her breath.

He didn't lean back into her but also didn't move away. She slid her hand between her nose and the drool, and prayed he wouldn't give her the opportunity to prove she'd follow through with her ultimatum. She didn't know if she could.

Chapter TWELVE

Matthew poured Hi-C into the Dixie cups lined up on the plastic tray. On another tray, he counted out two vanilla crème cookies for each child. He stacked the juice tray on the cookie tray and carried them both balanced on his left arm, grabbing a bag of napkins before taking the snacks to the fellowship room, where the children sat on matted carpet squares, waiting to eat.

It was his fourth year helping with Vacation Bible School at Temple Methodist, the church he called his own. He'd come as a participant the first summer he'd moved in with his aunt, when he was eleven. Lacie was a few weeks old and crying all night, and when Heather saw the hand-painted banner announcing the free VBS for kids four to twelve, she dumped him and the other girls off there so she could have three hours of extra sleep.

He'd been to church on occasion, with his mother, in those few times she tried to go sober, when she attended meetings and lit candles and tried to be all spiritual. But he never learned the story of Jesus— acted out before him in mangy felt shapes—until that week, and when his teacher asked if he wanted Jesus to live in his heart, he raised his hand, along with the rest of the children.

He could still hear some then, with his hearing aids, and the pianist taught them all to sing "No, Not One" for the end-of-week parents' day and barbeque. He sang as loudly as he could, not caring that the others stared at him, snickering and poking each other, and holding their ears. It wasn't for them. His song was for Jesus, who heard him perfectly, the way he would sound when he was in heaven—or so Mrs. Merry had told him.

> There's not a friend like the lowly Jesus.
> No, not one. No, not one.
> None else could heal all our soul's diseases.
> No, not one. No, not one.
>
> Jesus knows all about our struggles.
> He will guide 'til the day is done.
> There's not a friend like the lowly Jesus.
> No, not one. No, not one.

They gave all the children a golden cross on a fluorescent cord, thin and rubbery like licorice. He chose the green-corded one, and wore the necklace every day under his shirt, until all the gold flaked away and the hanging loop broke off, and no amount of Gorilla Glue would fix it. And he attended church nearly every Sunday after that, Temple Methodist being only a third of a mile from his aunt's apartment. He rode his bike or walked in the winter. Sometimes someone from the church would pick him up if the weather turned sour. Matthew tried to get Jaylyn and Skye to go with him—after all, they had prayed the prayer, too.

Jesus is in your heart now, he'd told them.

"Give me a break," Jaylyn had said. "We just wanted the free ice cream coupons."

He passed out the cookies and juice to the children. The younger ones—the four-, five-, and six-year-olds—touching fingertips to their lips, then flapping their hand forward as if blowing a kiss. *Thank you.* He'd taught them earlier in the week.

With the food finished, the children were led back to their classrooms duckling-style, one behind the other in a line, and Matthew collected the crumpled cups and napkins most left on the floor. He piled the mats one on another and took them outside, shook the crumbs onto the back lawn. He swept the floor in the fellowship room, washed the serving trays. Then he sat reading the Bible, waiting for the day to end so he could walk Sienna and Lacie home.

The VBS committee didn't have anything else for him to do. Maybe the women would have been happier if he didn't volunteer to help. Each year they gave him snack and clean-up duty, and he didn't mind. But the distance remained between him and the church members, a Sunday assortment of fifty or so senior citizens—farmers born and raised, staid in the old ways—and a handful of young families looking for a back-to-basics style of worship, without guitars and drums, and streamers. Matthew didn't doubt they cared about him with proper Christian love, and the pastor had begun adding sermon notes to the bulletin, for him. But beyond that, it was a handshake and a smile, maybe a "How's school?" if someone felt particularly chatty. He couldn't blame any of them for not knowing what to do with a sick, deaf kid who used to show up to services with mismatched shoes and gum in his hair.

At noon, he walked Lacie and Sienna back to the apartment. Heather was home, and when he wrote he was going out for a while, she said, "Don't forget I work at three." He rode his bike down to the school. The library, Phil's Steak n' Bake, or the school ball field—they were where his peers hung out.

There was nowhere else.

Matthew hoped to see Ellie at the field, and she was there with a couple girl friends, watching the boys play baseball—just a pickup game, six against five, the dust swirling over their feet as they danced into position, then set, punching their gloves and bending low to the ground. The inning ended with a high fly ball to shallow left, the shortstop backpedaling onto the singed grass to catch it. He ran in and waved at Ellie. She waved back.

Why am I doing this to myself?

The ballplayers packed up their bats and trotted to their cars, shoving each other and spitting sunflower seeds into the grass. The girls jumped up to follow. Matthew bent down, pretending to fix his bicycle chain, hoping not to be seen behind the bleachers. But he saw feet in flip-flops with pink-painted toenails.

He looked up.

"Matt, hey. How are you? I haven't seen you all summer," Ellie said.

I've been busy. You know. With stuff.

"We're all going to Phil's for a soda. Want to come with?"

Yes, he wanted to go, wanted to pack all his spare minutes together and spend them with her. He'd been crazy about her since that day last November when she'd come to his church with her family for her cousin's baptism. Before then, Matthew had seen her around the hallways at school; he knew she was smart, and always smiled, at him, at everyone. But he'd never had a reason to speak to her.

That day, however, at the reception, between the cake and punch and all the conversation he couldn't understand, she'd found him sitting in the corner, alone, and asked, "Why did the chicken cross the Möbius strip?"

He blinked. Then he felt a little grin on his lips, and he pulled out his pad and wrote, To get to the same side.

"You got it," she said, smiling, her braces ringed with blue and orange bands, the school's colors. "I heard you are a math geek."

You know what a geek is, right?

"Yeah, of course."

What?

"A nerd."

No, before that. It's real meaning.

She shook her head.

Someone who bites the heads off live chickens.

"Oh, that's gross. You're not serious."

Really.

"I'm going to go home and look that up."

Go right ahead.

"I will."

The next day at school, he had found a folded sheet of paper in the vent of his locker. When he opened it, a widemouthed man peered out at him, and a cartoon rooster head stared down the man's throat. Above the chicken's head, a thought bubble had been drawn, and it read, *Help! I'd rather be crossing a Möbius strip!*

He turned to her now, shook his head.

"You sure? There's room in the back of Teddy's truck for your bike."

The shortstop. Teddy Derboven.

No thanks.

My aunt's going to work soon, and I have to watch my cousins.

"Well, okay. I'll see you, then."

She turned away, to her friends, and all three girls walked to the parking lot, Ellie's floral skirt swishing just below her knees. And Matthew biked home, knowing the math geek never got the girl, especially with a shortstop flexing and waving at her.

Chapter THIRTEEN

Benjamin heard the telephone ringing, though in his sleep he saw the sound coming from a machine gun. After four rings he opened his eyes, stretched backward to grab the receiver.

"Yeah."

"Patil, we got a fire." Wesley.

"Where?"

"At the Hoogendoorn place. East side."

"I'm coming."

Abbi had left the bed already, her pillow in her place. The baby slept in the bassinet with her fists near her ears, arms bent out from her shoulders in little L's. He tucked his pillow next to Abbi's and, after shimmying into his socks and pants, went into the basement to find Abbi at her sewing machine.

"There's a field fire I have to go to," he said, standing behind her. She wore a tank top, and in another time he would have kissed the knob of bone at the base of her neck, the one that protruded from her back when she hunched over.

"Okay." The needle continued up and down. She didn't turn.

"What are you making?"

"Something for the baby."

She couldn't even tell him something as small as what. He breathed a deep, disjointed breath. "Don't stay down here too long. You won't hear her if she wakes up."

She switched off the machine light. "I'll finish later. Do you want something for breakfast?"

"No time," he said.

～

Thirty-foot flames burned in a field of wheat stubble, backed up against a grassed waterway. The lone Temple fire truck hammered the inferno with water, men in rubber coats guiding the hose. The flames shrunk, bowed to the firefighters in submission, until the hose went limp and dry, and then they were up again, big, orange marionettes of fire dancing and jerking their way over the green and across another harvested field.

Benjamin crossed to Wesley, who stood with the fire chief.

"Out of water," Wesley said.

"We've called in the Lippman and Hensley trucks. They're on their way," the chief said.

Benjamin shielded his eyes, looked toward the fire, beyond it where two neighboring farmers sat on their tractors, disc implements hooked to the back, slicing grooves in the earth. "Looks like folks are trying to dig a fire line down there. I'll head over, keep an eye out."

Wesley nodded.

Benjamin started his car, the smoke dense and black enough to obscure his sight. Like the sandstorms in Afghanistan. Those were red, though, and loud, a freight train plowing through the desert. He honked, hoping anyone in his way would hear and move, crept down the road, past the fire, and eased the steering wheel to the left. Out of the corner of his eye he saw a reddish glare and two round lights.

The fire truck slammed into his car, Benjamin's head cracking against the driver's-side window. Smoke seeped around him, filling the Durango. He pawed at the door handle, his fingers sliding off it once, twice, before his arm dropped to his thigh. He turned his head, watched the black air curl into the passenger seat, thickening, stretching until it looked like a man. And then it was a man. Stephen, sitting right there, made of smoke and sorrow. Benjamin managed to flip his arm up, palm flapping against his face, and rubbed his eyes.

You sure got your bell rung, the smoke-man said.

You're dead, Benjamin thought. He heard shouting from far, far away.

Yes sirree. How are the toes?

Gone. Benjamin rolled his head from one shoulder to the other, then back, glass shards tumbling down his face. Coughed. *I can't breathe.*

Smoke will do that. Remember that fire outside Kabul? Man, that was smoke.

The one that killed the shop owner.

Black, black smoke. Like tar pouring into the sky.

What was his name?

Farhad.

Yeah. Him. He sold Doritos. And Hershey's. He remembered the chocolate but not the man. How was it some memories had wads of chewed gum on them, sticking to the bottom of his shoe, refusing to shake off, and others floated away, like wind, like clouds.

Like smoke.

That was some time, man, smoke-Stephen said. *And afterward we grabbed hands and prayed, and the guys laughed at us, but we didn't care. We were alive.*

For a while.

You should be praying now. Not talking to a dead man.

Benjamin coughed again. *I can't.*

Don't give me that, Sergeant.

This is all in my head.

Then I'm just saying what you already know.

The shouting closed in on Benjamin, in his ear. Words. He knew they were words, knew words had meaning, but he couldn't match the sounds with the pictures they conjured in his mind. The passenger-side door was pried open, and Stephen disappeared the way he came, in a pocket of smoke.

Hands against his head. Fingers tugging down his lower eyelids, pressed on the inside of his wrist. And then Wesley strapped a brace around his neck and the hands were back on him, wriggling him from the car, onto a board, into a box. A metal box.

An ambulance.

He had taken bodies out of ambulances in Afghanistan, unloaded the dead and piled them into helicopters. He knew who they were. Most of them.

⟶

He woke to a still but heavy fullness, a kind of whooshing sound, and blinked his eyes to clear the solid sleep from their corners. Squinted at the harsh white ceiling.

"The lights," he said, mouth dry as snakeskin.

"I'll get them." A familiar voice. Wesley. His face appeared over Benjamin. "You're in the hospital."

"I'm thirsty."

Wesley guided a striped bendy straw between Benjamin's lips, red and white, like a candy cane. The water tasted like warm plastic. He tried to turn his head; it was stuck. His hand skittered up his thigh, his abdomen, felt something cold and hard around his neck.

"You're okay," Wesley said. "Just a strain. And a concussion."

"What . . . I don't remember . . ."

"The fire truck. Couldn't see it through the smoke, I guess."

He saw the hazy bulge of a white gauze pad out of the corner of his eye, a ghost in his peripheral vision. His head pulsed rhythmically, the IV in his arm filling him with something to keep the pain away. But it lurked underneath the drugs. It always hurt later.

He touched the bandage above his left ear.

"Fourteen sutures," Wesley said.

If only all wounds closed so easily.

"I called Abbi. She's on her way," the deputy told him.

Benjamin closed his eyes, said nothing.

"You two having some trouble?"

"We're fine."

Wesley nodded once, slow and burdened, rolling his lips in until only his mustache could be seen. "I was in 'Nam, you know. Saw some nasty garbage. Not as much as some, though. Came home and my wife left me. Not Renée. My first wife. She should have left. I beat the tar out of her. More than once."

He said it in a flat, blue voice, and Benjamin rolled his eyes to the pastel-patterned wall. He thought of the time—the one time—he had grabbed Abbi. Hard, at the upper arm. She didn't move, but pressed back into the wall with stuttering breath, her nostrils open, her eyes wide. His grip loosened as he looked on her stricken face; he let go of her and put his fist through the wall. The living room mirror had jumped from the nail and to the floor. The glass didn't shatter; it cracked. Three long, jagged lightning bolts through the center.

He'd tried to ignore the hole for several days, but by doing so he thought about it more, turning his head when he passed it, spinning away from the doorway before going into the room. And then, when he saw Abbi had slid the table over so the hole would be blocked by a lamp, he took an afternoon to repair the wall. It had done nothing for his marriage.

"Guess you need to rest," Wesley said.

"Guess so."

"Well, then, I'll be 'round tomorrow. And after that, I suppose."

Benjamin licked his lips. "You could just call, see how I'm doing. You'll save gas that way."

"Patil," Wesley said, "I won't get that mileage reimbursement, then."

Chapter FOURTEEN

Abbi went to the meeting to get out of the house, away from Benjamin, whose week of required recovery time couldn't end soon enough. She took Silvia, despite his protests.

"You can leave her with me," he said. "I'm fine."

"It's for mothers of preschoolers," she said. "I can't go without one."

She could, but wouldn't. Somewhere in the back of her mind, the place she only went when she felt brave or when the Holy Spirit prodded, she wondered if Benjamin didn't turn purposely in front of that fire truck.

She never wore pants in the summer, but today she put on a pair of loose linen ones, too long on her, cuffs frayed from dragging on the ground. She pushed her hair up under a cotton snood and slid a clear retainer stud through her nostril. She didn't want to be known as Deputy Patil's wife today.

When they first moved to Beck County, he'd told her, "Population five thousand. Small enough to at least know of most everybody, and big enough not to." He worked on the knowing, and she worked on the not, but after three years even those she'd never been introduced to had an idea who she was—the freaky, peace-activist vegan with the hairy legs.

To be fair, most people who knew her weren't like that. Hardly anyone, really. But she was in a foul mood. Her size tens hadn't fit this morning. She wanted to hide from herself, not everyone else. If she wanted to be able to think of anything but her weight this week, she'd have to stop at the Shop and Go, for a bottle of senna. The prunes weren't cutting it anymore.

"You're wearing pants? It's sweltering outside," Benjamin said.

"Oh, now you're looking at me?" she snapped. *I'm such an awful wife.*

He stared for a moment, shook his head a little. "I need the car at one," he said, and closed himself in the bathroom. She turned the other way, stomped outside to the car, loaded down with baby and bag. Two different directions. They were always turning away from one another, even when going to the same place.

She bumped Silvia's head while putting her into the car seat. The baby wailed, and Abbi jumped in the front seat and started the car; the motion would calm Silvia. *Lord, is this what you really want for me?* She didn't feel like a mother. After knowing since twenty she'd never have children, her constant concern for a baby now seemed unnatural. Even when she and Benjamin considered adoption, it was always a school-aged child, walking and talking, and potty-trained—a hard-to-place kid no one wanted. In the past, when confronted with a writhing, wailing infant held up before her, some other mother's prize, she'd told herself she simply wasn't a baby person. The truth or not, it didn't matter now. She needed to find some mothering instinct. Or at least be able to fake it.

The meeting, at the Baptist church in the next county, began at nine thirty. The sign out front read:

**WE USE DUCT TAPE TO FIX EVERYTHING—
GOD USED NAILS!**

A big-toothed woman greeted Abbi at the registration table, handed her a paper name tag and marker; skin flapped from the undersides of her otherwise skinny arms. "Welcome," she said, cheeks frozen in two rouged mounds with her smile. "You're new, aren't you? I'm Betsy Swell. I know, funny name, whichever way you look at it. Your daughter is gorgeous. How old is she?"

"A month."

"What a fun time. I love babies. And I love, love, love that little pouch thingy you have her in. I saw what's-her-name using one just like that in *People* a few months ago. Where'd you get it?"

"I made it."

"Oh, how crafty. I wish I knew how to sew." The woman licked her teeth, running her tongue over them like someone would over dry lips. "Just fill out this registration form and give it on back to me at the end. First visit is free. After that, there's a membership fee. It's all there, on the form."

"I can read it."

The woman giggled, high and springy. "If you can sew, you can read, right? Just go on in. Sit anywhere you'd like. We don't have assigned seating. Oh, wait. I think you have something stuck to your nose." She scraped the side of her right nostril with her fingernail. "Looks like a little piece of tape or something."

Abbi stood in the doorway, pressed up against the jamb, metal cold on her forearm. She scanned the tiny basement room for an empty chair, saw three of them, all squashed between chattering women, who drank coffee and laughed after every sip. She knew a dozen of them, should have known a few more. One of those *should knows* waved, pointing at the space next to her. Abbi squeezed in, sat sideways on the chair because there wasn't enough room for both her and Silvia between the table and the wall. A miniature metal washtub piled high with cheap, plastic baby dolls decorated her table—all the tables—their naked skin stamped with *Made in China for Dollar General*.

"Oh. My. Goodness. This is her, isn't it? The one they found? Janet keeps going on about it."

"It's her." The woman was Janet McGee's sister. She had come to church a few times. *Nicole . . . something.* Abbi snapped her fingers. *Nicole Webb.*

"Shanna," Nicole said to the girl on her right—they were both girls, really, about twenty, wearing lavender glitter nail polish and dark jeans—"this is that baby in the plastic bag."

"Really? Oh, she's so cute. How could anyone do such a thing?"

"You're gonna adopt her, right?" Nicole asked.

"We don't know yet," Abbi said.

"I hope they find those awful people who did it." Nicole bit her thumbnail, peeled off the top. Flicked it. "They deserve to be locked away forever."

"Where's your daughter?" Abbi asked.

"Nursery. You want me to show you where it is? Shanna's mother is working in there with the little ones."

"No, she's fine here." Abbi dove into the questions on the registration form, simply to avoid more questions—she had no plans of turning it in. Name. Birthday. Children. Anniversary. She had to think about that one. Dates didn't stick on her. There had been times when Benjamin woke her to breakfast in bed, and she'd look at him, mind ticking off the days of the week, until he took mercy on her and reminded her what the occasion was—if there was an occasion at all. Often there wasn't.

She missed that.

The woman from the registration tables tapped a microphone plugged into a karaoke machine.

"Hi, and welcome, all you ladies. I see some new faces today, so if some of you old crusties see a newbie, make sure you make them feel comfy and cozy here. Okay, then, let's open with a mighty word to our mighty God."

The room grew silent, sacred, except for a toddler crunching Cheerios, and another saying "Ba, ba, ba, ba," until his mother crammed a pacifier into his mouth. Then Betsy finished and introduced the guest speaker, who led the group in baby-massage techniques.

"That's right," the speaker said. "Massages aren't just for you and your hubby. Babies love them, too. It's calming for them, and it's a bonding experience between mother and child." She instructed everyone to take a plastic doll and a dab of oil, and practice the skills she showed them. "Don't be shy, now, ladies. Rub, rub, rub."

Betsy approached Abbi. "Oh, she's fast asleep," she said. "Why don't you go right ahead and stick her in the nursery, so you can have your hands free."

"I'd rather she stay with me."

"Well, okay, then. If you change your mind, I'll introduce you to the sweet sitters in the baby room and—"

"I already told her," Nicole said.

"Just remember this time is for mommies, too. A little break from it all," Betsy finished and headed to the next table to bother someone else.

After Baby Massage 101, another woman brought out canvas tote bags and glue guns. Everyone attached plastic flowers to their bags, including Abbi. As she alternated half-dollar-sized sunflower heads with umber buttons, she felt almost split in two, a meaningless craft project incompatible with the life she had at home. She looked around at the other women, wondered how many of them walked through life in halves—the public half who smiled and seemed so well-adjusted, and the private half slogging through her own personal hell.

In the car, she tossed the snood in the back seat, shook her hair loose, and rolled her pants to just below the knee. She fished her silver hoop from her bag, stuck it into her nose. She had time before Benjamin needed the car and didn't want to be home with him for any length of time.

But if she drove past the grocery, she'd stop and buy a bottle of laxative. She'd managed to go four months without taking them to purge, and each time she started using them again she found it more difficult to stop. So she drove around while Silvia continued napping until she slowed in front of a black metal mailbox with **RIGN Y** stuck to the side in gold letters, a magnetic yellow ribbon on the top. The driveway, nearly a mile long, slanted downward to the farmhouse, and Abbi could see dark specks moving on the porch, in the front yard. One of them was Lauren, she was almost certain.

Lord, when will she forgive me?

She went in and Benjamin left. She had no clue where he was going.

Abbi put in a load of laundry, then another. She washed the kitchen floor and took frozen black beans from the freezer to defrost for dinner. Bean burritos for her, with fresh salsa. Benjamin would eat them, too, if there was nothing else. A small plastic bag of ground beef stuck out from behind the ice cube tray. She grabbed that, too, and dropped it in a pot of lukewarm water.

She prepared a bottle for Silvia and, in the bedroom, stripped off the baby's wet diaper, cleaned her with a bamboo wipe. She looked at the tiny body, all torso and head, feet smaller than her hands. She traced the crease circling Silvia's chubby wrist, remembering the same line on her younger brother's, there for the longest time and then, suddenly, gone. How old had he been, then? Five, maybe six. From baby to boy overnight.

"Wait here," she said, going to the kitchen, shuffling through the spice cabinet for the bottle of apricot oil.

She unfolded an old beach towel from the linen closet and covered the bedsheets before rolling Silvia onto it. She spilled a few beads of oil into her fingers, rubbed her hands together to warm it. Then, placing both palms on the baby's chest, she fanned her hands up and around, making a heart shape over the rib cage. Down the arms,

massaging Silvia's palms with her thumbs. Over her legs, just beginning to plump and roll with fat.

Abbi shimmied out of her shirt, hands fisted to protect the fabric. She unclasped her bra, grabbing the baby in the armpits, laid her
on her chest, skin against skin, like a mother cradled her own right
after birth. She stroked Silvia's back, listening to her coo, then fuss
for lunch.

Sitting against the headboard, Abbi gathered the slippery little
body against her stomach; a drop of oil tickled as it slipped into her
navel. She reached for the bottle on the nightstand, turned it upside
down until a globe of formula bubbled on the rubber nipple. She
touched it to her breast, the white liquid quickly spreading on her skin.
Silvia turned her head and latched on, suckling as Abbi continued to
trickle formula down her skin, into the baby's mouth.

The front door slammed. Abbi yanked Silvia from her breast.
The baby screamed; Abbi bent over, drawing in a thick, fuzzy breath
to muffle her own scream, her nipple on fire from the quick release.
She heard Benjamin's limp-run down the hallway and, rolling Silvia
on the bed, managed back into her shirt before he barged through
the door.

"What's wrong? Is she okay?" he asked.

"You feed her." Abbi shoveled the infant, now purple with confusion, to Benjamin. A dark, greasy stain appeared on his shirt. "I'm
just . . . no good at it."

She went to her studio. With a wire, she cut a slab of cured clay
and smashed it onto the center of her potter's wheel. She sat, pushed
against the kick wheel, squeezed a sponge of water over the clay. Her
hands slid over the mound, slick as Silvia's oiled skin.

This she knew. What she'd felt with Silvia at her chest— No.
She didn't know that sense of motherhood, what she thought she
wanted, that thing others called bonding, or love, perhaps. The baby
wasn't hers. It would be at least six months before adoption could

be considered. Until then, the search for someone she belonged to—blood family, always thicker than strangers—continued. And if that someone was found, Silvia would be gone, and Abbi would feel it, like a nursing baby torn off her mother's breast. She couldn't go through that. She'd already lost her husband.

Chapter FIFTEEN

When he arrived at the Patil house, Matthew saw Abbi in the backyard, spreading sheets of newspaper over the ground, covering them with scraps of vegetables and fruit rinds and flower stems. She placed an unfired piece of pottery on each length of paper, rolling and securing them with copper wire.

He tapped her shoulder. What are you doing?

"I'm prepping my pottery for firing."

With rotting banana peels?

"Potassium can cause greenish hues on the stoneware. The other stuff will leave other colors. I hope. It's not an exact science. It's more of a throw-everything-in-and-see-what-happens."

You mean in the kiln?

"I mean in the hole. Put the pots in, some wood, some manure, light it on fire, and see what happens."

I dug the hole for you to burn garbage.

Abbi laughed. "Hey, you got paid for it, didn't you?"

Matthew laughed, too. He liked Abbi—not old enough to parent him, not young enough to be a peer. Not familiar enough to be a sister. But she wasn't like most people he knew, and it had nothing to do with the ink peeking from her tank top or the ring in her nose. His aunt had a couple of cheap, shaky tattoos—one on her ankle, one on her hip—and most of her boyfriends had had blue-green dragons or daggers or women on their biceps. Jaylyn pierced her navel without Heather knowing, not that his aunt cared when she found out.

Abbi seemed confident being a bit offbeat. Not in a phony I-don't-care-what-you-think way, like his cousins or the girls at school who did outlandish things in the name of individuality while glancing over their shoulders to see who watched. Abbi didn't hesitate to run to the store with clay in her hair, or turn handsprings in the backyard because she suddenly got the urge to. And she talked with him about things no one had spoken to him about before, asked questions as if he was her spiritual equal. Sometimes Matthew answered, and sometimes he shrugged and shook his head, but either way he enjoyed the fact that she even asked.

Can I take Silvia for a walk?

"Sure. Go ahead. It's a great day for it. Just be back before four thirty."

Stroller?

"We don't have one. When I take her out, I wear her."

Uh, no.

"Come on. You don't have to use the girly pouch. I have something more masculine."

???

Abbi carried Silvia, who'd been lying inside on a blanket, and said, "Ta da," as she unrolled a long, black cloth.

I don't get it.

"Hold her. No, against you. No. With her stomach to your chest."

He did, and Abbi wound the fabric around him, tying it at his waist.

I feel like a mummy.

"Have a nice time, King Tut."

Matthew walked away from the houses, out toward the farm roads, and he talked to Silvia because no one could hear him, and because he'd seen Abbi do it.

When Lacie was a baby, Heather had rarely said anything to her, didn't do much other than stick a bottle in her mouth when she couldn't get Skye or Jaylyn to do it. Or him. He didn't mind. But he never understood why his aunt kept having children. He couldn't say she didn't care about the girls, but she didn't act the way he thought a mother should. Not that he'd had any great example himself. It was more that he knew how mothers *shouldn't* act, knew plenty about that. He used to think he'd set his expectations too high, wanting a Maggie Seaver or a Clair Huxtable, loving and understanding and strong, but perhaps extinct in real life. Then he saw how Abbi parented Silvia, putting her first when she didn't feel like it—a child not even of her own flesh—and realized yes, some children honestly would rise up and call their mothers blessed.

He kissed Silvia atop her head. He was falling in love with her, too, which didn't surprise him. Since he'd first held Lacie, he'd always imagined being a father, one who didn't run out on his kid, leaving him with a druggie mother to face a life-threatening illness alone. Judging from the guys at school, with their rush to find someone to buy them beer on Friday nights, and their preoccupation with video games and girls, he didn't think he'd find many people his age who thought the same way. Not that Matthew wanted a child tomorrow. If he lived that long, there was college and marriage; the former would prove easier than the latter. He couldn't imagine anyone wanting to be his wife.

At least he couldn't pass his disease on.

Matthew circled back to the Patil house. Abbi had put away all her newspaper-wrapped pottery.

You're not going to fire them today?

"It's supposed to rain tonight. Did you have a nice walk?"

He nodded.

"Hold her. I'll unwind you." She did, and when she lifted Silvia away from his chest, the air rushed against the slightly sweaty place the baby deserted. It almost felt as if a hole was left there, in that cooled space, and if he hadn't been able to look down and see his T-shirt, he might have thought just that.

He felt the argument through the doorknob before he walked into the apartment, considered turning around and going—where?

Good question.

Matthew went inside. His aunt and Jaylyn were shouting at one another in the living room, ignoring him. He scooted past them and knocked twice on the girls' closed bedroom door. Knocked twice again. His code. If someone didn't want him to enter, she had time to let him know before he barged in. When none of the girls poked her head out to tell him to scram, he opened the door. Skye was leaning against her headboard, one foot up on the mattress as she held a nail polish brush over it. Wads of cotton puffed from between her toes. Matthew sat next to her.

What's it about this time?

She screwed on the bottle cap. "Some deputy showed up here."

Deputy Patil?

"No. The fat one. I guess Rebecka McClure went missing."

What's that have to do with any of us?

"You know how last week Becka and Jaylyn had that fight over Dan Pitts?"

He shook his head.

"Well, they did. Right outside the grocery before Jaylyn's shift. I guess Becka was there, flirting with Dan, and Jaylyn flipped out. Becka tore out a chunk of Jaylyn's hair."

They actually fought, fought?

"You're surprised?"

I guess not.

"Anyway, Jaylyn was so ticked she started telling everyone that Becka dumped that baby off in the field."

Matthew blinked, and his hand went to his chest, his T-shirt still slightly damp. Or maybe not. He couldn't tell with the window fan blowing on him. It's not true.

"Maybe."

How would Jaylyn know anything?

"She said she saw Becka crying in the girl's bathroom back in January, right after Christmas vacation. Said Becka told her she was pregnant."

She could be lying.

"Which one? I wouldn't put it past either of them." Skye stretched out her legs, brought the soles of her feet together. She pinched the cotton between her big and second toe, stretching the cumulus cloud into a stratus before pulling the whole ball free. It dangled for a moment from its wispy tail; Skye watched it, bobbing in the fan's breeze, and then grabbed the remaining cotton from her toes in two handfuls. She squeezed them, threw them on the floor. "I don't think Becka did it."

Matthew hoped not. Abbi had told him that if any of Silvia's relatives were found and they wanted her, that was where she'd end up. The thought of the McClures getting custody of Silvia . . . Well, it made him queasy. He didn't know them, not really, but once Rebecka had come to school with the skin on her stomach nearly scrubbed away, the wound all oozy and kind of yellowish because the scab hadn't had time to harden yet. He only saw it because she had lifted her sweater a little to scratch at it.

He wrote her a note asking what happened and tossed it on her desk while they switched their reading books over to their social studies ones—he was new to the school, and sat next to her in the sixth grade—and she looked startled that he'd even noticed.

She wrote back, *I fell,* and ignored him the rest of the year.

When he told Skye what happened, she had laughed at him. "You dummy. Her mom did that to her. She thinks Becka's got a demon."

A what?

"You know, a demon. Like in *The Exorcist*. Her mom uses sandpaper to scrub her wickedness away. That's what Aaron says, at least. He used to go to Becka's church."

Matthew never told the teacher, or anyone else, because then, at eleven, he still would have wanted to go back and be with his mother no matter what she did to him, a child's love for his parents the only love he had no ability to pick or choose. Now he knew better.

But Rebecka's parents seemed to have given up on her anyway. She no longer wore long skirts, but jeans with phrases like *you rock* and *so hot* scrawled in marker on the seat and legs. She ran with Jaylyn's crowd, or not, depending on who was fighting with whom over which guy. Still, he could see the McClures deciding to start over again with a grandchild, to fix the mistakes they made the first time around.

Would that mean less sandpaper, or more?

Skye swung her legs off the mattress and, using her freshly painted burgundy toes, raked the cotton under her bed.

They look nice, Matthew wrote, pointing to her nails.

"You don't know anything," she said, but smiled a little, shyly, pulling her feet back up onto the bed and rubbing her thumbs over the shiny color.

I know they look better than when Jaylyn does hers.

"That's 'cause she has gnome toes."

???

"Gnome toes. You've seen them. They're all bulby at the ends, and she doesn't even have pinky toenails. She paints right on the skin."

Gnome toes.

"That's what they look like to me."

And when was the last time you saw gnome toes?

She laughed. "Shut up."

You should smile more. It's nice.

Immediately he regretted his words as Skye's easy grin deflated. "There's not much to smile about."

You're wrong.

"C'mon, Matty, open your eyes. You live here, too." She curled up on the bed, kicking him away. "I hate it."

She cried with quiet little gulps, but instead of leaving, he stayed at the end of the mattress, all scrunched into himself so he wouldn't touch her. Not long after Lacie was born, his aunt had let what's-his-name—the boyfriend with the Fu Manchu—move in, and the two fought all the time, screaming and throwing things until he would give Heather a smack to shut her up. Sienna and Lacie slept through anything, but the three of them—Matthew and Skye and Jaylyn— would climb into one bed, each taking a turn being on the outside, holding the baseball bat or tennis racket, whatever was in arm's reach and could work as a weapon. The boyfriend never bothered with them, but they were all there, together, ready to protect one another should something happen.

So different now; they all pretended to sleep through the uncomfortable parts, ignoring the hurt, and each other. He didn't know how to react to the Skye in front of him now, the one who had tears instead of biting comebacks. So he did nothing until Jaylyn burst through the door, and said, "Get out."

And he went, because disappearing was something he knew how to do.

Chapter SIXTEEN

Benjamin sensed Abbi wasn't in the house as soon as he walked through the front door. Emptiness had its own personality; he had felt it inside enough to know it on the outside. When they first married, Abbi would always wake up before him; sometimes she'd go for a run, other times she'd make breakfast and read, standing, her back in the corner, where the countertops met. When he woke, he always knew before he opened his eyes—before he realized he was no longer sleeping—whether she was home or not.

He panicked now for a brief, irrational moment when too many terrible ideas clamored through his mind for him to separate them out into individual thoughts, and he was left with the rush of blood in his ears, an incoherent tangle of *what ifs* plopping heavily in his sinuses. He breathed deep and slow, willing the anxiety away, and the tangle unraveled in one long strand he could understand.

What if she's left me?

Absurd. Her battered Volvo sat in the driveway, and as he looked through the living room, into the kitchen, he saw the sliding glass door was open.

He filled a cup of water at the sink, eyes scanning the yard. In the only shaded corner, a teenaged boy sat cross-legged on a blanket, book in his lap. He leaned on one arm, positioned like a tent pole behind him. His other hand rested on Silvia's belly.

"Hey," Benjamin called. "You there."

The kid didn't look, didn't flinch.

Benjamin opened the screen door. "Hey, you. What are you doing?"

Nothing.

He crossed the grass, and the boy finally tilted his head up, flipped closed his book and dropped it, the sharp corner close to Silvia's cheek. Benjamin recognized him now. Matthew. Matthew Something. He snapped his fingers behind his back, thinking, trying to remember. Everyone in that apartment had a different last name. He'd been called there by neighbors—what?—at least four times in three years for domestic disturbances. Wesley had a couple calls logged, too. And Holbach.

Deputy. Matthew nodded sharply. A salute. Then he jerked his head sideways toward the ground. She's sleeping.

Benjamin crouched down for the baby; she rubbed her face against his shoulder before going limp in his arms. "Where's my wife?"

Nodding, Matthew first pointed to the shed, then to Silvia, holding out his arms.

"No, I'll take her."

Benjamin strode to the shed, tugged the iron latch. Abbi hunched over her wheel, earphones dangling from her head, arms red with clay. She looked up as the outside light passed over her hands, wiped them on her canvas painter coveralls. "You're home early," she said, shaking the wires from her ears.

"What's going on?"

"With what?

Benjamin tossed his head toward the yard.

"Matt?"

"You left him with the baby."

"I told you I hired him."

"No, you said you hired *someone*. To dig a hole, to mow the lawn."
Silvia shifted in his arms, and he readjusted his hold on her.

"He is mowing. But he's also been watching her," Abbi said, rinsing her arms in a bucket near her feet. "Just a couple days a week, so I can get some work done."

"You can't leave her with him."

She set her jaw, bucking against his words. She always reacted this way, stubborn and indignant, when Benjamin told her not to do something. "I already did."

"What if something happens?"

"I'm twenty feet away, Ben. You're acting like I dumped her with him for the month." Abbi unhooked the radio from her hip, dropped in on the workbench. "I'm just trying to get a little time to throw."

"Do it when I get home."

"It's too dark then."

"Before it gets dark."

"That's when I run."

"Then don't."

"He's deaf, Ben. He's not stupid."

"It's not that. He's . . . Look, there's been some issues at his home, between his aunt and her live-in. Several of her live-ins."

"I don't believe you're doing this." She stripped off her clay-hardened coveralls and hung them on the hook near the door. "Can I expect a lecture now about proverbial apples falling from trees? But not too far, right?"

"All I'm saying is we don't know this kid. We don't know his family."

"You seem to have some ideas about them."

"I'm trying to do what's best for Silvia."

"Really. By your logic, maybe Silvia shouldn't be around me. My parents were pretty bad, remember? My mother's a control freak and my father never spoke to any of us."

"Don't be—"

"Or you, for that matter. I mean, you're . . . Oh, wait—" she stepped around him, into the yard—"I guess I just proved your point."

Benjamin grabbed the door and, with all his anger, swung it closed. The latch clanged against the frame, and the door bounced open, swinging all the way around and banging against the shed wall.

Silvia woke, crying. He'd forgotten she was there, so accustomed was he to her warm little body against his chest. Abbi talked to Matthew under the tree while she folded the blanket. He nodded and looked at Benjamin. Nodded again.

Benjamin went inside with Silvia, into the spare bedroom, the unused crib piled with clean laundry and baby things, and locked the door. He sat in the rocker and read to her, first *Goodnight Moon*, then *Guess How Much I Love You*. She played with her toes and he joined her. "This little piggy went to the market, this little piggy stayed home," he said, nibbling each one in succession. Silvia responded with snuffles and coos.

His fingers tingled from the chair's arm cutting into his skin, and from Silvia's weight, so he laid her down on the play mat and turned on the plastic star suspended above it. A gift from Holbach and his wife. Silvia watched as the star lit up and played "Twinkle, Twinkle," cooed to it and kicked her legs. He stretched out next to her, their faces nearly touching, and he blew gently into her ear. She blinked and smiled, the first smile he hadn't coaxed from her by drawing his fingers over her cheeks and chin. She turned her head toward him, and he puffed into her face. Her eyes screwed closed again. Another smile, but this time she licked at the air.

He was afraid of Abbi. No, not of her, but of what she could do. He hadn't followed through with his not-quite-a-promise to deal with *things*. He had gone to the clinic that day Abbi took Silvia to the mother's meeting, not the local one, but four counties north. The doctor wrote him a prescription for Lexapro, but he hadn't filled it yet, and Abbi hadn't mentioned it again, either. But her threat nestled there between them, and he wondered how long she'd wait before forcing him to face all those things he'd been avoiding.

Trying to avoid.

Abbi knocked on the door, two gentle taps. "Ben, dinner's done."

She was afraid, too. He heard it in her voice. Afraid, maybe, that the next time instead of grabbing her, he'd do worse. Afraid, maybe, she'd find him dead one morning from another attempted overdose. Afraid just of him, perhaps, of who he'd become.

There were two of him now. Benjamin before the war, and Benjamin after. The man she knew, and the man she didn't want to know.

"I'll eat later," he said.

She didn't answer, but he still saw the shadow of her feet beneath the door. He heard her breathing, closed his eyes and pictured her standing with her head pressed into the crack of the door, her hot breath bouncing against the wood and back into her face. The doorknob trembled, and the feet disappeared down the hall.

⌒

He woke on the bedroom floor, head propped on a pile of clean laundry, Silvia asleep on his chest. Sliding his hand beneath her cheek, damp with sweat and drool, he moved her to the small area rug in front of the dresser and covered her with a blanket. Then he twisted right, left, cracking his stiff back.

He'd come out of the room only once last night. Abbi was in the basement; he heard the sewing machine, and she must have heard him walking, floorboards shifting beneath his weight. But she didn't come up to him, and he grabbed the bottle she'd already prepared for the baby and went back to the crib room.

Despite the hard bed, he had no nightmares. Hadn't had any

since Silvia came, at least not the kind with teeth, the half memory, half horror movies that made him scream and shake and hide in the bathroom, in the dry tub, waiting for Abbi to give up asking to come in. He'd stay there, too, curled up with the towels piled around him, staring at the night-light through the shower curtain, the one Abbi crafted by ironing layers of plastic grocery bags together. He'd always made sure he was back in bed before she woke, and then he started sleeping on the couch, or away from home—in his car, at work—so she wouldn't hear him reliving things over and over again.

He slept differently with the baby, though, never far enough down for the nightmares to find him. The sleep of a parent, always aware, waiting for a cry, or worse. The sleep of a soldier, with one eye open.

Getting off the floor, he carried Silvia to the bedroom. Abbi lay in bed, back toward him, sheet covering half her face. He put the baby into the Moses basket and pushed the wicker gently against Abbi. He didn't know if she was sleeping or not.

He was still in his uniform pants. He changed into a fresh pair, shaved, and left the house and headed over to the closest fast-food joint—Burger King—and ordered two large hash browns and a coffee. He didn't need to be at work for another forty-five minutes.

He ate the first sleeve of potatoes, pouring them into his mouth, as he drove past Wesley's house. Stopped, backed the Durango down the road and onto Wesley's lawn. Getting out of the truck, he closed the door noiselessly. When he moved his hand, he saw his greasy fingerprints on the navy paint. Finally, he willed himself to the front door. Knocked. Renée Wesley opened, house robe buttoned to her neck, three bald poodles yapping at her feet. "Ben, you all right?"

"Yeah. Is Wes . . . Ray around?"

"Come in. Come in. Ray," she shouted, "door's for you. Can I get you some coffee? Something cold?"

"No, I'm good."

Wesley lumbered into the room, suspenders over his undershirt, plush football-shaped slippers on his feet. He was a tree trunk of a man, chest as wide as a window, a soft layer of small-town monotony wrapped around his muscles. "I'm off today."

"I know," Benjamin said.

Wesley nodded. "Go check on that paper, Reenie." She shuffled out, dogs following. "Want to sit?"

"Let's go outside." Some things couldn't be discussed in living rooms decorated with swags of plastic flowers and lace doilies on the armrests.

In the driveway, Benjamin leaned back against the side of his car, hands in his pockets, mirror grinding against his ribs. He thought back to the day he found Silvia, to those kids, standing much the same way. "I'm not fine," he said.

"Don't suppose you are."

"I don't know what to do about it."

"You asking me?" Wesley snorted a quick, noisy puff of air from his nose. "Can't go around ignoring it, pretending it's not there. It finds its way out somehow. Mine in my anger. Yours in . . . what? No sleeping, no eating, from the looks of it. Probably more, since you're standing here. Sometimes it chews its way through, like it did with my pops. He served in the second war, came home and never spoke a word of it to anyone, not even my mother. He'd watch *The Longest Day* and try to wipe the tears before we saw them. Drank cream for his ulcers, until they got so bad his stomach bled and all those sores turned to cancer. That's how it got him. It gets everyone, I'm telling you."

"What did you do?"

"Lost everything. You don't want to go my way."

"And after that?"

"Scratched my way out. I'm still scratching."

"That's it?" Benjamin said, angry. He had expected solutions, not . . . whatever this was.

"What do you want me to say?"

"I want . . . I want to know how to make it stop."

"I can't say it does. It just gets less." Wesley opened the screen door to his house; it squeaked, bounced closed behind him. He pressed his spongy face into the screening, looking woven, distorted, monstrous. "Patil."

Benjamin waited.

"You go home and tell Abbi that this ain't her fault."

"She knows that."

"Tell her anyway."

⌒

She stood in front of the stove, arm stretched long, awkward, wooden spoon stirring the pot, unable to get closer because of the bulge at her middle. Silvia slept in the sling, and from the side Abbi looked pregnant, her hand resting on the lump, pushing the baby back from the gas flame. Benjamin came beside her, peered at the curried vegetables simmering and tinged yellow with spiciness. "The cauliflower was going bad," she said. "I had to use it."

"Smells fine."

"Do you want her? She fell asleep maybe ten minutes ago."

"No. She looks good on you."

She didn't respond, kept stirring, mushing the potatoes with the back of the spoon, trying hard not to look at him. He reached around, his hand covering the one she protected Silvia with, his fingers slipping between hers. "It's not you," he said.

The stirring stopped, her eyes still on the stove top, her nose growing pink, like a tomato in time-lapse photography. She rubbed her eye with the inside of her wrist, sniffled, and scraped the spoon around the side of the pot. "The curry," she said. "I think I put in too much."

"It's perfect." He took two dishes from the draining rack. "I'll set the table."

Chapter SEVENTEEN

Abbi knelt in the hole in her backyard, packing vases and pots into the sawdust and manure lining the bottom, and then sat on the edge and rolled out. She emptied boxes of Epsom salt over the bundles. After wiping the grit from her right eye with her shoulder, she lugged a sledgehammer from the shed and swung it at the wood pallets piled near the hole. The feedstore had given them to her for free; she needed only to haul them away. She'd crammed most of them in the back of her Volvo and tied the rest to the top.

The brittle wood splintered, pieces bouncing off at her ankles, but she continued to whack away, directing her frustration at the pallets. Using a rake and shovel, she scooped the pallet fragments into a wheelbarrow and, when she'd finished gently lining the hole with the larger pieces, dumped the scraps over them, stuffing wads of newsprint in the cracks. She went inside, leaving Silvia napping in the basket outside, and rummaged through the junk drawer until she found a butane lighter. Flicked the button. Again. No flame. She dropped it on the kitchen counter and continued to dig, pulled out a book of matches. Back at the hole, she lit the newspapers and stood watching until the wood ignited and the flames rose up.

She carried Silvia's basket with her, set her in the hallway outside the bathroom, and showered with the door open. After drying, she dressed in a tank top and recycled sari skirt and flopped onto the bed, legs spread on the cool sheets, arms stretched over her head.

Her muscles ached, but in a good way, and she sighed in contented exertion. She turned her head toward the nightstand; Benjamin had left his socks there again.

Things were better between them, and worse. She saw him looking at her sometimes, a little bit like he used to look at her before the war. He said good night and good morning now, kissed her cheek when he returned from work, touched her in safe places—stroked her index finger with his, tugged her hair—still, he was touching her. But the small victories only magnified the hours between, when he wasn't Benjamin, but a ghost of himself, and made Abbi crave more than he seemed able to give.

She heard pounding outside the house, a woman's voice shouting and banging against the front door, the picture window in the living room. Abbi jumped up to answer the door, ignoring Silvia, who woke at the noise and screamed. Janet was gasping on the patio step. "There's a fire in your backyard," she said.

"I want it there," Abbi told her. "I'm sorry. I should have let you know."

"Are you burning trash?"

"Pottery. I'm firing . . . Oh, just come in while I get the baby."

Abbi gathered the infant from the basket, shushing and bouncing her until she started to hiccup and the blotches on her face dissolved. Then she carried Silvia back to Janet and said, "I'll show you," and they crossed through the kitchen and outside, standing away from the fire, the flames already beginning to burn down. "I'm pit-firing some of the pottery."

"Not your floral ones?"

"Gosh, no. I'm just playing around with this. I fire my good stuff in the kiln."

Janet peeked over at the shed. "You're still making those?"

"Not as often as I'd like. But, yeah."

"I wasn't sure. You haven't shown me anything new . . . in a while."

"It's been a bit hectic around here."

"Oh, I know," Janet said. "I'm not trying to make you feel bad. I just like seeing them."

Abbi scuffed the toe of her sandal in the grass, crushed green blades sticking to the cork. When Janet first learned she was a potter, she had been fascinated by Abbi's work, and Abbi enjoyed having someone with whom to share her creations. But she had pulled away from that, too, especially as it became harder to pretend everything was hunky-dory in her life. She didn't have the energy to play happy, even for the short time it took to show off a vase. But she said, "I have a few pieces in there now," because as much as she'd been trying to avoid her neighbor, she was tired of speaking to walls. She had Genelise, but phone conversations weren't the same as face-to-face, and anyone she was face-to-face with lately—Benjamin, Matthew, Silvia—didn't talk back.

She missed Lauren.

How long had it been since they'd spoken? Thirteen months, at least. After three years rooming together in college, after she introduced Abbi to Benjamin, after their double wedding, after spending some part of every day together while Benjamin and Stephen were deployed, flinching at ringing telephones, watching CNN hours upon hours, waiting for e-mails or letters—after all that—Lauren's absence left a huge void.

Not by Abbi's choice. She had stayed by Lauren's side through it all. It had been easy, too, when she could go home and feel Benjamin next to her in bed. And Lauren made it easy; she didn't mope or hide, spending weeks in her pajamas with the shades drawn or crying each time she saw a news segment on Afghanistan. She acted . . . normal.

Until one day, after Abbi asked her to go out for a movie, Lauren said, "I can't."

"Okay, we can do it tomorrow."

"No, I can't. I just can't do this. Anymore."

"What? Do what?"

"See you."

"Lauren, whatever I did, I'm sorry. I would never—"

"You didn't do anything. Not really."

"Not really? What's that supposed to mean?"

"When I see you, I think of Stephen. I think how Ben's still here, and Stephen . . . He isn't."

"So then, what? You're blaming me for Ben being alive? How is that my fault?"

Lauren lowered her head. "It's not."

"Then what—?"

"It's God. I see you, and I get so angry at God for taking him. I don't want to feel like this. I can't."

"Laur—"

"Don't call me. I'll . . . give you a ring when I'm ready."

And Abbi had listened, praying—still praying—her friend would call.

She unlatched the door, hand unsteady with her memories, and stepped inside, watched the flecks of dust hovering, suspended, in the stream of light pouring in through the lone window. Reaching down, she plugged the standing lamp into the orange extension cord that ran from the outlet at the back of the house, and then flicked it on. More light, more dust. More shadows. "Here."

A metal utility shelf climbed one wall, ceramic pieces in various stages of completion on the shelves. Janet looked at the finished ones. "I love this," she said, picking a vase from the top shelf, there because of its height, nearly two feet tall and shaped like a long lily bud, the tips starting to open, each petal curling back and stamped with tiny floral vines. An earthy green glaze dripped from the top down to a smooth rust-colored finish. A thin, dark ruffle of clay grew up and surrounded the bottom half of the flower. "Oh, and this one." She pointed to a pitcher, the handle twisting like a tree branch and ending in a cluster of leaves, each one hand-sculpted with realistic detail. "Have you sold any lately?"

"Most people aren't paying two seventy-five for some clay and paint."

"And how many hours of your time? Fifteen? Twenty? They're worth it."

"I guess." Silvia's head bobbed against Abbi's shoulder; the infant sucked on her fist and squeaked with frustration. "I have to go in and feed her," she told Janet.

"I don't mind sitting and chatting over a bottle," Janet said. "If you don't mind."

"If you want. Grab that jar on the stump there, will you? It's sun tea."

Inside, she tried to prepare a bottle one-handed and dropped it. It bounced off the corner of the counter and broke. She brushed the glass shards beneath the counter with her feet; she'd sweep them later. Now she needed to feed Silvia, who wailed with hunger.

"Here, let me hold her," Janet said.

"Yeah, okay." Abbi gave her the baby and filled another bottle with formula. Janet took it and sat at the table, Silvia tucked in a cradle hold; she talked to the baby as she fed her, voice lilting and effortless. Abbi poured two glasses of the warm herbal tea and added ice. "It's unsweetened. Do you want sugar? Or, I have agave."

"No, I like it like this." Janet burped Silvia, shifted her to the other arm. "Hi, little girl. Yes, hello. You're so hungry, aren't you? Drink up. That's right. Drink up and grow big and strong."

Abbi never spoke to Silvia like that. She talked to her about practical things—how to sew a diaper, how to peel an avocado, giving step-by-step instructions, more to fill the silence than anything else. She wasn't sure she'd ever get the hang of the mothering thing. "You're good at that."

"Lots of practice. You remember, I have nine younger brothers and sisters."

"Are you and Silas still trying to have a baby?" Janet had two stepsons from her husband's first marriage, and Abbi knew she longed for a baby; the request had been on the prayer list at the church since Abbi and Benjamin started attending. Probably longer.

Janet tightened. "If God chooses to bless us." The woman shifted Silvia to her lap, squeezing her cheeks between her forefinger and thumb as she held her in a sitting position and slapped her back. After the baby burped, Janet wiped away a trickle of formula from the corner of Silvia's mouth and asked, "Diaper?"

"I'll do it," Abbi said, ducking around the corner into the living room to the basket filled with clean prefolds by the couch. She shook one open, grabbed Silvia by her armpits, and laid her on the kitchen table, pushing aside the glasses and napkins. She twisted and pinned and pulled up the diaper cover; her fingers tangled between Silvia's skin and the fabric, not yet nimble despite the daily practice. The baby peered up at her, smiled and kicked her legs. Abbi pulled the elastic band from her ponytail and shook her hair free over the baby's bare tummy. Silvia drew a scratchy, high-pitched breath. Her laugh.

"You don't see many of those anymore," Janet said. "My mother always used cloth diapers. She said it was because she was frugal."

"Huh."

"She always put them out on the clothesline. Said the sun bleached all the stains out better than Clorox. But you probably know that, since you hang yours."

"Yeah."

"You know, I wouldn't mind watching her a bit, if you ever need a sitter."

"Thanks for the offer, but I have a local boy here a couple afternoons a week. Giving me a break."

Though Matthew hadn't come Saturday to mow, or yesterday. Abbi would have been worried, but she'd seen him biking last night, in the distance, while she jogged. Her and Benjamin's fight had probably scared him away. She didn't want to police his comings and goings, but she hadn't realized how much she would miss his coming, even when she used him only as another pair of arms for Silvia so she could finally brush her teeth.

"I'm right next door. I could do that for you. Every day, even."

"I appreciate that. I really do. But Matt . . . he needs the money."

"What does he know about babies?"

Abbi looked at her. "What do you know about him?"

"His mother was in jail."

"Hmm." Abbi wasn't surprised. There had to be a good reason for him to be living with his aunt and her own four kids.

"For drugs," Janet said, unplucked brows wrinkling.

"Okay."

"I just mean . . ."

"I know what you mean," Abbi said. *What's wrong with these people?* And she winced as her judgmental spirit reared up inside her.

"Well," Janet said. She shimmied from the chair, sideways so as not to move it. "Well. Thanks for the tea."

⌒

The pit fire had burned out during the night, and by midmorning the ashes, though they still held enough heat to stick to the bottom of Abbi's sandals, were cool enough to allow her to ease into the hole and unload her pottery. Janet hung socks in mismatched pairs on the rusted clothes tree cemented in the center of her own backyard, steeling glances Abbi's way. Rolling each piece from the hole, she climbed out on her knees and one hand, her other arm tight around Silvia, who was wrapped against her chest. Sweat burned her eyes.

Only two of her pots had cracked; the others needed to be cleaned, but some splotches of red and umber showed through the soot, and coal black spots here and there. Empty plastic laundry basket on her hip, Janet stood where their yards met, her grass longer. Silas had told Benjamin it shaded itself that way, staying greener, but Abbi saw no difference in color, both lawns a dull yellow-gray. "Can I see them?" she asked.

"Sure."

Janet stepped gently over into Patil territory. "They're, uh, interesting."

Abbi chuckled. "You don't like them."

"I didn't say that. I guess I just prefer pretty things. Not that these aren't nice. I just—"

"Janet, it's fine. They're supposed to be primitive looking. And they're certainly not pretty." Abbi kicked some broken shards back into the pit. "Look, I'm sorry I got all snippy yesterday."

"No, I need to apologize," Janet said. "For talebearing about the Savoie boy's mother."

"You don't owe me anything. If you feel like you should apologize, apologize to him."

"I should. I will. If I see him. But you're here now, and I don't want you to think I'm some gossip, or something. I just was concerned about the baby. Can I . . . can I speak plainly for a moment?"

Abbi shrugged. "Uh, sure."

"I think, maybe, because of the type of person you are, you can be too trusting."

"I don't get you."

Janet brushed the soot from her hands. "You're one of those 'God is love' people. But there's more to Him than just love. And some people just are no good. I'm not saying Matt isn't. By all accounts, he's a smart, smart kid. He's actually in A.J.'s class now, skipped a grade just this year. And I hear he's already been accepted to USD. Got a full ride. Maybe you know that, maybe not. But still. That doesn't always mean much. And you have a baby now. You need to think about her, first of all."

"I do. And I trust Matt, or I would never leave her with him."

"Well, okay. And, seriously, if you need help with Silvia, just knock. You know I'm home most of the day."

"I will," Abbi said, and she watched Janet cross back into her own yard. Though, to Abbi, it seemed like another world.

Chapter EIGHTEEN

School started in a little more than two weeks, so his aunt piled Matthew and the girls into her car—Lacie between Heather and Jaylyn in the front, sharing a seat belt with her sister, the rest of them in the back—and drove to Pierre. Before heading over to the Wal-Mart, she pulled around the McDonald's drive-thru, ordered one super-sized Coke, six small fries, and a ten-piece chicken nuggets. Then she parked, pulled a hair from Jaylyn's head.

"Ouch," she said, slapping Heather's hand. "Why couldn't you use Lacie this time?"

"The girl at the window was blond. From a bottle. Stay here."

Heather came back minutes later carrying two boxes of chicken nuggets, tossed one over her shoulder to Skye. "Eat up. And don't ask for anything else until we get home."

They continued on to the department store, passing his mother's apartment complex. Matthew stared out the window, at the opposite side of the road.

Lacie twisted her neck around. "Matty, doesn't your mom—?"

Heather smacked her in the back of the head, and the little girl sunk back down behind the seat.

His aunt went into Pierre at least once a month. She never asked if he wanted to visit his mother; she just threw it out there—"I'm heading north for some shopping. Anyone need anything?"—and waited to see if he answered. He had gone almost every month in the beginning. And then he got tired of showing up and Melissa being there drunk, or high, or not being there at all. It wasn't that he saw more as he got older—she didn't do anything she hadn't done when he lived with her—he just saw deeper. And he hadn't wanted to deal with it anymore.

The little girls needed gym sneakers, so Heather took them to the shoe department. Jaylyn and Skye disappeared to look at clothes. Matthew wandered up and down the school supply aisles. He picked up three notebooks, leaving fingerprints on the shiny covers. A package of pencils, some folders. He'd have to get a couple pairs of jeans, and socks. There wouldn't be money left for anything else.

Even if it was his money.

He knew part of the reason—the biggest reason, probably—Heather took him in after his mother went to jail was the stipend. Nearly five hundred extra dollars a month. She used it for the household, for his cousins. For her own things. Occasionally for him. He tried not to mind. If he needed something else, he'd buy it himself. He could always find an odd job here and there. Plus, his babysitting for Abbi Patil, and the yard work. He hoped she'd keep him on, after the argument with her husband. Matthew had already saved close to two hundred dollars, thanks to her. It wouldn't be long before he'd be able to afford his trip to Buffalo.

There was a tap on his shoulder. Matthew turned.

"I thought that was you," Ellie said.

He gave one wave of his hand, low, near his hip. A cool wave, he hoped.

"School shopping?"

He nodded.

"Me, too. You still taking calculus?"

Another nod.

"Me, too." She wore her brown hair swept back in two braids. Not the Pippi Longstocking kind that hung freely and fluttered as she moved. She wove them flat against her head, the ends running down her back in two shiny zippers. Her skin was more freckled than not, clusters of umber dots packed so close that her face looked like it was covered with pennies. She was everything a girl-next-door should be— cute, but not beautiful, sweet, smart. He looked close at her upper lip. He didn't see hair, just more freckles. "It should be fun. Gosh, that's lame to say. I sound like a complete nerd. Not a geek."

Matthew laughed, shook his head.

"Well, I guess I'll see you in class, then."

And then Skye came down the isle. "Ellie, hey."

Please, don't say anything.

Skye smiled like the Cheshire cat. "We're going to a movie at the Grove tonight. Want to come?"

"You're going, Matt?" Ellie asked.

He hesitated a moment, then nodded.

"I'll have to check with my mom."

"Well, if you can come, just meet us there," Skye said. "At seven."

"Sure, okay. Thanks," Ellie said. "Well, bye." She looked over her shoulder once before turning the corner.

Matthew slapped Skye with the back of his hand.

"What?" she asked.

He hit her again, grinning.

"Yeah, well, you're paying."

⌒

He wore his collared shirt, combed his hair. He noticed he should get it cut before school began, but wouldn't. He was used to wearing it long, from when he wore hearing aids and grew his hair over his ears to hide them. Now he felt naked without its covering.

On the way out the door, Matthew stopped, an idea sparking as he looked at Skye in a pretty black blouse and orange flip-flops. She turned and told him to hurry. He raised one finger and, pulling his pad from his pocket, scrawled a note on his way back into the apartment, and gave it to Sienna.

"No way," she said. "Uh-uh."

Just call him and ask.

"Skye will strangle me."

I'll buy you those jeans Aunt Heather wouldn't get you today.

"Oh, fine." She dug the phone from between the couch cushions. "He won't come."

Yes he will.

Heather let Skye drive the car. They got there early and waited, and Ellie pulled to the curb in her mother's minivan. She had taken the braids from her hair; one silken ponytail hung over the front of her shoulder. She twisted the end around her finger.

Matthew tried not to smile too much.

The movie theater, in the adjacent county, had only one screen. He paid for all of them to see the Disney action movie, bought popcorn, too, and soda. And Sour Patch Kids for Skye. A bottle of water for him.

Go in and find seats. I'll be there in a minute, he wrote. And he counted to thirty in the restroom before sneaking back out to wait for Jared by the theater door. He checked his watch.

"What are you doing out here?" Skye asked, tugging on his sleeve. "The previews are over and your dream girl is waiting. Come on."

In the theater, he positioned himself between the girls in the nearly full theater with the tub of greasy popcorn on his lap so they could both reach it. He couldn't eat it—too much salt. He focused little attention on the movie. Should he try to put his arm around Ellie? Hold her hand? In the end, he sat there, hugging the cardboard container, nervously jiggling his legs and sliding his feet over the floor. At one point, Skye punched him in the knee.

The lights flickered on as soon as the credits began. Matthew stood and stretched, kicked the popcorn on the floor under the seat in front of him as they waited to leave. Shuffling up the aisle, Skye stopped; Matthew crashed against her back and saw Jared in the back row. She turned and glared at him. He shrugged.

Ellie squeezed ahead of them and gave Jared a quick hug and a sweet, bright smile. She spoke to him; he said something back, eyes drifting toward Skye, snapping back to Ellie's face.

Skye dragged Matthew into the lobby. "I'm gonna kill you," she said, and then raked her fingertips down her face, shook her head. She snagged Matthew's notebook from his pocket and tossed it at him. "Just ask her to get something to eat."

Ellie and Jared came out of the theater and he scribbled, *Are you hungry? Want to grab a burger?*

"Sure, okay," she said.

You, too? He showed the pad to Jared.

"I think I'll get home," he said. "Unless Skye wants something."

"I'm not hungry," Skye said. "You can give Matty a ride home, right, Ellie?"

"I guess."

"See you at home, then." She finally looked at Jared. Swallowed. "Good luck out there at DSU."

"Thanks," Jared said.

"Yeah, well, you worked hard for it." And Skye left with a twitch of the shoulder and a little wave.

Sorry, man.

"What the heck, right? I'll see you guys."

After Jared left, Matthew took out his pad again. *If you don't* want to go, you don't have to. If you're tired, or something. I can hitch.

"Oh, no. I'm good. Unless you're tired, or something."

He shook his head.

They jogged across the street to the Burger King. He opened the door for her, touched her on the back as she slipped inside, and they ordered at the counter; Ellie a coffee and a slice of apple pie, Matthew just the pie. She pulled a few bills from her back pocket, but he nudged her arm away, shook his head.

"You sure?" she asked, and he handed a ten to the cashier. They sat in a two-seater booth by the window.

Ellie tore open her plastic-wrapped package of flatware and played with it, standing the knife up inside the tines of the fork, then the spoon. Then she stacked the plastic creamer containers one atop the other, seven tall. She tried to add another and the tower fell.

I don't bite, he wrote, and pushed the pad across to her.

"I'm sorry," she said, squeezing one of the containers. "It's just . . . I don't know. I guess I don't know what to say."

Say anything.

"Anything."

Very funny. He took a bite of the pie. You can just ask me.

She smiled, hid half her face behind one hand and tilted her head. "I'm a moron."

No.

"Okay, then. What happened? To your hearing, I mean."

Alport Syndrome.

"What's that?"

Some genetic thing. It's rare. Causes kidney failure. Sometimes deafness. I got both.

"Is that why you leave school early sometimes?"

Dialysis three times a week.

"I'm sorry."

It's not your fault.

She curled the end of her ponytail around her finger. "Is it hard?"

What part?

"Any of it."

This part. The communication. His inability to say everything he had pent up inside. It was easier before he moved to Temple, when he lived with his mother in Sioux Falls and had daily interaction with others who used sign language—a few hard-of-hearing classmates, teachers, volunteers at the after-school center. And there were those who grew up with him, who had grown accustomed to his odd vowels and scrambled syllables, and understood him. When he came to Temple, the kids teased him about his deaf accent, and he stopped talking; now he had to concentrate so much to remember tongue angle and lip position, he didn't bother trying. And he didn't know anyone who signed, except the speech therapist that came to the school once a month, and Mrs. Healen at church, who remembered maybe a hundred words from her college days, and tended to improvise others, more charades than ASL.

He put his pen to his pad, lifted it again. Then he decided to be honest.

It's hard to fit everything I want to say on a scrap of paper.

⟶

She drove him home, and they both looked at each other and then away, not knowing how to end their night. Matthew finally wrote,

147

I'll save you a seat in math, ripped the page from his pad and gave it to Ellie.

"You won't have to. I hear there's only four of us."

Three. Jennifer Metternich bailed.

"Great. Now I'm the only girl."

You shouldn't be such a high achiever.

She laughed, and again he heard Woody Woodpecker in his head. "Me? You're the one graduating a year early."

Maybe.

"What do you mean, maybe?"

He shrugged. I don't know. Just, we'll see.

Ellie turned quiet; her cheeks fell, and she stared at her fingers, twisting the corner of the paper she held. Matthew guessed she thought he meant his illness. He didn't.

He meant Lacie.

He was a fixer. A caretaker. As a child, he had made certain to tuck a pillow under his mother's head and cover her with an afghan when he found her on the floor, passed out from too much coke. By the time he turned ten, he could sometimes shimmy her up onto the bed, or couch, depending on how far he needed to drag her. His first thoughts were always of her—when he joggled his key in the door, wondering if she'd be home or if he'd have to make his own supper of toast and peanut butter; when he woke in the morning, looking to see if she had bothered to wash his laundry the night before, or if he'd have to go another day without clean underpants.

And now those concerns fell on Lacie. Born only weeks after he came to live with his aunt, she was more a sister than a cousin, sometimes more a daughter for all the time he spent caring for her. He didn't want to leave her behind, alone, to witness the river of men flowing through the apartment, the constant cussing and bickering.

He needed to believe there was more for her than all that; maybe, somehow his presence gave her more than that.

It's late.

"Okay."

Come by next week, if you want.

"You, too. You know where I live, right?"

I can find it.

"I work for my dad during the day, but at the house. And I can take a break whenever I want. So, anytime. And bring your swimsuit. We have a pool."

He couldn't imagine swimming in front of her, letting her see his too-big head bobbing around on his twiggy neck and narrow shoulders. But he nodded and smiled an ill-fitting half smile before stepping out of the minivan and back into the real world.

Skye wasn't waiting for him; he'd expected her on the couch, ready to scratch out his eyes, or something equally estrogen-laced. The next morning, though, after he dressed, he stood outside the bathroom until Skye finally opened the door, and held his notebook up in front of him, for protection, I'M SORRY written in huge, dark letters over the entire page.

"You don't have a clue, Matty," she said.

You hate me.

"No." She reached up and shoved him in the head. "You can, I don't know, go to church and beg forgiveness or something."

Want to come? There's time for you to get ready.

"Buildings like that collapse on people like me."

Oh, stop.

"Well, just in case. I don't need any more surprises, do I?" And she closed her bedroom door behind her.

Chapter NINETEEN

When his parents came, he and his father left the women at the house and headed to the Badlands. It was their place, had been since Benjamin was a child, when he and Harish would go hiking there, first the small mounds on the side of the road, with the well-worn paths, then some higher peaks, and finally up and down the deep, craggy fissures carved by moisture and time. The prototypical scientist, Harish documented the erosion of the rocks, the changes in landscape, photographing the same areas of the terrain at least twice a year. Sometimes more. He'd then gather his pictures together and pore over them with magnifying glasses, engineer's scale, and grease pencils, marking and turning and documenting. "Benjamin, this is the overlook ten years ago, and here it is today. Do you see?"

"Yes, Baba."

"Fascinating."

The Badlands saved them as Harish slowly allowed himself to accept that his son wouldn't be following in his scientific footsteps. And Benjamin understood his decision grieved his father almost as deeply as if he had rejected Harish's faith in Christ.

The summer before he began college, the two of them went together into the buttes and spires for three days, came out covered in a chalky white dust. They didn't talk about anything outside the scope of their camping trip, but somewhere during that time they both came to an unspoken truce, neither one willing to lose the other over a career choice.

The forty-minute drive ended when Harish paid for the pass permit and parked at the side of the road near a collection of striated mounds, red and brown and yellow stripes banded around each butte. Sandstone, volcanic ash, and paleosols.

They strapped on their packs and climbed, first over a few packed footpaths, then up sheerer faces, jamming their boots into the soft rock and testing each handhold, having learned early on that even the firmest-looking ledges could crumble under the weight of a man. Benjamin hadn't done such climbing since he lost his toes and found his footing a bit hesitant, a bit unsure. He favored his left leg, going behind his father, debris spilling down into his face as Harish scaled the peak above him.

His father stopped, sat, and Benjamin caught up; they drank water and ate cashews, staring over the majestic formations. "'Lead me to the rock that is higher than I,'" Harish said. "'For You have been a refuge for me, a tower of strength against the enemy.'"

Benjamin tossed handfuls of stones down into the gaping crevice; they scrambled and bounced over the craggy outcroppings, and then fell silent. His father capped his canteen. "You did the same when you were a child."

"I like how it sounds."

"And how is that?"

"Like dragon scales."

On the way home, Harish wanted to stop for a meal, and inside the diner he picked up all the free publications near the counter—real estate magazines, weekly newspapers, tourist guides. They sat and ordered, Benjamin asking for a large coffee. The air-conditioning had dried the sweat on his skin, chilling him. "You're not going to say anything?" he finally said.

"If you want to talk, I will listen. You know that. But I do not think you want to. If you did, you would have said it to me by now."

"Maybe I want you to pry it out of me."

Harish paged through the *Beck County Register*. "Do you?"

"Don't read that," Benjamin said, sipping his coffee. More gossip column than journalism, the thin newspaper reported who went to whose birthday party, who had houseguests over the long holiday weekend, and the dates of the United Methodist Church's next ice cream socials. And included the sheriff's log.

"You are mentioned in here."

"Come on, Baba, you can't seriously look at this stuff and think . . ." He grabbed the paper from his father. "You want to hear how I'm in here? 'July twenty-ninth. Deputy Patil responded to a report of three cows and eleven calves in the middle of I-90, about four miles south of Temple. The owner's neighbor assisted the deputy in putting the cattle back in the pasture.' "

"Benjamin—"

"Wait. There's more. 'August first. Deputy Patil responded to a church in Lippmann for an out-of-state subject needing ministerial aid.' Another incident on August first. 'Deputy Patil responded to a motorist assist at the westbound rest area east of Temple. A wrecker was called for assistance, and Deputy Patil transported four people to a motel in Hensley.' "

"Tell me, what is the matter?"

"You have to ask? It's this—" Benjamin folded the paper and shook it. "All of this. Livestock and lost travelers. This is how I spend my days."

"And I fiddle with test tube, and lecture freshman who take my chemistry class because they know my teaching assistants will grade them lightly." Harish took off his silver-rimmed glasses and bent one bow before repositioning them on his nose. "We can trivialize all what we do. It does not change whether we do it well. You saved a life, *nannubala*. Do you not think the Lord put you in your job, in that field, for that reason?"

"Okay, fine. I saved one unwanted child. But how many lives have I taken?"

"You are angry."

"What was your first clue?"

The waitress brought their food; she slid the plates from her brown plastic tray to the table without making eye contact and hurried away.

Harish cut his baked potato down the center, and Benjamin watched his ritual. Butter pressed onto the back of the fork, painted over the entire white surface. Three shakes of salt over each half, then cut into fifteenths—four slices widthwise, two lengthwise. That was his father. Deliberate. Steady. Unmoving. No, unmoved. "Tell me, at whom are you so angry?"

Everyone.

Abbi, of course. Stephen, for getting himself killed and leaving Benjamin alone to deal with it all. Everyone who looked at him and thought he was fine. Everyone who looked at him and pitied him.

And he was so, so angry with himself. He had no idea where that list began, or ended.

Benjamin stabbed his overcooked carrots. "I don't know."

"You have been in prayer, yes?"

"No."

They ate, their eyes not traveling past the other's chin. Harish diced his steak into polite bites. Benjamin hacked at the tough poultry, gnawing on chunks, working his jaw as he did as a teenager with braces, when he snuck Bubbalicious in the bathroom and chewed three or four pieces at a time. A thread of chicken lodged between his molars, and he tried to work it out with his tongue. It didn't come loose. He dropped his knife

and fork on the table and cupped his forehead in his hands, palms pressing into his eyes until he saw violet and blue and green blobs swirling
behind his lids, and flashes of crackly white lightning.

"This is your dark night of the soul," his father said.

Benjamin looked up, blinked until his vision cleared. "What did
you say?"

"'Oh, night that guided me, Oh, night more lovely than the dawn,
Oh, night that joined Beloved with lover, Lover transformed in the
Beloved.'"

"How do you—?"

"Benjamin, Benjamin. Do you think honestly I would know nothing of what my son holds closest to him?" Harish slid his napkin under
the lip of his dish. "You were seventeen, I believe, and you carried that
book with you all the places you went. Always it was curled in your
back pocket. What kind of father would I be if I failed to notice?"

"You read it."

"The librarian laughed when I checked it out. In all my years at
USD, I did not ever take anything from the library unrelated to the
sciences. And not since."

"You read it," Benjamin said again. He'd never doubted either of
his parents would have worked their fingers to bloody nubs for him,
even though the words "I love you" weren't common—or uncom-
mon—in his home. His father supported them. He came to all Benjamin's spelling bees, debate matches, science fairs. He stood on the
sidelines in November, shivering, while Benjamin played soccer, and
played badly. All good parent things to do. But in that instant he saw
the depth of his father's love for him. The book. A book the man would
never have glanced at on his own, but for his son he slogged through
it, the archaic language, the poetry, the abstract theological musings
he and his plain analytical faith had little use for. *O God, this is the love
I have for Silvia. Is your love for me really infinitely more than this?*

Why can't I feel it?

"Yes, Benjamin. I read it," Harish said.

"I'm sinking," Benjamin said.

"You cannot sink. Nothing can snatch you from His hand."

"What if I let go?"

"No."

"You don't know I won't. Neither do I." Benjamin shredded his napkin. "Can we get out of here?"

"Of course."

Harish folded the newspapers, tucked them under his arm and paid. The sun beat on the car, and when Benjamin got in he shivered from the heat, folded his arms behind his back. They pressed into the leather. It burned for a minute, and then his bare skin adjusted, and he closed his eyes so his father wouldn't speak to him.

He had found the book at a used bookstore, one not far from the college, a deceptively small storefront, but inside room after room after nook filled with all kinds of printed pages. He hadn't been looking for anything in particular when he found the coverless paperback, picking it up because the title intrigued him. *Dark Night of the Soul*.

He almost put it back when he read the author, St. John of the Cross, was some sort of mystic, and a Catholic at that, but when he skimmed the first line of the poem, it drew him in, and he had to read the entire book, to follow the journey of the bride of Christ—the soul—to her love, the Lord himself. A journey through darkness to light. A journey home. But in no way an easy journey. In fact, there were times in the night where the soul was desolate, lost, and feeling completely disconnected from God.

St. John pushed on during the blackness, coming out the other side with a refined faith, an intimate knowledge of the Divine. He saw struggle as a blessing, and Benjamin had prayed for his own dark night, wanting the kind of spiritual awakening St. John had experienced.

Well, he had what he asked for. What a fool. He wondered if he'd make it out at all.

Chapter TWENTY

"Abbi. Abbi, where is your flour?"

Slinging Silvia, she found Sangita cooking in the kitchen, her hair knotted at the base of her neck, flashing gold and green as she moved around the kitchen in her *kurta* with gilt embroidery, her red *churidar* tightly gathered at her ankles. A matching crimson *dupatta* draped across her shoulders. Abbi had only seen her dressed traditionally, but usually in a more casual cotton *salwar kameez*.

Whatever she wore, it hadn't been enough to keep her from feeling Benjamin's bones through both their clothes. She'd seen Sangita wince as she hugged him earlier. The woman loved her son—maybe too much, if that was possible. Abbi didn't know. Benjamin suffered from the opposite affliction she did. His parents heaped all their expectations on him; hers none at all.

Harish and Sangita had never been anything but kind to her, but Abbi hadn't been able to find her place with them. She felt as if Benjamin's mother was always looking at her, wishing she was Maharashtrian, or at least a Republican. Benjamin, of course, told her she was being ridiculous. Whether she was or not, she needed Sangita now, to help her figure out how to help Benjamin.

"You wanted flour?" Abbi said. "It's right up here."

"I see that flour. It is darker than I need. You have white?"

"I have spelt in the basement. It's close in texture to all-purpose."

She brought the glass jar up from her cellar pantry, and Sangita screwed off the lid, rubbed the flour between thumb and forefinger. "Is good."

"Good. Is there something I can do?" Abbi asked.

Sangita kept her sleek head bent as she kneaded dough for *naan*. "You hold that baby too much."

"Maybe chop something? I can't mess that up."

"Thank you to ask, but I not need help."

"Ben does."

The woman made a dry, barking sound, clearing only air from her throat.

"Sangita, please. I know you don't like to talk about things, but you're his mother. And I don't know what to do for him." Abbi sighed, shook her head. "I love him."

The woman slapped the dough into a disc. "Benjamin go always his own way."

"What's that supposed to mean?"

"He do what he do. That job. That army. You. He have his own mind."

"Okay, fine. But what am I supposed to do?"

"You cook. You wash clothes. You pray."

"You're kidding, right?"

"You are only a wife. You cannot make a husband do what they not think themselves of doing. That is how it is."

"That's easy for you to say. You're not watching him disappear a little more each day."

Sangita turned, looked at Abbi. "Not easy," she said, tapping three fingers just beneath her collarbone on the left side of her chest, her hand fanned out like a star. Her heart. "Not easy at all. I hear in his voice when he calls. My boy is in much pain. I know it."

"I know it, too. That's why there has to be something else," Abbi said, petulant, like a child who finds only a package of underwear after tearing through the wrapping of her birthday present.

"If there is, I have not an idea." Sangita poured a few scattered drops of oil into a bowl, swirled it to coat the sides. She dropped the ball of dough into it and covered it with a plain white dishcloth. "You hold that baby too much."

Abbi sighed. Conversation over. "How long until dinner?"

"Always we eat at five."

"I'm going to go take a walk, get Silvia out for some air. Do you want to come?"

"*Nako.*"

"That's a no, right?"

Sangita nodded once, wiping her just-washed hands on her apron. She reached out, touched Abbi's sleeve. "*Kanyaratna*, I know what it is like to be part of hard marriage. But Benjamin, he is not hard man. Have thanks for that."

Abbi shook her head. "Ben always told me you and Harish—"

"Not Harish. My first marriages. They were to . . . hard men."

"I'm sorry."

"No, no. These things make me what I am. Make me look not to men but to God. Is good, and is past." She lifted the pot's lid, stirred. "I make *amti bhaat bhaji*."

Lentil dal, rice and vegetable. "My favorite," Abbi said.

"I know it."

⌒

She pondered Sangita's words as she walked with Silvia, unhappy with the advice. She wasn't a sit-and-do-nothing type person. Her initial instinct was always to act, then consider the consequences. Benjamin liked to talk first. She wished he'd open his mouth and tell her what happened in Afghanistan, but she figured she'd lost that privilege, to be in *that* part of his life.

Others wondered, when they first married, how a soldier and a pacifist could live beneath the same roof of their tiny loft apartment.

But Benjamin wasn't really a soldier then, and she a pacifist in name only. He went off to shoot at things one weekend a month, coming home afterward to shower away the smell of mock combat, wash and roll his fatigues into a bag he kept in the trunk of his car until the next training exercise. And she spouted the flaws of the just-war theory and "blessed are the peacemakers" from a comfy armchair at the coffee shop two blocks from the college. Neither thought they'd be forced to become who they said they were.

And then the war started.

For two years they waited for Benjamin's deployment, knowing it would happen. After he left, Abbi drove three hours every Tuesday to Vermillion to stand on the corner of Cherry and Pine with a smattering of college kids and retired professionals, carrying a red tagboard sign reading *What Would Jesus Bomb?* on one side and *Peace Takes Brains* on the other.

When the local newspaper learned she was a soldier's wife, they asked to profile her, and she agreed, not taking a moment to consider Benjamin's feelings. Or anyone else's.

She didn't tell Lauren about the story, and when her friend saw it, glaring above the front-page fold of Sunday's thick edition, she met Abbi in the church parking lot and dumped the newsprint pages on her feet. Sale circulars cartwheeled across the gravel, glossy full-color tumbleweeds.

"This isn't helping them," Lauren shouted, and then hugged her fiercely, fingers digging into her upper arms. "You're not the only one who wants them home."

Abbi knew she wasn't. One weekend she traveled to a protest in Washington, D.C., stood shoulder to shoulder with wives and girl-friends and sisters. Mothers. Daughters. So close she smelled their angry breath—some coffee-coated, some fruity, some tinged with nicotine or alcohol—as they shouted their pain to anyone who would listen. They used blame as their balm of Gilead, their way to keep from going mad, to make sense of the empty pillow next to them, the unused car keys hanging beside the front door. It helped—some.

People were supportive of her, for the most part. A few—like the neighborhood egg lady, Marie Vilhauser—believed Abbi's pacifism betrayed not only Benjamin and the other soldiers, but America, and Jesus himself, but the rest came alongside her and, despite their disagreeing beliefs, worked hard to see her as *Abbi* and not as *that left-wing commie liberal.*

She, however, was less than charitable toward them, becoming distant and snappish. She hated that they carried on with their farming, and shopping, and whatever else they did, maybe offering up a prayer on Thursdays and Sundays for Benjamin's safety, but otherwise totally unaffected by the happenings on the other side of the globe. They turned off their televisions, but it was in her living room, her bedroom, her heart every single moment of every single day.

By the time Benjamin returned home, she had wedged the war between her and everyone else. And now, as she tried to retrace her steps, to mend the holes she had poked through her relationships, a tired embarrassment kept her from fully reconciling. She just was too ashamed of her behavior. Self-loathing, she was good at. Apologizing, not so much.

Silvia's cries pierced Abbi's thoughts, and she jogged home, the bouncing calming the cranky baby. Benjamin sat on the front steps, waiting for her. "You okay?" he asked.

"Why wouldn't I be?"

"You spent the afternoon with my mother. Alone."

"She's hungry," Abbi said.

He took the baby. "I'll go feed her."

"Ben, wait," she said. "What does *kanyaratna* mean?"

"Daughter. But in an endearing way, like saying "she's a gem." Mom called you that?"

"Yeah."

"You must have done something right, then."

"That's a change." She smoothed Silvia's hair. "Are you okay?"

They stood close, only the baby separating them. Benjamin touched Silvia's head, too, but avoided Abbi's fingers. "Why wouldn't I be?" he said. "I'll see you inside."

~

She was exhausted from the short weekend visit, mentally more than physically, and Sunday night she flopped back on the bed with a sigh, her feet still on the floor. She listened to Benjamin rattling through the refrigerator, the cabinets. His parents had left after church, a small blessing that they decided not to stay for lunch. Abbi had spent the afternoon and evening in her studio, coming in only when the dim light gave her a headache.

The phone rang.

"Abbi, you getting that?" Benjamin called, but she ignored him. The answering machine kicked on, and she heard a voice through the walls, then Benjamin said, "Hello. Wait, hold on. You there?" He carried the cordless receiver into the bedroom, held it out to her. "It's for you."

"Genelise?" Abbi asked. No one else called her.

"My mother."

"Why are you giving me the phone?"

"She wants to talk to you."

Abbi sat up, took the phone. "Um, hello?"

Benjamin stared at her.

"We need to pray. Now, for Benjamin. We pray every day together," Sangita said.

"Okay, I guess."

Benjamin still hadn't left the room. He changed out of his clothes, slowly, listening.

"He there. You listen. Tomorrow I call in the morning."

"That would be better."

"Now, you listen." Sangita prayed for her son in a Marathi-English hybrid. Abbi had difficulty understanding the words, but her spirit knew. She closed her eyes until her mother-in-law said, "Amen. Okay, I call tomorrow. Good night."

"Bye." Abbi pressed the Off button. "Here." She tossed Benjamin the phone and fell back onto the mattress again.

"You didn't say much," he said.

"You know your mother."

"What did she want?"

"To pray," she said, and then added, "for you."

Benjamin got an odd, crumbly look on his face; he blinked rapidly and then shut his eyes, took a stilted breath. "Thank you," he said.

"I'm your wife. That's my job."

"Job," he mumbled. "Yeah."

"That's not how I—"

"It's okay, really. Trust me, I know I'm lucky to have that much." He climbed into bed, removed his socks beneath the sheet, balling them and leaving them on the nightstand for the morning. "You coming to bed?"

She nodded. "After I change Silvia."

"Good night," Benjamin said, and turned out the light.

Chapter TWENTY-ONE

He'd knocked on every door in Beck County. No one knew where Silvia had come from. Benjamin didn't know if he should be relieved or not, didn't want to think about it. Today was one of the hard days, like the ones he had before Silvia, when he had to hide from people so they wouldn't see him struggling. He straddled the ravine between a civilian's life and a soldier's, curling the toes he had left into the earth on either side to keep his balance. But the banks of the ravine kept moving, wide at some points, narrow at others. On the easy days there was hardly a crack between the banks. Today the ravine was so wide, his legs wouldn't stretch any farther. The doctor said the new medication would help—she wrote him a prescription the day Abbi went to that mothers' meeting—and it had, until he'd gone into Dunkin' Donuts this morning for a coffee and bear claw, and the television mounted in the corner showed scenes from Afghanistan.

He'd swallowed the war whole, and then came home and started regurgitating up pieces. He moved his desk into the corner so his back wouldn't be exposed, and found himself always positioned by doors, just in case. He swerved around trash on the side of the road. He replayed combat scenarios in his head over and over, searching for alternative outcomes. But no matter how many times he watched and rewound, the end stayed the same. Stephen dead; him looking on, helpless. If he'd acted with honor, he'd be dead, too.

I should be.

Benjamin checked into the office. Roubideau looked him over. "We tracked down the McClure girl," the sheriff said. "With a friend or a friend's cousin over in Aberdeen. Holbach's on his way to pick her up."

"And?"

"She's not the one who left the kid, if that's what you're asking."

"But she ran."

"Seems the Grant girl was tellin' the truth, or some bit of it. Rebecka McClure did find herself pregnant back earlier this year. But she terminated. Left town 'cause she got scared about her parents finding out."

"They must know now."

"If they do, it wasn't from us."

"Rebecka McClure is just sixteen," Benjamin said.

"Don't I know it." Roubideau squinted at him again. "Take the rest of the day off. You look like you need it. That kid still keeping you up nights?"

Benjamin nodded.

"Better you than me."

"That's why you never had children."

The sheriff chuckled. "Or a wife, for that matter. Or a goldfish. Too much trouble for me. I got all I need with this job."

Instead of going home, Benjamin went to the library, and the books welcomed him. He hadn't been born a reader. As a child, his parents assumed he would follow his father into the sciences, and he thought the same because they did. But they didn't know such things—titrations and quadratics and dissections—didn't come easy for him. He excelled because he worked harder than anyone else, the pages in his loose-leaf binder constantly reinforced with white donuts of gummed paper and smudged with graphite marks. And his father patted his hair and brought home back issues of *Biomacromolecules* and

Organometallics, which Benjamin faithfully slogged through, dizzy with jargon by the time he finished. He never allowed himself to consider he hadn't an interest in any of it.

When he was fifteen, he had to read *The Great Gatsby* for English class. Mrs. Grace dropped a pile of thin books on each of the front desks, and the students passed them over their shoulders with groans and protests. Benjamin ran his hand over the cover. Bigger than the shiny pocket-paperback size, and matte, and bound tight, it was the first brand-new book, without a crease or sticky fingerprint, he'd ever received in school.

He opened the book wide enough to see the words, but not so wide as to damage the spine, and he read.

After that, he always kept a book with him. Sometimes he read at night with a flashlight, and when the batteries died, he left his bedroom door open so the light from the hall bathroom fell on the end of his bed, and he'd put his feet on his pillow and squint at the type. Other times he'd hide the book between his legs, beneath his desk during history, and Mr. Scott ignored him as long as he scored nineties on his quizzes.

His father said science tied people together—everyone had the same cellular components, the same DNA—but books, Benjamin thought, formed tighter, more intimate connections. He walked the mall, the campus, the airport, looking at those who passed, trying to decipher the words within the person. Which words did they share? Had that mother comforting her crying toddler read *Anna Karenina*? Did *The Count of Monte Cristo* stand sentry on the bookshelf of the businessman in the food line, the one whose shirt poked through his pants zipper and who still had a ball of toilet tissue stuck to his face, below his ear, where his razor cut him? What about titans of the past—presidents and kings and explorers? What books had they experienced along with him, an insignificant Desi boy who still forgot to throw his dirty clothes in the hamper?

Now he read to fill his head with other things, the words and plots shoving out the past, for a moment at least. He couldn't read and think at the same time.

The library, recently remodeled, had three restrooms—the men's and women's near the circulation desk, and a small bathroom in a back corner. It was there he read; he felt safe in the cramped space. Rarely did anyone come to use that bathroom, and if the doorknob rattled and a knock came, he said, "One minute," hiding his books beneath his shirt and exiting to sit at the table near the door until the room was free again.

He took two books—a John Grisham novel and a nonfiction one about money management he grabbed from the *To Be Reshelved* pile—back there now, and locked the bathroom door. His first thought was the same thought he had every time he was in there—*What was the designer thinking?* The top half of the walls were built with some sort of modern brick, white and full of holes, most of which were now plugged with pen caps and chewing gum, cigarette butts, and tubes of rolled paper. He had fished one of those papers out once, using the tweezers from the Swiss Army knife on his key ring. *I want to die*, it had read.

He hadn't looked at another.

The hardcover in his lap wore a clear plastic wrap. It crinkled as he opened it, and he played the *Who Read This Last?* game, looking for clues in the pages. Sometimes it was a certain perfume, and he wondered if it was an old lady's scent or a young woman's. Other times it was cheesy fingerprints marching in the margins, some snack-food junkie. Today he found scribbles. Dozens of stray pencil marks. He stared at them, imagined them beginning to move. It looked like a person. Like Stephen.

Hey, the doodle man said.

Why won't you leave me alone? Benjamin thought.

I'm not asking to be here.

Then go away.

Man, you got it all wrong. You won't let me go.

Benjamin blinked. *I killed you.*

Nah, I was dead already.

No. I heard you screaming. I saw you. Your eyes were open; they were right on me. And I . . . Oh, God, I didn't move.

You were scared.

A soldier isn't allowed to be scared.

You're not a soldier anymore.

Shut up, Benjamin thought, and slammed the book closed. He washed his face and looked in the mirror. He needed to run the clippers over his hair; it was longer now, furry almost. He liked to keep it short, rough, like a cat's tongue. "Get it together, Ben," he said. He knew Stephen wasn't there, that he was talking to himself. He did it anyway.

He dumped the books on the windowsill next to the bathroom door and got in his car. He couldn't go home, not feeling the way he did. He thought of Silvia; she wouldn't know if he didn't go home tonight. She didn't need *him.* Someone, yes. A warm body to feed and clothe and cuddle her. But any arms could do that. Abbi's, another foster family three counties away, whoever. It didn't matter that he found her; she was nothing to him.

He'd seen pieces of dead children in Afghanistan, after the detonation of suicide bombs or IEDs. And that boy, about eleven, who'd walked by near the end of a firefight. He stepped over the body of an insurgent and hesitated, his foot against the man's AKM assault rifle.

Don't touch it. Just keep walking, Benjamin had thought. *Oh, Jesus, please let him keep walking.* And Stephen, beside him, had whispered, "Don't pick it up, kid." But the boy bent down, wrapped his dusty hand around the barrel, and then jerked backward, hit by a smattering of gunfire, falling onto the dead insurgent.

Somehow, Silvia had become matted into his war, a sweet, bright face in the tangle of sand and smoke, the one who made it, despite being left to suffocate in a grocery sack. The one he'd found, and saved.

He ordered battered fish, fries, and a Dr. Pepper at Phil's, took the food to his car and picked at the meal. He hated the bouncing up and down, the mood swings. They controlled him.

After listening to some ball game for a while, he went back to the county building, to the familiar confines of the holding cell. It was where he belonged, alone. He sat with his head in his hands, in his undershirt, his bare feet on the floor, and heard the office door open. Benjamin didn't move. Where could he go?

Footsteps, and then, "Come home."

He lifted his head. Abbi stood there, in the doorway of the cell, Silvia asleep in the car seat hanging against her thigh. She set the baby on the floor.

"The door . . . I locked it. I know I did," he said.

Abbi held a ring up, jingling it at eye level, two silver keys twitching. "Your spares. From the junk drawer."

"How did you—?"

"I drove around looking for you the first few times you didn't come home. And other times, when I couldn't sleep. You were always here." She stepped toward him, her feet in sandals; she'd wear them until the first snow, or the second. When she reached him, she took his head in her hands, fingers touching at the nape of his neck, and rubbed her thumbs along the rims of his ears. She always teased him about the ripples in the cartilage, saying it looked like little mice had nibbled on them while he slept.

"Come home," she said again.

"Abbi."

"Silvia and I, we need you."

"You don't need anyone."

She didn't. She was like the sunflowers he occasionally saw while driving down I-90, not on the side of the road but in it, the only bloom for miles, growing from a crack in the pavement, thriving despite the heat and fumes.

"How can you say that?" Abbi asked.

"It's true."

"Ben, I'm a train wreck."

"Stop."

"I am. But I'm worse without you." She sighed. "And I've been without you for a long time. Too long."

He pulled her close, face pressed into her belly. Abbi squeezed tighter, arms around his head; she bent down and kissed his hair, his forehead, his nose. "Come on. I'll follow you," she whispered.

He slipped on his shirt and shoes, stuffed his socks in his back pants pocket, and smoothed the blanket on the bunk. He drove home, Abbi's headlights behind him, and when they pulled into the driveway he took Silvia's seat from the car and brought her inside.

They stumbled against each other and, leaving Silvia strapped in the carrier near the sofa, they found the bed and made love, awkwardly and still dressed. Afterward, they untangled their jeans and dumped their clothes over the side of the mattress, and lay on top of the sheet, legs scissored together, her face in his neck, her arm across his chest, their fingers twined. Then Silvia began crying, and Benjamin said, "I'll get her."

Abbi slipped beneath the blanket, and he returned with the baby, bottle in her mouth. Silvia finished the formula, and he burped her, rocking her and singing until she fell asleep. Instead of moving her to the crib, he tucked her into the bed between them, no longer a stone buffer but an anchor, holding him and Abbi steady through the storm.

They floundered in the morning, not uncomfortable but clumsy, like grade-schoolers with crushes, pulling hair and kicking each other under the lunch table. They sat across from each other, Benjamin sneaking glances at his wife through the steam floating above his coffee mug, each one longer, until their eyes met and he smiled quietly. Looked into the black liquid, and then back up at Abbi, waiting for her to look up at him. He liked how her eyes felt on him.

He had no idea where to go from there, with Abbi. She seemed nervous and unsure, too, tapping her grapefruit spoon on the edge of the plate. Twice she stretched her hand out, her fingers as long as she could make them until they nearly touched his. Both times she hesitated, then picked up her glass instead.

"Any plans for the day?" he asked.

She shrugged. "Not really. No. You?"

"Work, obviously. Then home."

"For dinner?"

"Yes."

"Okay."

"Okay," he said, standing. He leaned across the table, his body stopping and starting, stopping and starting as he went in for a kiss. Their lips touched, flattening like pillows—soft, clean, flannel-cased pillows. "I'll be home before six."

She looked at him now, and he held her gaze. It was the longest they'd *seen* each other, and her eyes said she wanted to trust him, but didn't. He knew the feeling. His eyes probably said the same thing.

He waited until school was over, drove to Matthew's home. Inside the apartment he heard shouting, and the door flew open with a "What?" from an overweight teenaged girl. She stared up, and he noticed an eruption of pimples in the center of her forehead. She'd tried to conceal them, but the makeup had crumbled away sometime during the school day, and now they peered out at him, seven fiery mounds with white eyes.

The girl seemed nervous; her fist tightened on the doorknob, skin thinning over her knuckles, and she swallowed, saying, "I didn't know you were a deputy."

"I'm looking for Matthew Savoie."

She blinked. "Matty?"

"Is he here?"

"Skye, you trying to cool the neighborhood? Close the darn door already. I—" The woman stopped next to the girl. She grabbed a handful of hair at the back of her neck, lifted it into the air and let it fall. Again. And tossed her head. "Oh, Deputy, can I help you with something?"

"I'm looking for your nephew."

"Is there some sort of problem?"

"No, no problem. I just need to speak with him for a moment."

"He's at dialysis now. Won't be home until eight-ish."

"Dialysis?" Abbi hadn't told him the boy was sick. Did she know?

"There's a center in Hollings."

"Thanks for your time, Ms. Benson."

"Why don't you leave your number, and I'll have him get back to you," the woman said. She tugged at the bottom of her shirt, pulling the neckline down to reveal more cleavage. Beside her, the girl snorted and rolled her eyes, fading back into the apartment.

He scratched his chin—rubbed it, really, his palm flat against the pointy bone, his wedding ring clearly visible. "It's fine. I'll just take a ride over to see him now."

⌣

At the dialysis center, a nurse pointed to Matthew, eyes closed in a recliner-type chair, two thin tubes snaking from his arm. Benjamin wheeled a small stool beside the boy's station and waited, unsure if he was asleep or resting but not wanting to disturb him. And to check, Benjamin would have had to touch him. He felt oddly discomfited doing that; a touch meant more to him than to most people.

A book tented on the boy's lap—something about the seven most famous unsolved mathematics proofs of the millennium. Benjamin shifted on the stool, listening to the hissing and whistles in the room. At one time, he would have prayed in stretches like this, in the waiting. Stephen told him he was better at the empty moments than anyone else, and there had been many of those in the desert. The other guys had played cards and had spitting contests, pocking the sand with foamy blobs of saliva and mucus and Skoal. They had drunk vodka colored blue and shipped in mouthwash bottles by Sergeant Wilkinson's mother. Or they'd complained—about what they missed from home, about what they wouldn't miss from Afghanistan.

But Benjamin had sat quietly, if not actually praying words, working to see God in the grenades and latrines and the MREs. And he had always managed to find some glint of His goodness, somewhere, every day. Now . . . He shook his head, and with his lips rolled under his teeth, grunted softly.

Now I don't want to see it. The good only magnifies the bad.

Matthew's book fell to one side, and the boy's eyes opened. He reached for the paperback, then turned his head and saw Benjamin, groped for his notepad. What's wrong? How did you know I—

Benjamin waved to get his attention. "Your aunt. And nothing's wrong. I came to apologize. For the other day."

You didn't do anything.

"I did enough to keep you from coming over the last couple weeks."

He saw Matthew write, I should have called, and

reached over to pinch the tip of the pen between his fingers, stopping it from moving. Matthew glanced at him.

"Look, Abbi really appreciates your help. And after three days of rain our lawn looks like the Amazon. So, if you're feeling up to it, I hope you do come back. We're not as odd as we seem."

The boy smiled a little. I will. Tomorrow.

"Good." He motioned to the book. "You planning on solving one of those?"

Not me.

Benjamin paused. He stared at the boy's scrawl and realized he had no idea what meaning to put on it. *Not me, I'm not smart enough to do something like that? Not me, I won't have enough time?*

Just how sick was he?

Benjamin wasn't sure he should ask. Matthew had a reason for not telling them, and Benjamin understood all about hiding weakness. A pride thing. A guy thing. Or, simply a thing humans suffered because of this sin-drenched world. He wouldn't put the kid in a position of having to answer, when he was still trying to figure out his own questions.

"Then, tomorrow," Benjamin said.

Matthew nodded.

In the truck, Benjamin smiled at the thought of going home. More specifically, of going home to his family. To his wife and baby. He turned on the radio. And he whistled.

Chapter TWENTY-TWO

Abbi dreaded going to her yearly exam, but because of her history she couldn't miss it. She was at an increased risk for cervical cancer, so she put up with the prodding and swabbing so both she and Benjamin would have peace of mind. He more so than her. He knew her appointments came around September, and by the end of the month, if she hadn't given him any sort of update, he'd begin pestering her to go and get checked.

She read *Good Housekeeping* magazine in the waiting room, with Silvia, and the nurse called her name. Abbi perspired as they approached the scale in the hallway and the nurse said, "Step on." She removed her shoes—that would shave off a pound or two—and got on the wobbling platform. Squeezed her eyes shut. Each year she told herself she wouldn't look, and each year she did anyway. One hundred sixty-eight pounds. Eleven pounds heavier than last weigh-in.

She only learned her weight during these appointments; Benjamin didn't allow a scale in the house, and she loved him for that. As a child, her mother had weighed her every day, sometimes two or three times, until Abbi turned thirteen and decided to refuse.

She wasn't chubby; she was fat, despite her mother putting her on a perpetual diet from the time the scale inched over fifty pounds when she turned five. She went to kindergarten with her Care Bears lunch box stuffed with mustard and lettuce sandwiches on thin, low-calorie bread, celery sticks, and a thermos of skim milk, while the other kids traded Ding-Dongs and Handi-Snacks. She wanted nothing more than to smear that salty cheese onto crackers with a little red plastic stick.

Sometimes she kept to the diet. Sometimes she snuck food. Not from home—her mother always knew exactly how many packages of granola bars remained in each box, exactly how each orange was positioned in the fruit drawer. In elementary school, she'd take change from the ashtray of her father's car to buy a sixty-five-cent ice cream, or two. By junior high she'd chuck her packed lunch in the trash and feast on chips, Slush Puppies—with tons of syrup and very little ice— and tater tots, purchased with her babysitting money.

She wasn't the fat outcast; that was Joy-Marie Ingersman, with dandruff and body odor, who wore stirrup pants and her brother's peeling Nirvana T-shirts every day. Abbi's parents had money and status—a lawyer and a state senator. She wore trendy clothes and let the popular girls copy her Spanish homework. The in-crowd kept her around for the ego boost. "Oh, Abbi," they'd say, "you're so lucky you can eat whatever you want. If I gain five pounds, Coach will kick me off the cheerleading squad."

She refused to go away to college as any kind of fat girl, and spent the summer first walking, then jogging, then running the wooded trails behind the YMCA, listening to the trees and birds, stopping to eat a handful of sour wild-buffalo berries when the trail erased in the brambles. She ate little more than that, slept too much to escape the hunger headaches, and the pounds fell off—more than thirty.

But the food kept getting in the way, and she knew she hadn't the willpower to be anorexic. She tried vomiting a few times, once with her finger but mostly by poking her toothbrush into the back of her throat. And she wasn't cut out for that, either—the chunks of chewed carrot or sugar snap peas forced into her nose from the heaving, the pain of blowing them out, or the coughing fits from sniffing them back down her throat.

With the laxatives came freedom. Oh, she cramped the first few times she took them, sat on the toilet with her toes curled, breathing as if she were in labor, until her body adjusted to her daily senna regimen and she ate what she wanted and popped those pills, and the weight stayed gone.

And then Benjamin came along and caught her dipping into the laxative bottle, just twice, but enough for him to understand. He told her she was beautiful, and she made it out to be less than it was—"Just once a week, really. Not even."—and managed to cut back to a couple of episodes a month, after big meals or during exams when she had no time to exercise.

After they married, she stopped—she had to. She couldn't bolt to the toilet every morning without suspicion—except for his weekends away with the Guard, and even then, she found she didn't need or want them as much. She didn't purge to be thin, not really. She did it for the same reason she binged, some bizarre paradox of simultaneous self-soothing and self-loathing that not even coming face-to-face with the living Christ at nineteen could end.

That bothered her most of all; each time she swallowed those pills, or drank a half-dozen glasses of Metamucil, or simply binged until she felt as if her stomach would split, she denied the reality of Jesus' sacrifice. He died so she wouldn't have to allow the bulimia to overcome her. But some part of her didn't want to give it up. She feared if she stopped the purging, she'd end up that fat girl again. That scared her more than grieving God.

The nurse handed Abbi a paper blanket for her lap, and after her exam the receptionists passed Silvia around. Then Abbi went home and ate, and didn't stop until Benjamin came through the door.

⁓

"I have to grab some groceries," she said to Matthew, standing over him.

He wrote on his pad and held it up to her—I'LL be here—from his back, on the floor with Silvia, his legs sprawled in the opposite direction of hers, their faces inches apart. The baby giggled each time Matthew made a noise or smacked kisses on her lips.

Abbi nudged him with her ankle. "The sky's about to open up. Come with me, and I'll bring you home when I'm done. You don't want to get stuck riding home in the rain."

My bike?

"Ben can drop it off tonight or in the morning."

Matthew stood with Silvia, ambled across the living room with wide, uncoordinated steps, his teenaged sneakers too large at the end of his thin legs. Thunder cracked, loud enough to vibrate the front window, and Silvia tensed, arching her back and crying her startled cry. Matthew squinted at Abbi.

"Thunder. It scared her."

He nodded and cuddled the baby close. Abbi gave him a smocked blouse and tiny shorts to dress her in and then bent over and tied a red bandana around her own hair. "Let's get out of here before it starts pouring."

She took the diaper bag and an umbrella, and Matthew carried the baby, strapping her into the car seat and remaining next to her in the back. The rain pelted the windshield in plump, explosive drops as soon as Abbi backed from the driveway. "Good timing," she said, forgetting for a moment Matthew couldn't hear her. She didn't repeat her words.

Pulling up in front of the Food Mart, she saw a girl standing out front, under the roof overhang, smoking. She tucked the cigarette behind her back, dropped it, one foot stealthily smothering the butt. Abbi cut the engine and the headlights, turned around to Matthew, who looked up.

"That's your cousin out front?"

Matthew glanced out the window. Shrugged. Abbi looked toward the store again; the girl was gone. "She must have gone inside. If I see her, I'll ask if she wants a ride. Stay here, okay?"

Abbi darted from the car through the glass doors, shaking off the rain and greeting Martha, the cashier. She made a bit of small talk about Silvia, and with a shopping basket over her arm, grabbed a container of strawberries, a bottle of Head & Shoulders for Benjamin, a cucumber, and two boxes of prunes. She had come only for the prunes but didn't want to admit that to herself, or the cashier. And Benjamin had run out of shampoo that morning.

As she paid, she saw the smoking girl plucking videos from the rack near the front of the store, glancing at the back of the cases for a second before sticking them back. "Skye, right?"

The girl fumbled with the movie she held; it slipped from her hand, clattering to the linoleum. She left it there. "Sorry. Yeah. Hi, um, Mrs. Patil."

"Do you need a ride?" Abbi asked.

"Uh, no. It's okay. I'm just gonna wait out the rain here. These storms, you know. They're loud but they don't, uh, really like, last long."

"I have Matt in the car, and I'm going that way."

Skye finally bent down to retrieve the dropped video. She jammed it into the rack, knocking two more out. Swearing softly, she picked those up, too. Wiped the back of her hand across her upper lip. Abbi went over to her. "Look," she said in Skye's ear. "Relax. Matt didn't see it, and I won't say anything about you-know-what out front." She took the movies from the girl and placed them on their proper shelves. "Come on."

"Okay, yeah," Skye said.

They scampered to the car, Abbi slamming the driver's side door and dropping the grocery bag between her and Skye. "I found her," she said to Matthew, who smiled and waved at his cousin.

"Hey," Skye said, barely glancing over her shoulder. She jerked too hard on the seat belt and it jammed. Again. A third time. "Ugh. Stupid thing."

"It does that sometimes," Abbi told her, though it never did. "Pull slowly."

Finally Skye buckled herself in, and Abbi drove carefully through the rain, the drops long and thin now, like needles. The teenager plucked at her thumbnail. *Click, click. Click, click. Click.* And when Abbi stopped at the curb of the apartment, Skye jumped from the car, closing the seat belt in the door.

Matthew saw it, pointed.

"Don't worry about it. I'll fix it when I get home. Thanks for all your help today, and I'll see you Thursday."

He nodded, and before going inside came around to the passenger door, opened it, and tugged the belt back into place. Abbi rolled her eyes, waving him away with a laugh. The kid was too perfect; she wasn't surprised his cousin didn't want him to know she'd been smoking.

Chapter TWENTY-THREE

He turned off the lawn mower and waited for his bones to stop vibrating, then maneuvered the machine into the back of the shed, in the corner behind Abbi's pottery wheel. He was careful not to bump anything; once he'd knocked some sort of urn off the worktable and had debated against telling Abbi, thought he might leave the broken pieces and pretend he knew nothing of what happened. But Matthew couldn't, of course, and he gathered the shards in some newspaper and brought them into the house with a long note of apology scribbled on three notepad pages with promises of repayment and working for free. Abbi read the first line—*I'm So Sorry*—and dropped the pieces in the trash can, except one. She squeezed that piece until it crumbled and let the dust fall through her fingers, brushed it on her shorts.

"Just some clay and paint," she said, and it was one of the few times he'd been certain her tone would have told him something more.

Untangling the weed trimmer from the rakes and shovels, he tried to wiggle it from the small space but lost his grip on the handle. He shook his left hand. His skin felt too tight, and when he pressed his thumbnail into each fingertip, he knew he'd lost sensation. He had been worried about this after he woke this morning with his access arm twisted under his body, his hand rubbery numb, as if he'd slept on it most of the night.

He pressed his right palm against his fistula, feeling for the thrill, the whoosh of blood through his joined veined and artery. It was gone. He gritted his teeth and jerked his head forward in frustration, punched his outer thigh with his right fist. Then he went inside to find Abbi and the deputy.

They sat at the table—she with a grapefruit and a bowl of some curly grain, he with a buttered bagel. They spoke softly, fingers almost touching.

"Matt," Abbi said. "There's bagels, and cinnamon quinoa on the stove, and lots of fruit. Help yourself."

I need help.

"What's wrong?" Benjamin asked, shoulders going rigid.

He held out his arm. *I think I have a clot. In my access. Please call this number and tell them.*

Benjamin nodded, took the pad. "I will," he said, and flipped his phone from his belt.

They're closed Saturday. Someone will be on call.

Benjamin dialed, wrote another number, pressed a button and dialed again. Abbi got up from the table, Silvia swaddled against her chest in the black fabric wrap. "This is because of us, isn't it? We worked you too hard."

He shook his head.

Benjamin snapped his phone closed. "The nurse said to go to the hospital. Let me call your aunt."

"No," Matthew said slowly—N's were difficult, having the same tongue position as L and H—making sure to feel the sound vibrate through his face, to keep it buzzing. He shook his head again, harder.

Abbi and Benjamin looked at one another, as if startled by his voice.

"She needs to know. She'll probably want to take you herself," Benjamin said.

No. I'll go by ambulance, if you'll call for me.

"Matt . . ."

Please, just call the ambulance.

"I'll drive you," Abbi said.

"We'll take the Durango," Benjamin said. "You stay with Silvia."

"I'm coming."

"I'm not speeding with the baby in the car."

"I'll leave her with the McGees."

"Fine. Hurry," Benjamin said, and Abbi took a tote bag from near the front door and left. They followed her, Benjamin strapping himself into the front of the truck, Matthew behind him. Abbi returned and slipped into the back seat, as well.

"Can I do anything?" she asked.

He shook his head. It's not as bad as you think.

"I don't believe you."

Matthew leaned his head back and closed his eyes. They'd remove the clot. That was nothing—a nick in the skin, a balloon catheter, a couple hours of day surgery. He needed to hope there wouldn't be continued clotting. A failed access meant an operation to create another fistula in his other arm. He shouldn't complain; people spent years in dialysis. For him, it'd been, what? Fourteen months?

He felt a flutter against his wristbone, then another, saw Abbi's fingers tapping him. "Can I pray, at least?"

He nodded, and she took his hand and squeezed. Her prayer fell into her lap as she bowed her head, so he could only agree with her moving lips. She didn't look up until Benjamin pulled into the hospital parking lot.

They walked on either side of him, sentinels, Abbi holding on to his upper arm, the deputy close enough so their shoulders kept bumping. He thought of that song, the one Ellie had sung the solo part for at the spring concert. "Someone to Watch Over Me." Or, two someones. His first someones, really.

Mother. He couldn't say she'd never looked out for him; she'd had moments of lucidity, periods of days, weeks sometimes, when her blood and brain weren't boiling with drugs. In those times she tried to be a parent, making his favorite grilled cheese sandwiches with tater tots and reminding him to wash his face before bed. But mostly he remembered her strung out, passed out, or out of luck. He had to believe she would have been a better mom if she hadn't been full up with poison. Had to.

He didn't remember his father at all.

And he didn't remember a time when he hadn't been going deaf, though he didn't know it. How would he have? He couldn't hear through ears other than his own, and those ears heard bubbly, dim, underwater sounds. He learned to talk that way, from the television, listening to words through cotton, and by the time he turned five it had been clear there was a problem. If his mother hadn't been a junkie, she would have known he spoke differently than other kids his age. Instead, he went to kindergarten, and when his teacher realized he had speech delays, she arranged for a hearing test. The school nurse squashed his head between a pair of heavy, padded headphones, telling him to raise his hand when he heard the beep. By then, he'd lost nearly fifty percent of his hearing in one ear, close to ninety percent in the other.

The doctor didn't find the kidney damage until later, at eleven, when Matt stopped peeing and fell asleep each day in class, couldn't walk from one end of the soccer field to the other without gasping for air. The genetic testing showed he had Alport Syndrome, a rare disorder passed down maternally. Had his mother taken him to be examined when he was three and had blood in his urine, early intervention may have prolonged the life of his kidneys.

He had to believe she wanted to be a better mother, but couldn't.

The sidewalks leading to the emergency room were dusty gray and still ridged with newness. There were prints in the cement, leaf fossils, oblong and pointed at the ends. They must have fallen from the trees lining the path onto the still-wet concrete. Not many, one or two per rectangular slab, but Matthew noticed them because he was looking down rather than ahead. He felt the sting of loneliness. If something should happen to him, who would feel it?

Lacie, of course, for a while. But her attachment to him was like a child's to a pet gerbil, passionate while the thing lived, weeping during the shoebox funeral in the backyard, then rapidly fading as something new—a guinea pig, a first crush—came along. None of his other cousins, nor his aunt. Not his mother. He was only a blip, a point on an infinite plane. No one would miss him. He knew it but kept putting one foot in front of the other, moving through each day, clutching at his numbers and his Lord, telling himself he needed nothing else.

Three point one four one five nine two six five three five eight nine seven nine three two three eight four six two six four three three eight three two seven five zero . . .

Inside the hospital, Benjamin explained the situation to the woman at the reception desk. He talked with his hand, gesturing, raking his fingernails over the top of his head. "Do you have your insurance card?" he asked Matthew.

My wallet is home.

The receptionist entered Matthew's information into the computer from the page he wrote it on, and told them to sit and wait. "He would have gotten in quicker if he'd gone by ambulance," he said to Abbi, perhaps forgetting Matthew would see his words.

"This is better," Abbi replied, touching Matthew's knee.

He looked at her and a smile twitched at one corner of his mouth.

Abbi plucked the pad and pen from his hand. *You can have the money for your trip. We'll give it to you.*

Matthew mouthed, *No*, shaking his head.

"Yes," Abbi said. "I'm not saying you can't come back and work. But if you can't . . . If the doctor says you can't, I mean, then Ben and I will give it to you. We want to. No one should miss their senior trip. It's your only one, you know."

He shrugged and nodded a little, and she said, "Good, it's settled." And she reached one arm around his shoulder, pressed her other hand against the side of his head and pulled him into her, kissing him on his hair, above his ear. Then she stood and took the deputy's phone from his belt. "I'm calling Janet. How long do you think we'll be here?"

Matthew tapped her shoulder. *I can wait by myself.*

"No, no. I'm just worried she might need more diapers or something. Ben, did you leave the front door open?"

"Sorry. I locked it. Habit."

"There's still a key in the shed, though. Right?"

"On the beam to the left of the door."

She dialed, wandering around the corner. When she came back, she again sat next to Matthew. This time, he touched her hand. She squeezed back, and didn't let go.

Chapter TWENTY-FOUR

After showering and dressing, Benjamin kissed Silvia on the top of the head and said good-bye to Abbi. "Maybe we can go out to dinner after work."

"A date?" Abbi asked.

"Nah," Benjamin said. "I'm just tired of tofu."

He drove to the county building, and before he managed to get inside, Wesley came out. "Let's go," he said.

"Where?"

"The school. Something to do with your case. I'll drive."

Inside a classroom adjacent to the front entrance, a teacher was hanging a glittery *Welcome Students* banner on a pocked bulletin board. A preschool staff day. Benjamin touched the brim of his hat; the woman nodded back.

The principal was waiting for them. "Thanks for coming so quickly," she said.

"What's going on?" Benjamin asked.

"In the technology lab," she said, walking briskly down the hall. The deputies followed her into a room with fifteen computers. "One of the students was looking for a Web site she visited a few weeks ago and found something, well, disturbing in the browser's history."

"Which was?" Wesley asked.

"I should show you." She clicked on a window and it opened. "Three weeks ago. Someone was in here looking at this."

Benjamin scanned the page, a newspaper article dated two years ago, about a teenaged mother who left her newborn in a Nevada McDonald's restroom. "There must be more, if you called us."

"Six sites, all about girls abandoning their babies, five of them having to do with sentencing. Plus sites with Baby Moses law information, state law sites." The principal sighed. "It's one of our girls."

"The computers are password protected?" Benjamin asked.

"Well, yes. But I'm sure the student who found this wasn't pregnant. Kids tell each other their log-in information, write it in the covers of their notebooks. You know. They're kids."

"We'll need a list of everyone who's used the computers recently," Wesley said.

She handed him two sheets of paper. "Already done. There's a list with those who have logged in during the past month, and also a list of those who have signed in at the door saying they're here to use the lab. But there's no guarantee she's on here. Students let their friends in at other entrances. People are in and out. Doors are unlocked all day. It's summer. Things just aren't monitored as closely."

"You checked out all the pregnancy rumors," Benjamin said to Wesley. "There wasn't anything on any of them?"

"It had to be someone who hid it," Wesley said, his monster shoulders heaving up and down.

"Karen, were there any girls who suddenly started wearing baggy clothes, or seemed to gain weight quickly?"

The principal shook her head. "Not that I noticed. I can check again with Pam. And Tina. As guidance counselor and nurse, they'd hear more of it than anyone."

"I was hoping . . ." Benjamin rubbed the back of his head. *Velcro*, he thought. He needed a haircut. "I really thought it was someone not from around here."

"Keep your ear to the ground," Wesley said to Karen. "Teachers, too. Can't imagine a secret like this staying bottled up for too long. Especially with school starting in a couple of days."

"I'll call if I hear anything," she said.

Without speaking, the two men walked down the hallway, Benjamin running his hand over the shiny metal handles protruding from the blue lockers—empty now, but on Wednesday they'd be filled with books, decorated with photos and stickers, a multitude of teen-aged angst padlocked away. Wesley waved at the main office secretary on the way out the door, and as he climbed into the Durango, said, "This will get around. Someone will talk."

"Whoever she is, she's feeling remorse," Benjamin said. "If she didn't care, she wouldn't be looking at all that."

"Unless she thinks she's about to get caught," Wesley said. "And it could be the father checking things out, not the mother."

"I hate this. Now every time I see a kid, I'll wonder, Did she do it? Did he?" Benjamin counted the names on the lists. "I'll divvy these up between the three of us. Holbach will take some. There are no addresses, though. We'll have to get those from Karen."

"You hungry?"

"It's barely noon."

"I didn't have breakfast," Wesley said. "Like salmon stew?"

"No."

"I do," Wesley said, and he turned left, then right, then right again and pulled into his driveway. "Renée makes it twice a week."

Inside, Wesley filled two bright turquoise dishes with the leftovers, stuck them in the microwave one at a time. He dropped a bargain-sized bottle of ketchup on the table along with a jumble of flatware and napkins. "Water okay?"

"Whatever."

"Ignore the blue plates. Reenie read some article says blue plates make you eat less. Ugly as dirt, but she had to have 'em. Says she lost ten pounds since she got 'em. I don't see a difference." Wesley stripped off his uniform shirt, hung it on the back of his chair. He sat in front of his meal in his undershirt. "I'm a slob when I eat. I know it. Can't keep food off myself to save my life."

Wesley paused—giving thanks, maybe—before stabbing a hunk of fish and chewing it. He shook on salt, garlic powder, and stirred. Then he squeezed ketchup over the plate, threads of red zigzagging across the potatoes and celery. Like blood. He whipped it all together. "Eat, eat," he said.

Benjamin tried a carrot, not chewing but mashing it with his tongue against the roof of his mouth before swallowing. He sprinkled on some salt, too.

"I know," Wesley said. "I love her, but my wife loves her stuff bland as bread. Still great, though."

"Wes, did you . . . kill anyone?"

Wesley wiped his mouth. "Not exactly mealtime conversation."

"Did you?"

"Yes."

He looked at Wesley's stew, the ketchup mixed with the gravy, all muddied and brown. Like Stephen's blood in the sand. "Me, too."

"That's war."

"How can you be so cavalier?"

"I choose not to think about it."

"Because you don't, or because you don't want to?"

"Ain't no difference."

"It's a lot different, Wes. Either it just doesn't come to mind, or you fight to keep it out of your head."

"You're trying too hard to figure it all out. Leave it be. Whoever is dead, is dead. Whoever's living . . . Well, you got it. That's just the way it is."

Benjamin poked at his stew, fork scraping against the dish. "How many?"

"Don't know," Wesley said, his broad shoulders moving up and down.

"Honest."

"As the day is long. Not like I counted. I got off thousands of rounds and watched dozens of men fall. My bullet, someone else's. Don't matter."

"I know who I killed."

"You know their names? Birthdays? Favorite colors?" Wesley wiped his mouth. "You don't know a darn thing."

"I know his face," Benjamin said. "The first one. We were in the street in Kabul, and he looked at me, and he was terrified of dying. I saw it, clear as daylight. He looked at me like, 'What am I doing here?' and I thought the same exact thing. 'What am I doing here, with my gun pointed at some stupid kid?' He was a kid—just had this fuzz on his lip, couldn't have been more than seventeen. Then he reached for his weapon and I shot him."

His finger twitched with the memory, and he grabbed one hand in the other, squeezed. *Just a little pressure and bam. That's all, folks. He was there in a bright red puddle with half his skull imbedded in the wall behind him, and I'm feeling like the big man. Oh yeah. All righty.*

Until later, when the adrenaline had sweat out, and it grew quiet and dark, and the springs of his cot squawked beneath the weight of his guilt each time he moved. And he did too much moving that night, and the nights after, flopping from back to stomach, knowing some mother would be waiting forever for her boy to come home. He hadn't realized it would be so hard, when ideologies turned to people, and people bled.

"So, what are you saying? You wish you never went over there? Wish you were never a soldier at all?"

Benjamin couldn't say that. If he did, it would be admitting the futility of it all—Stephen, his foot, his decaying marriage, that dead boy, those bodies he unloaded. All of it for nothing. "No."

"Then stop your complaining and start living."

"It's not that easy."

Wesley plucked a fleck of fish from his undershirt. "I know."

⌒

Abbi wore a dress, the one he liked, the one she bought when they first married, beige with a bold fern design and sleeveless, swishing just above her knee. It tied at the side, as if it wrapped around her; but it didn't really, he knew. He had tried to open it that way once. Abbi laughed at his confusion when the dress didn't fall off, and said, "It's a faux wrap dress. *Faux* being the operative word."

He pouted. "How am I supposed to get you out of it, then?"

"Try the zipper," she had told him.

He smiled tenderly now, watched her with a toothbrush hanging from her mouth, filling baby bottles. She said, "I'm almost ready," through the white foam, and scooted down the hallway. He followed her to the bathroom. She spat, rinsed. "What are you grinning at?"

"Nothing," he said.

"Well, stop it. You're making me paranoid. Go get the baby."

Benjamin strapped Silvia into the detachable car seat and dangled a plush monkey above her. "One little monkey jumping on the bed. She fell off and bumped her head. Mama called the doctor and the doctor said, 'No more monkeys jumping on the bed.'" He bent down to her, wriggled his face against her belly, dotted her bare legs with kisses. "Are you my little monkey? You are. You're Daddy's little monkey." She giggled and kicked him in the eye.

"I'm ready," Abbi said, tugging a green sweater over her dress. A jade donut-shaped pendant hung on a cord around her neck; his eyes slipped down from the necklace over her body, down her legs, to the knots of muscle balled in each calf, more pronounced by her hemp platform sandals. Her skin glistened, and he smelled melons. Sweet, sugary melons.

"You shaved," he said.

"You like it."

They took the Volvo, and Abbi drove. They ended up in a tourist town, the main attraction a neo-Moorish building covered in ears of colored corn and other grains that created themed murals. "Want to stop at the Corn Palace?" Benjamin said as they passed. "Silvia's first tourist trap."

Abbi rolled her eyes.

"Just asking."

He carried the baby into a Chinese restaurant, and he and Abbi took turns sitting with her as the other plated their food at the buffet. They ate for several minutes in silence, then Benjamin said, "We had a bit of a break in the case today," and he told her what he could while she listened, twirling lo mein on her fork.

"What does it mean?" she asked finally.

"That at least one of Silvia's parents goes to school in Temple. Or maybe someone who knows who her parents are. Most likely it's the mother, though."

"Poor girl."

"I know you didn't just say what I thought you said."

Abbi sipped her iced tea through a straw. "I did."

"Look at that child on the bench next to you. How can you even—?"

"Because I do. Have you even considered how scared and confused this girl must have been to do what she did?"

"Or maybe she just wanted to get rid of her kid. You hear about teenagers at their proms, giving birth in a toilet stall and dumping the babies in the trash before going back out and partying."

"Which is my point. What healthy, sane person thinks no one will find a newborn in a school bathroom?"

"And if Simon Wayne hadn't been trying to make out with his

girlfriend, no one would've found Silvia. She'd be dead, Abbi. It was just dumb—"

"Don't you dare say *luck*."

Benjamin swished his soda. "Your problem is you think everyone is basically good."

"No," Abbi said, "I think we all bear God's image. It's not the same thing, but it's why I try to give people the benefit of the doubt."

He'd forgotten how to do that, trust people first and think later. A man who did that in a war got his head blown off. "You're such a bleeding heart. Let's just gather for a big ol' group hug and the world will be a better place."

"Not a bad idea," she said, and she laughed. "Remember our first date?"

"That vegetarian place. Gag. You made me eat wheat meat."

"I didn't make you do anything, Benjamin Patil. You choked that down all by your little lonesome. And, if I remember correctly, it was your idea to take me there."

"To impress you. It didn't work. We argued the whole meal."

"Like this," she said.

A grin pulled at one corner of his mouth. "Yeah. Like this."

"And I did come back for more."

"Masochist."

"Takes one to know one."

The waitress appeared, gathering their dirty plates. "You finish?" she asked. They both nodded, and she slipped the check onto the table, two fortune cookies on top. Benjamin held one out to Abbi, the plastic wrapper crinkling as she took it from his hand, her fingers gliding over his wrist and palm. "You first," she said.

He cracked his cookie open, like an egg, on the side of the table. " 'You display the wonderful traits of charm and courtesy.' "

"They obviously haven't lived with you lately."

"Ouch."

"Sorry," Abbi said quickly. "I didn't—"

"No, I deserved that." He yanked a napkin from the metal dispenser, swept the crumbs and greasy bits of fried rice onto the carpet. "I am trying."

"I know. I am, too. I think I am, anyway. Sometimes." She sipped her drink again, now watery from the melted ice, wrinkled her nose. "Let's get out of here."

"Wait. Your fortune."

Abbi ripped open the wrapper and broke her cookie into two neat halves. Read the slip of paper.

"Come on. I told you mine," Benjamin prodded. "What's it say?"

She looked at him. "I love you."

The words hung there between the clattering silverware and jumbled conversations around them. He couldn't remember the last time she'd said that to him, or he to her. And he couldn't remember why he'd stopped saying it. But it was back now, fluttering like an exotic bird, one everyone had thought extinct but was really only hidden in the thick, dark canopy of angry words and bruised hopes.

He stood, an odd, light feeling in his stomach. *Happiness? It could be.* "Now I think we can go."

"You drive," she said, and tucked the fortune in the diaper bag.

"Hey. What's it really say?"

"I told you."

Benjamin inserted the car seat into its base, started the car. He touched Abbi's smooth knee, beneath her dress. "Thank you. For trying."

"It's not much."

"Yes it is," he said. "I love you, too."

Chapter TWENTY-FIVE

There was a knock on the door, and this time it didn't seem out of the ordinary to Abbi. People had been knocking for weeks—neighbors, church ladies, co-workers from the grocery or her time substitute teaching—all coming to see Silvia. At first Abbi took the meals they offered and, with some excuse about nap time or bottle time, closed the door, leaving them hovering on the patio. The food stopped but the visits didn't, so she started inviting people in. They held Silvia and between uneasy silences asked the requisite baby questions—"Is she a good baby for you?" "How long is she sleeping at night?"—until eventually words ran out and the guests excused themselves to run to the market, or the hairdresser, or get home to grab the kids off the bus.

Still, they came back. The conversations grew longer and the silences nearly disappeared, and Abbi began to realize this baby that someone didn't want was closing not only the wounds between her and Benjamin, but between her and the town.

"I'm coming," Abbi called as the knock came again. Marie Vilhauser, she guessed. The old crone has been coming by every few days with a small basket of eggs. For the baby. "You go ahead and shake up one of these in her bottle," she had told Abbi. "She'll grow up strong as a bison."

So Abbi opened the door with her head tilted down, expecting to be staring at the wrinkled woman's flaky scalp, but saw instead a gray T-shirt with *PENN STATE* printed across the chest in blue-flocked letters. She'd seen that shirt more times than she could count, and looked up, her heart pulsing thick and joyful behind her entire rib cage.

"Hi," Lauren said.

The corner of the metal screen door scraped Abbi's ankle as she flung herself onto her friend, weeping. Lauren cried with her, hugging back. And they laughed, Abbi smearing the tears over her cheeks as she wiped them away.

"What are you doing here? Come in. Where are the kids?"

"I left them at home," Lauren said. "You're bleeding."

"It's nothing. A little scratch. I just can't believe you're here."

"You're really bleeding."

Abbi inspected her leg. The cut wasn't deep, but it was long with tiny pearls of blood sprouting up every few centimeters. Lauren couldn't stand the sight of blood. Abbi tugged her sock over the wound. "All better," she said.

"You nut."

"Sit, sit. Do you want something? Tea? Anything?"

"I'm good, really," Lauren said, dropping her long body onto the couch. Long, broad, and flat, that was how Lauren was built. Nearly six feet tall, with wide hips and shoulders, and straight through the waist. But not fat. Flat—no curves in the front or back, and even her face seemed pressed in, with wide-set eyes and a wide, low-bridged nose. She scooped a shredded Kleenex from her pocket. "Here. Take half."

"It's paper," Abbi said.

"Yes, but it's recycled paper. I wiped Stevie's nose with it and forgot to throw it out before I washed my jeans."

"Thanks. I'll pass." Abbi sniffed and watched her friend blow into the pre-used tissue. She wanted to tell Lauren how much she had missed her, but it would come out wrong. "I've really missed you," she said anyway, and it was wrong, all morose and accusatory, like telling someone her favorite grandmother died, but wouldn't have if she'd been there a few hours earlier.

"I've missed you, too. I should have come sooner. I wanted to. I just . . . didn't know how," Lauren said. She scratched her knee. "I knew you'd do it, eventually."

"What?"

"Motherhood."

Abbi glanced down the hallway, where Silvia napped, the baby she was trying not to love. "I'm not a mother."

Lauren hesitated. "Is Ben at work?"

"Yeah."

"How is he?"

Abbi couldn't tell the truth. She had a husband. Lauren did not. Who was she to complain? "Fine. Great. We're both great."

"Liar."

"How do you know?"

"Kathy. She talked to Sangita."

Not surprising Sangita would talk to Stephen's mom about Ben. "And that's why you're here?"

Lauren crossed her legs, her arms over her stomach. "You were there for me, and I left you to deal with this all by yourself."

"Lauren—"

"No, really. That's not a best friend. That's a jerk. I'm so sorry."

"Stop it. You don't have to apologize. It was easier for me to be there for you."

"The last time I checked, God didn't call us to easy," Lauren said. She nudged Abbi's foot with her own. "Tell me what's going on."

"I don't know. Ben won't talk to me. I mean, he says stuff. At least he does now that the baby's here. But it's not anything about . . . anything."

"He's depressed."

"Yeah, but it's more than that." Abbi pulled up her legs, rested her chin on her knee. "I don't know." Her thighs pushed against her gut, her diaphragm. She couldn't draw a deep breath. "That idiotic war."

"You and Ben were having problems long before he went away, Abbi."

"Not like this."

"No, you were the one not talking then."

Lauren was right.

Every woman had what she believed were the wrong reasons for getting hitched. Money. Pregnancy. Family pressure. Abbi could add her own wrong reason. Love. *Ha, ha*. Both hers for Benjamin and his for her.

It had been good in the beginning—that first year of marriage while she finished school and he worked at the mall as a security guard. They still played the part of college kids, living in a loft apartment, washing laundry in the bathtub because they hadn't enough money for the machines, eating off their laps in front of the television. They celebrated everything by making love, from her B+ on an art history test to his finding a deal on a package of clearance bungee cords at Wally World. They saw their friends every day, sipped coffee together and talked like their conversations could impact everything from teenaged apathy to Tibetan independence.

She'd never had a man love her with his abandon. He'd shown her by telling her how he felt—so unlike any other boy or man she'd known, her own father included—which was why his silence now was so devastating. It wasn't *him*. He had showed her by doing all sorts of special little things for her, like changing her monitor background to her new favorite painting, or ordering a case of her favorite cherry pie Lärabars, which she couldn't find anywhere closer than Sioux Falls. And she had loved him because he made her feel like a princess (and she hated to admit that, especially to herself). She had loved him because he looked at her as if she were the only woman in the world.

And then she couldn't stand him looking at her as if she were the only woman in the world.

It changed when Benjamin took the job in Temple. She became a deputy's wife, and people knew her only that way. They had no friends, not like the ones in college, without responsibility to children or career or grown-up obligations. Stephen and Lauren lived twenty minutes away, but they had a real life now, with him working Lauren's parents' farm and her pregnant. So it was the *Abbi & Benjamin Show*. Evenings together. Weekends together. Just the two of them. And Abbi started itching, suddenly allergic to Benjamin's undivided attention. She spent more time in her studio, out running, on the computer—but with her avoidance came the guilt.

She knew guilt, couldn't remember a time when she didn't feel guilty about something—her weight, her binge eating, the ninth grade boys groping her in the band room. Deceiving Benjamin about the state of her uterus. That only intensified her desire to hide, and her self-loathing.

Her year of laxative abstinence ended, and she set her alarm for three in the morning, taking the pills then so she wouldn't have to go to the bathroom until Benjamin left for work. She snapped at him more, found all sorts of silly reasons to be angry. And he, feeling her slipping away, squeezed tighter, trying harder to please her, suffocating her. When news came his National Guard unit would be mobilizing, Abbi had been relieved. The two months Benjamin spent at Fort Dix, where she figured nothing bad could happen to him—it was only training, right?—were the best months of her time in Temple. Only after he shipped out to Afghanistan did the shame come crashing down, and hard. What kind of woman wanted her husband in a war zone?

More guilt. More bingeing. More purging and exercise and withdrawing from everyone around her.

She was sick; she knew it. The twisted truth of it all was that she needed to be in control, of her weight, her bowels. Her husband. And when he came home and began treating her the way she'd been treating him, giving her what she had once wanted—space, silence, inattention—she couldn't handle it.

How dare he pull away? He's supposed to love me. He's supposed to look at me like I'm the only person in the world who matters to him.

She wanted to be left alone on her terms.

She wanted to be loved on her terms.

I want, I want, I want.

"You're right," she told Lauren.

"I know I'm right."

"You don't have to be so smug about it."

"What are friends for," Lauren said.

Silvia, on the kitchen table in her basket, began to cry. Abbi picked her up, and Lauren said, "Oh, let me hold her."

"Go right ahead. You're the baby person."

Lauren cuddled her, cooing and kissing and making faces. "What did you name her again?"

"Silvia."

"I bet Ben regrets ever making you read *The Bell Jar.*"

"Not *that* Sylvia. The one from Shakespeare. Spelled with two I's."

"She's beautiful," Lauren said. "I miss this. I want ten more."

"One will be the death of me." Abbi gave her friend a warm bottle. "Do you really think you'll have more?"

"If I get my way. Don't know what God's plan is, but I can't say I have any intentions of becoming a nun anytime soon."

Abbi leaned back cross-legged on the couch, watching Lauren acting motherly, and asked, "Are you doing okay?"

"I am. Really. Sometimes I miss him. At night, mostly. But I have so much to be thankful for."

"That didn't just come out of your mouth," Abbi said with a snort.

Lauren kicked her, laughed. "I know, I know. It sounds trite. But that doesn't make it any less true."

They visited awhile longer, until Lauren needed to get home to her children. Abbi hugged her again, not wanting to let go. Lauren shined. The first day they met, in the dorm, Abbi had seen that glow about her, and it convinced her to go to that first Campus Crusade meeting. And after everything, Lauren still had that shimmer. Abbi silently admitted her envy. She wanted that kind of faith.

Chapter TWENTY-SIX

He wasn't in homeroom with Ellie. The forty-three seniors, divided in half, alphabetically, the H's and S's split. Matthew found his desk, class schedule waiting for him, and saw calculus in the first-period slot. Glanced at the clock above the door. Seven minutes until the bell.

Lord, I'm so nervous. Am I allowed to feel this way about a girl?

He hadn't seen Ellie since that night at the movies. She never did show up at the apartment, not that he honestly expected her to. He hoped, yes, but with a kind of futile hope more like tossing pennies in the fountain at the shopping mall. He'd loved doing that as a little boy. And when he didn't have pennies—which was almost always—he would grab a handful of gravel and stick it in his pocket, and wish on the pebbles he threw in the water. Wishes for his mother to get clean, for his hearing to come back, to find the Godzilla Rampage game under the Christmas tree.

He didn't need wishes now. He could pray. But he wouldn't pray for silly, inconsequential things, and making some girl like him fell decidedly into that category.

He'd considered sacrificing his hair for Ellie, biking over to the one-chair salon her mother had in their garage for a trim, but he didn't have the guts; it would have killed him to show up and have Ellie treat him like just some geek in her calculus class. If she'd wanted to see him, she would have.

In homeroom no one talked to him.

The bell rang; he knew because everyone suddenly jumped from their seats and scrambled out of the room. Matthew waited a minute more before venturing out to the hallway. Ellie stood near the door, dressed in a pink blouse and pleated plaid skirt. White tights. Black buckle shoes. And those braids. "I thought I'd walk with you," she said.

He smiled a little, not wanting to hope, and wishing he'd bought a new shirt for the first day of school, or at least worn one without dark grease splotches staining the front, Lacie's buttery handprints from her hug that morning.

They slipped into the mathematics room. Ellie took a seat front row center, spilling her books and folders onto the desk before smoothing her skirt under and sitting. Matthew hesitated, and she said to him, "You're not going to stand there all day, are you?"

So he sat next to her and dropped his books, exposing his forearms. The gauze seemed so much whiter with Ellie staring at it; he'd hardly noticed it this morning.

"Are you okay? Your arm . . ."

Touching the bandage, he shrugged off her concern, a quick jerk of the shoulder, a wrinkle of the nose.

"Matt, really."

It's nothing.

"Would you tell me if it was?"

Mr. Brandt entered and handed out syllabi and classroom policies to the three students in the class, and gave Matthew several more pages. Notes for the week. All the teachers provided notes for him. While he lectured, Mr. Brandt occasionally remembered to speak toward the class, but mostly he talked into the blackboard, whirling every few minutes to say, "Oh, Matt, sorry. Did you get that?"

Matthew gave a thumbs-up.

They had time at the end of class to work on their homework

assignment. Ellie leaned over and tapped his arm. "When do you have lunch?"

5th period.

"Darn. I have it sixth. But I have English next," Ellie said. "How about you?"

Same.

"I'll walk with you. I just have to stop at my locker first."

I don't need a babysitter.

Ellie tugged on one of her braids, wove it through her fingers. Over, under, over. "What's that supposed to mean?"

You're a smart girl.

She shook her head. "Fine," she said, and swished out of the room.

In English, she sat between her friends—who wasn't her friend?—and didn't look at him. He couldn't concentrate at all, scribbled in the margins of his notebook. In fourth-period history, she ignored him again.

At lunchtime, Matthew picked a plate of goulash from the cafeteria line and took his tray outside. He straddled the low wall, in front of the gymnasium, and poked at his canned peaches. His stomach burned.

Someone touched his shoulder.

"Hey," Ellie said.

You said you had lunch next period.

"I'm skipping Spanish." She sat beside him, crossed her legs, tucking her skirt between her thighs so it wouldn't blow up. "I thought you might, you know, stop by."

I thought you might.

"I couldn't. My grandmother got sick and my folks went out to see her. I had to take care of my little sister. I asked Jaylyn to tell you."

When?

"When I called."

When was that?

"The day after we went to the movies."

He wanted to strangle Jaylyn. *She didn't tell me.*

"Really? Oh, that's good. Well, I mean, it isn't good, but it's better than what I figured."

Which is?

Her ears turned pink; she pulled on one, twisting her lobe, stretching it like Silly Putty. He thought she was blushing, but couldn't be certain beneath all those freckles. "That you don't like me."

You're crazy.

"It's a simple categorical syllogism. People don't come over when they don't like you. You didn't come over. Hence . . . Well, you're a smart boy."

That doesn't work. Your middle is undistributed.

"Now you're just showing off."

Yeah. I am.

They sat without talking, and he watched the wisps of hair shivering around her face, the ones that had escaped from her braids. *I thought you were seeing Teddy Derboven.*

"Seriously? Come on. He flunked Algebra One. And Two."

All the girls drool over him.

"I'm not all the girls," she said, and she wriggled a black-and-white-marbled composition notebook from the bottom of her pile. "This is for you."

Matthew looked at her, shook his head slightly. Ellie opened the cover, and turquoise words twirled across the first page, and the second and third, each *i* dotted with a daisy, each *t* crossed with an ocean ripple. "I thought we could write to each other. Like, instead of a phone call, if you think of something you want to tell me, you can write it down. I have one, too. We can switch them every day."

He wanted to kiss her.

It was more than a crush, though. More than a pretty girl paying attention to him. For the first time in five long years, someone wanted to climb into his head and know him, peer into all the not-so-silent corners. Nothing was quiet about him, not when she was around.

He pinched the corner of the surgical tape holding the gauze pad over part of his access, pulled it up slowly, his skin releasing from the stickiness, exposing a small incision, scabbed over and greasy with Neosporin. His fistula bulged, like a garden hose snaked beneath his skin. Ellie reached down to touch it, traced the bulge with her soft fingers, inner elbow to wrist, then slipped her hand into his.

⌒

He went to Abbi as she folded laundry on the couch, diapers and boxer shorts and panties. It embarrassed him a little, watching her untwist bras from socks and then sling them around her shoulders; the cups dangled at her chest or bulged from the sides of her neck. At home he'd fold Sienna's and Lacie's underclothes, but not the older girls', and certainly not his aunt's silky thongs and lingerie. He didn't even like taking them from the dryer, but he would if he had to.

He looked at his feet, but at Abbi's tap on his knee, he looked up.

"Hey, what's up? You feeling okay?"

He nodded. She always asked if he felt okay now, and he almost hated to admit he liked it, her concern. He didn't get it much from anywhere else.

Since the day of his clot, his relationship with the Patils had shifted. He wasn't *that kid who mows the lawn* anymore, but, honestly, he wasn't quite sure what he had become. He knew, however, he trusted Abbi and the deputy—something else he'd never had.

I need a favor.

"As long as it's legal."

Do you have a credit card?

"Yes, I do." She dropped her bras on the top of the laundry pile, a nest of straps and hooks.

I want to buy something on-line.

"I said legal, remember."

A bracelet.

"A bracelet?"

Yeah. There's this girl.

"A girl?"

Are you going to repeat everything I write?

"Sorry," she said, grinning. "I just . . . Sure. Absolutely. I can order it for you."

He followed her to the computer, set on a board across stacked milk crates. She typed in the address he gave her, and he pointed to the center photo, a polished sterling bangle with an awkward bend in it.

"This one?"

Matthew nodded.

"Are you sure? It looks mangled."

It's a Möbius strip.

"What's that?"

He took a sheet of paper from the printer, folded the long edge of the page, scoring the crease with his nail, then ripped the strip over the edge of the tabletop. He gave the paper a half twist and, snagging a piece of transparent tape from the dispenser next to the keyboard, joined the ends together.

Watch, he wrote, and then drew a star in the center of the tape. He placed her finger on the ink spot, guided it along the surface of the paper until she reached the seam again, but on the side without the star.

"I'm on the opposite side."

There's only one side. Keep going.

And she did, dragging her fingertip along the smooth paper until it returned to the star. "That's kinda cool."

Of course it's cool. It's math.

"Math, huh? How romantic."

I think so.

"Does she?"

We'll see.

"Whatever happened to flowers and chocolate? And poetry?"

I don't think it works if she has to read it to herself.

"You do have a point." And she left it there—no apology. "Does this girl have a name?"

Ellie.

"So, when are you and Ellie coming for dinner?"

He shook his head.

"You have to. Ben and I need to check her out. How about Friday?"

Dialysis.

"Shoot. Right. Saturday, then. Or Tuesday, or Thursday."

Saturday.

She clicked on the bracelet, typed in the payment information. "I'll send it to your address."

He touched her shoulder, shook his head again. *Here, please.* Someone at the apartment would open it.

"Okay, here it is," Abbi said. "I'm happy for you, Matt."

Me too.

He couldn't remember the last time he had been able to say that.

Chapter TWENTY-SEVEN

They came up the driveway together, Matthew and the girl, and Abbi smiled at how they walked, close but not touching, he stumbling to match his strides to her shorter ones. She heard whistling, short bursts of sound between whispery puffs of air, and then a female voice before the knock on the storm door. Her knock, not his, dainty and hesitant. "Come in, you two," Abbi said. "Ellie, right?"

The girl held out her freckled hand. "Mrs. Patil, thanks for inviting us."

"It's Abbi. Please. And you're welcome anytime. I hope you like Indian."

"I've never had it," Ellie said, and Matthew shrugged.

"Something new, then. I made it mild."

"Because my darling wife can't handle anything spicy," Benjamin said, Silvia against his waist, dangling from his arm. "Not because she was concerned about the two of you. You must be Ellie."

See, you're popular.

"At least I know you couldn't have told them that much. I've looked in your notepad," Ellie said.

Matthew leaned toward her, nudging her with his whole body. She shoved him back, and they both glanced at each other, then away, smiling and blushing. Benjamin laughed. "To be sixteen again."

Ellie's 17.

"An older woman. I'm impressed."

"Leave the boy alone and set the table," Abbi said. "Matt, he's joking. Just ignore him."

"I'll hold the baby," Ellie offered, and she and Matthew sat at the kitchen table while Abbi finished the meal, passing Silvia between them, holding her in the air over their faces and performing to make her smile—blowing raspberries against her bare stomach, speaking in high-pitched voices, and jiggling her until she cooed. Abbi couldn't help but look on in wonder at how Matthew adored Ellie, how his eyes followed every flick of her braids, each time she crossed her ankles.

Boys had never looked at her that way. Boys had never looked at her, period—not until she let Travis Harrington stick his hands up her shirt.

It had been Jessica Bloomquist's thirteenth birthday party. A boy-girl party, all the hormones shut downstairs in the finished basement, with everyone eating pizza and drinking orange Crush, and wondering when the making out would begin.

It didn't take long.

Jessica lifted a plastic sand bucket from behind the couch and said, "Let's see who gets the closet first. I'm the birthday girl, so I pick." She pulled out two scraps of paper, her own name on one, and on the other, the name of the boy she liked. She laughed. "I got my birthday wish, and I haven't even blown out the candles yet. Who'll time us? Seven minutes, okay?"

So she and the kid closed themselves in the dark, and the rest of them pretended to watch television and play pool, listening for any sounds from the closet. Finally someone opened the door, and they came out from between the garment bags and parted like the Red Sea, girls following Jessica to one side, behind the sofa, boys clustering near the mini-refrigerator.

"He kissed me three times," Jessica said, covering her face with her hands, peering out between her fingers. "Twice with tongue."

Couples went in and out of the closet while Abbi drank too much soda and ate half a bowl of Doritos, and then her turn came. She saw Travis ram his finger down his throat in not-so-mock disgust before he squeezed in beside her.

He smelled like pepperoni and cologne. She didn't want to think about what she smelled like, a cold, clammy dampness in the armpits of her silk blouse. She hadn't put on deodorant because the short sleeves on her blouse were loose and fluttery, and she didn't want anyone to see white streaks of Secret if she lifted her arms.

"Sorry you got stuck with me," she said, flattening herself against the wall to find space that didn't exist. Travis did the same, pushing several garment bags on the floor.

"I guess we'd better do at least *something*," Travis said.

"Okay." But she didn't mean it. She couldn't remember a time when her mind churned faster, flying from one thought to the next, a car radio scanning for the perfect mood music. And she wanted to cry, her throat tightening like the previous year when she tripped and fell while going up onstage for her art award during the sixth grade moving-up day, and everyone saw her underpants. Including Travis.

She didn't want her first kiss to be with Hairy Harrington, his pale legs carpeted in super-long strands of straight, black fur, and who threw rounds of bologna up into the air during lunchtime, catching them on his face with a splat before eating them.

Walk out, walk out, she thought, but his open mouth clamped over hers, like a suckerfish.

She kept her eyes open, waiting for the kiss to be done, telling herself, *This isn't so bad*, as Travis's hard nub of a tongue speared her own. But he kept going, panting through his nose, and Abbi didn't have the courage to push him away. He'd tell the whole school she was a prude.

And then his left hand was under her shirt and on her breast.

She'd been aware of it hopping around, from her waist, to her bare lower back, and then flat against her ribs. She'd hoped the time would end before it landed anywhere she didn't want it to, but there it was, a warm lump under her shirt, unmoving, and the kissing stopped, as if Travis was shocked he'd made it so far and waited for her to reach up and shove his hand away.

"I knew you were cool," he said, and dove back into her mouth, his fingers kneading and twisting first above her bra and then, because she still did nothing, beneath it. *Seven minutes can't last forever*, and finally the light poured in. She turned her back to the door and managed, somehow, to pull down her shirt and wipe the fat ring of spit off her face before joining the girls on the couch.

"So?" Jessica asked.

"He kissed me with tongue, too."

After that night, Abbi found herself with a reputation. She liked the attention more than she hated it, and she did hate it; no girl starts junior high thinking she'd be *that girl*. But she finally had an identity outside her weight—which had been all those around her ever noticed—and she took it, even if it meant a quick feel in a dark closet.

Soon, though, the groping progressed. It had to, if she wanted to keep her value. She watched her life slip out of control and had no idea how to stop it, because how could she start saying no when all along she'd been saying yes?

At twenty, after years of pain and irregular bleeding, she finally went for an exam. The doctor diagnosed pelvic inflammatory disease caused by untreated chlamydia, telling her, from the extensive scarring in her fallopian tubes, it wasn't her first episode. And then he told her she would probably never be able to get pregnant. She'd been a Christian for a year then, abstinent for two, and just figured, *This is what I get for what I did.* She never meant for Benjamin to suffer along with her.

~~⌒~~

After dinner they played Scrabble, Abbi managing to scrounge together only one five-letter word while the others stacked and strategized their way to a three-way rout, Benjamin coming out on top, Ellie and Matthew tying for second. She scored nearly seventy points less than them, and declared herself an artist, not a wordsmith.

"How many points for spelling *sore loser*?" Benjamin asked.

"Ha, ha," Abbi said. "Winner gets to change Silvia."

I'll do it.

"The menfolk sticking together. I like," Benjamin said. "But no, I will take care of diaper duty."

"Mrs. Patil, can I call my mom?" Ellie asked. "She's going to come get us."

"Yes, of course. But please call me Abbi."

"You're making her feel old," Benjamin said.

This was her Benjamin, talkative and witty. This was the man she fell in love with, and she hadn't realized how much she missed it until now. She watched him pin the diaper on Silvia, knowing it would leak if she didn't fix it. And she would, in the bathroom, quickly, so he didn't find out. Matthew saw it, too. He flicked his head toward Benjamin with an amused half grin, and Abbi touched her finger to her lips. The boy smiled wider, opened his pad. *It won't be my lap she's peeing on.*

"There. Done," Benjamin said. "A work of art. Like origami."

Matthew snorted.

"Origami?" Abbi said, handing Benjamin a bottle.

"That's right."

"I think you'd better stick with literary analogies."

"There's no way I can compare a diaper to great literature. That's why I chose art. Most of it is . . . Well, most of it is what comes in diapers."

"I can name a few stinkers you made me read. Like *The Brothers Karamazov*."

"You wound me."

Abbi laughed. "Not as much as that book did me."

Now, children. Play nice.

"Oh, really," Benjamin said, standing, passing the baby to Abbi. He pinned Matthew's shoulders against his side, beneath his arm, and rubbed his knuckles into the top of the boy's head.

Ellie returned from calling her mother and stared at them all. "Did I miss something?"

"Nothing at all," Benjamin said, releasing Matthew. "Except your boyfriend, being a smart-mouth."

"He doesn't know how to be anything but smart," Ellie said.

"No kidding," Benjamin said.

After Matthew and Ellie left, Abbi cleaned the kitchen, and Benjamin helped, rinsing the plates before loading them in the dishwasher, scrubbing the burner plates of the stove where the rice water boiled over and cooked on. She said, "I like her. Ellie, I mean."

"So, you approve?" Benjamin threw the sponge into the sink.

"I do."

"I'm sure Matt will be relieved."

"I think he was happy to show her off a little."

"Well, I doubt he gets to do that at home," Benjamin said.

"He really has it bad for her. I think it's adorable."

"I have it bad. Am I adorable?"

"I don't know. Are you?"

"I certainly think so."

"Well, then, maybe you are. Let me check." She kissed him. "You taste pretty adorable."

"It's from the *dahi bhaat*. Which was very, very good, though I have the sinking suspicion you used soy yogurt."

"You know I did," she said, laughing.

"So, you going to bed now?"

"I have a little sewing I wanted to get done, and then I'll be up."

"How long?"

Abbi shrugged. "Not too long."

"How long is not too long?"

"Why? Do you have something in mind?"

"No," Benjamin said, rolling his eyes toward the ceiling and batting his lashes.

"You're terrible. I promise I won't be long."

He sighed. "Apparently, I'm not adorable enough."

She gave him a little shove down the hallway, and said, "Don't forget Silvia," and Benjamin hoisted her to his shoulder with another sigh. "Ew, she's wet through. How come she never does that for you?"

"Because I know how to fold a diaper." She laughed again. "Give her here."

"No, no, no. I'll get her in a quick bath, and by the time I'm done, I expect you to be upstairs. In bed. Preferably naked."

Abbi kissed him again. "You expect it, huh?"

"Mm-hmm."

"Okay."

Benjamin craned his neck backward, raised his eyebrows. "What, no argument?"

"I'm tired of arguing," she said.

"Good," he said, smoothing her hair behind her ear. "Me, too."

Chapter TWENTY-EIGHT

Heather had found a new man—Walter. They met at the dry cleaner. He drove a semi and had a couple of boys who lived with an ex-wife in Sioux Falls. He saw them when he passed through on a job. Matthew didn't like or dislike him. He couldn't say he'd liked or disliked many of Heather's boyfriends. They usually weren't around long enough.

Heather thought this one would keep; he could tell. She hoped he would, at least. She invited him to dinner on Saturday and made the little girls take baths, and the older girls dress appropriately. To his aunt, that meant Skye wasn't clad head-to-toe in black, or in sweatpants, and Jaylyn covered her bikini with shorts and a T-shirt.

She didn't want competition.

Walter brought flowers and wore a tie, and he took his shoes off at the front door. Heather dripped all over him, picking lint off his shoulder, tracing the tattoo on the back of his hand—any excuse to touch him.

"Call me Whip," he said, when Matthew shook his hand.

"He's deaf," Jaylyn said. "He can't call you anything."

"Shut up, Lynnie," Lacie said.

"Don't tell me to shut up, you little—"

"Both of you shut up," Heather said, and then sighed with embarrassment. "Girls. Try living with four of them."

Walter, standing behind Matthew, squeezed his shoulder and planted a little pat on the upper arm. Lacie gave an exaggerated five-year-old frown, all eyebrows and lips, and flapped her arms in exasperation. "You gotta look at him if you're gonna talk to him. Never mind, I'll do it. He said, 'I bet this one' "—she pointed to herself—" 'never gives you any trouble.' "

Matthew ruffled Lacie's hair, and they all sat to eat. Heather had covered the table with a beige cloth. She wore a lime green half apron, ruffled around her waist, and served spoonfuls of Potato Buds and tough strips of cheap flank steak. And frozen broccoli boiled until near disintegration. They didn't eat on paper plates, however, and Matthew knew he'd end up washing the dishes, even though it was Jaylyn's job. She'd leave them piled on the counter until they stunk.

They all talked too much, vying for attention, and Matthew couldn't keep up with all the threads of conversation. He closed his eyes, disappearing, alone in his head. He was invisible, hidden from the world. And he stayed that way, jaw in his palm, until someone knocked his elbow out from beneath his chin. Skye. "Come on," she said. "It's that time again."

The photo albums came out. Heather's tradition, when she found a man she wanted to keep. Her way of sucking him into the family. She started with Jaylyn's infant pictures, flipping the plastic-wrapped pages and pointing to each snapshot—"Here she is, three days old. Oh, here's her first bath. And this is her with her grandmother."—before passing the book around the circle for everyone else to see. She was on the couch with Walter, Lacie crowded between them, the little girl dipping her hand into Walter's shirt pocket, for more Mike & Ikes. She liked him. She liked any man Heather brought home, desperate for a father, one who wouldn't change every six weeks—even though she did see her dad occasionally. She and Skye were full sisters, not like the others, sharing a father who lived four states away but who sent Christmas gifts and made a phone call a couple times a year, and sometimes came by for a week in the summer.

It wasn't enough.

Skye's album came around next. Jaylyn tossed it on Matt's lap, and he was about to pass it on to Sienna when he noticed one of the infant photos. Dark hair, but not much. One unruly eyebrow that fanned the wrong way, reaching across the bridge of her nose. The other neat and growing smooth to the right. Full lips, but small above her square chin—puckered, not spread wide. And thick, stubby eyelashes.

He knew this face.

Silvia's face.

His suspicion filled his cheeks, hot and pulsing. He turned toward Skye. She was still paging through Jaylyn's album, her face tilted away from him. But he read her body—back slouched, neck loose, legs splayed on the carpet. Relaxed, unconcerned.

He had to be wrong.

Taking out his notebook, he wrote, You were funny Looking, on a half-used page and ripped it from the spiral. He slid the book onto her knees and flattened the note next to the baby photo.

Skye laughed, crumpled the page and threw it at him. "Oh, you should talk," she said, flipping through the album until she found a picture of the two of them, hanging upside down on the monkey bars, their shirts around their noses, bellies showing. "Look at you. If that's not funny looking, I don't know what is."

Matthew couldn't stay there. Closing himself in the bathroom, he filled his cupped hands with icy water and splattered it on his face. *Think. Think. When was the baby found?*

The day before he went to see his mother.

He remembered lying on the couch, TV on, volume off, watching a replay of the press conference on the eleven o'clock news. The heat. The plans for the next day whirling like bumper cars, crashing against one another and the inside of his skull, keeping him awake. And he'd taken the cushions off the couch, moving them to the floor, hoping to be cooler, be calmer about his trip.

Where had Skye been that day? He'd had dialysis. Didn't see her before then. What about after? *Think. Think.* He couldn't recall. No, wait. He could. She didn't come to dinner that night. Heather called her, and she said she wasn't hungry. And the next morning she looked tired and drawn, and he didn't take the time to find out why, because he was annoyed she hadn't looked at him when she spoke. Because Jaylyn was being such a pain. Because he was distracted with his plans to go see his mother.

The doorknob rattled. He opened it. "Matty, I gotta go," Lacie said. He held out his arm toward the toilet, bowed a little, like he was presenting something wonderful to her. "You're crazy," she said, slamming the door.

In the living room, they'd moved on to videos. Sienna's dance recital from last year played on the television. Everyone laughed and pointed. Even Skye. Matthew snuck into the kitchen and washed the dishes, scrubbing each plate until his fingers stuck to them when he ran them over the center. He thought of the Palmolive commercial. Squeaky clean.

Skye yanked on his hair. "Jaylyn's supposed to do that."

He shrugged, tried not to stare, but his eyes crawled over her anyway. Her face, her stomach. She didn't look different. He couldn't believe she'd be able to dump her own child in a field, leaving it to die.

"What's wrong with you? You look weird. Are you sick or something?"

He shook his head.

"All right," she said, eyebrows—one still lifting the wrong way—up. "If you say so."

Matthew rinsed the frying pan, the scalded broccoli pot. He dried his hands, took his pillbox from the cabinet and poured the night's doses into his mouth, held them there until he could no longer stand the taste, yellow and sulfured on his tongue. He imagined urine tasted

this way, spit the pills into the sink, swallowing back the vomit claw-
ing up his throat.

He couldn't believe it. Not Skye.

"Matt," Heather said, coming beside him. "Skye says you're sick.
Should I call the doctor?"

A show for Walter, the concern. Matthew shook his head. My
pills went down the wrong pipe. I'm okay.

"Well, okay then. Whip and I are going out for a bit. Make sure
Sienna and Lacie are in bed by nine." And she squeezed him, an odd
sideways hug, her head bumping against his shoulder.

He nodded and, after she and Walter left, counted out his medication again and took it with water.

The albums were on the coffee table, the little girls transfixed
to the television. He found Skye's book, the blue one with silver
edging, and wiggled the baby picture from the plastic page, into his
back pocket.

He managed to somehow get through the weekend, and when
school came Monday, Ellie took one look at him before homeroom
and asked, "What's wrong?"

I don't know.

"Are you sick?"

He shook his head.

"Matt, you promised."

I know. But I can't talk about this yet.

"When can you?"

I don't know.

"Matt—"

"I don't know. Okay?"

She flinched at the sound of his voice. "Okay. Sure. Whatever."

On Tuesday, he and Ellie barely spoke. And when the final bell rang, he took the bus home, and then pedaled over to the Patil house. Silvia slept in her basket, and as soon as he walked in, Abbi went out to the shed. He didn't want to pull the photo from his pocket, but had to. Holding it above the baby's face, he saw Skye's head on Silvia's body. He closed his eyes, praying he was wrong, and moved the picture aside. Looked down. And he saw two Skyes looking back at him. Same eyes and eyelashes, same crooked eyebrow, same chin and mouth. The nose was different, Silvia's smaller and flatter, pushed into her forehead.

He rocked back, landing hard on his tailbone, his spine against the couch. And he sat there, staring at Silvia from between his knees. Sat there until his feet tingled and Abbi and Benjamin walked in through the sliding back door, laughing. He tickled her side, she wrestled his hand away, twisting his arm around her. "She's still asleep?" Abbi asked. "Did she even wake up at all?"

Matthew shook his head.

"She'll be up all night. Do you want to stay for dinner? You're welcome to call Ellie to come, too."

He stood, stomped his feet on the floor. *Things to do.*

"Okay, then. We'll see you Thursday," Abbi said, and he nodded and left, flinging one leg over the seat of his bicycle. He stopped, got off the bike, let it drop onto the driveway, walked two steps back to the door. Stopped again. His hands were balled in fists at his sides. He opened them, flapped them, turned to the bicycle, then back to the door. And then to the bicycle again. He climbed on and pedaled away.

Chapter TWENTY-NINE

Benjamin had a feeling.

He couldn't explain it, more a hunch than anything else. But he drove to the field where he found Silvia, stood where he first saw the bag. When he'd gone over his notes again this morning, something so simple had occurred to him. Silvia had been approximately three hours old when she arrived at the hospital—an hour drive from Temple. So, that made her two hours old at the time he pulled her from the plastic.

How far could a young mother get two hours after giving birth?

A thin creek ran from Silvia's pond to another about thirty yards away. Three more cottonwoods guarded that one, though the grasses weren't nearly as high. He paced the distance off. What if the girl had been there all along? He snapped on a pair of latex gloves and combed the weeds. Near the trunk of one tree he found a patch of loose earth, brushed it with his fingers and saw the tiniest fleck of silver. He picked it up, wiped it on his pants. An earring. The stud kind, with a skull-and-crossbones design. Maybe it had nothing to do with the case at all, but Benjamin didn't believe that. He was almost positive the mother had watched him pull Silvia from the bag. She'd most likely been startled by the teenaged lovebirds and hid. Had she put Silvia in the bag before she'd seen them in the distance, or after?

Maybe she hadn't been trying to asphyxiate her baby at all but only wanted to hide her until Simon and Tallah passed through.

Now I sound like Abbi, defending the person who tried to kill my daughter.

And in doing so, trying to defend his own actions.

All this time, Benjamin had been ready to condemn the person who'd abandoned Silvia. But when the sandstorm cleared and he shed the protective jargon of the battlefield, he wasn't any different. Both of them cowered in the distance, looking on. Both of them waiting there for someone to die, too afraid to do the honorable thing. Stephen was his Silvia.

His squad had been returning from a convoy escort, Benjamin riding shotgun in the second of three armored Humvees. Ahead of him, he watched Stephen's head and torso shimmy on the roof of the first Humvee, hunkered behind the mounted .50-caliber machine gun. Other than the rumbling of their vehicles, the streets of Kabul were quiet.

And then the road ballooned up under Stephen's Humvee with a thundering roar, a furious elephant rising from the pavement. The vehicle flipped, and Benjamin watched the blast toss his friend's body low through the air, bouncing off the road. Glass and debris hailed over his windshield as SPC Groves, Benjamin's Humvee driver, swore and maneuvered around the wreckage, then stopped.

Small-arms fire crackled, and Benjamin scanned the buildings to the left, looking for insurgents. In his peripheral vision he saw a flash; a rocket-launched grenade plowed into the ground in front of his vehicle. More gunshots, also from in front of them. "Out," Benjamin ordered, and they opened the doors, using them as shields as they scampered behind the Humvee. They returned fire, one sniper falling from a window above them.

He saw Stephen then, in the middle of the street, a hole ripped in his gut. He had his hand pressed into it, the blood soaking his uniform, a seeping black stain on the fabric. But his hand was red, a deep raw-meat color, and thick, clinging to his fingertips. Pomegranate juice. That was what it looked like, and Benjamin closed his eyes and saw Abbi, cutting fresh pomegranates, plucking the seeds out of the rind with her ruby-stained fingertips. *Oh, Lord*, Benjamin thought. *Let him be dead.*

But Stephen moved, curling his head up enough to see the pit in his stomach, patting the shallow pool of blood between his hipbones, with almost childlike wonder, as a toddler would splash in a puddle. Then his head lolled to one side; his eyes found Benjamin's, and he managed to scoot his arm from his belly to the dirt, dragging it up toward his shoulder, the wing of a sand angel, reaching toward Benjamin. Blood trickled from the corner of his lips as he moved them open and closed.

Benjamin didn't know if words came out; if they did, he couldn't hear them amidst the shouting and the gunfire. But he understood what Stephen asked. *Come get me. Pull me out of here. Don't let me die alone.*

And he didn't go. He was scared of dying himself.

A spray of bullets pinged against the Humvee and thumped across the ground, kicking up dust. Benjamin covered his head, and when he looked again at Stephen, his friend's face was pocked with lead, one eye still open. The other had been shot away.

Another explosion, near Benjamin's feet, and that was the last he remembered. He regained consciousness sometime later and was airlifted to Landstuhl. Groves had been killed in the same blast that took Benjamin's toes. Toes, for crying out loud. That was it. Stephen dead. Groves dead. Another of his unit DOA at the hospital, a fourth man paralyzed from the chest down.

And there he was, medically retired because he couldn't run without a limp, slowly putting the pieces of his life back together when so many others had no pieces at all. Survivor's guilt, maybe. But also complete discontent with "the Lord's ways are not our ways" platitudes of those around him. Yeah, no kidding. He got it. But he didn't have to like it. It brought no comfort, having a God he couldn't understand.

He walked back over to Silvia's pond, picked up a rock and smashed it down into the water with all his strength. The surface waved and bubbled, humps of muddy water rising, reaching up over the banks. At the center of the rippling he saw a face. Stephen's face.

Hey, said the ripple man.

I don't need this right now.

Then don't talk to me.

If I stop, I'll have no one.

There's your wife.

Yeah. Benjamin looked into the sky, dropping his head back as far as it would go; he felt the stretch in his throat. *I'm afraid she's going to leave me.*

You're afraid of a lot of things.

Shut up.

If you don't want her to leave, don't make it easy for her to go.

Benjamin stared into the water again. *I don't need advice from you.*

The ripples thinned as he heard his words in Stephen's voice say, *You don't need me at all.*

Then the surface of the pond went silent, and his friend's absence pushed through his thoughts. Benjamin had always had Stephen, since their mothers were pregnant together. He knew he was a fool for pretending to have these conversations, but he didn't want to give Stephen up now.

⌒

He went to the school with the earring and showed it to the principal.

"I don't recognize it, if that's what you're asking."

"Are there any students who would be more likely to wear something like this?"

"I can think of a few off the top of my head."

"Girls?"

Karen shook her head. "Boys, mostly. But maybe one of their girlfriends. You want me to ask around?"

"No," Benjamin said. "Not yet. I don't want to spook anyone. Just keep an eye out."

"Will do."

Benjamin planned on going back to the office, but instead of pulling off the highway at Temple, he drove past the exit, kept driving. He knew where he was going but thought about anything else until, nearly two hours later, he pulled into the driveway of a white raised-ranch house.

He knocked on the door, and Katherine Duhamel answered. Her eyes widened, and she said, "Benjamin," and hugged him tightly. Her wig scratched his cheek; it didn't feel like real hair at all, smelled sort of synthetic—or maybe he'd imagined it. For years, Katherine had carried an extra sixty pounds smeared over her thighs and middle, the remnant of five kids in eight years, and late-night snacking to stave off sleep as she made lunches or finished laundry. After Stephen died, her weight fell off, and so did her hair.

"Mrs. Duhamel. Sorry I didn't call first."

"My goodness, Ben, you're twenty-six years old. It's Kathy."

"I don't think you'll ever be anything but Mrs. Duhamel."

"Fine, have it your way. But don't ever think you need to call before coming over." She opened the basement door and called, "Les, come up here."

"Hon, have you seen my wrench? The one with the blue tape on the hand— Ben." Leslie Duhamel grabbed Benjamin by the back of the head and embraced him, pounding him on the shoulder a couple of times. "It's good to see you, son. It's been too long."

"Are you sure?" Benjamin asked.

"There's no reason to stay away from this house."

"How's that pipe coming?" Katherine asked, poking Leslie in his fleshy stomach.

"I'm a physicist, not a plumber."

"He says that every time, Ben. But does he call someone? Nope. I think he takes delight in having a reason to bang on things." She lowered her voice. "And do some swearing."

"Oh, stop," Leslie said. "Don't listen to her. Come on, sit down. Tell us what's going on. How's Abbi? She's not with you?"

"No. I just . . . thought I'd come by."

"Ben, can I get you a drink? Coffee? Lemonade?" Katherine asked.

"Don't trouble yourself. Just whatever you have made is fine."

He sat with Leslie on the floral couch in the sunny, mismatched family room, across from a wall of photographs. Benjamin had never seen more pictures in one place: yellowing, candid shots of Christmases and birthdays, of weddings and graduations, posed family portraits, and others of no particular occasion. And pictures of Stephen—in his Class A's, black tie slightly off-center. And of Ben, too. There were more photos of him hanging in the Duhamels' family room than in his own home.

He wasn't being fair. His folks weren't the Duhamels, no matter how much he had wished they were while growing up. What did children know about the pain they caused their parents? His never took him aside to explain things, to speak with him about culture or tradition. He hadn't understood them, and he'd wanted what Stephen had. Man, that must have hurt, and hurt deep.

Katherine returned with a clear glass pitcher of lemonade rattling with ice and slices of citrus. She plucked a mint leaf off the sprig on the tray and dropped one into each glass, then filled them. "Here you go, Ben," she said. "Help yourself to a cookie, too. Oatmeal raisin-cranberry. I know you like them."

She frosted her cookies with a confectioner's glaze, and he bit into the soft disc of cinnamon and dried fruit. He'd forgotten how much he missed real cookies, having eaten Abbi's vegan cardboard for so long. She did bake for him, but never followed the recipe, always trying to substitute applesauce for oil, or halving the sugar. "These are so good," he told her, catching crumbs as they fell from his mouth. "Sorry."

"So did I miss all the news?" asked Katherine.

"He hasn't told me a thing yet," said Leslie.

Benjamin broke another cookie in half. "There's not much to tell, really."

"You found that baby, didn't you?" Katherine asked.

"Well, yeah." He swallowed. "We're fostering her now. Silvia. The baby, I mean."

"Your mother mentioned that," Katherine said. "How is Abbi enjoying motherhood?"

"She's . . . adjusting. We both are."

"It's a lot, I know." Katherine swirled the ice in the bottom of her glass. "We just saw Lauren last weekend. Stevie is walking now, and Kate is such the little chatterbox. She said she's spoken with Abbi."

Benjamin nodded. "She came by a couple weeks ago."

"Oh good. Good for both of them," Katherine said. "They need each other."

"Any news around here?" Benjamin asked.

"Tina got engaged," Leslie said. "A nice boy she met at school. We like him. They're planning their wedding for the weekend after Thanksgiving. Lance and Brianne are expecting their third. Due in, what? January?"

"February," Katherine said.

"And Phillip. He joined up with the Guard."

The ice in the pitcher shifted, tinkling against the glass, sinking below the lemonade. "You let him," Benjamin said.

"Not like we had a choice, Ben. He's a grown man," Leslie said.

"He's twenty."

"You and Stephen were eighteen. You couldn't wait, remember? We're proud of Phillip wanting to serve his country. What happened to Stephen doesn't change that. Our son died a hero, fighting for us. That's the price of freedom."

"Is it?" Benjamin asked. He thought of Abbi and her protest signs.

"Darn right," Leslie said. "We miss our boy, but there's no shame in any of it."

Katherine touched Benjamin's knee. "And no blame," she said.

He sat on his hands so he wouldn't fidget with his fingers or hair or the piping on the couch. Looked at his feet. "I need you to forgive me."

"Ben, there's nothing to forgive," Katherine said.

"I don't care if you think that or not. I need you to forgive me for not bringing him home. I need—" He wept, and Katherine held him like only a soldier's mother could.

She whispered, "We forgive you," and his body shook against her in this place he grew up in, a safe place where they believed in what he did, and wouldn't question his grief or his honor.

A place without Abbi.

For all their healing, Benjamin still needed some distance between him and his wife. When that newspaper article had been published, the one with the photo of Abbi at the protest, someone e-mailed it to the guys in his unit, and they said to Benjamin, "What's wrong with your woman? Can't you keep her on a leash?" Before then, he'd never wanted Abbi to be any different than who she was—idealistic, passionate, uninhibited. Wild, even. But he also never thought she would flaunt her opposition to all he held firm with such a blatant disregard for his own passions and ideals.

He returned home torn in two—loving her, wanting her, but also distrusting her. Looking at her as if she, too, was an enemy combatant. How could she be for him and against him at the same time? If he asked her to choose a side, he couldn't be certain she would pick his.

When he was dry, Leslie gripped his arm and told him to come back whenever he needed. "Despite what the commercials say, no man is called to be an army of one." And Katherine said, "We pray for you every night," and gave him a bag of cookies for the ride home.

Chapter THIRTY

After worship, they went to the McGees' for Sunday dinner. Abbi brought a fruit salad and watched Silas grill thick steaks on the small back deck while Benjamin played horseshoes with the boys in the yard. Silvia napped in the sling. "Don't worry," Janet said. "I made a pasta salad."

"Thanks," Abbi said.

"You can lay the baby down on the bed in A.J.'s room. Window's right there. We can open it up and you'll be able to listen in on her."

"She's fine here."

"Hon, will you watch the grill?" Silas asked. "Looks like the boys need some help down there."

"Go show them how it's done," Janet said with a laugh.

Silas took the horseshoes from eleven-year-old Dillon, forming one team. Benjamin and Silas's older son, A.J., stood at the opposite post. They all flung the metal U's around, joking and clanging as Janet turned the steaks.

"I can't believe how big the boys are," Abbi said. "I feel old."

"Don't give me that. In ten years, maybe you can start complaining. We're going to eat inside," Janet said. "Don't call the guys yet. I need to finish setting the table."

"I'll help."

Abbi folded a paper napkin beside each plate as Janet mixed

the pasta and poured milk into all the glasses. Abbi kept her mouth shut.

"So," Janet said, "Ben seems well."

"He's fine."

"He seems it. Not so, oh, I don't know. Not so down, I guess. He's seemed a little . . . down lately."

You think? "He's good."

"That's good. I mean, we all know it can be hard getting back on your feet after what Ben went through. Well, not that we *know* it. Obviously. But, you know." Janet fumbled through the refrigerator, emerged with several bottles of salad dressing. "And you're okay?"

Abbi posed. "What you see is what you get."

"Oh good. Good. The ladies started working through Proverbs a couple weeks ago. You probably read that in the bulletin. You can bring the baby, if you want. No one will mind."

"Hmm. You made a ton of food," Abbi said, dodging the need for a response.

"I cook when I don't know what else to do." Janet dropped mismatched forks and knives on each napkin. "Abbi, we . . . I mean . . . Boy, I don't know how to say this without sounding like your mother, but we really hope you'll come back to Bible study."

"Who's *we*?"

"Well, the ladies. As I said before, we miss you and your, you know, unique perspective." Janet pressed her thumb down on each finger until it popped. "And, I mean, now that Ben is doing better—"

"Was there something wrong with him before?" Abbi asked, her words tinged with the frustration of the past year. Now Janet came to her with an *Oh, we knew something was wrong with your husband, but now that he's not a basket case, c'mon back to Bible study.* Why couldn't she have said something eight months ago?

Janet pivoted her wrists, cracking them, too. "Well, you know. He seemed to be kind of . . . down."

"Down," Abbi whispered. Then the tears came, and she couldn't stop them; she yanked a napkin from under the flatware, knife bouncing on the linoleum, and ground the paper against her eyes. "Is not speaking to his wife, down? Not touching her? Losing thirty pounds. Sleeping in his car. Overdosing on—" She stopped. She hadn't meant to reveal that much.

"Abbi, we didn't know," Janet said.

"Please, don't."

"You never told us."

"Ben was a walking neon advertisement for, well, for something a whole heck of a lot more than just down. And, I mean, you live next door. I know you saw his car missing at night—saw, heard, I don't know. . . . What did I need to tell you?"

"The truth, for one. Every week at church someone has asked you if things were okay. You said yes."

"But you could see him."

"Abbi, you said nothing was wrong. Ben said nothing was wrong. What were we supposed to do?"

Silvia woke, looked up at Abbi and smiled a gummy baby grin, and Abbi shifted her into her chest and hugged her, the top of her head warm under Abbi's chin. Abbi wiped her wet cheeks on Silvia's hair. "I needed someone to say it first."

"I thought about it. I think we all did. But I was afraid if I tried to push a little more, you'd just dig your head deeper into the ground. I mean, come on. We couldn't even get you over for dinner. And you practically stopped talking to me. To anyone. It hurt, Abbi. I thought we were friends." Janet ran her fingers over the creases at the back of Silvia's neck.

"I guess I did it to myself."

"No, no. I'm sorry, too. It wasn't all your fault. But how do you help someone who acts like they don't want help? How do you say the hard things out loud? None of us were really prepared for Ben to come home and hurt like he did." Janet sniffed away her own tears. "We all messed up."

Abbi shrugged. "So, what now?"

"Well," Janet said, lifting the lid off the steak. "I nuke this meat, you call the guys in, and we eat."

"Sounds good to me."

"And I promise I won't talk around things with you. If I want to know something, I'll be direct and ask."

"I can't promise I'll answer," Abbi said. "But I'll make an attempt."

"Okay." Janet gave her a quick hug, baby between them, only their shoulders bumping.

The men and boys trampled through the kitchen, tracking dirt and grass from their sneakers, and dropped into their chairs. "Wash up," Janet said, and they groaned but soaped in the sink and sat again. Silas said grace, all of them holding hands, Abbi and Benjamin peeking before the amen, legs tangled under the table. Dillon complained the milk was warm, and plunked ice cubes into everyone's glass without asking. And Benjamin raised his eyebrows as Abbi sipped the milk and tried to pick around the cubes of cheese in both the green and pasta salads. Still, several pieces ended up on her plate, and she cut them small enough to swallow without chewing.

꩜

After putting Silvia to bed, Benjamin and Abbi snuggled on the sofa, her legs over his, and they talked the way they used to, when they first met—one of them choosing a random word, and the other recounting a memory the word conjured. Abbi surveyed the room. "Lamp," she said.

"I don't think I've told you the broken lamp story," Benjamin said. She shook her head. "When Stephen and I were, oh, I think nine, maybe ten, we had both signed up for little league. Well, we were playing ball at my house. No, in my house, in the living room, which was a huge no-no. But we were. And I ended up knocking over my mother's lamp, the one she brought with her from India when she first came here. It broke, and Stephen knew I would be in major trouble, so he told my mom he did it. He even gave her all the money he'd been saving for a new bicycle to pay to fix it. 'I'm taking one for the team,' he said."

And then Ben winced, as if everything he remembered about Stephen came roaring to the surface, a sudden jolt of pain, like a brain freeze after sucking down a Slush Puppie. He smoothed his hand over his head. "Your turn."

"Okay."

"Umm. Kumquat."

"What?"

"You heard me."

"Why on earth do you think I have a kumquat story?"

"I just like to say it. Kumquat. Kummmquaaaat. You try. I bet you can't say it without laughing."

"Kum—" She giggled.

"You lose."

"No, no. Let me try again."

"Go ahead. You can't do it."

She laughed before the first syllable was out of her mouth. "No fair. You planted the laughing seed."

"I'd like to see that tree."

"Stop. You know what I mean. Just pick something else."

"All right, fine. How about dot."

"Dot, as in, dot, dot, dot?" she asked, stabbing the air with her index finger three times.

"Dot, as in, 'circle, circle, dot, dot, now I have my cootie shot.'" He nibbled her earlobe. "I hope you have yours."

"Oh, groan."

"I'm waiting. Dot, dot, dot . . ."

"Okay, this one's easy."

"Not like kumquat."

"Do you want to hear it?"

"Sorry, sorry. Go right ahead."

So she told him how, when Lauren first mentioned him, she told Abbi he was Indian, "With a dot, not a feather. And really nice."

"If he's so nice, why aren't you dating him?" Abbi had said.

"I might be, if I hadn't met Stephen first."

"He's in the Guard?"

"Yeah."

"I'm not really into soldiers. Give me a nice beat poet any day."

Lauren snorted. "Oh, you've had lots of luck with the beat poets."

"What did you tell him about me?"

"That you're a hippie wannabe and a pacifist. And you don't shave."

"Hey. I shave sometimes."

And then Abbi told Benjamin how she met him and tried not to love him from their first date, when he took her to that vegetarian restaurant thirty minutes out of their way, and choked down a seitan and mushroom stir-fry. She had tried not to love him, had reminded herself of his ripple-edged ears, and his buttoned-down shirts and leather belt. "But it was too late," she said. "You'd infected me."

"Really?" He grinned, cheeks puffed with pleasure.

"Really, really."

"It must have been the cooties," Benjamin said.

"You're impossible. Do you want a word, or not?"

"Of course."

She saw Silvia's rattle on the floor. "Baby."

He didn't hesitate. "The day I found her, I called you. After I brought her to the hospital. I wanted to hear your voice. You weren't here. I just listened to the answering machine and hung up." He traced her collarbone, one finger on either side. "We wouldn't be here without her."

"I know."

"I want more."

"Than what?" she asked, though she understood him perfectly.

"No. More babies. More children."

"Ben, everything's so up in the air with Silvia as it is. I couldn't even—"

"I don't mean right now. Just, sometime. Do you think you might be open to considering it sometime?"

"Yes," she said. And she meant it. Not because she thought Benjamin would leave her if she said no, or because of her guilt or a desire to appease him. But because she wanted to. She enjoyed being a mother, after all.

Chapter THIRTY-ONE

He waited on the stoop until he saw Abbi's green bumper-stickered car kicking up dust as she turned the corner and pulled in front of the apartment. Matthew sprang to his feet and yanked the passenger-door handle. Abbi turned off the car, stepped out. "I know, I'm running late. Silvia had a really awful diaper right as I was walking out the door. I had to bathe her."

He made quick circles with his hands, pulled on the door handle again.

"No, don't worry. It's not that kind of thing. We have time." She lifted the baby from the back seat. "Your aunt's inside?"

She knows I'm going with you. You don't need to see her.

"Matt, I'm not leaving without saying hello. Which one?"

He pointed to the middle door, wiped his palms on his pants.

Abbi knocked, and Lacie answered. "Who are you?"

"Is your mom here?"

"I guess," Lacie said and, leaving the door wide open, spun into the apartment.

A moment later, Heather stepped outside. "You taking him now?"

Abbi nodded. "We shouldn't be later than dinner. But I'll call if we will be. And I promise I won't bring him home hungry."

"Fine by me." Heather lit a cigarette, took a drag and held it up near her shoulder. "That her? The one from the field?"

"Yes, this is Silvia," Abbi said, turning the baby around so Heather could see her. Matthew stopped breathing, realized it only when waves of tightness pulsed in his chest, down his arms. Any moment his aunt's memory would click in, and she'd run inside and grab Skye's photo album, flip through the pages to find the picture, the carbon copy of Silvia. But it wouldn't be there, because he had it in the pocket of his good pants, folded at the bottom of his clothing tote.

He stepped backward, dizzy, as Heather dropped her cigarette on the stoop and stepped on it, took Silvia's feet in her hands, knocking her tiny heels together. "How are you, pretty girl? I had babies like you. Yes, I did. Yes, I did, sweet feet."

Silvia broke into a gummy smile and drooled, bringing her fists to her mouth.

The blinds rippled in the front window, fingers separating two of the thick vertical strips. Fingers too large to be either of the littler girls, and Jaylyn wasn't home. He and Abbi needed to leave before— What? Would Skye come out? He couldn't give her that chance.

Matthew nudged Abbi with his toe. When she looked at him, he tapped the back of his bare wrist.

"Oh, right. We're going. Thanks for letting me borrow him," Abbi said.

"He's all yours," Heather said, and shut the door.

They drove to Ellie's house, and Abbi went inside to talk to her mother, too, asking Matthew to watch the baby for a sec. When they came out, he gave up the front seat to Ellie. "I don't mind the back," she said, but with a crinkle of his lips and a jerk of the shoulder he climbed in back next to Silvia.

Ellie and Abbi talked as they drove, and laughed. He had no idea what they were saying. Every so often a weird feeling crawled over him, and he looked up to see Abbi's face smiling at him in the rearview mirror. Otherwise he kept his eyes on Silvia; he couldn't stop seeing Skye in her. And he thought of his cousin, not a friend really, but a cohort. They had grown closer these past five years.

When he'd first come to live with them, the girls had been inseparable—both a bit chubby, both brunettes, Jaylyn's hair more cocoa, Skye's a deep mahogany. And both miserable toward him. Hiding his shoes before the bus came, forcing him to wear too-small girl's sneakers to school. Dropping his hearing aids into the toilet for him to fish out. Sprinkling cayenne pepper in his peanut butter sandwiches.

But Skye stayed small and round and awkward, as Jaylyn grew up and thinned out and only had use for her sister when she needed to borrow a couple of bucks for nail polish, or wanted someone to lie to Heather for her. And as they grew apart, Skye didn't seek out Matthew as much as she fell in with him, both of them alone together at the apartment in the evenings, or stuck watching the little girls. They shared small frustrations, an occasional secret, and Matthew dragged her to church a time or two.

He didn't know her, though. So much of what happened around him was lost in the silences, intentionally or not. But he saw her disappearing. He never dared approach her about it. They weren't that close, and he spent so much energy surviving that when he finally had a moment to consider Skye, he didn't want to deal with another problem.

He wouldn't blame himself for Silvia, for the circumstances that put her here, in the back of Abbi's Volvo. And, no, maybe it wasn't his responsibility to save Skye from herself, or Jaylyn, or his aunt, or the slurry of low expectations. But he should have done something. If he had, he might not be in this predicament—deciding if two families will be torn apart, wondering if secrets like this ever lose their teeth.

He leaned toward not telling. He thought he could keep it to himself, a sin of omission, a lie for the greater good—like Rahab, who'd been counted righteous for her deception, or the midwives in Egypt. How could he think Skye would be better off if everyone knew what she'd done? And what would happen to Silvia? Would the Patils be allowed to keep her, or would she end up in some other foster home? As her grandmother, would his aunt get custody of her?

God forbid.

They crossed the bridge into Pierre and turned toward the park on the river, right past his mother's apartment. He saw her window, a grinning paper jack-o'-lantern taped in it, two black bat cutouts on either side. He stared up at it until Abbi opened his door.

"Unbuckle Silvia, will you?"

He did, and she wiggled the baby into the sling she wore. Ellie took his hand as they followed Abbi to a woman with green hair and rings in her cheek and eyebrows. He wouldn't call what she had in her ears piercings; they looked more like something in *National Geographic*— round, quarter-sized discs in the center of each earlobe.

"Genelise," Abbi said, "This is Matthew, and Ellie."

"Glad you could come," the woman said, offering her tattooed hand to them. "Feel free to mingle, or whatever."

"Where's Neal?"

"Uh . . ." Genelise spun around. "There. With Greg."

"Come on. I want you to meet someone," Abbi said. She tapped the shoulder of a man in loose jeans and a hooded sweatshirt, his hair clipped short. "Neal, this is the guy I was telling you about. Matthew, my sanity-keeper."

"The pleasure's mine," Neal said. And signed. He wore bright sapphire hearing aids behind his ears.

It's nice to meet you, Matthew signed back. Then, remembering Ellie at his side, he pulled out his pad and translated.

"You don't have to do that," Ellie said. She tugged on his belt loop. "I'm going to go over there and . . . find something to do."

"I'll go, too," Abbi said, and they wandered away together, to a picnic table under a wood pavilion where people sat, eating.

Abbi said you don't get a chance to sign too often. Neal's mouth moved with his fingers. Matthew had no idea if sounds were coming out, too.

Is it that obvious? Matthew signed back.

No. You're fine. Come meet my wife, but don't laugh. She's an awful signer. She's not deaf. She just loves me.

So Neal introduced him to Constance, an almost-bursting pregnant woman about Abbi's age, with sleek black bangs and almond eyes. She made a few clumsy attempts to sign to him before Neal took pity and told her that Matthew read lips. "I blame it all on these fingers, Matt," she said. "How could anyone move swollen, preggo fingers like this?"

When are you due?

"Yesterday," she said.

He and Neal talked some more about nothing in particular, but the conversation was soothing in the motions and the understanding that went along with them. Not only the literal meaning of the signs but beneath that—a common struggle, a kinship. Matthew didn't know this man's story, didn't need to. They shared something, and for those thirty minutes he was unfettered. No pen and paper. Only his words, straight from his head to his hands.

People left the park, some with a few cans of vegetables in their arms, others with a grocery sack of clothing. Matthew helped clean up the food and loaded the extras into the back of Genelise's Prius. The woman hugged Abbi and said, "I'll call you," and then gave both Matthew and Ellie a quick squeeze.

"So," Abbi said, "is there anything you want to do while we're here? Shopping? I can tolerate the mall, but please don't say Wal-Mart."

Kmart?

"Don't be smart," Abbi said, giving him an elbow in the ribs.

"He doesn't know how to be anything else," Ellie said.

Matthew looked across the street, at the bluish-grayish apartments. The two saddest colors, together in one place. He didn't quite know what he would get out of a visit. Maybe he wanted his mother to know he was all right without her—despite her. Wanted her to see it with her own eyes. Maybe he wanted to rub it in. He didn't let himself think about it too long.

"So, the mall?" Abbi asked.

"Sounds good to me," Ellie said.

I'd like to see my mother. If that's okay.

They looked at him, at each other, and Abbi finally said, "Yeah, sure. Of course. Does she live far from here?"

Over there, he wrote, pointing.

"In those buildings?" Abbi asked.

He nodded, and walked across the street. Ellie suddenly came up next to him and slipped her hand into his. He stopped, looking up at the jack-o'-lantern's black triangle eyes. Can you guys wait here? I want to see if she's even around.

Ellie squished his hand.

Matthew jogged to the back of the apartment complex and jammed his thumb against each of the eight white plastic buzzers beside the entrance, pulling on the door until it opened. He climbed the steps and paused in front of his mother's apartment, his knuckles against the cool metal.

And he knocked.

Melissa opened the door in stretchy jeans and a tight, black T-shirt dotted with lint. "What are you doing here?"

I was in town.

"Yeah, right."

I was. With friends. I thought I'd stop in.

"And say hey? Have a nice little tea party? What?"

He shrugged.

"Where are they? These friends of yours."

Matthew squeezed past his mother, his back scraping against the molding, and twisted the thin stick hanging next to the vertical blinds. He spread the metal slats, leaving fingerprints in the thick dust, and pointed. That's Abbi Patil. I babysit for her, and mow her lawn.

She raked her hand through her hair, an orangey blond on the bottom, dark brown at the roots, and flapped the loose strands off her fingers. "Who's the other one?"

Ellie. My girlfriend.

"She pregnant? Is that why you're here?"

No.

"I was pregnant with you at your age."

I know.

"You think you're smarter than that, don't you?"

He shrugged again. So did she. "Bring them up."

Matthew banged on the window. Abbi and Ellie looked up, and he motioned for them to come, met them at the downstairs door. When they got back to his mother's apartment, Melissa had changed into a different black shirt, this one tighter with a deep V-neck, and pointy black shoes. She'd had boots with toes like that when he lived with her—her witch's shoes, he called them. She called them her going-out boots. Out, without him. They could be the same pair.

"I got Coke. And diet root beer," Melissa said. "Root beer used to be Matt's favorite. He'd eat it on his Cocoa Krispies. Bet he didn't tell you that."

"No," Ellie said, nestling into his side. "Not yet anyway."

"I bet he didn't." His mother grabbed a couple of glasses from the draining tray. "Anyway, there's water, too. What can I get you?"

"I'll have water," Ellie said.

"Me, too," Abbi added. And Matthew nodded.

"Suit yourselves," Melissa said. She filled the glasses from the tap and handed them around. "Well, sit."

Matthew sat on the futon with Ellie on one side and Abbi on the other. His mother came in from the kitchen after disappearing for a moment, sat on the cracked leather chair. She sipped her drink. It looked like cola, but Matthew doubted it. He wrote, I have to move. I can't see, and dragged a chair over from the dining table, positioned it so he was one corner of a trapezium. He was always on the corners. He held his glass between his knees, condensation seeping through his jeans.

"So, what brings you all out this way?" Melissa asked.

"A friend of mine, her church gives out food in the park," Abbi said. "We came up to help." She spread a flannel receiving blanket on the floor, and after changing Silvia's diaper, laid her on it. Everyone watched as Silvia rolled from her back to her side, her arm stuck under her body. She whimpered until Abbi scooted her over all the way, and then she lifted up on her arms, a baby push-up.

"Cute," Melissa said. "Your first?"

"Yes."

"Matt said he watches her."

"I need a sitter, and he needs to make some money for a school trip. It works out for both of us."

"School trip? Where you going?" Melissa asked.

"New York City," Abbi said. "Right, Matt?"

He glanced at Ellie and slowly bobbed his head up and down once. She wrapped the end of her braid around her finger.

"You going, too?" Melissa asked Ellie.

"I don't know," she said.

We should head out. We told Aunt Heather

we would be home by now. He hopped up, showed the notepad around.

Abbi gathered the baby's things, and Ellie picked up Silvia. Matthew opened the door, the hallway air as stale and depressed as the air in the apartment. He stood in the intersection of his past and his present, his life a Venn diagram, the blue circle and the red circle overlapping purple in his mother's living room. Set A and set B. This visit wasn't the good idea he had hoped it would be. He hadn't moved very far beyond his childhood, not when confronted with the root beer and the breakfast cereal, and his mother trying to take an interest in his life.

He slapped the doorframe.

"It was nice to meet you, Mrs. Savoie," Ellie said. "I hope we can, maybe, you know, see you again."

"You know where I am," Melissa said.

Matthew walked down the stairs, and then ran, slipping near the bottom and jamming his wrists as he caught himself. He slammed into the metal bar across the glass door and, once outside, bent over—his hands on his knees, his head down. He sucked down the autumn sky, tasted the leaves, the decomposing earth.

Then a hand warmed his back. Ellie's hand, and he spun around and squashed her in his arms. Abbi was there, too, shaking him gently. Ellie pulled away, turned him around. His mother waited there. "This is for you," she said, handing him a square of lined paper. "Since you're heading that way, anyway."

He unfolded the paper. His father's phone number.

And then Melissa went one way, and the rest of them went the other, and they drove home in silence.

Abbi dropped Ellie off first; Matthew didn't move from the back seat, and Abbi slowed, coasting to a stop at the side of the road. She looked at him over her seat. "There isn't a class trip, is there?"

He shook his head.

"What's going on, Matt?"

I need a kidney transplant. I was hoping my father might be a match.

"Is that what you need the money for?"

Yes. I want to go talk to him. In person.

"Why didn't you say anything to me and Ben?"

What could you do?

"Well, we could pay for you to go see him, for one. You don't have to be watching Silvia and mowing lawns."

I like watching Silvia.

"That's not the point."

Abbi, this is something I want to do on my own.

She flattened her lips together. "Haven't you been on your own long enough?"

And then she dropped him at the apartment, and he found Sienna in front of the television, and Skye in her bedroom, both Heather and Jaylyn gone, and Lacie eating Cheetos, her fingers and face smeared orange.

"Matty, I'm starved. Skye won't make me anything to eat."

So Matthew made grilled cheese sandwiches and warmed two cans of tomato soup. He washed a load of laundry, packed the lunches for the next day, and put Lacie and Sienna in the shower.

When Heather came in with Whip, he and the little girls were on the couch watching a movie, subtitles on, microwave popcorn on their laps.

"Where's Skye?" Heather asked.

"In her room," Sienna said. "Where else?"

"And Jaylyn?"

Sienna shrugged. "She went out with Leo," Lacie said. "Even when you said not to. I told her you said not to."

"Go to bed, both of you."

"It's early," Sienna said.

"I don't care. Whip and I want the TV."

I'll tuck you in.

"I don't need to be tucked in," Sienna said.

"I do. I do," said Lacie. "Carry me."

"Matt, you take Jaylyn's bed," Heather said. "She's not here. She'll get the couch."

He stood up, and Lacie jumped on his back, and he galloped to her bed, dropping her. She laughed, snuggled beneath the Barbie comforter and brushed her hair from her face. "Kiss, please."

He kissed her forehead. Sienna climbed onto the top bunk. He motioned to her, and she hung her head upside down over the edge of the mattress. He kissed her, too.

Skye lay with her face toward the wall, earphones clamped over her head. Matthew changed into his pajamas in the bathroom, brushed his teeth. He took his medication. Back in the bedroom, he touched Skye's shoulder, gave her a little shake. She didn't respond, so he crawled into the bunk and read for a while, enjoying the extra room to stretch out.

Finally Skye got up, left and came back. He took his pad from under the pillow but couldn't find the pen. Skye bent over. When she stood back up she held the pen, gave it to him.

He bit off the cap.

She covered his hand with hers. "Just . . . turn off that lamp. I can't sleep with it on."

He did, and the bunk beds rocked from Skye turning beneath him. She was torturing herself over Silvia. At least, he hoped that was the case. It would be a lot worse if she wasn't.

Chapter THIRTY-TWO

Benjamin arrived home to children's voices, shouting and giggling floating out from behind the house. He shut the truck's door and carried the two grocery sacks to the backyard, where Matthew's two younger cousins were chasing each other. "Hi, Deputy Patil," Lacie said, racing over to him. "Miss Abbi said we can eat dinner here."

"You're it," Sienna said, slamming into Lacie's back.

"Not fair. I called time."

"No you didn't."

"Yes I did."

"Nuh-huh. Did she, Deputy?" Sienna asked.

"I'm staying out of this," Benjamin said. "Where's Matt?"

"Inside with the baby," Lacie told him. She slapped Sienna on the arm. "You're it."

"Hey, we weren't playing yet," Sienna shouted, taking off after her sprinting sister.

Matthew sat at the kitchen table, head in his books, Silvia asleep in the basket in front of him. He glanced up as Benjamin closed the sliding door, raised his pencil.

"What are you working on?"

Matthew held up the book, finger inside it marking his page. *AP Physics.*

"Fun, fun."

The boy chuckled. Hope you don't mind the girls here.

"Of course not."

My aunt doesn't want them home alone anymore. Sienna nearly burned down the apartment trying to heat up a pizza.

"They're young to be by themselves."

I know. Sometimes my older cousins aren't the best at being where they say they'll be.

And Benjamin saw how responsibility hunched Matthew's shoulders, his burdens chasing him 'round in circles until he was so dizzy he couldn't see he wasn't these girls' father. He was older than he should be, worrying about kidneys and children, and probably much more that Benjamin didn't know about. He shook his head, remembering his biggest teenaged concerns—pimples and school dances, and his mother's odd clothing.

He watched the two little girls in the backyard—now playing campfire, roasting leaves over a cold pile of twigs—and tenderly picked up Silvia and bundled her into his chest. He couldn't believe how much she'd grown over the past three and a half months. A smile spasmed at the corners of her mouth as she slept, and his heart with it.

Benjamin knocked on the table. "Where's Abbi?" he asked.

Matthew pointed down the hall.

She was showering, and Benjamin silently entered the steamy room, watching her shadow flicker behind the curtain. The water stopped running, and the towel hanging on the curtain rod disappeared into the tub before Abbi stepped onto the bath mat.

"Oh, shoot," she said when she saw him. She unwrapped the towel from her waist and hit him with it. "You scared me."

"Shhh. Don't do that. You'll wake the—"

Silvia opened her eyes and cried. Benjamin bounced her, touching his nose to her own, saying "Boop" each time, until the baby calmed and reached for his face.

"You're a good dad," Abbi said. She turned her head upside down and buffed her hair with the towel, her shins and thighs, first one leg, then the other. She straightened, and Benjamin pulled the hand towel from the holder on the wall, patted the drops of water from her back. "Thanks."

"Don't mention it," he said, kissing her neck.

"Mmm. That tickles."

"Tickles? I'm offended." He kissed her again, behind the ear.

"Ben, Matt's in the kitchen."

"He can't hear us."

She snickered. "You're terrible."

"Two seconds ago you were telling me that I was good."

"Well, maybe you can change my mind again," she said, pulling on her shirt, "but after dinner."

"Now *you're* terrible."

"Did Matt tell you his cousins are eating here tonight?"

"Yep. So much for a quick dinner."

"Or a good one." Abbi sprinkled baking powder on her hands, dabbed her armpits. "Those kids have got to be the pickiest eaters I've ever met. I finally got them to agree to spaghetti, but without sauce. Only butter. And salt."

"Consider it a taste of what's to come in, oh, about two more years."

"You're resorting to puns now?"

"Torturous, isn't it? I promise I'll stop, if you'll just go over across the hall and take off that shirt of yours—"

She opened the bathroom door, the cool air sucking the steam into the hall. "Don't make me start quoting Galatians, Mr. Self-Control."

"Look," he said, following Abbi into the kitchen, "Matt's not even here."

"Why don't you go out and play with him and the girls? Run off some of that energy," she said, plucking Silvia from his arms and motioning toward the sliding door. And then she kissed him long and soft on the lips. "But not too much."

"Tease," he said.

Outside, the girls threw a playground ball over Matthew's head as he made feeble attempts to intercept it, pretending to trip, or bouncing it off his head. Lacie and Sienna giggled and pointed, calling, "Matty's a monkey, Matty's a monkey." Sienna slung the ball past her sister. It rolled toward Benjamin, and he popped it into the air with the toe of his boot, juggled it on his knees.

"Cool," Sienna said. "I didn't know old guys could do that, too."

"Old guy? Well, this old guy challenges you three to a game of dodge ball." Benjamin stretched the garden hose across the lawn. "You all stay on that side. I'll be over here."

They lobbed the ball back and forth until Abbi called them in to eat. The girls bickered and gabbed enough for all of them. Benjamin enjoyed the sheer exasperation on his wife's face as Lacie knocked over her milk and Sienna tried to convince her sister the noodles were honest-to-goodness dead worms while both of them kicked each other under the table when they thought no one was looking. Then Lacie asked for dessert, and Abbi offered some carob and cranberry bars.

"These brownies taste funny," Sienna complained.

Matthew rapped the table, shook his head, but Abbi touched his arm. "It's fine." And then to Sienna, "I like to call them healthy brownies. They don't have any yucky stuff in them."

"I think I like the yucky stuff," Lacie said.

Tell me they are not always like this, Abbi mouthed to Matthew while the girls wiggled into their jackets near the front door.

Don't you want a dozen?

"Don't worry. Ours will be an angel," Benjamin said.

She glared at him. "Just go."

"Okay, then. I'll be back soon." He winked. "Very soon."

"Take your time. I need a long, hot bath after this meal."

He gave the kids a ride home, letting them off in front of the apartment, the girls bouncing out of the Durango and inside. Matthew seemed reluctant to get out. The dome light stayed on because neither Lacie nor Sienna had closed the back door. Benjamin shifted in his seat, and Matthew turned toward him. "You okay?"

He nodded and shrugged all at once, picked at the corner of his thumbnail.

"You're good with them. The girls."

What's your father like?

Benjamin blinked at the unexpected question. "He's different than me. Brilliant. A scientist. You two would probably get along. He's just who he is."

But he was good to you.

"Oh yeah. Absolutely. The best. Even if I might have not thought it at the time."

Don't know much about mine. He played baseball. Minor League stuff. Wrecked his knee and sort of flickered out of our lives. At least that's what my mom told me. I can't remember him.

"Abbi said your mother gave you his number."

Did she tell you the rest?

"Yes."

What do you think?

"You're asking me? I don't know. I guess you need to be realistic about it. There's no guarantee he's going to be, I don't know . . ."

He didn't want to see Matthew hurt; the kid had been through so much already.

I don't have expectations, Ben.

"I'm not trying to talk you out of it. It's probably good, you know, to have some idea where you come from."

What about Silvia? Do you think she should know about everything?

"Well, I mean, we'll tell her, of course. One day. I don't know when." Benjamin squirted wiper fluid on the windshield, and the blades swished back and forth twice. "Matt, what's wrong? Tell me so I can stop tripping over myself here. I don't tiptoe well. I'm much better with direct."

I was just thinking of Silvia's father.

He waited for more, but Matthew only tapped his pen against his knee. "What about him?"

What if he doesn't know he has a daughter? What if he never knows?

"Come on. Really. How could he not know? Eventually he'd be asking where the baby went to."

What if Silvia's mother kept it from him?

"I sincerely doubt that's the case."

But it could happen?

"Well, yeah."

And what if it did?

"What aren't you telling me?"

Matthew turned his head. *Nothing.*

He's lying. Benjamin squeezed the steering wheel, ripples of nausea high in his chest, behind his ribs. "Hypothetically speaking, if we found the birth mother, and she told us the father didn't know she was pregnant, we would have to find him and ask if he wanted to . . . parent Sil—the child."

Hypothetically speaking, what if he said yes?

"He would take custody of the child. And that would be that."

No, it wouldn't. They both knew it.

And what if, hypothetically speaking, you never find out who left Silvia?

"Then whoever did it gets away with attempted murder, and Silvia lives happily ever after with two parents who love her."

His words were daggers, and he almost thanked God the boy couldn't hear his tone. Almost. He started praying and stopped.

Matthew's pen hovered above his pad, trembling. He touched the point to the paper, to his tongue, to his paper again. His fingers tensed, relaxed, and he stuck the pen in his mouth again, the opposite side now, clamping the cap between his teeth while he scribbled, *Thanks,* then closed the pen. He slipped off the seat, closing the passenger side door and the one behind it, and let himself into the apartment, head hung deep between his shoulders.

Benjamin started home, and on the dark stretch of road between two fields his queasiness returned. He parked the Durango, scraped his hand along the door for the handle, and leaning out over the gravel, dry-heaved in the raw, slumbering air. Autumn air. Nothing came up, and he was glad. He didn't deserve the relief of vomiting. *What have I done?* Not what he should have done—he should have told Matthew that whatever he knew or didn't know, or thought he knew, he could say it aloud. No. Benjamin told him to stuff his secret deep, camouflaged beneath disquieting thoughts of poor Silvia growing up without the Patils. Not in so many words. But they both understood what Benjamin had meant. And he did mean it. He'd rather Matthew live with whatever information he may have—with the consequences of carrying it around with him, everywhere and forever—than live without his daughter. Who was Matthew but the lawn boy and some drug addict's son? Who was he that Benjamin would consider sacrific-ing Silvia for some kid he had only known a couple of months?

No one. He was no one.

What's wrong with me? I should want only the truth.

But he didn't. He wanted Silvia.

He was tempted not to go home, but his need to protect his baby compelled him back to the house. Abbi waited for him, dressed in a sheer, gauzy nightgown. "What took you so long?" She kissed him. "Mmm. Your nose is cold."

"I'm exhausted. I'm going to bed." Her strap had fallen from her shoulder, and he repositioned it.

"Ben?"

"You're right. Those kids are whirlwinds. I just need some sleep."

"Okay, sure. Okay. I'm going to go . . . take a shower."

"Another one?"

"I never did take that bath, and like you said, those kids . . ." She closed herself in the bathroom, and the water came on. Benjamin pressed his ear to the door. He thought he heard sniffling, and then Abbi switched on the vent fan, drowning out any evidence of her tears.

Silvia slept in the basket on the floor of their bedroom. He nudged it close to his side of the bed, lying down on his stomach with his arm hanging over the edge of the mattress, his hand resting on the baby's chest. Up, down. Up, down. Each breath carried her a littler further from him. *You can't take her. You hear me? You can't take her.* He didn't consider it a prayer, more of a threat. And if he lost her, he wouldn't pray again.

Chapter THIRTY-THREE

The phone rang, and Abbi pounced on it so it wouldn't wake the baby.

"Abbi, it's Janet. Listen, is everything all right?"

Say no. "Yeah, fine. Why?"

"Al said . . . Well, he said Ben seems, um, down again. And after church Sunday, you both . . . Look, I'm not trying to be nosy, but you . . . I mean, after . . ."

"You're right. But I don't know what's wrong. He won't tell me. It's like time's rewound three months, and here we are again."

"Did something happen?"

"No." Abbi banged her fist on the wall. "Nothing between us, I don't think. Things have been really good. I mean, he was the old Ben. Not totally, but he was trying. We both were."

"I wish I could do more than pray."

"Praying is more than enough."

"Well, then, I can do that."

"Thanks. I mean it." And then Abbi started to cry. "I don't think I can do this again, Janet."

"You can. If you need anything . . . Really, anything . . ."

"I do. Could you maybe watch Silvia for a couple hours? I'll bring her there."

"No, no. I'll come over. Do you need me now?"

"If you can."

"I'm on my way."

When Janet arrived, Abbi showed her where to find the bottles and formula, gave her an all-in-one diaper so she didn't have to fuss with pins and folding, and after kissing Silvia good-bye, she drove straight to the Rigney farm.

"Abbi, hey," Lauren said, nudging open the warped screen door. "Are you okay?"

"No. It's Ben."

"Well, get in here." She held Stevie on her hip, his hands gooey with something orange, mucus bubbling from his nose as he screamed. He crammed his face against Lauren's shoulder, snot smearing over his cheek, on her sweater. She pinned his arms and swept a wet washcloth around his face. Then she cleaned his hands. "He hates having his face wiped."

As soon as she put the toddler down, he stopped wailing and walked over to the dog dish, flopped on his diapered bottom and raked a handful of small, round nuggets toward his mouth. Lauren sighed, scooped him up, and pried open his fingers. "Look at what you have to look forward to," she said. "Let's go in the family room. It's baby-proofed."

Abbi fell into the recliner, and Lauren drew the gate across the doorway. Stevie crawled to a pile of board books and picked one up, chewed the corner. "Where's Katie?"

"Napping. I was just about to put this little man down before you came."

"I'm sorry. Go ahead. I can wait. Or I can just call later. . . ."

"No, tell me what's going on."

"That's the problem. I have no idea. It's Ben. He really was doing better . . . and then last Thursday he comes home and, poof, he won't talk to me. Won't even look at me."

"Where'd he come home from? Work?"

"Dropping Matt and his cousins at home."

Stevie abandoned the books and crawled over to Abbi, pulled himself up on her leg. Lauren grabbed him around the belly, tickled him, and then settled him into her lap to nurse. The little boy closed his eyes, twirled a strand of his mother's hair. "He'll be out in two seconds," Lauren said. "And you're sure nothing happened after he dropped Matt at his house?"

"I'm not sure of anything. I can't get any answers out of him."

"Maybe you're not asking the right question."

"What is that supposed to mean?"

Lauren unlatched Stevie, and Abbi pushed away a stab of envy at the bond between her friend and the child. She'd never have that. "He'd been talking to you before this?" Lauren asked.

"I just said that."

"About what?"

"Everything."

"Really?"

"Yes."

"Hmm." Lauren laid Stevie on the area rug and covered him with a blanket. "Has he told you about Afghanistan?"

"Well, no, but—"

"What about what's been bothering him all this time?"

"No, but that's not the point. I—"

"What have you been talking about?"

Abbi scratched the back of her neck. There had been plenty of words filling the spaces between them. Always regarding Silvia; they could find things to say all day about her—from her expressions, to giggles, to the color of her dirty diapers. About who would unload the dishwasher or change the toilet paper roll. And flirting, lots of silliness and innuendo. But nothing deeply personal. "Stuff," she said.

"He doesn't trust you, Abbi."

"Of course he does."

"I don't think so. Not with the parts that are truly him."

"We can't all have what you and Stephen had."

"You could be a lot closer to it than you are. Don't you get it? How can he open up to you when you're against everything he is?"

"I am not."

"He goes to the other side of the world to fight for you to have the freedom to stand on that stupid street corner with your stupid signs. He does it because he thinks it's right. But he knows you think he's no better than an ignorant, bloodthirsty redneck. How can he confide in you about anything?"

"This isn't about Ben and me. It's about you and me. You're still ticked about the protesting."

"Yeah, I am. But don't you see? If it bothers *me* so much, how much do you think it bothers Ben? How can he tell you anything about what happened to him over there when he knows you think he's reaping what he's sown?"

"I'm not going to lie and tell him I think he's some great hero for slaughtering people. He knew who I was when he married me."

"And you knew who he was."

Silence. They both watched Stevie drool in his sleep, his silky hair curling from the perspiration at the back of his neck. Abbi moved to the floor, next to him. Ran her finger over the dimples in the back of his hand. "He looks like Stephen," she said.

"Not as much as Kate. That girl is her father. Personality, too."

"I'm sorry, Lauren. That you're alone."

"If you think someone can be alone living with her parents and two kids, you've never tried it."

"You know what I mean."

"I'm not alone. I have God. I have my church. I have all those things people tell you that you have after you lose someone, and you just roll your eyes and think *They don't get it*, because it just hurts too much to believe them. You're alone. Not me. And you're going to be more alone if you don't get your head on straight and deal with this. Your marriage isn't going to stand up under it for long."

"This is what drives me insane. You sit here and say all this. But you and Stephen . . . You were perfect together. Ben and I, we screwed it all up. Everything we tried to convince ourselves wasn't going to matter—it all exploded in our faces."

Lauren smacked her lips. "You want out, then?"

"I didn't say that."

"Then what?"

"I don't know." Abbi lay back on the floor, turned her head away from Lauren. She saw under the chair, puffs of dust and hair clinging to the leg. She blew, watching one ball slide across the wood floor, colliding with another, both of them scampering into the corner. "I shouldn't have married him."

"Once you're married, there aren't any *shouldn't*s. There's just what is. How you move on from here, that's up to you."

Abbi closed her eyes. "I love him."

"Then let it go, Abbi. Go home and ask Ben to forgive you."

"For what?" Defensiveness rose up in her again.

"Everything up to this point."

"I'm sorry, but I'm not going to apologize for what I did, or what I believe, or—"

"I, I, I. That's your biggest problem. Not Ben. Not the war. All you see is what you do, and what he does. You're two individuals floating around out there, acting like, well, two individuals. Not like a pair. Not like one flesh."

"We're not you and Stephen."

"Oh, will you stop it with that? I don't care if you're oil and water. Keep shaking. Keep trying. It takes effort. But that's just the way it is."

They both looked up at the ceiling, watching the hanging lamp jounce as something bounced over the floor upstairs. "Katie's up,"

Lauren said, and then the four-year-old danced down the stairs into her mother's arms, pigtails matted to her cheeks.

"I'm hungry," she complained.

"Shh. Not so loud, honey. Stevie's sleeping."

"I'm hungry," Katie repeated in an exaggerated whisper. "And you said we can make cookies."

"Okay, cookies it is. Maybe Aunt Abbi wants to join us?"

"I think I'll head out. Silvia, you know."

"Yes," Lauren said. "I do."

"Lauren . . . Thanks."

"Yeah, well, if your best friend can't tell you you're being a selfish j-e-r-k, who can?"

"No fair, Mommy," Katie said. "I can't know what you said. What did you say?"

"I said it's time to make cookies." Lauren scooped up her daughter and planted squishy kisses all over her face and neck, Katie's chubby legs flailing in the air. "Call me if you need anything."

Before going home, Abbi picked up a few things at the Food Mart, avoiding the pharmacy aisle, grabbed a couple of books from the library. Killing time. Her head buzzed with Lauren's admonition. *She's right, she's right.* Abbi knew it could be done, being a half and a whole at the same time—Lauren did it. But it required dying to self, something she'd been unwilling to do. She had spent her entire marriage preserving her identity, afraid of melting into some black puddle of *what Benjamin wanted*, rather than who she was. A Stepford wife. A perfect, plastic, meat-eating, gun-toting Conservative.

She hadn't taken her marriage seriously. To her, it had been a lucky coin, a worry stone in her pants pocket. Something she carried with her and rubbed without thinking; she knew it was there—always there—but she never looked at it. Never took it out unless she needed something.

She was tired of excuses. She wanted what Lauren and Stephen had had. She didn't want to settle.

On the road, Abbi glanced in her rearview mirror, and she instinctively slammed on the brakes. *Where is Silvia?*

At home. At home with Janet.

The panic drained away, flooding her pelvis with warmth, and then it evaporated. Other than her evening jogs—down to three or less a week now—and a few hours in her studio when Matthew came, she hadn't been without Silvia hanging on her body or within earshot. The baby had become a piece of her, a transplanted finger, a toe, grafted into her skin.

Her baby.

⌒

Benjamin, home from work and in jeans and a T-shirt, held Silvia in the kitchen. No, didn't just hold her. Clutched her. His eyes, moist and bloodshot, didn't move from the baby's face. "Janet said you went to see Lauren. Is everything okay?"

"No."

"What's wrong?"

"Us."

He tilted his head toward the ceiling, sucked his lips in between his teeth. "I'm not in the mood for this now."

"I don't care."

"I'm going . . . out. Can I have the Volvo keys? I'll take Silvia with me."

Benjamin stepped around her, but she grabbed his arm. "You're not doing this to me, Ben. You need to stay here and deal with this. I'm so sick of you checking out on me."

"Me? Me checking out? Oh, you're one to talk. You've been gone since we moved here."

"You're right."

He stopped, keys hanging in his fingers. "What?"

"I said you're right."

"No you didn't. You couldn't have. I'm never right, remember?"

"Ben, please. I'm trying to talk to you." She closed her eyes, sighed. "I'm trying to say I'm sorry."

"For what?"

"I couldn't even begin to list everything."

"Try."

"You're enjoying this."

"Mmm, yeah," he said.

"Stop it." She swung her arm up to punch him in the shoulder—lightly, jokingly—but Benjamin caught her fist, drew it down to his chest, holding it there. She opened her hand, felt his heart beating against her palm.

"You don't need to apologize," he said.

Pulling away, she said, "Why do you do that? You're not supposed to be all sweet and understanding. Just let me say that I screwed up. I tried to sabotage our marriage. I couldn't handle you loving me. Like you said, I pulled away. I think . . . No, I *know* one of the reasons I protested so hard was to hurt you. I mean, I meant it, but I didn't want you to think I wouldn't do it just because of you. I needed you to know I was still me—"

"Abbi—"

"—and I wasn't going to change—"

"Abbi. Stop."

"—and I certainly wasn't going—"

"Just stop," he said, not shouting, but close.

She didn't. "Why can't you just tell me why you're angry? Last week we were doing better. Good, even. And now you won't even look at me."

"It's not about you. Or us." Benjamin buffed the top of his head, dug his fingertips into his scalp. "It's Silvia."

And all at once her anger disappeared. "What? I don't . . ."

"We might be close to finding out who her moth— Who left her. There's some new evidence, and it's possible there might be some . . . other relatives out there, who might not realize she—I mean, Silvia—is part of their . . . well, part of their family."

"She's part of *our* family."

"Look, we don't know anything for certain. And I didn't want to say anything until there was something more substantial."

"Then why did you?"

"Darn it, Abbi. Don't put this back on me. You asked. I answered. Period."

She dragged a kitchen chair out from beneath the table, dropped into it, all rubbery-boned, like when she was in fifth grade and her class soaked a chicken skeleton in vinegar. "When will you know?"

Benjamin shrugged. "Tomorrow. Never. Somewhere in between?"

"That's helpful."

The cupboards stared at her—dark, whorled eye knots and shiny gold-handled noses. She wanted to get behind them, to eat, to think about the food swelling in her stomach and puckering the back of her thighs. She wanted Benjamin to leave so she could fill herself and hate herself, and feel something familiar. Not this uncertainty, this almost pain, not knowing if it should come or go. "Are you still going out?"

"No."

"I am," she said, jiggling the keys from her fingers. She unbuckled the car seat and threw it in the Durango. Then she drove the Volvo back to the grocery, bought a jumbo bag of baby carrots, and ate all of them sitting in the car on a farm road, sometimes shoving six or seven in her mouth at a time, sometimes slicing one into little rounds with her front teeth. She opened the trunk, unzipped the jumper cable bag, and from between the wires removed another small pouch.

Unbuttoned that, and shook out four senna tablets—all that were left. She scrunched them in her hand and went home, downing them with a glass of water from the kitchen sink.

Benjamin was already in bed, curled around Silvia but not asleep. Abbi changed to her pajamas and said, "I'm going to read for a while. In the living room."

"You can stay in here. I'm not tired. I'm just . . . watching her."

"Nah. I'll just be a bit."

On the couch, she lay flat on her back, feet elevated on the arm. She brushed her hands over her face, still smelling the senna on her skin.

⌒⟶

Matthew showed up Tuesday afternoon, like always. She was still in her robe and told him she didn't need him. She hadn't slept at all last night. Neither had Benjamin; she heard him up every couple of hours, in the bathroom, in the kitchen. She pretended to sleep, and did her pacing while he pretended to sleep. She didn't go into the bedroom, didn't want to be close to the baby.

She had spent the day floating around, disembodied, with Silvia on the floor, in the Moses basket, away from her. Abbi changed her, of course, and picked her up if she cried. Fed her. But when Abbi finished those things, she got away from her, looking on from a distance, willing the space between them to grow.

Are you sick? Matthew asked, as he stood at the door, smudges of sleeplessness beneath his eyes, too.

She nodded. "You don't want to catch this."

I can stay, really. You go nap. Or shower. Or both.

"I look that bad?"

He shook his head. I didn't mean—

Abbi put her hand over his. "Joke, joke."

Please, let me do this for you.

Matthew itched his forearm, his upper arm, swiped at his neck.

"Are you okay?"

He nodded. *Let me help.*

"Yeah, fine. Whatever. Come in," she said.

She did go take a nap, or tried to, and eventually her headache weighed down her eyelids, and she dozed for a while. When she woke, she didn't bother to dress—it was almost five, and she'd be back to bed in a few more hours anyway. Matthew waited in the living room, in the recliner, Silvia bound up against him much the same way Benjamin had held her the evening before, tight to his ribs, arms rigid and protective. He jumped up, held her out to Abbi.

"Just . . . put her over there."

He hesitated, and then rolled her from his arms into the basket.

I'm going.

"Oh, Matt. Sorry. I'm just out of it."

No. I'm sorry.

"You don't have anything to be sorry for. Thanks for the nap. It helped."

Did it?

She fixed the collar of his rugby-style shirt. "Go on. Get out of here."

I'm sorry.

"Matt, I just told you there's nothing for you to be sorry about."

The boy hesitated, and then hugged her before running out the door.

Chapter THIRTY-FOUR

He woke with the same resolve he'd had that other Thursday nearly four months ago, the day he went to Pierre to speak with his mother. There was no heat today, no sun. Just the low rumble of traffic from the interstate and autumn on the wind's breath, the smell of decay and earth puffing through the cracked window.

Lacie charged into the room, jumped on him, her knobby knees digging into his ribs.

"Wake up, wake up," she said. "I'm hungry."

Matthew rolled up his blanket and smoothed it over the humped back of the couch, threw his pillow into the corner, atop his clothing tote, and allowed Lacie to grab his index finger and pull him to the kitchen. "Pancakes," she said.

He shook his head, pulled out a box of instant oatmeal and another of frosted cornflakes.

"Is there any apple left?"

He turned the oatmeal box over; a package of maple-flavored fell to the counter, another of peaches 'n cream.

Lacie scrunched up her face, bottom lip pushed out. "Cereal, I guess."

He poured a bowl for her and one for Sienna, then fried three eggs, scooping each one onto a fork and eating it in a single bite. He dropped a couple slices of bread in the toaster; they popped up and he buttered them for the girls, made two more pieces for himself. Lacie wanted cinnamon and sugar on hers. And when Sienna clamored into the dining area, she reached across the table to snatch Lacie's toast. Lacie flailed at her hand, knocking her own orange juice over, spilling it into Sienna's bowl.

"Stupid," Sienna said, hurling her toast at her sister. It stuck, butter side, to Lacie's shirt.

Matthew stepped between them, sent Lacie down the hall to change her shirt while he cleaned the mess and then sat down next to Sienna. Do you have to instigate like that?

"I don't even know what that means."

It means start problems.

"Why should she get cinnamon toast and not me?"

You want toast? He pounded the sugar bowl onto the table, grabbed a fistful and flung it on her now-soggy bread. "There," he said, not caring how it sounded.

"Matty, what's got into you?" Sienna asked.

Closing his eyes, he inhaled, held his breath until he couldn't anymore. Not long. Maybe thirty-five seconds.

How could she know her life, her family, would change forever today?

And this was why he needed to tell, because of his cousins' lives without their fathers. Because of his own life. If the person who fathered Silvia had something to do with her abandonment, so be it. Abbi and the deputy would keep her and raise her with more love than Matthew hoped to ever know from human parents. But if he didn't know, well, Matthew owed the truth to Silvia.

He wanted her to have better than he did. And he was fairly sure he knew the dad. If so, Matthew could say with enough certainty that Jared Whalen would want to be there for his daughter. That in and of itself made the gamble of *telling* worth it to him.

He only prayed Skye would forgive him someday.

He left the apartment, crossing the courtyard shoeless, his flannel pants dragging in the dirt. He nestled into the swing, tracing circles in the sand with his big toes before digging his feet in and kicking up a cloud of dust. Lacie ran over to him, clean purple shirt matched with her pink pants, and plowed into his chest with a hug. Her face vibrated against his breastbone. He pulled her away, shrugged his whole body.

"I said I'm sorry Sienna and I was fighting."

Standing, he picked her up. She wrapped her legs around his waist, and he sat on the swing again. Lacie grinned. Matthew saw the ripples of her new tooth poking up through the gum, in the empty space on the bottom. They held on to the chain together, his fists above hers, and pumped the swing, a four-legged beast rising higher into the air.

"Jump, jump," she said, and he wrapped one arm around her, felt her legs tighten around him again, and at the peak of the swing's arc, he wriggled off the seat, and for a moment they were flying. He couldn't see the ground because her hair tangled over his face; his feet hit the hard-packed sand, knees buckling, but he kept his balance.

"Again," Lacie said, but he put his hand on her shoulder and walked her back into the apartment.

Matthew hurried to dress, not bothering to rinse his feet, downed his pills and slapped some water on his face from the kitchen sink. Once the bathroom was free, he had just enough time to brush his teeth and hair before Skye told him the bus had come, and they climbed onto it in size order—Lacie skipping up the steps in front, he in the back, shoulders sunken beneath the weight of his backpack, and his secret, which by eleven tonight he guessed would be broadcast across all of South Dakota.

⁓

He somehow made it through his classes. Ellie knew something was eating at him. "Do you want to talk about it yet?"

Tomorrow.

"Always tomorrow."

I mean it this time.

By the final bell, Matthew's resolve had faded to a wisp of hesitancy. He told Jaylyn he was staying after school, and when the buses pulled away he walked to the county courthouse and sat against the trunk of an elm across from the sheriff's entrance until his feet went numb from the pressure on his tailbone. He stretched his legs; they slipped over the fallen yellow leaves, smooth as skin, and sweet, like an overripe apple. Dead but not dead. Not crispy corpse brown, but heading there soon. A day. A week. Nothing could save them.

A deputy stepped out of the building. Not Benjamin. He drove away. Matthew screwed his fingers into the ground, digging wormholes. He couldn't bring himself to stand. The door across the street opened again, and this time it was Benjamin. He started his squad vehicle, and Matthew folded his knees to his chest and tucked his head down. *If he drives past me, Lord, I'll go home. If he stops, I'll tell him. If he sees me. I promise.*

Drive past, drive past. Oh, please, drive past.

He saw the curb of the road from beneath his hair, and tires, slowing in front of him. And then boots in the grass and a hand on the top of his head. He looked up.

"Matt, you okay?" Benjamin asked.

Matthew sucked his lips between his teeth, bit them. He stood, using the tree trunk as support, and flipped open his pad. *If someone knew who Silvia belonged to, would you want to know?*

"Yes."

Even if it meant you'd lose her?

Benjamin pressed two fingers against the outside of his ear, dragged them down the side of his face, his neck, skin puckering around the pressure, turning pink, like the precursor to a bruise. "Tell me."

But Matthew couldn't yet, not before speaking to Skye. He went to the deputy first because, if he hadn't, he would have gone home and put off the confrontation. For a day, perhaps, a week. Longer. And the more time that passed, the easier it would be to ignore, like sand in an oyster, the irritant coated in calcium carbonate, each concentric layer drawing him further from the truth. Still, he needed to warn his cousin.

He wrote, Wait in the office. I'll call you. In an hour.

"Matthew, you can't . . . Please, who is it? Just say it."

An hour. I promise.

He walked home, head empty. He tried to think, to pray, but couldn't keep a single word contained; they floated up into the darkening sky. He turned to the numbers. To pi. *Three point one four one five nine two six five three five eight nine seven nine three two three eight four six two six four three three eight three two seven five zero . . .*

Skye was sitting on the stoop at the apartment, watching Lacie build castles in the sandbox with Tara Blye, the second-grader three doors down. She sucked on a cigarette, blew the smoke out her nose.

Since when do you smoke?

She shrugged. "Since I started."

He settled next to her, pad on his knee, tapping the pen on the paper.

Skye ground her butt out on the step, tossed it. "I know you know."

Matthew saw only the side of her mouth, and wasn't quite

certain he'd read her lips right. He scooted around, in front of her.
What?

"You know."

About?

"Her."

How?

"The picture. You took the picture." She dug another cigarette out from somewhere down her shirt, the lighter from beneath her thigh. She flicked the button once, twice. No flame. Her arm fell to her lap. "I knew you'd figure it out, once you started working for them."

She's Jared's.

Skye nodded.

Did he know? Does he?

"No. Have you told?"

Not yet. Not really. I'm going to. Tonight. Deputy Patil is waiting for my call.

"I wouldn't expect anything less."

I have to.

"Yeah. I know."

I'm sorry.

"I didn't mean for this to happen, Matty," she said, her eyes focused on something off to the side—her burned-out butt, maybe—not on his face. If he could have looked away, too, he would have. "I got pregnant, and then it was just too late to do anything about it, and all I kept hearing in my head was Ma telling Jaylyn and me that we better not bring any babies home, or we could find someplace else to live. I know she meant it. She made Jaylyn get rid of two. And Jared was planning college, and I didn't want to ruin that for him. I figured Ma or Jaylyn or someone would notice eventually, but no one did.

"I woke up that morning just feeling . . . I don't know, kind of sick. Like, nauseous. And I just packed my swimsuit and towel in my backpack, and a lunch, and started walking. I thought it was too early for the baby to come. But I was wading in Hopston's pond, and the sick feeling turned to pain, and there was blood and water. I sat in the weeds and started to push, and she was there.

"I cut the cord and tied it with my shoelace, like in the movies. She didn't even cry. And I . . . I panicked. I can't even tell you why I thought it was a good idea to leave her. But I did. I put her in my lunch bag, tied the handles, and pushed her into the tall grass. I should have at least wrapped her in the towel, but I was afraid someone would recognize it, like evidence, or something.

"Then I started walking across the field. Wandering, really. I told myself if she cried, I'd go back for her. But she still didn't. And this terrible, sharp pain cut through my stomach, and I felt like I had to push again. For a minute I thought I was having twins, but then this blob fell out of me. They don't show you that part in the movies.

"I ripped part of the towel off and stuffed it in my underpants, wrapped the blob in the big piece. But then Tallah and her stupid boyfriend showed up, and I got scared, and I left the towel and hid against the closest cottonwood. I watched as Simon tripped over it, and called the sheriff. I watched as the deputy came and found her.

"Somehow I made it home. I showered. I bagged my bloody clothes and shoes and threw them in the dumpster out back of the school. And I waited for the knock on the door. But it didn't come. Until now."

She sniffed. "I'm going to jail."

You don't know that.

"Yeah, I do. The Internet's a wonderful thing."

Maybe you'll get leniency or something.

"For what? I left my baby to die." She scrubbed away her tears with her thumb knuckles. "Let's get this over with. Make your call, or whatever."

Matthew nodded, his fingertips skating over her shoulder as he went inside and dialed 711, pressed the phone into the TTY hub. He watched until the red light stopped its lazy blink.

HELLO RO#45435F HERE, NBR TO DIAL PLS QQ GA, the screen read.

He typed the number for the sheriff's station and waited.

THK YOU DIALING PLS HD. . . . RINGING 1. . . . 2. . . . 3. . . . 4. . . . HELLO QQ (EXPLAINING RELAY PLS HD) GA.

I WOULD LIKE TO SPEAK TO DEPUTY PATIL, Matthew typed.

HOLD PLEASE. And then, PATIL HERE. MATT IS THAT YOU QQ GA.

Matthew typed, YES. METHODIST CHURCH, 30 MINUTES GA.

The screen read, I WILL BE THERE GA.

SKSK, he typed, and then he knocked on Jaylyn's door. I have to go out. You need to make dinner for the girls.

"Tell Skye to do it."

She's going out with me.

"Why? What for?"

Just take care of the girls.

He wrote a note to Sienna, telling her he was leaving. She didn't lift her face from the television.

Outside, Skye was still slumped on the stoop. "They coming?"

Matthew shook his head. Not here. At the church down the road. I didn't want everyone to see.

She touched his arm, almost smiled. "Lacie, get your butt over here."

The little girl came running. "I didn't do nothing."

"Just get inside and wash up for supper. Matty and I gotta run an errand real quick."

"I'll make sure Sienna saves some food for you. You know what a hog she can be."

"Yeah, great," Skye said, and she hugged her. "You be good."

"Ow, stop. You're crushing me," Lacie said, wriggling away and charging into the apartment.

After the door slammed, Matthew turned and started walking, Skye beside him on his right, out of the parking lot, onto the road. Head down, he watched her feet against the asphalt, heels of her blue tennis shoes dragging.

Three point one four one five nine two six five three five eight nine seven nine three two three eight four six two six four three three eight three two seven five zero . . .

Twilight fell differently on overcast days. When the sun was out, it stretched over the earth, wrapping each tree, each car and house and blade of grass in its pink-orange arms until it tumbled beneath the horizon, the light snapping away in an instant. But when clouds packed the sky and the world was already ashen, the darkness crept in slowly until suddenly it was dark, and no one had noticed it coming. That was how Matthew felt as he and Skye reached the church, sat on the green wood steps leading to the front door—the world went black between Skye's confession and this place, and he hadn't realized it until he looked up the road and saw two bright headlights inching toward them.

The Durango stopped, still idling, and Benjamin stepped from the car. He said something, in the shadows. Matthew couldn't make it out. But Skye nodded and stood, put her arms behind her back, one wrist over the other, hands forming wings. As Benjamin took handcuffs from his belt, Matthew jumped off the steps, grabbed the deputy's arm. "I have to, Matt," he said.

Matthew gave Benjamin a little shove, yanked his pad from his pocket and fell back onto the steps. He wrote, John 16:33, folded the page over and over until it was more a tube than a rectangle and he couldn't fold it anymore. Benjamin closed Skye in the back seat, walked around the car. Matthew yanked the handle—*please, please*—he needed to give Skye his note.

"You can't get in there," Benjamin said, coming back around to him.

Give this to her. Promise me. Matthew opened the deputy's hand and crammed the paper ball into it.

Benjamin's fingers tightened around it. He scrunched his lips, nodded. "Get in front. I'll give you a lift home."

But Matthew shook his head and ran, down the road alone until the Dodge Durango passed him, and then alone again.

Matthew entered the house to Jaylyn screaming at Heather, Heather screaming at Jaylyn, Sienna complaining as they kept crossing in front of the television, where Tom and Jerry raced around the globe. Lacie, middle fingers jammed deep into her ears, shouted, "Stop, you two. Why won't you stop?"

When they saw him, it did stop, and Heather asked, "Where's Skye?"

Sheriff's office, he wrote.

"What for? What's going on?"

Maybe you should just go down there.

Heather looked at him, opening her mouth as if she wanted to yell some more, but instead slung her purse over her arm and said, "Put the girls to bed," before leaving.

"You better tell me," Jaylyn said.

"No," he managed.

"I can't understand anything that comes out of your stupid mouth."

Understand this. I'm not telling you.

"Retard."

Jaylyn stomped off to her bedroom, cordless phone in hand, and Matthew sent Sienna with her.

"It's too early," she whined.

I don't care. I'm tired and want the couch.

"You've been so mean today."

Good.

"Jerk."

"I don't think you're a jerk," Lacie said. "Or a retard."

He picked her up and spun her, once, twice, three times, until he couldn't keep his balance. Then he helped her brush her teeth and tucked her into Heather's bed. She slept there now; his aunt needed a warm body next to her.

But he couldn't sleep, didn't try. He waited in the dark, eyes open and toward the door, and when he saw a crack of light, he turned his head into the back cushion, pretending to sleep. Even when the brightness penetrated his closed lids he still didn't move. Not until someone wrenched him by the arm, onto the floor.

"Get out," Heather said. Shouted. He knew by the tendons straining through her neck, the wide-open mouth, like the Munch print Abbi once showed him. He sprung to his feet, and with one hand snapped open his pad. His aunt tore it from him, hurled it across the room.

"I don't want any of your notes. I want you out of my house."

She hefted his clothing tote from beside the couch and, standing on the stoop, flung it into the night. The girls appeared from their rooms, Jaylyn pale and confused against the white wall, Lacie sobbing, Sienna holding on to her.

"Now go," Heather said.

He went, shoeless, into the playground, and the door shut behind him. He gathered his clothes, pulled on a sweatshirt, and closed the rest in the plastic bin. Then he tried to balance the bin on the handlebars of his bicycle. He rode ten feet before the tote spilled forward. He picked everything up again and, after shoving the bin into the shrubs next to the building, rode down the street toward the church, pedals poking into the soles of his feet.

The building was unlocked; he knew it would be. He thought he'd sleep on a pew but must have made more noise than he realized. Perhaps the door hinges gave him away, squealing in the night, or his bike when he dropped it in the gravel. Whatever it was, the pastor found him and, without a question, guided Matthew to the back bedroom in the parsonage.

Chapter THIRTY-FIVE

They stood together just inside the door of the family services office, Abbi's body rigid, Silvia caged against her, tears dripping silently off her jawbone and onto the sleeping baby's head. Benjamin, no more than a hand's length away, didn't dare reach for her.

Four days. It had taken only four days to undo the past four months.

He didn't have a chance to explain to Abbi, to soften the blow. He had called her to say he wouldn't be coming home until late, and as soon as she heard his voice, she understood.

"What's going on?" she had asked.

"I don't know yet."

"You know enough to be at work still."

He sighed. "We have Silvia's mother in custody."

"Just her mother?"

"Abbi."

"No. No, no, no. You fix this, Ben, I mean it. You don't come home until you fix it."

But when he had walked into the living room a few minutes after one in the morning, Abbi was sitting in the chair facing the door, Silvia sleeping in her lap. He bent down to hug her, but she said, "Don't touch me." So he went to bed alone, in his clothes, watching fuzzy gray spots spark as he stared at the ceiling in the darkness, until the first splashes of sun spilled over the windowsills and he abandoned all hope of sleep, only to find Abbi still in the chair, still stiff and alert, eyes on the door.

"No one's coming today," he said, and she wept, clamping her torso to her knees, gulping and wheezing and pressing the baby into her belly until Silvia, too, began to wail. He'd never seen Abbi break down like that before. If she ever cried, it was a few tears and done. "No sense wasting time on the wet stuff," she'd always said.

Now he took an envelope from his shirt pocket, handed it to Cheyenne. "We wrote a few things down for the Whalens. About Silvia. Things they might find helpful to know."

"I'll make sure they get it," she said.

"We'd like to see him."

"Ben—"

"Just ask."

She nodded and left the room, returning minutes later with a lumpy, dark-haired boy and a lumpier woman, both of whom Benjamin had met numerous times since he'd moved here. The boy wore a clip-on tie and cleared his throat several times before shaking Benjamin's hand. "I don't suppose there's any good thing to say right now," Jared said.

He's been told. One of the other deputies, or Cheyenne—someone— let this kid know Silvia had been loved.

Benjamin knew a few things about him, too. Knew he was the first in his family to go to college, accepted to a handful of schools but chose Dakota State University to be close to his mother. Knew his father had died when he was in junior high. Had a Marine for an older brother, a sister who married right out of high school, with three kids and a husband who worked as an assistant manager at Taco John's. Decent people. Salt of the earth.

Salt in his wounds.

"I suppose not," Benjamin said.

Jared looked at Abbi, at Silvia. "She never told me. Skye, I mean. I didn't . . ." He unclipped his tie, rolled it into his pants pocket. Opened the top button of his shirt. "I wish she just would have told me."

"Well, you know now." The words came out ugly, sponging up the bile in his throat. He was the sore loser.

"She'll have a good home, I promise you that. My mom's gonna move to Madison, watch her when I'm in class. And I'll do . . . whatever I need to do. I know how to do that. My dad, he was a good man. He showed me what it means . . . to be a man."

Yeah, right. The kid turned eighteen a couple of months ago, and Benjamin was back to feeling old, ancient, really. He expected Jared, after a few sleepless nights, would feel the years piling on, too.

They stood around trying not to look at Abbi, at the baby in her arms. The grandmother whispered to her son.

"Well," Cheyenne said finally, "the Whalens have a bit of a ride home."

Benjamin popped his jaw, stretching it as far to the right as it could go, nodded. He turned to Abbi, slid his arms against hers, beneath Silvia. Abbi wouldn't let go. Her hazel eyes held his—they seemed gray today, matching her shirt and her mood—pleading with him, accusing him. She blamed him, for bringing Silvia into their home, for letting her leave.

I'm sorry, he mouthed, pressing his arms up into the infant's body until he was supporting all the weight and Abbi nothing at all. She dropped her arms and went. He listened to her footfalls down the hallway. One door crashed open, then another, more quietly than the first. He heard both snap closed.

I've lost her.

He couldn't bear to wake the baby. "Good-bye, sweet *kanyaratna. Me tujhashi prem karto,*" he whispered, kissing her on the forehead before holding her out to Jared, like a doctor in the delivery room. "Here."

The boy untangled his hands from his pockets and took the small body against his, bumping and shifting her until she was settled in his arms. Silvia arched her back, ballooning her lips in a sleepy pucker before rubbing her face and sighing, nodding off again. "She's heavy," Jared said.

"Sixteen pounds."

"I didn't expect . . ." The boy's voice disintegrated as he looked down on her. He sniffled, turned his head and wiped his eye on his shoulder. "She looks like her mother. Good thing."

"Just . . . enjoy her," Benjamin said.

"Mr. Patil, we, I mean, my mom and me talked about it, and this isn't anywhere near anything much, but, if you want to, we'd like you and your wife to come visit sometime. If you want to. And we can send pictures and stuff. E-mails, or whatever. To let you know she's doing good."

He meant it sincerely, Benjamin knew. But it burned, seeing his daughter in another man's arms. Just like he still woke some mornings and—throwing back the blankets and settling his feet on the cool wood floor—was startled to see his deformed foot, he expected he'd be reaching for Silvia in the bed at night, brushing the back of his hand in the air where the bassinet had been, frantically wondering where she'd gone before realizing he never had her to begin with.

His, but not his.

"I appreciate that," he said. "Really. But I think I'll have to talk to Abbi and let you know."

Jared nodded. "I'm sorry."

"You and me both."

⁓

When they pulled into the driveway she was out of the car before he had a chance to switch it off, and he didn't, leaving it to idle as she hopped the two patio steps in one stride. At the front door, she turned back to him, and he opened the driver's side door and stood behind it, guarded, one foot on the blacktop, head above the window. "I'm going to . . . take a drive," he said.

She stared at him for a moment, then shut herself in the house.

And he drove, sped, needle close to one hundred. The highway stretched before him, billboards cluttering the side of the road. *Free Donuts for Newlyweds at Wall Drug. Wall Drug—80 Ft. Dinosaur. Have You Dug Wall Drug?* He passed half a dozen lonely cars, glancing in at the drivers. No singles. All had at least two passengers, most with children in the back seats.

He hurt all over—not physically. His bones had been jarred when Stephen's Humvee overturned, every muscle fiber bruised by the blasts around him. But this wasn't the same. Now he was all dry veins and dead space inside, as if even his cells knew Silvia had kept him alive, and now they desiccated in mourning.

Badlands 12 miles.

The rocks rose up around him, and after parking the Durango, he walked, wearing his church shoes and dress pants, straight out to the first hill. He climbed it, the setting sun's shadows making it difficult to discern the rolls and dips in the terrain. His shoe snagged in a divot, and he fell forward, skinning his palms, listening to the familiar sound of loose stones cascading over the ledges. He examined his hands, pinpricks of blood in the dust, shook the sting away. Then he ran with his imperfect gait—a limp, a shimmy—down the footpath, between the towering mounds, kicking through low brush, ignoring the threat of rattlesnakes.

The cool autumn air scraped his windpipe, and he swallowed to alleviate the metallic dryness. He stopped, looking up at the steep face to his left. He began his ascent, arms quivering as he lifted his body over shelves and outcroppings. Sweat and dust burned his eyes. He lost his footing, slipping down the rocks on his belly, fingers grappling for any hold, and when the friction slowed him, he flattened his cheek to the rock, arms spread wide, hugging it, breathing deep, his heartbeat the loudest sound around him. His muscles twitched from the fear surging through his blood, until finally he calmed and began to climb again.

He reached the top, panting, hands on his knees. Then he straightened and, digging his fingernails into his raw palms, bellowed until he emptied his lungs of air. The sun, a compact red disc teetering on the horizon, quivered with his cry. The clouds rippled gray and pink and silver above him, choppy like the sea in Boston Harbor on that windswept day, when his parents took him to see the USS *Constitution* and made him walk the Freedom Trail in the rain. Too much sky. Enough to drown in.

He sat and waited in the gloaming, still able to see the skeletons of the buttes in the distance, confessing the glory of creation. He bit the side of his tongue to keep from shouting his confession.

He hated God.

This was beyond a dark night of the soul, beyond doubt and feeling disconnected. *How did I get here?*

After Stephen died, Ben had woken up in Germany, and then the U.S. government shipped him back to the good ol' States, where he spent two months rehabilitating at Walter Reed, learning how to walk without toes. He kept his Bible in the drawer beside his bed, but didn't open it. Couldn't. He didn't want to read the promises, refused to feel Christ's love for him. He was mad at God, and himself— for forsaking Stephen. *"Greater love has no one than this, that he lay down his life for his friends."*

Yeah, right. He had cowered behind the Humvee and thought only of his own skin. He owed God more than that. So he pushed Him away, pushed and pushed until it was no wonder he couldn't find his way back to Him.

Benjamin had heard the stories of the persecuted church, and of ordinary people, how the trials they faced drew them to the Lord. His struggles tore him away, and it was because he'd always had a comfortable, easy journey. Nothing had prepared him for the upheaval that true pain could wreak on the soul. His faith had no calluses.

The moon emerged from the cloud cover, a bright, thin crescent, and behind that the remainder of the moon glowed ashen in the earth's reflected light. Earthshine. Some people called it the old moon in the new moon's arms. He saw his own arms, around Silvia.

⌒

He woke up, cold under his jacket, stiff in the back seat of the Durango, his good black pants torn at the knee and dusty. Sitting up, he groaned, flipped into the front and started the engine. Cranked on the heat.

He had spent the night in a motel parking lot, could have rented a room but had no desire to be comfortable. The corners of his lips split when he yawned. He wiped them with his thumb, drove to the closest convenience store and bought two coffees. Made it about eight miles outside Temple when he noticed flashing lights in his rearview mirror. He eased onto the shoulder, opened his window. Wesley ambled over to the passenger side, let himself in. "I called the house looking for you."

"What did Abbi tell you?"

"Nothing. She didn't answer. Someone else did, told me you weren't home. What you doing here, Ben?"

"Driving."

"You should be with your wife."

Benjamin sipped his coffee, scalding his tongue. He turned the key back toward him so he could put the window up. "I'm heading there."

"Were you?"

"Yes."

"Why weren't you with her when she needed you?"

"She doesn't need me."

"She's hurting as much as you are. Probably more. Her baby gone. Her husband gone, too."

"Silvia wasn't her baby," Benjamin mumbled.

"I'm guessing biology doesn't matter. Seems you already got that one figured out on your own, though."

"Get out."

Wesley nudged the door open, a shrill buzzer echoing in the truck. "Go home to your wife."

Chapter THIRTY-SIX

After Benjamin left her, just drove away and left her, Abbi leaned against the fat, white molding in the doorway between the living room and kitchen, and slid down the slick wood to the floor. She stayed there, listening. There was nothing to hear.

She'd spent the past four months worrying about Silvia—was she crying, hungry, wet, tired, needing to be cuddled?—having her hanging on her body, on her mind. Abbi felt naked. All this time she'd been hiding behind the baby, too. *Such a big responsibility for an itty-bitty babe. How sick is that? Save Benjamin. Save me. No wonder you took her. . . .*

Abbi crawled from the floor to the couch, her head pushed up against one arm, her toes skimming the other. The drawstring at her waist felt suddenly tight. She shifted, but it still cut into her skin. The knot opened as she pulled one side of the ribbon, and she stretched the skirt as wide as possible, looking down at her stomach. She knew each roll and lump on her body, and even though Benjamin refused to keep a scale in the house, she could tell the difference between 150 pounds and 170. She was at the high end now. Not enough exercise, not enough laxatives. Too much attention to Silvia and not enough to herself.

"You dumb, fat slob."

She went to the kitchen and downed two bowls of granola and soy milk, then the crumbs at the bottom of the box. She couldn't handle open boxes, nearly empty containers. They pestered her, and she was unable to get them out of her mind, there, in the cupboards or freezer, waiting for her to finish them. Then she ate a bag of flax chips, four slices of toast with coconut oil and sea salt, the remainder of the baby carrots, and an avocado. In the bathroom she pulled her skirt low on the hips, hauled up her shirt and twisted it into her bra, her stomach hard with food. She stood sideways in front of the mirror and hated herself, the bulge in her middle. Her jeans, she needed to try them on. She wriggled into the size tens; they wouldn't zip. She peeled them off, kicked them off her foot and onto the bed, and tried on the twelves. They were tight, too tight. When did she try them on last? She couldn't remember. A month. More than that. A few weeks after Silvia showed up.

She searched all her hiding places—her winter boots, the underside of the nightstand drawer, the hidden pocket of her rarely used camping backpack. There were no pills in the house. She grabbed her car keys and drove to the Food Mart, ignored the *Hellos* and the *Are you doing okay?*s and headed to the pharmacy aisle. She knew where they were—first the pain relievers, then the cold remedies, then the antacids and laxatives. She picked up a bottle of natural senna, squeezed it in her hand; it fit there, round and smooth and cool. But she tucked it back in line. Needing more than that today, she plucked a box of Fleet off the shelf. One hundred tablets. She read the ingredients. *Bisacodyl 5 mg.* Some horrid, gut-burning chemical. She paid for them and ripped them open before she was out of the store, tossing the empty box in the garbage can outside.

In her car, she pushed the tiny orange dots through the foil backing, one after another until she'd emptied one plastic square. She sucked all twenty-five pills from the palm of her hand; they stuck to her tongue, sweet, like candy. She poked out another twenty-five and swallowed those, too. Then she drove home, dropped the empty laxative packaging out the window, stuck the full ones in the elastic of her waistband. She felt the little bumps against her skin. They calmed her. She knew she could eat another fifty pills' worth of food before having to go back to the store. How much was that? In college, before she met Benjamin, she had taken eight senna tablets a day, whether she needed them or not. If she ran out, she could think of nothing but getting to the pharmacy and buying more, the empty bottle haunting her, each forkful of food an adversary she could feel adhering to her fat cells.

Abbi drove past the red car on the shoulder in front of her house as she pulled into the driveway, the sporty kind, low to the ground and feisty. A reporter, she thought. But, no. Lauren appeared.

"Hi," she said, not moving toward her.

"Nice car."

"I borrowed it. Mine's in the shop."

"What are you doing here?"

"I heard. On the news."

"You came for me?"

"Yeah."

They made their way to the kitchen. Lauren filled the teakettle with water and cranked the burner to high. "Where's Ben?" she asked.

"He ran away. Like always."

The kettle's wet bottom sizzled as the stove heated, and Abbi reached atop the refrigerator for a box of tea, standing on tiptoe. Her skirt shifted and the Fleet packages rattled down her leg. Lauren picked them up, fanned them in her fingers like a couple of aces.

"I couldn't help it," Abbi said.

"Com'ere," Lauren said, pulling her close. Abbi started to cry, trembling a little, sniffling.

The kettle screeched, and Abbi moved out of Lauren's embrace to move it off the burner. She took out her stoneware teapot, the one she'd made—the one Benjamin, soon after returning from

Afghanistan, dropped and broke the spout off and then tried to glue back on without her knowing. She knew, but never said anything. He had held his breath each time she used it, always offering to wash it for her so she wouldn't find the crack in the glaze, until finally she decided not to take it out unless he wasn't home.

There had been times she had screamed at him for chipping other bowls and cups and platters she'd made, literally gone into rages about him not caring about things that were pieces of her. But that was before he'd left for Afghanistan, when pottery seemed important. How could he know she didn't give a flying flip about some cooked clay with a bit of paint spattered over it now? She wanted him whole.

She wanted him home.

She steeped some lime-ginger rooibos in the pot and poured a cup for Lauren, one for herself. They sat, first at the table, then in the living room when the chairs grew hard and the tea cold. And when Abbi stretched out on the couch, Lauren cleaned the kitchen and left her be. She loved that about Lauren. She didn't force things; she wasn't afraid of the silences.

The cramps woke her. Subtle at first, slithery through her intestines, with a sort of gassy nausea in her middle. She wormed upright, pulled her knees into her chest and burped out some air. Groaned softly.

"How many?" Lauren asked. She was watching a movie on her notebook computer.

"You don't want to know."

"Can I do anything?"

Abbi shook her head, groaned again, in disgust this time. "I'm so stupid."

And then the cramps came hard and fast, a jackhammer, and her whole body tensed in the wave of pain. She held her breath, squeezing the edge of the couch cushion with one hand. She tried to get to the bathroom before the cramping came again, but she was too slow; she squatted in the hallway, panting as the pain subsided, and crawled to the toilet.

The diarrhea poured out of her, like water. She wet a washcloth and cleaned herself, but feeling the familiar spasms in her gut, sat back down on the toilet.

She stayed in the bathroom, sitting on the floor between bouts, wedged in the corner where the wall and tub met. Lauren gave her a pillow, a blanket; she waited outside the door, reading to her—Psalms and Lamentations—washed the soiled towels and brought her clean ones. Finally, when the pangs produced only dry pressure, she stumbled across the hall to bed, changed her clothes. "Don't leave," she said.

"I won't. Just let me call my parents and let them know." She did, and then flopped on her back on Abbi's side of the bed. Abbi balled up on Benjamin's side, near the empty bassinet, in his smell, sporty and sour and thick. Her shirt rose, exposing a half-moon of flesh above the elastic waistband of her flannel pants, and she shivered from the air and pills.

⌒

She woke to the smell of meat. The bed was empty beside her, but she heard whistling from the kitchen, the *beep beep beep* of the microwave. She wound the extra blanket around her from ribs to ankles and followed the flesh-filled smoke down the hall.

"Carnivore," she said.

"I'm surprised you keep bacon in the house," Lauren said. "All those poor little piggies."

"Ben buys it."

"Want something else? I'm cooking."

"I can't. It will go right through me." And she tugged the belt loop of Lauren's jeans. "Thank you. For staying."

"Abbi, this is the church. We're called to bear each other's burdens.

Where else would I be but here?" Lauren flipped the bacon. "Mom's dropping off the kids here. She has an appointment, and I didn't want to leave you. I wasn't sure how long you'd sleep."

"You don't have to stay now. I'm okay."

"I don't think so."

"I'm going in the shower. I probably stink." Abbi hiked the blanket a bit higher. "Lauren, how did you get over being angry with God?"

Her friend plunged her hands into her pockets, leaned back against the counter and sighed. "God. He did it. Not me. I probably could have stayed ticked off forever. But He didn't leave me there. If you step out and trust Him, He'll do the same. He'll show you that you don't need anything else but Him."

"I do trust Him."

"This coming from the woman who eats Ex-Lax like candy."

Lauren's words devoured her, forcing her faith down the throat, through the stomach and intestines, coating it with half-digested excuses and gooey truth. She couldn't remember a time when she'd gone to God first. It was always the refrigerator, the laxatives, the road. And then, after she had purged and exercised herself dry, she went to Him, insides empty, head clear, dust and sweat washed away.

Oh, she prayed while she ran, but she wasn't running to pray. She ran to fit into her size tens; the prayer was incidental, something to boost her spiritual ego. *Yes, I prayed today for an hour. And I read my Bible, fasted on Sunday, and didn't kill a single animal, contribute to global warming, or support a Chinese sweatshop this week. Go me.*

She locked the door and twisted on the water, unwrapped herself. Then she kneeled on the blanket and, forehead against the floor, begged forgiveness, laying her idols before the Lord. She thought of the men who prophesied in Jesus' name, who healed the sick and cast out demons, the ones He told to depart from Him.

"Oh, please, please. Don't say you never knew me."

The shower ran cold by the time she stepped in. She washed

gently, raw from the night before, and dried off, wrapping the blanket back around her to go into the bedroom and dress. A knock at the door. She peeked out the crack, and Lauren said, "There's a woman here to see you. She said she's your neighbor and she has pie."

Janet. "Don't let her in."

"I already did."

"Fine, okay. Just tell her . . . I'll be there in a minute."

When she returned to the kitchen, Lauren and Janet each sat with an untouched piece of pie in front of them.

"I don't know if you'd feel like eating or not, but when I don't know what else to do, cook, remember? Want some?"

"Ah, not really. Not right now."

"No eggs. No butter, no milk. Nothing you don't eat."

"I appreciate it, but my stomach isn't up for it."

Another knock on the door. Lauren jumped up, banging her thigh on the table, tripping over the chair leg. Katie dashed in and wrapped her arms around Abbi's pelvis, her head ramming her sensitive stomach. "Oh, pie. Can I have some?"

"Abbi?" Lauren held Stevie, who grabbed for the table lamp, and cried when his mother moved out of reach.

"Go. Go. The kids don't need to be cooped up here."

"You sure?"

"Yeah, it's fine."

"Okay, then. You call if you need anything. I mean it."

"I will," Abbi said, bumping her cheek against Lauren's, her lips smacking at the air.

She wiped the crumbs from the table to keep her hands busy; then she took the broom from the pantry and swept them into a pile. The cat sniffed at the mound, walked through it, tracking dust and crust morsels back across the floor. Abbi didn't bother sweeping again. She leaned the broom handle against the counter, and as soon as she stepped away, it slid and bounced off the stainless steel trash-can lid, echoing like a drum. She jerked at the sound even though she'd watched the broom fall. "I'm sorry. I'm really not up for company today."

"This is the day you need it most," Janet said, sliding a tract across the table to her, dark blue with a lighter blue tear in the center, and white script asking, *Why Did This Happen to Me?* "Jesus sees. Turn to Him."

"Janet, don't do this now."

"I know it hurts. I know you don't understand the big picture. But He does. And even in this time of hurt He deserves to be praised. 'The Lord gave, the Lord has taken away. Blessed be the name of the Lord.' That's what His holy Word says."

"Does it now?" Abbi snatched the dishrag from the sink and squeezed. "I must have missed that part, given that I'm only one of those 'God is love' people. But that's okay. That's fine. You're here to help me see the error of my ways. And while you're at it, why don't you tell me how you felt when your child was ripped from your arms. Oh, that's right. You don't have any kids. You praise God for that lately?"

Good one, Abbi. Thirty minutes ago you were prostrate before the Lord, begging forgiveness. Now look at you. Yeah, you meant what you said.

Janet stood, slowly, a stunned flatness glazing her eyes. "I . . . I'm just going to go. You can return the pie pan wh-when you're finished with it."

She went, and Abbi took the pan and a fork, stomped down on the waste can's foot pedal, and scraped every last bit of pie into the trash.

Chapter THIRTY-SEVEN

Breakfast tasted better when he didn't have to make it, Matthew decided, the fat, soggy waffles drowned in syrup and margarine on his plate. He cut them on the grid lines, dividing each one into nine even squares. Mrs. Larsen added batter to her cast-iron waffle maker, dropped the lid, and put it on the burner. "There's more coming," she said.

In the two weeks he'd stayed with them, Mrs. Larsen made breakfast every day. Sometimes pancakes, sometimes ham and eggs and hash browns. Waffles. Cheesy casseroles. Matthew didn't think she allowed cold cereal in the house.

He saw the syrup ripple in the little glass pitcher in front of him, looked up. Pastor Larsen, dressed in a pale green shirt and striped tie, had sat down at the end of the table. Matthew had never seen him without a tie—even at night, reading his newspaper with socks off and feet up; then he loosened it so the polyester hung slack around his neck, but he didn't remove it.

"I forgot to tell you I got a ride for you for Monday. Posie Peppmuller said she'd be there to pick you up at two thirty." Pastor Larsen winked. "You know that means she'll be waiting at ten to two."

Matthew nodded, signed *thank you.*

"We're glad to do it."

He hadn't taken the medi-bus to dialysis in two weeks, either. The first day he'd stayed at the Larsen house, he scribbled a note to

the pastor, asking him to call the center to change his pickup loca-
tion. He didn't want to wait at the apartment complex, though he
could have.

"I can take you, pick you up," Pastor Larsen said.

I don't want to be any trouble.

"It's no trouble."

If you're not too busy. I can just tell them
the change when I get there today.

"Don't do that. We'll get someone to take you wherever you
need to go. Whenever."

That is being trouble.

"How long have you been going to that place?"

A year. About.

"Every day?"

Matthew shook his head. 3 days a week.

"How come you never told anyone about it?"

He shrugged.

"It's no secret that we've not been the best we could be toward
you," Pastor Larsen said. He patted the side of Matthew's head. "We
told ourselves we didn't want to stick our noses where they didn't
belong, but really we had no clue what to do for you, boy. This is
something we can do. Let us."

So Matthew did. And he had to admit he'd enjoyed the shorter
rides, getting home a bit more than an hour earlier each night, leaving
school only twenty minutes before the end of the day.

He had a bed now, too. And a bedroom, a closet for his things, a
desk and dresser. He wasn't sure how long he'd stay with the Larsens.
Pastor said as long as he needed to be there. Matthew didn't expect
Heather would let him back into the apartment. Ever.

The first day after Skye's arrest, Matthew had gone to school
despite his exhaustion and the putrid feeling in his gut. He wanted

to see Lacie, and he needed to see the nurse. Heather hadn't tossed his medication out with him. The pastor brought him early, and he waited on the sidewalk until Lacie bounded off the bus and into his arms. "Mommy said bad things about you."

He pressed her into his rib cage, rocked her back and forth. Sienna walked past, eyes thin slits of disdain. And then Jaylyn, hair still wet from her morning shower and sleek in a ponytail. She carried two backpacks. Hers. And his.

"Hey," she said. "Thought you might need this."

Thanks.

"Your pills are in there. I don't know if I got all of them. I was . . . in a hurry."

I'll check.

"You okay?"

I guess.

"You have a place to stay?"

What do you care?

"Lacie, go inside," Jaylyn said, prying the little girl's arms from around Matthew's waist.

"I don't want to," Lacie said.

"I don't care. Go."

"Wait for me Monday, too, Matty." Matthew nodded, and Lacie stuck her tongue out at her sister before disappearing into the school.

Jaylyn slipped her ponytail through her O-shaped fingers, and when she got to the end she stuck her hair in her mouth, chewed it. She wore no makeup. "Lacie cried all night for you." He turned his head, and she stepped around in front of him. "Ma will come around. She will. She's just, you know, being all mama lion."

Doesn't matter.

"Matt, I . . . Well, class time, you know. I'll see you."

He had nodded and watched her walk off, alone.

Two weeks later, he still stood on the curb, waiting for the bus and Lacie's hug, Sienna's angry glare. He received both, and Jaylyn again needed to twist his youngest cousin away from him to get her into the building.

"Jaylyn said you could come over today," Lacie told Matthew. Her little cold hands snaked up the back of his shirt, knotting together at the small of his back so Jaylyn couldn't pull her off too easily.

He looked at both of them.

"Ma's working late. So, if you want to, you can," Jaylyn said.

Why, do you need me to watch the girLS? With both him and Skye gone, he knew the brunt of the responsibility fell on her. Something new. He wanted to believe that the truce between them had grown from her realization of all he'd done for her sisters. Her, as well. But he still didn't trust her.

"It's not like that."

Sienna wiLL teLL.

"There's no secret. I mentioned it to Ma already. She doesn't care. She knows she screwed up. She just won't say it, ya know? If you moved your stuff back in tomorrow, she wouldn't blink twice. It would be like you'd never left."

"You have to come home, Matty," Lacie said, bouncing up and down in place. "Jaylyn doesn't swing with me, and she leaves big dry clumps in the macaroni and cheese. And she rips all the snarls out of my hair, and—"

"Enough. I have a complex already," Jaylyn said. "So, you coming?"

Lacie clasped her hands together under her chin. Her bangs tangled in her eyelids as she jumped around him, blinking. She swiped them away. "Please, please, please?"

Okay. But just a visit. And only if ELLie can come.

"Matty and Ellie, sitting in a tree, K-I-S-S-I-N-G," Lacie said.

"We'll see you then," Jaylyn said, pulling her sister into the building by the strap of her backpack.

"First comes love. Then comes marriage. Then comes—"

Jaylyn clamped her hand over Lacie's mouth. "Stop."

Matthew already knew the rest.

Then comes baby in the baby carriage.

He missed Silvia. But more so, he missed Abbi and the deputy. There were people now trying to know him—Pastor Larsen, his wife, the kids at school since he'd developed a bit of celebrity status—but the Patils had been there for him first. They'd cared for him, and he'd trampled them with his convoluted sense of moral absolutes.

He knew he did the *right* thing. But was the right thing ever the wrong thing? He wasn't certain anymore.

Ellie waited for him outside homeroom. "What's wrong?" she asked when he didn't return her smile.

What are you doing after school?

"Drama rehearsal. Why?"

Can you skip?

She picked a long, dark hair from his shirt. Lacie's hair. "If you need me to."

I do.

"Okay, then." Her forehead creased, freckles bunching together. "Want to tell me what's going on?"

Lacie wants me to visit.

"Matt, I—"

"Hey, Savoie." Teddy Derboven held out his fist, and Matthew bumped it with his own. "You, me, lunch," he said, and disappeared into the classroom.

Ellie shook her head.

What? I don't care that he failed algebra.

"He cares that you didn't."

Stop.

"Vanity of vanities."

Ha, ha.

"You laugh now. Next week he'll be asking to copy your government homework."

Speaking from experience?

"Maybe."

You can copy my homework anytime.

"Like I need to."

⟶

They walked to his aunt's apartment after school. It took half an hour, but Matthew didn't care. He spent the entire time with his fingers laced through Ellie's, their connected arms a pendulum between them, her silver Möbius bracelet cutting into his inner wrist. He loved her, but he hadn't told her. He didn't know if she felt the same way and wouldn't be the first to say it. At least not yet. Whenever he thought about it, he wanted to run over to the Patils' house and ask Abbi her advice. In reality, Abbi probably wouldn't speak to him again.

He didn't blame her.

Lacie waited on the stoop for him, thin jacket open, no hat. "Matty, push me," she said, darting toward the swing. He caught her before she got there, whirled her around and knelt in front of her, his fingers working the metal teeth into the zipper.

"It won't close," she said. "It's broken. But I'm not cold."

She wriggled onto the swing, and he gave her several underdoggies, holding her high in the air before running beneath her. Then he pushed her feet as she pumped her legs forward, straight at him. She giggled when he pretended she'd kicked him in the nose. Ellie watched, leaning against the building.

After a while, Lacie jumped off the swing, hands bright pink.

"Okay, I am cold. You're coming in, right? I want to show you my spelling test. Mommy hung it on the 'frigerator 'cause I got a ninety-two. I really only got a ninety, but then I spelled the super secret bonus word right, so Mrs. Swell gave me two more points. Know what the bonus word was?"

Matthew shrugged.

"Paper. Only me and Darrell Pendleton got it right. But he gets everything right, so it doesn't count much for him. Know how I knew it? It was on my pencil." She pulled him through the door and unzipped her backpack. "See? Paper Mate. I guess it's sorta cheating. But not really. Come see. There's a butterfly sticker on it, and it gets all sparkly when you shake it."

He looked at the test and gave Lacie a squeeze. She grabbed the paper and showed it to Ellie. "See? I can be smart like Matty, too."

"That's pretty smart," Ellie said.

Sienna threw her empty Pepsi bottle at them. "I can't hear," she said from the couch, TV on.

The apartment was more of a mess than usual, the kitchen counter piled with dirty pans and dishes. Two full bags of garbage, black plastic stretched almost gray, leaned against the overflowing pail. Sticky splotches dotted the kitchen table, some fuzzy with lint, others crusted over. And stuff. Just lots of random things dropped everywhere, and left there.

"Matty, make macaroni and cheese for me. Please, please," Lacie said.

He nodded, pulling up his sleeves, and Lacie said, "Don't start yet. Let me get Jaylyn so you can show her how to do it right."

Without being asked, Ellie rinsed the sponge, squeezed it out. Smelled it. She opened the cabinet beneath the sink and found a cello-wrapped package of sponges, pushed the old one into the trash can, and then washed the table. Matthew boiled water, and Jaylyn came into the room.

"Sorry, I didn't know you were here yet," she said.

"Watch him," Lacie said.

"I will," Jaylyn said.

Lacie moved her mouth, shaking her head and shoulder, scowling. She hooked each corner of her lips with her fingers when Jaylyn turned to the stove, stretching her mouth, teeth and gums exposed. Matthew chuckled.

"She made a face, didn't she?" Jaylyn asked. "She's such a brat these days."

Ellie started on the dishes, and Matthew grabbed one of the freshly washed pots, added milk and butter, and the orange powdered cheese. He whisked until the mixture thickened and bubbled, and poured it over the strained pasta.

"That's too much effort for Kraft," Jaylyn said.

But not too much for Lacie.

He spooned the elbows into a bowl and slid it across the table to his cousin, sending a spoon down after it. He prepared another dish for Sienna, but set her place with a fork. Both girls got a cup of milk, and he cut the last apple and dropped a few slices on two saucers near the macaroni bowls. *Want some?*

"Not now," Jaylyn said.

He held the pot up toward Ellie.

"Sure, I'll eat," she said.

He gave her a bowl and peeled a tangerine for her, too.

She wiggled her eyebrows at him. "Nutritious and monochromatic."

I don't know about the nutritious part.

She smiled, squeezed his arm.

Jaylyn hovered while he finished tidying the kitchen, wiping counters and putting dishes away. He spilled the remaining pasta into a Tupperware and left it on the counter, one corner of the cover open so condensation would dissipate.

Ellie chatted with all the girls, engaging even Sienna. He wasn't surprised. Ellie sparkled, and it was infectious. They finished eating, and Lacie dragged Ellie down the hall, into her bedroom. Sienna followed, and before disappearing around the corner, Matthew saw her tell her sister, "You better not touch my nail polish."

"You're pretty popular 'round school these days," Jaylyn said, taking a Yoplait from the refrigerator. She peeled off the tin lid and licked it.

Matthew shrugged. The double whammy of dating Ellie and turning in Skye had transformed him into some sort of local celebrity. Kids took time to talk to him now, sat with him at lunch. They invited him places. He couldn't say he hadn't enjoyed it a bit, maybe more, despite knowing how empty such curiosity could be, and how fleeting.

"Ellie's nice."

I know.

"She likes you."

He grinned, though he tried to hide it, turning his face against his shoulder.

Have you talked to Skye?

"She calls."

How is she?

"Holding her own. You gonna get out there?"

He shrugged.

"She asks about you. She's totally ticked at what Ma did."

Matthew looked at her. Did you know?

"No," Jaylyn said. "And yes. I mean, I wasn't surprised when I found out. I think the idea was there the whole time, even before the baby was found. I just didn't let myself go there."

He understood. He probably knew, too—and didn't want to know.

"So, are you coming home?"

It's hard work, isn't it?

"That's not why I'm asking."

Right. When was the last time someone did the dishes?

"Things are different when you're here, Matt. I'm not talking about the cleaning and cooking. It's . . . more than that."

I'm not sure yet. I kind of like the quiet.

"I don't blame you." Jaylyn scraped the last of the blueberry yogurt from the container, dropped the spoon into the sink. "I applied to college, you know."

Really?

"I mean, just MTCC, but it's more than I was planning. They have a radiology program. I can handle two more years of school. And I think . . . Well, I think now it's okay to want more. For myself, I mean."

Lacie darted into the kitchen, forehead slamming into Matthew's ribs. She twirled. "Ellie did it," she said, her hair intricately braided and her fingernails painted. "I look better than Sienna, don't I?" He saw the other two girls, Sienna with dark curls and lip gloss, Ellie with her hair clipped in all sorts of crazy directions, green eye shadow above one eye, purple above the other.

"Don't laugh," she said. "Your cousins have a future in cosmetology."

"Tell Sienna I look prettier, Matty," Lacie said.

"Do not," said Sienna.

"You both look gorgeous," Jaylyn said.

Everyone flinched suddenly, turning toward the front door. Matthew did the same; Aunt Heather stepped in, kicked off her heels and dropped her oversized bag on top of them. She noticed Matthew, nodded ever so subtly, and said, "Jaylyn, heat me up some meat loaf. I'm gonna change."

Matthew hugged both his younger cousins.

"Don't forget to wait for me tomorrow," Lacie said.

He gave her a double thumbs-up, and he and Ellie buttoned their coats to go, but not before he lugged both garbage bags to the curb.

"You okay?" Ellie asked, looping her arm around his.

Yes, he signed. She knew that one, learned more every day.

"You sure?"

~~Do you think I did the right~~ I mean, would you have done it, if it were you? Your sister? Would you have turned her in?

"I don't think so."

He froze, swallowed. His fingertips went cold and told himself to breathe, that he only imagined his throat closing up.

Ellie stopped, too. "No, Matt, I didn't mean—"

He brushed her away. Don't apologize. I asked.

"Matt, stop. I don't mean it like you're taking it."

You just told me I did the wrong thing.

"You're putting words in my mouth. I said I wouldn't have been able to do it." She took his hand. "That's why it was you."

And she kissed him.

Chapter THIRTY-EIGHT

He stacked the boxes, filled with baby clothing and toys, in the empty room and pushed them up against the dismantled crib. The Whalens didn't take many of the items Benjamin had offered them—a few outfits, a stuffed bunny, the bottles. The grandmother said they didn't need much, but Benjamin figured they didn't want anything smelling like the Patils' detergent, imprinted with their memory. Abbi leaned in the doorway, arms locked across her chest; she held her elbows and swayed a little. She always rocked when she stood now. Habit. Or perhaps she tried to soothe herself, the way Silvia would be comforted if she still slept in Abbi's arms.

"I'll take this stuff to the Salvation Army on Saturday," he said.

"I can do it tomorrow," Abbi said.

"I said I would."

"You said you would two weeks ago."

"And you could have had everything packed up two weeks ago. I'm not the only one who lives here."

"I wasn't sure you did that anymore."

Benjamin flipped another empty box over, a smaller one, stretched the packing tape across the bottom seam, tearing the cellophane with his teeth. "Just . . . don't."

Shrugging, she said, "Whatever."

Benjamin stood, knees cracking, and threw the tape dispenser into the box. "Fine."

He brought the box to the kitchen and opened what they both had been calling "the baby cabinet," a skinny door in the upper corner, next to the canned-vegetable turntable. *"Where are the bibs? In the baby cabinet. I can't find the diaper balm. Look in the baby cabinet . . ."* He swept everything from the shelves into the waiting cardboard box and sealed it, piled it atop the other ones, back in the bedroom. Abbi hadn't moved from the doorway.

"You can't erase her like that," she said.

"She's gone, Abbi. Gone. And we're right back to where we were before she came." Silvia's presence had been only a Band-Aid. The growth in their relationship, the changes for the better, the effort—it all had been nothing but a mirage, brought on by sleepless nights and the empty promises of the family Benjamin had always hoped for. The past weeks had been nothing short of torturous. He went to work. He poked at his food and avoided his wife. She did the same.

"We don't have to be," Abbi said.

He wanted to wrap himself around her, be comforted by her and to comfort her, and he wanted to scream and shake her until the loss emptied out of both of them. He wanted to beg her forgiveness for deserting her when she needed him, and he wanted to ignore her until she gave up on him, gave him the easy way out. "Don't put this all on me. You're not doing anything to change it, either."

"I know," Abbi said, then mumbled something else.

"What?" he said, the strip of tape he held folding over on itself. He couldn't peel it apart, crumpled it in his hand. It stuck to his fingers, and he shook his arm.

"I think I'm going to go stay with Genelise for a while."

"You're leaving?"

"I'm can't sit around and watch you slip away again."

"You are leaving." And, suddenly, the things he'd feared most in the world collided with reality, and Benjamin felt . . . What? Shock?

Relief? No, more like an odd satisfaction that he had brought this about, and had been right all along. "I knew you would."

"Don't you get it?" Abbi said, elbows at her sides, arms out like she wanted to strangle someone. She dug her finger into her face instead, bending at the waist and groaning, "*Burgh*. All I want is for you to make an attempt."

"Oh, yes. I forgot. Everyone else is so completely well adjusted after they lose a child. Thank you for that reminder."

She moved to him, close enough that he smelled her breath, heard the thickened saliva in her mouth. Ketosis breath, acrid and sticky from lack of food. She crammed her hands into her back pockets. "I lost her, too, you know."

He blew a puff of air through his nose. "You didn't even want her."

"Fine. You're absolutely right. I'm glad I don't have to deal with this bull anymore."

"Don't get all high-and-mighty. You're walking out on me."

"You're choosing that baby over me, Ben. Not even a baby. The memory of a child we knew might not ever be ours. What do you expect me to do?"

"Understand," he shouted. "No, just forget it. You stay here. I'll leave."

He took the Durango, and simply drove. Turning left, turning right, he didn't think about it. He'd left his wallet in the house, so he couldn't stay at a motel. It was too cold to spend all night in the truck. And anyone he could stay with—well, they'd take Abbi's side over his. And they should. He knew she was right.

He didn't want to lose her, too. But he didn't want to fight for her, either. The pain had made him lazy.

The gravel crackled beneath his tires, and he noticed the road ended. He parked, punched out the headlights, green steps disappearing in the night beyond his windshield. He closed the truck door quietly, pushing it until it was nearly shut, leaned against it until the inside dome light flickered out.

He was at the Methodist church, where it ended. Or began. He hoped the door was locked but knew it wouldn't be. It swung open and he went in, the back pew creaking as he dropped into it. He wouldn't pray. He refused.

Victor Hugo's words came to his head. *"There are thoughts which are prayers. There are moments when, whatever the posture of the body, the soul is on its knees."*

I'm not on my knees.

Years ago, in Sunday school, his fourth grade teacher had told the class there were two types of prayer—ones for help, and ones of praise. Benjamin took this to heart, and every time he approached the Lord, he first thanked Him for who He was and what He'd done, then he moved on to his list of petitions, each one chronicled in his prayer notebook with date, time, and response, if possible.

After Stephen, he found he wanted no help, and had no praise. He didn't know how to fill the spaces with anything else. He'd been taught never to shake his fist at God. So he said nothing at all.

Don't fool yourself. You've been praying all along.

"No."

"In the same way the Spirit also helps our weakness; for we do not know how to pray as we should, but the Spirit Himself intercedes for us with groanings too deep for words."

Oh, he'd groaned. All those sighs and fears and trepidations he clung to in protest of God's promises, what he considered the antithesis of prayer was prayer itself. Benjamin had challenged God to a game of Who Can Keep Quiet the Longest—like he and Stephen used to play on rainy days and long car rides that felt like eternities—and both had lost. The Lord hadn't stopped speaking to him at all, and for all Benjamin's bravado, his soul had continued to seek God even as his flesh rebelled in confusion.

He soaked in the silence for some time, and when it felt like it would overwhelm him, he shifted in the seat so the old wood creaked and buckled. He folded his hands, resting his forearms on the pew in front of him, leaned forward so his knuckles pressed against his forehead.

Now that he wanted to say something, he didn't know how to begin. Lack of practice. Lack of faith. He believed God would hear, but not answer. He didn't deserve an answer. But for the sake of Christ, maybe He would.

"Why have you forsaken me?" The words leaked out. He didn't want to be in darkness anymore. He opened the pew Bible to Psalm 22, read the words aloud. Prayed them. " 'My God, my God, why have you forsaken me? Why are you so far from saving me, so far from the words of my groaning? O my God, I cry out by day, but you do not answer, by night, and am not silent.' "

And he continued, feeling each word as his own. The roaring lions tore at him; his strength was dry as dust, his heart melted inside his chest like wax. But the song didn't stay in the depths of David's anguish. And, by the end, Benjamin had been lifted from there, too. He read on. " 'The poor will eat and be satisfied; they who seek the Lord will praise him—may your hearts live forever! All the ends of the earth will remember and turn to the Lord, and all the families of the nations will bow down before him, for dominion belongs to the Lord and he rules over the nations. All the rich of the earth will feast and worship; all who go down to the dust will kneel before him— those who cannot keep themselves alive. Posterity will serve him; future generations will be told about the Lord. They will proclaim his righteousness to a people yet unborn—for he has done it.'

"Amen, and amen. I believe, Lord. Help my unbelief."

Forgive me.

He sped home. Abbi's car wasn't in the driveway. He rushed inside, flung open the closet, his belts clattering to the floor. Her clothes hung straight and silent. It meant nothing. She'd leave without them.

He found Genelise's number in the phone book, dialed. No one answered. He left a message. Called Lauren.

"She's not here, Ben. What's going on?"

"Nothing. But if she shows up, have her call me."

He paced. Prayed. Pleaded with God for his marriage. Finally, he decided he couldn't wait for her. He'd drive up to Pierre and bring her home. He collected his wallet from the nightstand, and when he returned to the living room, Abbi stood there, coat open, army green knit hat fighting to stay over her hair, a small paper bag folded in her hand. "I went to the grocery," she said, unrolling the bag.

She took out a green and white box, no bigger than a deck of cards. *Fleet*, it read. She rubbed the cardboard flat between her thumb and fingers. Empty.

"I couldn't . . . I threw them out the window when I was driving home. I pulled over and thought about looking for them in the street. I didn't, though. I'm trusting He's enough, even without Silvia." She started to cry. "Even without you."

"What about with me?"

"Don't, Ben. Don't do this unless you mean it."

"I do. I swear. I will do whatever you ask of me, whatever it takes to keep you here. I don't want to be without you."

She charged into him, sobbing, and they fell back on the couch, holding each other without speaking. Finally, Abbi said, "I hate to be unromantic, but I have to pee," and when she returned, she pressed a small kraft-paper box into his hand. "Happy birthday."

"It's not until Tuesday."

"I know."

He shook the gift, held it to his ear. "Is it a composter?"

"I wish."

"A million dollars?"

"You'll have to open it and see."

He tugged the end of the raffia ribbon, wiggled off the cover. In the cotton sat a glazed pottery circle, a tiny footprint in the center. Silvia's footprint. He squeezed it, turned it over. Abbi had glued a translucent frame to the back, and in it a piece of yellow paper on which she had written, *The Lord gave, and the Lord has taken away. Blessed be the name of the Lord.*

"We didn't have to have her at all," she said.

"I know." He embraced her again, kissing her ear, the side of her head. Finally he let go and said, "Isn't this little frame plastic?"

"Shut up," she said. "Jerk."

"I couldn't resist."

"Oh, there's one more." She took another brown box from her coat pocket, identical to the first.

"Is this one a million dollars?" he asked, something rattling within.

"I'm not telling," she said, "but maybe you'd better open it in the bedroom."

In his half sleep, his arm snaked across the bed and touched something soft. He thought, *Abbi*, and he was right. She was there when he opened his eyes, sheet pulled into her armpit, hands bent under her chin like a child. She was facing him.

He shifted, leaned toward her. Kissed her bare upper arm. She brushed it away, mistaking it for an insect, it seemed, an annoyance. He smiled, kissed her again, on the shoulder this time.

She's beautiful, he thought, had thought hundreds of times.

Gingerly, he left the bed, dressed, and snuck into the backyard. The sun wasn't up yet, though the early golden glow on the dead fields stretched until they butted against the sky. He sat on the damp grass with his back to the sunrise, legs straight out in front of him, arms locked behind him, and watched the stars melt away into the morning.

A shadow grew behind him, as if a man stood off to his right, long and lanky, like Stephen.

Looks like someone got lucky last night, the shadow man said.

Don't be an idiot, Benjamin thought.

The shadow quivered, laughing. *I'm gonna take off now.*

I'm sorry I left you.

Man, it's all good. Where I am now, can't say I mind being there—know what I mean? Anyway, what kind of God lets a man decide who lives and who dies? Not any God I serve.

You're right, for once.

For once? Who told you to marry that girl of yours?

Not you.

I thought it.

Right. Benjamin's elbows hurt. He stretched the joints and lay back, overgrown grass prickling behind his ears. *Guess I should stop talking to myself.*

Sounds like a plan to me.

Yeah, me too.

Well then, I'll be heading out. See you someday.

"See you someday," Benjamin said.

He kinked his neck up and around so he would see the hackberry tree casting the shadow, reddish fruit peeking through the leaves. Just a tree.

"Hey, you," Abbi said. She crossed the lawn, barefoot. "What are you doing out here?"

"Thinking."

"Want company?"

"I could handle some," he said, and Abbi snuggled against his side, head on his collarbone. Her hair smelled like almonds. He breathed deep.

"You need to mow," she said.

"I was spoiled by Matt."

"Ben, we—"

"I know." He sighed. "But in a few days. I need time to decompress."

"Do you think he's okay?"

"Better than us, probably."

Abbi coughed. "That's not too hard."

"Let's go in," Benjamin said, standing, yanking Abbi to her feet. He looked back at the tree—still only a tree—and at the sun falling through the branches in separate shafts of light. He ran his hand through the closest beam, thanking God his dark night had ended.

Chapter THIRTY-NINE

She baked two pies, both with apples and cranberries, wrapped one and put it in the refrigerator for Benjamin and carried the other to the McGees with the vase that Janet had admired the day of the pit fire. Knocked. Janet opened the door.

"I have pie," Abbi said. "It's apple. I guess, sometimes when you don't know what else to do, you should just bring food. And some clay and paint."

Janet smiled a little, invited Abbi inside. The storm door shut behind her in three stilted hisses, and she carried the plate into the kitchen. Janet held the vase, hugging it, pressing her index finger into the point of each sculpted leaf. "You didn't have to do this."

"Well, it was just sitting there in the shed."

Janet opened a drawer, took out a knife and server. "Would you like a slice? Coffee or tea, maybe?"

"I'm good, really. I only wanted to come and apologize for being so cruel."

"I owe *you* an apology."

"I don't think so."

"Yes," Janet said. "I've been so jealous of you, I could hardly see straight. Because they gave you Silvia."

"Janet, I don't—"

"We can't have children, Silas and I. No, not Silas. Me. I can't." She chopped at the pie, dropped the sticky knife on the pink Formica counter. "I thought if I did everything right, God would bless us. And I tried and tried, and still no baby. But you come along—you and your tattoos and your protests and your *unique perspective* and, well, you got her."

"She's gone now."

"And I was glad. I didn't want to be, but I was."

Abbi chuckled wryly, masked her face in her hands and shook her head. "It's no big deal. Trust me. I've thought a lot worse about you."

"I'm sorry."

"You can't be sorry for my self-righteousness."

"I'm sorry I acted in a way that made you think badly of me."

"Enough of the apologies already. You're sorry. I'm sorry. Done. All right?"

Janet nodded. "Are you sure you don't want some pie?"

"Well . . . since you twisted my arm."

They sat and talked between forkfuls of too-dry crust and too-sweet filling—Janet telling of growing up with nine siblings, and small crumbs of her faith journey Abbi hadn't heard before. Abbi recounted a few of the struggles between her and Benjamin, a few of the graces the Lord had shown her. And when Abbi went to leave, she felt a tapping in her spirit, like an annoyingly persistent woodpecker outside her window, hunting for grubs when she wanted to nap. *Tell her,* the knocking said. *Tell her.*

But that's mine, Abbi thought. *It's not for anyone else.*

"Thank you for coming over," Janet said.

"No biggie. Oh, if you didn't notice, I baked the pie in your pan, so you don't have to worry about returning it."

"My nana always did that. 'Don't ever send it back empty,' she used to say to all us girls."

Tell her.

"Well, I'll see you, then," Abbi said, and she stood on the flagstone path as Janet closed the door, the tapping now more of a poke, stronger with each step she took toward home. "Okay, fine. I get the point."

She rang Janet's doorbell, and the woman looked out with concern. "Did you forget something?"

"No. Well, yes. I just . . . I wanted to tell you I understand. I can't have children, either. I know, it's not exactly the kind of thing people discuss at parties around the punch bowl, but if you ever want to talk, well, you know where I am."

"Thanks," Janet said, swiping her thumb under one eye. "Not yet. But sometime."

And Abbi nodded, inhaled, filling like a balloon, an unexpected buoyancy overtaking her, and on her way back to the house she played hopscotch on the umber stones, her toes nimbly avoiding the cracks.

⟶

They were getting ready for worship, running late as usual, though they couldn't use Silvia as an excuse anymore. *How hard is it for two adults to get out of the house on time?* That was the issue, both of them underestimating the time it took to ready themselves, and then snipping and shoving each other as the minutes ticked down—half of Benjamin's face smeared with Barbasol, Abbi still undressed and, with no time to iron, trying to find something unwrinkled to wear after leaving her laundry half folded in the basket all week.

"We need to remember to do all this Saturday night," he said, and they both snorted, knowing neither of them would. "I need coffee."

"Sorry. Didn't make any."

Abbi did remember it was Communion Sunday, but she refused to fast. She wouldn't again, not until she could do so without thinking of her weight. Or at least control those thoughts. Right now, food still held too much power over her. Without the laxatives to fall back on, she did battle with every bite—*Do I need it? Why do I want it? How much will I gain from it?*—sometimes thinking of nothing else but the two pear muffins on the counter for hours at a time, until she either ate them and felt miserable about her lack of self-discipline, or threw them out and berated herself for wasting food.

Not that she hadn't eaten from the trash before.

They were getting shorter, though, those obsessive times, and fewer. Most days she didn't let the internal arguments go on for more than a few minutes without turning to prayer, but it was nowhere near automatic yet. She trusted it would become easier, as she reached upward for help first, not into the refrigerator.

The announcements were over when she and Benjamin slipped through the church door, he easing it closed so it wouldn't slam accusatorily behind them, and they took their seats in the back row. Benjamin sang and prayed and nudged her with his elbow when she stared out the window. When the Communion tray came around, he didn't partake, but they stood together at the benediction, arms around each other's waists. Benjamin started it, as a reminder to go out as one, and work to stay one during the week.

After the service, they chatted for a while, people asking how they were managing without Silvia. Except for that afternoon with Janet McGee, no one had made any direct references to the past year, and that was fine by Abbi. She wasn't looking for anything other than what was already happening—the congregation folding in around her and Benjamin, making it easy for them to reattach to the body without fanfare or guilt. They followed the Yates family home for lunch, but before getting out of the Durango, Abbi reached across the armrest and touched the corduroy cuff of Benjamin's jacket. "Hey, you good?" she asked.

He nodded. "I didn't feel ready today. I'm still a lot more angry than I'm willing to admit."

"The table is for sinners, you know."

"I know. And I don't. If that makes any sense."

"Perfectly, and not at all," she told him, and laughed.

"I love you," he said.

At home, Benjamin paced the house. He opened all the kitchen cabinets, organizing measuring cups and colanders, washed down the stove. "The hinge is broken in the pantry."

"It's only been like that for five months," Abbi said, embroidering a napkin on the couch. She'd found a set of the cutest vintage Swiss-dotted cloth napkins at the Baptist church's white elephant sale, and planned to give them to Janet for Christmas after she stitched teapots on each of them.

"Hyperbole."

"Nope. It happened the day after my birthday." She stuck her needle into the fabric and went to him. "What's wrong?"

"Nothing."

"Right. You always rearrange cabinets and wander aimlessly in eight hundred square feet for hours on end."

"I think we should ask Matt to come live with us."

"Well, maybe that would work if we weren't both—um, what's the word?—completely avoiding him. And he avoiding us, it would seem."

He burnished the crown of his skull with his palm, like a child rubbing a balloon on his hair, trying to make it stick to the wall. "I've been planning to go over there."

"You said that three weeks ago. Anyway, he's still staying with the Larsens."

"Why should he be there when he could be here?"

"Why should he be *here* when he could be *there*?"

"You don't want him to come?"

"I didn't say that." She opened the bread box, snagged a slice of raisin bread. She thought about taking a bite, stopped. *Stop me, Lord. I'm not hungry.* Instead of eating it, she plucked out each raisin, crushing it against the butcher-block counter with her thumb. Benjamin covered her hand. "He's not a replacement part, Ben."

"I can't believe you'd even think I'd be thinking that."

"Then what are you thinking? I mean, where is this even coming from?"

"I don't know," he said. "You're right. I haven't been able to go see him. I've tried. I've driven past the Larsen place every day since we first talked about it. But I can't stop. I don't want him to think I blame him at all, but I'm still worried about what I might say to him, how I might look at him. Which is why I don't think this is my idea. No matter how I try to shake it off, it won't leave."

"He might just come because he thinks he owes us something. The kid is already pulled in a thousand directions. I don't want us to add to that."

"Maybe, then, we could pray about it."

She balled up the tattered bread and pitched it into the trash. "I can do that."

"Together. Now."

Benjamin kneeled in the middle of the kitchen floor, holding out his hands to her, and she took them, crouched down so their kneecaps touched. And as he made his request known, by prayer and supplication, Abbi's eyes filled with tears and ran over with thanksgiving. She had her husband back.

Chapter FORTY

Ellie's mother wouldn't let her drive all the way to Lester, so Matthew decided to take the bus. He could have asked Jaylyn, or Pastor Larsen, or anyone else at the church, but he wanted the time alone. It had nothing to do with burdening someone. He didn't have use for the money now anyway. He wouldn't be traveling to New York to see his father.

He wasn't playing the martyr, still wanted the transplant. But right now he wanted it more than his father's love. He wouldn't go there feeling the way he did. So he prayed, waiting for God to change his heart.

At the bus station, Ellie hugged him and asked, "Are you sure you don't want me to go? I will."

He shook his head.

"Well, okay. Have someone call me before you leave, and I'll be here to pick you up."

I will.

"Promise me, Matthew Savoie. I know you. I don't want you hitchhiking back. I mean it."

Yes, Mom.

"Promise."

I promise.

She took both his hands in hers, their fingers interlaced. "Promise again, now, so I know your fingers aren't crossed."

"I promise," he said.

"Okay, I believe you. Matt, I . . . I think Skye will be glad to see you."

We'll see.

He found a window seat, waved to her from the bus.

She signed, *I love you.*

He rubbed the glass with his sleeve, but Ellie disappeared into the building.

He tried to count cottonwoods on the ride, mostly scraggly clusters of no more than ten, all gnarly and half naked. They looked ancient, but the trees only lived sixty or seventy years. He couldn't seem to keep the numbers in his head, though, because of Ellie, and her sign.

Did she mean it, mean it?

Taxis waited outside the bus station in Lester. Matthew chose the plainest cabbie, the one without tattoos or turbans or feathers hanging from his rearview mirror, and showed him the back cover of his pad. Then he scrawled Central South Dakota Juvenile Service Center on an inside page.

Nine minutes later, Matthew stood on the concrete sidewalk, staring at a choppy brick building, juts and boxes stacked together at various heights and depths. He asked the driver to wait.

"It's forty cents a minute," the cabbie told him.

Matthew nodded and walked to the door, counting each line he stepped over. The guard might turn him away; visitors under eighteen needed to be accompanied by an adult. Matthew had snuck into the high school office and stole a blank ID card, and at home he altered his birth date to add a couple of years and laminated the card with another photo using clear packing tape. He prayed quickly that the guard would be too lazy to press for more information, though he figured God wouldn't hear any prayer involving lies and fraud.

He was on his own for this one.

I'm here to see Skye Becker.

The guard reached for his pad, but Matthew shook his head and turned it over.

"Brother?" he asked.

Cousin. But I have permission from the caseworker.

"Got ID?"

He searched through his backpack, untangling his card from a nest of tens and twenties, dropping several coins on the floor. The guard gave a disinterested glance at Matthew's photo and typed his name into the computer. "Okay, sign here," he said, pushing a clipboard across the counter. Matthew did, and clipped on his plastic visitor badge. "Bag in the coatroom, then step over here."

After dropping two quarters in a locker, Matthew took the key and stepped through the metal detector. Another officer pat-searched him, and he was led into the visitation room—white cinder-block walls, round white tables, white floor—sterile and clean, as if the center were trying to wash away the crimes of those inside. The chairs were gray plastic with fat legs. Matthew sat with his back against a wall. Several teens in blue scrub-like outfits shared low conversations with family.

A guard escorted Skye into the room. She looked thinner, her hair pulled back into a rubber band.

"You came."

Matthew tried to smile. Jaylyn said she thought you wanted me to.

"I did. I do. I just wasn't sure if you would."

Why wouldn't I?

"I figured you'd be home torturing yourself over all this."

I'm okay.

"I bet. Anyone with you?"

He shook his head. How are you?

"Okay, really."

Five months in here. Not too bad.

"Better than a year, in some ways. In others, it seems like it should be a whole lot more."

You're just as good at torture as I am.

She dragged her middle finger on the table, toward her. "I told Ma none of this was your fault. She'd just rather blame someone else than her own sorry self for her part."

It's fine.

"You ever gonna go back there? To live, I mean."

I don't know.

"Maybe you could move in with Ellie."

He rolled his eyes, crumpled a page from his notepad and threw it at her.

"I forgot. Good boys like you don't do things like that."

Skye.

"Oh, stop. I'm just messing with you." She scratched at a scab on her elbow. "It's weird. There really is something sorta . . . clean about the truth. I don't think I would have been able to stay quiet forever. Then again, maybe I would have. I don't know."

Matthew bumped her hand with his. I don't think you would have.

"You have a better opinion of me than I probably deserve."

They talked for a while, her about the daily routine, about some of the other girls, him about school. About Ellie. Finally, he wrote, I should go, jerking his head toward the clock on the wall. I took the bus. Last one back is in forty minutes.

"Okay. It was good seeing you."

You too.

"You'll come again, right?"

Yeah.

"My caseworker will wonder if you don't. I told her you were practically my brother and integral to my recovery process. Pretty good, huh?"

I'm impressed.

"Yeah, well, I didn't come up with it on my own. Hey, Matt?" She lifted her hips off the chair to reach into her pocket, pulled out a wrinkled square of lined paper. Pressed it into his hand.

"These things I have spoken to you, so that in Me you may have peace. In the world you have tribulation, but take courage; I have overcome the world."

Matthew hugged her, hard. *See you soon.*

He gathered his things from the locker and took the cab back to the station. He asked the woman at the ticket window to call Ellie for him, and she clenched her jaw but did it. When the bus pulled into Hollings, Ellie was there, waiting outside with her coat zipped up over her nose. She held his hand, and they walked to her mother's minivan. As the engine idled, she asked, "Did it go okay?"

He nodded.

"Good. That's . . . good." She played with the buttons on the dashboard, turning on the heat, the front and rear defroster as the windows clouded with their breath. She scratched her fingernails over her tights. Striped today. Gray and pink and purple and red. She jiggled her leg. "I'm glad."

Question?

"Okay."

Do you know what this means? He copied the sign she made earlier.

She nodded.

What?

"I love you."

Do you?

"That was really stupid of me."

Do you?????

"Yes."

I do too.

Ellie smiled, ever so slightly. "Do what?"

Clever girl, he wrote.

"You already knew that, and you're not getting out of answering."

Matthew looked at her. "I love you," he said.

"I guess we're even now," she said, and then turned her head away. He saw her reflection in the dark window. She grinned, her hand covering half of her face.

He tapped her knee with his pad. Both of us, even?

"Matthew Savoie, if you make a math joke right now, I'll punch you. I mean it."

I wouldn't dream of telling you that the derivative of an even function would just make us . . . odd.

She swung at him, and as her momentum carried her forward, he kissed her, only their second kiss—not the quick, puckery kiss she gave him walking home a few weeks ago, but the sweetest, softest kiss he ever dared imagine. Finally, Ellie sat back and said, "I guess there are worse things than being odd."

Like, without you, Matthew wrote.

"Yeah. That," Ellie said, and kissed him again.

Still aglow with Ellie's declaration the day before, he ran the twenty yards from Pastor Larsen's house to the church for Sunday service. He sat in the third pew from the front, closest to the wall so he could see Mrs. Healen. Not that she helped much.

He closed his eyes, breathed in the old wood smell, musty and pious, and he thanked God for Ellie once more, as he did almost every time he thought of her. He prayed for Skye, for all his cousins. And for Silvia.

And Abbi and the deputy.

I miss them, Lord. Please, please let them forgive me.

Someone brushed past his knees, stepping on his feet despite his tucking them under the seat. The person settled next to him, close enough he felt the heat radiating off the person's leg onto his own. The entire pew had been empty when Matthew came in five minutes ago. *Why can't they move down?*

And then the someone squeezed his arm.

His eyes popped open; from the paisley-clad thigh he knew who it was, but he turned his head anyway to see Abbi, and Benjamin beside her. She enclosed him in her arms and, clasping her hands against his shoulder, drew him against her, the top of her head crushing his ear, hurting him.

He didn't care.

Chapter FORTY-ONE

"Okay," Benjamin said. "Everyone out. You'll need boots."

In the back seat of the Volvo, Matthew and Ellie zipped their coats and wiggled on their mittens. He jammed a knit hat over his hair while she untied her ponytail and ran a brush through hers. They laughed as they tumbled from the car and jogged along the guardrail, then over it, tromping through long locks of dead, brown grass and snow on the side of the road.

Benjamin opened the door for Abbi. "It's freezing," she said.

"Come on. This is the last one."

"They better not want to do this on the way back."

The teenagers had already slid down the embankment and stood together in front of the *Welcome to New York* sign, inside arms around each other, outside arms pointing up at the lettering above their heads. Benjamin snapped a photo. "Wait. One more," he said.

It felt good to be standing, to be out of the cramped car. Benjamin pushed his chest forward and his shoulders back, waggling his head from side to side until his neck popped. Twenty hours of driving, no matter how it was broken up, did a number on a man's bones.

"Your turn," Ellie said, climbing up the small hill. It had been her idea to stop and take a picture at each state line, and she hadn't had to do much to persuade Matthew—smile and ask. She lost her footing, and Matthew, walking behind her, instinctively flattened his hands against her rear to stop her from slipping.

"Hey now," Benjamin said. "No getting fresh. I've sworn on my life to Ellie's parents I'd return her exactly the way she was when we took her."

Matthew buried his hands in his coat, face blazing red, and Abbi gave Benjamin a small punch in the arm. "Oh, stop. Leave the boy alone."

Benjamin laughed. "He knows I'm joking. Right, Matt?"

The boy shook with an embarrassed shrug and reached for the camera. Benjamin handed it to him and jumped down into the ditch. Abbi followed, and they posed in front of the sign. "Okay, got it," Ellie said.

As he walked back to the car, a lump of cold thudded against the back of Benjamin's head, and then wetness in his collar, trickling down his back. He spun, and another snowball hit him in the side of the face. All three of them—Abbi, Ellie, and Matthew—stood with misshapen hunks of snow in their gloved hands. His hands were bare, and his fingers froze before he could properly pack the snow; his projectiles fell to dust as he flung them toward his attackers.

And then they all dropped their snowballs. "Uh, Ben. Turn around," Abbi said.

A state police car pulled in behind the Volvo, lights spinning silently. Benjamin took out his badge and approached the trooper, who glanced at it, saying, "Someone's going to get themselves killed out here, fooling around like that."

"I'm sorry, Officer. We're all just a bit rowdy from being cooped up in the car for the last twelve hundred miles."

"How far you heading?"

"Buffalo."

"Well, that's only 'bout an hour and a half drive from here. I think you rowdy folks can handle that."

The trooper waited until they all strapped back into the car, and Benjamin steered out into the oncoming traffic. After the trooper car passed them, Matthew passed his notepad up to Benjamin. I don't think Ellie's parents would appreciate her coming home with a police record.

"Ha, ha." Benjamin tossed the pad over his shoulder.

Ellie caught it and, after skimming the note, giggled.

"I don't need comments from the peanut gallery back there," Benjamin said.

After Ellie repeated his comment to Matt, she said, "Matt wants to know if you know where the term *peanut gallery* comes from."

"*Howdy Doody,*" Benjamin said.

"No, before that," Ellie read from Matthew's pad.

"Kindly remind our little smarty-pants friend that I made no promises to get him home safely, so if he doesn't watch it, I'll accidentally forget him at the next rest stop."

In the rearview mirror he watched as Ellie repeated his comment to Matthew, who broke out in a wide grin. He wrote something back to her.

"What'd he say?" Benjamin asked.

"That you'd miss him too much to ever do that."

"He's right," Abbi said.

He is right.

Matthew had been living with them since the week before Thanksgiving, both of them knowing the boy only agreed to it because he still felt guilty about his part in their losing Silvia, and the first couple of weeks had been uncomfortable as all of them tried too hard.

But now, nearly a month and a half later, Benjamin couldn't imagine their home without him. Any remaining awkward moments were only because he and his wife sometimes forgot they now had a teenager in their house, not an infant. They left little sticky notes on the bathroom and bedroom mirrors reminding each other that clothing was no longer optional. And Matthew made a lot of noise before entering any room. They had worried when it started, him seemingly so klutzy, dropping things or banging against walls. He finally told them he did it on purpose; he'd come into the kitchen one morning when Benjamin and Abbi were kissing, and he wanted to make sure to warn them before he stumbled upon them in a more intimate situation.

They added locking doors to their sticky-note reminders.

The trip to Buffalo had started with a phone call. Abbi somehow convinced Matthew to let her call his father, and Jimmy Savoie wanted to see his son. He hadn't known Matthew was sick. He didn't even know the boy wasn't living with Melissa anymore. Yes, yes, he said, he could have done a bit of digging, found the number and called. But the way he and Matthew's mother had parted—well, he figured Melissa wouldn't have let him talk to his son anyway.

"But tell him . . . ." Jimmy had said. "Tell him I still have that picture of him, from that day we went to the fair, the day his face turned blue from the snow cone—tell him I have that one on the mantel. Tell him he has brothers."

Matthew said he didn't remember the fair, or the blue ice. But when Benjamin told him they'd take him out to New York over Christmas vacation, he'd agreed.

They had left on Sunday, early, suitcases and snacks crammed in the trunk, pillows and blankets mounded between them, and drove twelve hours, spending the night in a cheap motel outside Chicago— he and Matthew in one full-sized bed, Abbi and Ellie in the other. The next morning they logged another six hours, stopping in Cleveland so Matthew could have a dialysis session, staying another night. Then another two hours today.

Abbi turned around. "Anyone want to stop for breakfast?"

Benjamin glanced in the mirror again, saw Ellie look at Matthew. He shook his head. "No, I think we're good," Ellie said.

"Well, there's some granola back there. And fruit in the cooler. I think a couple sandwiches from yesterday."

His wife was worried about Matthew. So was he. Benjamin hadn't had a moment to talk—really talk—about how Matthew felt being so close to the end of this leg of the journey.

He loved the boy. He didn't think, after Silvia, he'd be able to love a child so freely again. And it wasn't like with the baby, an overwhelming instant of emotion crashing over him. It came on in bits and spurts, surprising him, because who outside of God himself would have known a brilliant, deaf kid, a vegan hippie, and a toeless soldier would find themselves some sort of family?

They didn't get only Matthew, though. Ellie came over nearly every evening, and more afternoons than not, Benjamin found Sienna and Lacie playing Polly Pockets in the living room, or sitting at the kitchen table, Matthew helping with homework. Even Jaylyn showed up a couple of times a week. And Heather, once. She had been looking for the girls, and Abbi invited her to dinner. She stayed, uncomfortable and self-conscious, but there nonetheless. Slowly, like rock candy crystals, they all piggybacked on one another, growing thicker and stronger and sweeter.

He reached across the armrest and threaded his fingers through Abbi's, smiled at her and mouthed *I love you.* She covered their hands with her other one, picked at his knuckles. Things were better between them. They tried now, every day, working hard at loving, like the blistering, sweaty task it was, the unnatural discipline of denying oneself. He grilled his own steak when he wanted it; she bought him paper napkins and disposable razors while grocery shopping. They didn't meet in the middle, but above it, in that place neither could reach alone, but in Christ was possible. Not all the time. Not even most of the time. But when they did, they could rejoice in the magnitude of the tiny victory and think, *Yes, God is growing us.*

They drove in silence, no radio, no scribbling in the back seat, and after all the hours and the planning and the wondering, they were in

Buffalo. Benjamin pulled in to the first gas station he found, and Abbi asked Ellie to help her get coffee for all of them.

Benjamin checked the directions to the Savoie house. "About fifteen minutes more," he told Matthew.

Matthew nodded.

"You okay?"

More nodding.

"You're sure?"

Ben, I'm fine.

"I don't think you need to be concerned. Abbi said she got the sense he'd be open to a transplant, and—"

Matt stopped him with a shake of his head. *It's not about that. Not really. Not now. Not anymore.*

"I know."

I never really thanked you. Both of you.

"You don't owe us anything."

I didn't say owe. I said thank.

"You're welcome, kiddo. And so much more."

The women returned, and Benjamin navigated through Buffalo. Eventually he turned into the Savoie driveway, a little bungalow with asbestos siding and a basketball hoop cemented into the oil-stained blacktop. They all got out of the car.

"Do you want us to go in with you?" Benjamin asked.

Matthew shook his head.

"You don't have to do this alone," Abbi said.

I'm not alone.

"Should we wait, or maybe come back in an hour?" Benjamin asked.

The boy looked toward the house, where a lanky man with a dark blond beard looked out from behind a glass storm door covered in paper snowflakes and gummy Christmas clings. Do you mind staying here? In the car?

"We're not going anywhere."

And then Matthew was in the house, the three of them inside the Volvo, alternating between idling the engine so the heater would work, and sitting with the cold pressing in on them.

"He'll be fine," Abbi said. "He will."

"Relax," Benjamin told her, pushing up the armrest so she could slide over against him. He draped his arm over her, and she rested her head against his chest.

There were two of him now—Benjamin before Silvia, and Benjamin after. He'd have been a liar if he said he still didn't think of her every day, still didn't get angry he had to give her back. The Whalens were sending a photo of her every week. At first Benjamin deleted them from his inbox without opening the e-mail. Then curiosity overcame him, and this dark-eyed, apple-cheeked cherub smiled at him from the computer monitor, two teeth poking up from her bottom gums. Jared asked them to visit, but neither he nor Abbi were ready for it. Not yet. The summer, they said. Maybe on her first birthday.

The front door opened again, and Matthew waved, gesturing for them to come inside. "He wants us," Abbi said, and Benjamin heard the relief in her voice, and they ran from the car, through the sleet, into the Savoie home, where Matthew waited for them, not alone.

Acknowledgments

My sincerest gratitude and appreciation to all who helped in my research for *Watch Over Me*:

Tishia Chambers, who patiently and honestly explained her experiences as a deaf woman in a hearing world.

Officer Denny Pottebaum of the Sioux Falls Police Department, for his expertise regarding child abandonment laws.

Shirlena Freund, Kelly Kingrey-Edwards, Joy Maynard, Mellymommy, Manda Troutman, and Shanna Wright, for answering my foster care questions; Loretta Tschetter, for her South Dakotan eyes and ears; Rebecca, for her personal insights into familial relationships within the Indian culture; the Alport Syndrome Foundation; and all those men and women who have served in Iraq and Afghanistan, and have bravely posted their stories on-line so others might know they are not alone.

A huge thank-you to my editor, Karen Schurrer, who endured the verb tense-change nightmare with me; to Dave Long, for his keen insight and chauffer service around Dallas; to Noelle Buss and her marketing magic; and to all those at Bethany House Publishers who work not only on my behalf but on behalf of the Kingdom.

My thanks to Bill Jensen, my agent and one of my biggest fans. To everyone at Redeemer Church, Greater Glens Falls Christian Home-schoolers, and Gentle Christian Mothers who uphold me in prayer. To Sharon and Krista, for welcoming Jacob into your homes each week. And to Jo, Marilyn, and Kay, just because.

To my parents, for their never-ending love and support, and for learning to share. To Jacob, for grudgingly agreeing to let me dedicate this book to him—I adore the person God is growing you to be. And to Chris, without qualifiers, for allowing Him to use a silly little card to do a "wicked awesome" thing.

A past winner of Associated Press awards for her journalism, CHRISTA PARRISH now teaches literature and writing to high school students, is a homeschool mom, and lives near Saratoga Springs, New York. Her first novel, *Home Another Way*, was a finalist for the 2009 ECPA Christian Book Award for fiction.